LOVE

AGAINST ALL ODDS, TRUE LOVE

HAS NO

ENDURES AMID THE VIETNAM WAR

COUNTRY

A NOVEL BY

ERNEST BRAWLEY

Copyright © 2021 by Ernest Brawley

For information regarding permission, please write to:
info@barringerpublishing.com
Barringer Publishing, Naples, Florida
www.barringerpublishing.com

Cover art by Amy Ecenbarger
Image of landing strip, helicopter, skin abrasions and sack all from Shutterstock, with standard license.

Design and layout by Linda S. Duider
Cape Coral, Florida

ISBN: 978-1-954396-05-0
Library of Congress Cataloging-in-Publication Data
Love Has No Country / Brawley

Printed in U.S.A.

NOTE TO THE READER

Several people have asked me whether I was personally involved in the CIA's Shadow War in Thailand and Lao during the Sixties and Seventies. My answer has been that I am a US Army veteran and a retired government employee. I had occasion to visit Burma, Thailand, Laos, Cambodia, and Vietnam during the war years, but I have never worked for the CIA. My late friend and colleague, Captain Asa Baber, USMC, bears a slight resemblance to Zachary Ogle, the covert ops shadow warrior who is the male protagonist of this story. The firebase commander, Jimmy Love, resembles the infamous old CIA military operative, Tony Poe. My dear friend, Kanchana Namjaiyen, is a medical professional from Southeast Asia who is in some ways reminiscent of the book's female protagonist, Nittaya Aromdée. Those are the facts. The rest—including some scrambling of geography, historical details and dates—is fiction.

Love seeketh not Itself to please,
Nor for itself hath any care;
But for another gives its ease,
And builds a Heaven in Hells despair.

—William Blake

*I dedicate this novel to my
two beloved granddaughters,
Bianca and Aria.*

CONTENTS

Part III

Part IV

Part I

CHAPTER ONE

Hollywood

On the bright, sunny morning of December 4, 2020, a little Filipino-American mailman in shorts and knee-socks pushes a three-wheeled postal cart up a root-buckled sidewalk in Bronson Canyon, a neighborhood of old, yet well-kept, clapboard bungalows and enormous shade trees. He parks his cart outside a small, white, Craftsman house with a pepper tree, a fringe of roses out front and an only slightly obscured view of the Hollywood Sign on Mount Lee, a couple of miles to the north. He draws out several letters, opens the mailbox by the front fence, slides them in, slams it shut and heads up the street.

Inside the bungalow, a crusty, old, sometime scriptwriter named Zachary Ogle hears the rattle of the mailbox. Rising stiffly from his coffee and *Los Angeles Times*, he leaves his breakfast nook, crosses his old-fashioned, front parlor, and steps out his squeaky screen door.

Waving at the departing postman, he reaches a large,

weathered hand into the mailbox, retrieves the letters, carries them into the house, tosses them on a lamp table and is about to return to his *LA Times* when he notices the exotic return address on one of the letters and his mouth flies open in astonishment.

> Ms. Katay Aromdée Kim
> 7 Suk Road, Vientiane 10001
> People's Republic of Laos

He grabs the letter, rips it open, and starts to read.

November 28, 2020

Dear Mr. Ogle:

Do not ask how I obtained your address. Let us just say it was a miracle of modern cybernetics. It helped that your name is apparently not common in the USA, I knew your place of birth, and you were very much in the news in the year 1973.

Now brace yourself for a shock, sir. Recently, I was going through my grandmother's old bamboo chest and discovered some photographs and diaries that lead me to believe you may be my grandfather. Please have a look at the enclosed pictures and let me know what you think.

Squinting and shaking his bald dome to rid its antique

interior of cobwebs, Zack lays the letter down on his breakfast nook table without getting past the first two paragraphs.

He sweeps its surface with his hand, as though he might find the answer to the riddle of its words in its folds and creases, plucks the photographs from the envelope and fans them out on the table, face down.

Someone has penned a line or two of Lao on the back of each photo. He has not read a word of the language in fifty years, yet the Asian characters magically transform themselves into English before his eyes, as in an old Frank Capra film set in the *Mysterious East*.

The first photo reads, "Zack and me, Firebase Juliet, Nam Noy, Laos, July 27, 1971."

He turns it over gingerly, like a poker draw, and finds that it is yellow with age, tattered around the edges from handling.

It shows two young people in their twenties sitting on a pile of ten-kilo rice bags at the edge of a jungle landing strip, with an Air America Twin-Pak helicopter warming up behind them. They're wearing camouflage, Vietnam War era, military fatigues called "tiger suits," and are both armed to the teeth.

The young man, an early, luxuriantly haired, version of the present-day Zachary Ogle, sits behind the young woman. Long and lithe and not at all your fragile "Oriental Flower" of lore, with a beauty so striking and exotic that it seems enhanced by her drab military gear, she leans back against his chest with her hands resting on his knees while his thick muscular arms enfold her slender waist.

Heads together, they smile at the camera as if there were no other place on earth they would rather be.

The second photo says, "Cybèle on her wedding day, Luang Prabang, March 5, 1995."

It shows a tall, slender, Eurasian girl of about twenty-one. Her long, black hair, festooned with golden jewelry, rises a foot above her head in an elaborate structure meant to evoke an antique Buddhist temple. She has outlined her large, unexpectedly blue eyes in kohl to emphasize their upward slant. Her face is oval, exquisitely proportioned, and much like that of the young woman in the first photo, although her coloring is a shade or two lighter and there is something in the shape of her mouth that seems a bit more sensitive and vulnerable.

She wears a traditional Laotian wedding gown, which consists of a long-sleeved, jasmine blouse, a red and gold shoulder-scarf with red, flower-like decorations and a long, crimson, skirt with gold trimmings.

She is apparently looking at a monk, or a shrine, for she has bowed her head in prayer, and her hands are raised above her breast and pressed together in a Buddhist salutation called "Wai."

Although her looks are far more Asian than Caucasian, something in her aspect points in the direction of blue-eyed Mr. Zachary Ogle.

The last photo reads, "Katay, at school in Vientiane, October 13, 2014."

It shows a pretty, petite, Asian girl about seventeen years old. Dressed in a white blouse, short tartan skirt and white knee socks, she stands at the front gate of a large, concrete school building beside a solemn, little, security guard in a pseudo-military uniform.

Cocking her head, causing a wisp of long black hair to

partially veil one dark, slanted eye, she grins confidently at the camera, with her index and middle fingers raised in a V sign.

After scrutinizing the photographs, a second time, and stuffing them back in the envelope, Zack takes up the letter again and begins to read.

Yet he does not get far because suddenly his mouth feels dry, and the room starts spinning.

He drops the letter and starts thumping his faltering, old heart with a fist.

His eyes roll up in his head and he falls forward, striking the tabletop with a bang, upsetting his cup.

The spilled coffee runs over the photos and starts dripping on the floor.

Yet, in the scenario that old, screenwriter Zack instantly concocts, his visceral reaction to the photos is rejected as "over the top." He sees himself conquering his emotions and calmly sipping his coffee, while considering the far-reaching ramifications of certain past events.

Given that memory is fallible, especially when burdened by an unacknowledged state of impaired consciousness, Zack's recall of experiences five decades in the past is amazingly accurate.

The years fall away, and it all comes back to him, from first to last, in living technicolor.

CHAPTER TWO

Temptation

After forty-seven Search & Destroy missions, fifteen Body Counts and one unrestful R & R, after a year-long contribution to the pacification of the militant and impervious peasantry of Quang Nghai province, with nothing to show for it but a thousand-yard stare, the Presidio of San Francisco seemed a sanitary *Paradiso*, a Switzerland for my soul.

Every morning, I awakened on crisp, white sheets, in the basement of a quaint, brick barracks built in the era of sailing ships, when the U.S. Army wore blue and rode around on horses.

Sniffing sea fog and cypress trees out my window, I would leap up, do eleven minutes of Canadian Air Force exercises and take a long hot shower. Then I'd slip into my starched fatigues and spit-shined combat boots, clamp my billed cap upon my head, and jog down Infantry Terrace to the mess hall with nothing more important on my mind than what was for breakfast, or what to do with all my boundless excess energy.

Next, it was off to Presidio Headquarters on Battery Dynamite Road where I did make-work in the G-2 Section while a civilian clerk in the Military Records Section processed my discharge papers.

So, while Cambodia and Laos got B-52ed into firewood, and the butcher's bill in Vietnam surpassed that of the Korean War, and universities across the United States exploded in anti-war violence, I collated mimeographed copies of the Daily Intelligence Report and conducted an imaginary love affair with my commanding officer, a beautiful WAC major nearly twice my age.

A Cajun from Louisiana with a sultry, French-inflected, Southern drawl, Major Duval was tall, dark, and voluptuous, with fluffy, blunt-cut hair. As I remember her now, she had the sensual pouting mouth, the sloe-eyed look, and the cigarette saturated voice of the actress Jeanne Moreau in Francois Truffaut's *Jules and Jim*. Only her crow's-feet, and the wrinkles around her mouth, told of her long career as a warrior woman.

My itch for the major may seem like nothing more than a horny young GI's fantasy of upward sexual mobility. Yet, incredibly enough, it was beginning to look like my itch might just get scratched.

At Presidio HQ, the betting was even money, and the odds got better every time Major Duval tidied her coif when she caught my eye, or complimented my job performance for trifling reasons, or took me aside for "briefings" that had only the slightest relevance to my paltry duties.

The office crew in G-2 thought it hilarious and kidded me about it relentlessly.

Keesha, the civilian key punch operator, said, "I just cain't figger out what the major see in a peckerwood like you, still wet behind the ears."

Captain Ponce said, "It must be those curly locks."

Sergeant Major Wasson said, "It must be, 'cuz it sure as hell ain't his purty manners."

"It's the medals," I said, and the REMFs (Rear Echelon Mother Fuckers) of XVth Corps didn't say much back to that because I had a chest full of medals, including the Silver Star.

Only I knew they were unearned and ill-gotten, collected after the third annual Tet Offensive of 1970 when, for reasons of "morale," the Army was handing them out like C-Ration candy.

I earned the Silver Star on an S & D mission near some nameless little *ville* outside Phan Rang. My first "valorous action" of the morning was to lead my squad splashing across a rice paddy, screaming, "Fuck yo commie mommy!" after a gang of little, black pajama-clad, VC irregulars as they ducked and flopped in the mud to avoid our automatic weapons fire.

My second "valorous action" was to submit—with only the most fainthearted resistance—to the repeated orders of my bloodthirsty company commander to take no prisoners, inflate the Body Count, and incinerate the rice-stocks and hootches of the *ville*.

From my present perspective, I realize that I paid a heavy price indeed for that moment of glory. I will carry with me to the grave the sight of those newly widowed, little mama-sans and orphaned baby-sans crying *"Do luong, do luong!"* for mercy as they watched their world go up in flames.

A few days before my release from active duty, Major Duval

shocked her staff—and settled their bets—when she stepped into our office, crooked a finger at me, and said in her languid, Terrebonne Parish drawl, "Sergeant Ogle, y'all come with me now, you hear? I got a proposal to put to you."

Ignoring my office-mates' winks and rolling eyes, I dropped what I was doing, followed her out the door, down the hall, and into her office.

She locked the door behind us and motioned me into a seat beside her desk. Sweeping her green uniform skirt beneath her with a little flounce of her curvaceous hips, she settled in her swivel chair and fixed me with a smile that I can only describe now as incandescent.

While in military terms nothing inappropriate had yet occurred, the air between us crackled with electricity.

Thrilling though I might have found the major's unspoken invitation, I can't say I was completely surprised because I'd always had a way with women.

Younger women said I was cute because I looked like a dark-haired Jimmy Dean and had a real smooth rap.

Older women didn't say why but latched right onto me. My secret with them was my orphan routine, which I had perfected over the years, and consisted of lapsing into little boy talk at strategic moments. They found it irresistible, if applied with discretion.

In adolescence, I even conducted a love affair with one of my county-appointed foster mothers. That is, until her barber husband came home unexpectedly during one of our summertime daily doubles, beat me black and blue with a razor strop, accused me of a bunch of thefts I did not commit, and turned me back to the County of Los Angeles.

Which put me in Los Padrinos Juvenile Hall.

From which I thought I might never escape.

"Sergeant, ya'll be getting out here directly, *non?*" said Major Duval, perusing my DD-214 papers before her on the desk.

"Yes, Ma'am."

"Twenty-four years old, just a few credits short of your bachelor's degree. Scored off the charts on your GCT intelligence test. Made sergeant in a year and a bit. You were a squad leader in the Battle of Quang Nghai. Earned yourself a bunch of medals. And apparently you got a way with languages."

"I do my best."

"Alors, Sergent, dites-moi la vérité; est-ce que vous parlez français bien, ou non?"

"Pas mal, Madame Commandante, pas mal de tout. J'ai pratiqué beaucoup avec les jeunes filles colons au Vietnam."

"Well, I do declare!" she said, employing an archaic southernism that I found utterly endearing. "Not bad, not bad at all! Now let me ask you something else. What're you figuring on doing, now that you're back in the World?"

"To tell the truth, Major, I haven't given it much thought."

"Uh-huh. Well, I see here that you're getting pretty short time."

"Six and a wake-up, Major."

"Well, listen here, son. I might have a job opportunity for you when you get your discharge. Why don't you pop by my private quarters tomorrow, Saturday, at about 1100 hours—It's house number B132 on Sherman Road—and we'll talk some more about it, *non?*"

The major was not leering when she said this. She seemed quite serious. Obviously, she had convinced herself that all she said was the truth, and she possessed no ulterior motives.

Next morning, I got up an hour beforehand, showered, shaved, and trimmed my mustache in conformance to Army regulations.

After a quick shot of coffee in the mess hall, I hiked briskly up the hill and under the Golden Gate Bridge Approach toward her cottage in the Presidio Woods.

The fog was still very thick and hung in an impenetrable blanket, just a few feet above the tips of the tallest trees. A fine, misty drizzle was falling. It dropped from the wind-twisted limbs of Monterey pines, off the green umbrella of the cypress trees, and formed crystal globules on the bracken ferns. The air smelled of damp eucalyptus leaf.

I took a shortcut through the wildest part of the woods. I was all alone. Not a grunt in sight. All I could hear was the crunch of my civilian, Frye boots on the pine needles, and the nostalgic and altogether pleasant sound of automobiles racing over slick pavement at a distance.

The Hurt Locker, Vietnam, had been hot, clamorous, sharp, deadly, and bright, a detonation of sights and sounds—too real.

Here in the foggy, Pacific woods, Zen woods, all was cold, quiet, and obscure—unreal.

After the opium-tipped, paranoid reality of Phan Rang and Tuy Hoa and treacherous Route 1 . . . of the 2nd Brigade, the Screaming Eagles . . . the true meaning of things was no longer important to me.

After you've been overrun by howling, little, yellow fellows wearing weeds in their hair, after you've watched your petrified twenty-two-year-old LT call down in despair your own artillery upon your head, after you've seen your two best friends blown into slaughterhouse scraps before your eyes, you are too glad to just be walking and talking to give a shit about anything else.

I had never been one for self-analysis, in any case. The origin of whatever psychological problems I had—self-destructive impulses, difficulty sustaining close relationships—was so predictable and obvious for an abandoned child such as myself that I thought, *Why bother?*

I managed to cope well enough. I had not done the hard prison time that so many of my old dormitory mates from Juvenile Hall had done. I'd only been fired from a couple of jobs, maintained a B average in college, did fine in the Army. So, I figured, "Hey, why not leave well enough alone?"

And though I had a compulsion to write in my journal every day, and felt incomplete if I didn't, I mostly wrote about my observations of others, and the world around me, and events I was involved in.

Sure, I had strong emotions, the principal among them being fear, but I rarely if ever reflected on them, even in combat.

Of course, that would all change later when I fell in love.

Oddly enough, though, as I've grown older and my fires have dampened somewhat, I've found myself writing in my journals less and less, while exploring my inner conflicts and motivations more and more.

Humping it up Presidio Hill that day, with the horror of Nam behind me, I remember being so happy I felt I might faint.

All my life stretched out blankly before me like a long and

empty book at the printer's shop, with not a word on any page, only a "THE END" after many heavy numbers.

"What am I gonna do?" I asked the air.

"What's it matter?" I was pleased to believe it responded.

Every dogface has his day, and this was to be mine.

"How you doin' there, boy?" the major called, beaming a smile at me across her yard.

It was a positively radiant smile. She had the kind of olive skin that wrinkles only a little with age, and it stretched smoothly across her high, elegant cheekbones.

"Morning, Major Duval, I'm doing just fine," I replied, crunching up toward her across fallen gum tree leaves, leaves that fall summer, autumn, winter, and spring.

Standing above me on the damp crabgrass in a black turtleneck sweater and tight, hip-hugging, bell-bottom jeans that accentuated her tiny waist, her vast and still-fecund hips and breasts, the major was looking me over as well.

I'd dressed very carefully, as she had. Those who habitually wear military uniforms are extremely conscious of the way they look the first time people see them in civvies.

I was wearing bell-bottoms and a black turtleneck as well, along with a tight-fitting leather jacket. I'd made extra sure that not an article of my attire looked too pressed, too clean, too Dacron shiny and PX-new. I wore puka beads around my neck and a turquoise bracelet around one of my wrists.

So had the major.

Yet neither of us had succeeded in our disguises.

"Well, I do declare," she said. "Damn. If we don't look like the Tony Twins."

We were both happy for the excuse to laugh. She pressed my hand as if we were old friends.

"Come on into the house, hon, and let's have us our little talk."

"All right, Major."

"Now, you don't have to call me 'Major' at home. Call me Desirée."

"What?"

"Desirée. You know, like Napoleon's fiancée?"

"Wow."

"You like it?"

"Fantastic," I said. "It's so Old World and . . . *romantique.*"

"*Merci, jeune homme, vous êtes très gentil.*"

"*Mais je vous en prie, madame.* And you can call me Zack if you like."

Just as we reached her front porch, the fog suddenly lifted; we were bathed in sunlight, and Major Duval turned to regard the view of Alcatraz.

"Whoo, it's really something when that fog rolls back!"

She waved her hand toward the sunlit side of the bay.

"You know, this here is the prettiest damn state in the Union."

"The weirdest," I said, just to make talk.

Actually, I could not conceive of living anywhere else.

"Oh, I don't know about that. There's locos all over nowadays," she said, showing me inside, motioning me to take a seat on her living room sofa. "Look at those yoyos back in New York, blowing up that police station.

"Hell, even the Army's loaded with psychos. I had this big, fat, Cane River Creole for a commanding officer one time, over in Germany. And you're not going to believe this. Everyone knew he was a fool. Him and his skinny, little, high yellow wife.

"Then one day he has a heart attack at his desk, and we took off his jacket and we could see his pants been cut clean away around his behind."

"What?"

"His trousers, boy. Had 'em cut out around his butt, covered up by his jacket. And it was puckered black and blue from beating. A freak—him and his wife. We hushed it all up and gave him an honorable military funeral because his brother was a big shot in the colored quarter of Baton Rouge.

"But all I could think was—here's a man I worked with every day. From my own state of Louisiana! And he was always impeccable. But under that beautifully pressed and tailored forest green Army jacket of his, and all his service ribbons, his bare buns were sticking out.

"And let me tell you, that created quite a little stir around there. He was cleared for 'Top Secret.' If the Russians or East Germans ever got a hold of him, they could've blackmailed his octoroon ass from here to Dixie and back."

"I'll bet!" I said, attempting to laugh, as she stepped into the kitchen to pour us some coffee.

Truth was, though, I was puzzled. Not so much by her story as by the expression on her face when she told it. I was a bit titillated as well, despite myself, and didn't know why.

Except—I was reminded of Eugènie Lassnier, a pretty Eurasian girl I met one time when I was on leave in Saigon.

She worked at a place called *Bar Toi et Moi* on To Do Street, owned by a notorious Frenchwoman named *Maman Bich* who was purportedly her stepmother.

Anyway, one evening Eugènie and I were sitting at the bar having a chat and she said, *"Tu sais, je deteste de faire amour dans le cul. Enculer. Compris? C'est dégolasse!"*

From which I understood that someone had once performed anal intercourse upon her, and she didn't like it. But since she'd brought up the subject *a propos* of absolutely nothing, and since her manner of indicating her disgust was purposely insincere, I perceived that she was not disgusted at all, that her feigned aversion was meant to evoke a positive response from me.

And it worked.

I took her upstairs and did what she secretly wanted me to do, and she responded with gusto.

Later, after a long and hot double bath, I recall, we were strolling under the rolled barbed wire and banyan trees of pretty John F. Kennedy Park, across the street from the tall French Catholic Cathedral, when Eugènie leaned into me and whispered, *"Je joue, je joue encore, ça coule!* I'm still coming!"

And I believed I understood then ... something of the psychology of human perversity that I'd never understood before.

Eugènie may have been a complicated little prostitute, but I found a sweetness in her, a depth of soul.

On the morning when I had to return to my base, she insisted on accompanying me to the US military bus stop at Rùa Hồ.

Swinging on my arm, leaning on my shoulder, she smiled fondly up at me like a devoted fiancée.

When we reached the big open market at Ben Thanh, she stopped and asked me what the year of my birth was. When I told her it was 1945, she took me to a fabric vendor and bought me a lightweight, cream-colored, silk scarf, of a kind that Southeast Asians sometimes wear as a combination sweat sop and mosquito guard. Except that this one had a pattern of little "Hear No Evil, See No Evil, Speak No Evil" monkeys printed on it.

"*C'est pour la bonne chance, pour vous garder hors de danger, parce que vous êtes né dans l'année du singe,*" she said. "It's for good luck, to keep you from danger, because you were born in the Year of the Monkey."

And it worked!

I wore that scarf until it was tattered, yellow, and smelled like swamp water. But I was never wounded. Never got a scratch.

Only one other grunt in my platoon had that kind of luck. A black dude from Harlem named Malcolm McGee. Then, at least from what I heard, he got mugged and killed on his third day back in the world.

When Desirée popped out of the kitchen carrying a tray full of coffee and croissants and sat down beside me at the coffee table, I suddenly felt reckless and audacious, like I had nothing to lose. So, I told her a somewhat sanitized version of Eugènie's story, testing her.

When I was finished, she affected shock and said, "That is dis-gusting! You oughta be ashamed of yourself!"

Yet, she acted just as I had expected she might, with a sharp intake of breath and an increase of the pulse beat in her neck.

All through breakfast, we chatted of inconsequential things, squinting at each other in the bright sunlight that streamed in through her front windows, squirming in our seats, each of us hoping it would be the other who would get up the nerve to break the ice.

By the time we were finished, it had come to the point where I figured I was going to have to make my move. Yet I was afraid to make it, despite the encouragement her eyes appeared to be giving me. I hoped she'd make some more overt sign, for there to be no mistaking her desires.

I recollected several times in my life when, bedazzled by a woman's beauty, deceived by my lust, I'd been sure that she was beckoning, and made my move, only to be angrily admonished, or turned down flat, or even slapped in the face.

I knew how we men fool ourselves with women, convince ourselves that the most innocent glance is an invitation, and act upon our illusions.

I was also aware of how certain women provoke us falsely, just to prove their power.

And I could not take the slightest chance of offending this woman who, after all, was my commanding officer, and held my discharge papers, my life, in her hands.

"You know, I was wondering all night long, son," the major said, when we'd finished eating and were seated closely together on her sofa, "how you ever got by on your own, with no mom or dad, no family at all."

"Let me tell you, it wasn't easy," I said, in my little boy voice. "Sometimes it was kind of touch and go."

"Why, you poor baby; come here and let Mama give you a hug," she said, raising her arms to me.

"Ooooh," I moaned, she moaned, and we fell over sideways on the sofa.

I crawled then upon the sweet expanse of my commanding

officer and got off instantaneously into my Army-issue boxer shorts. I tore at her sweater and jerked it around her neck while her head lolled back against the sofa. Ripped her bra off. Threw it in a corner.

Then, as I put it later in my journal, "I went down upon her marvels, her mams. Sucked nip and mum till she begged me quit, else she die of excess. Slid those jeans down her broad-bottomed beam and we rolled like a boat upon the waters, heaved like the sea. The tide rose higher. The wind yelled. And there we were again, atop another wondrous wave, a tidal flow, a frothy blow and ebb. Then on to uncharted fathoms, unplumbed depths, down and down to rest at last in womb, homeroom, essence."

When at last we broke it off to grab a breath, she held my head between her breasts, stroked my hair and said, "Say, you know, boy, the reason I first had my eye on you is—I thought of you for this job I told you about, when you get your discharge?

"Some old government boy come by G-2 and wants to know if I got anyone to recommend. Says he needs a smart, well-educated, young combat vet with French and Southeast Asian language abilities who's just about to get out. Some kind of undercover work.

"'Right now, we got too many of those goddamn Ivy Leaguers working for us,' he says. 'People starting to talk.' So, he's looking for a clever, young fellow from a working-class background. Po' boy like you. 'Show them Libs in Congress we can play it straight,' he says. Pay's good. Twelve times what you're getting now."

"Sounds great, but this sounds better," I said, and blew into her cleavage.

"Ooooh, that tickles!" she protested and clamped down hard

upon my head and held it tighter and tighter in her lactiferous cleft until I surrendered all resistance and whistled like a white-bellied mammal in a fish net for mercy.

CHAPTER THREE

The Hurt Locker

If Major Duval had told me that six months to the day after our first and only carnal encounter, I'd be strapped to the metal floor of a rickety old C-47, spiraling toward the Mekong River in a precipitous, missile-avoiding, corkscrew landing approach, I'd have told her she must be out of her tree.

My sense of surreal familiarity only deepened when I clanged down the steps a few minutes later with a groggy gang of hung-over airmen just back from R & R and got smacked by the torrid heat and paddy-stench of upcountry rainy season. And my sinking sensation reached bottom as I hotfooted across the steaming blacktop toward the control tower of the Royal Thai Air Force base at Nakhon Phanom and glimpsed the cloud-ringed jungle mountains of Laos on the horizon and a pair of Air America Hueys going *whap-whap-whap* as they prepped for take-off.

And I asked myself for the umpteenth time, since I'd

embarked upon this my second perilous *Journey to the East,* how in the Lord Buddha's name my duplicitous commander had ever seduced me into revisiting a region of the world that I'd sworn on the putative grave of my absent mother to never set foot in again.

To be sure, the tax-free salary was nothing to sniff at, socked away as it was in a numbered Swiss account. Yet how could it ever compensate for the likely ending of my young life in a pile of buffalo dung?

I wondered if the major hadn't worked some kind of Cajun *juju* on me.

Or maybe the nameless "government man" she'd introduced me to at the Saint Francis Hotel had laced my drink with one of those mind-altering, will-defeating drugs of movie lore.

"Probably, though, the bitch read me like a book," I confessed to myself as a scrawny little Thai customs official with a thin mustache, flanked by a stout, black, scowling US Air Policeman, scrutinized my papers in the Ad Building. "Played the old 'Mommy Card' on me—The Queen of Hearts."

It was all so obvious, so pathetic.

I had conspired yet again in my own defeat.

It was nothing new. I'd run scams on myself like this forever. Like breaking out of Juvie Hall, just when I had a nice new foster home lined up. Or volunteering for military service at the height of the Vietnam War when I could have easily evaded it by going to graduate school . . .

In short, my beautiful, young, Hollywood starlet mommy, with the shiny platinum hair, sky-blue eyes, and electric-crimson lipstick, who abandoned me at the age of four and nightly haunted my dreams, had managed yet again to punish me for the crime of being.

I am the whore, I thought, not Major Duval.

And like the whore I was, I had signed on the dotted line— in opposition to all my hopes and dreams, all the dictates of reason—to three years as a "contract employee" for an obvious front organization called "Air-Sea Supply," with an address in Nakhon Phanom, Thailand.

An unsigned oral addendum to the contract specified five months of training in Covert Ops and Special Warfare at Camp Peary in York County, Virginia, followed by a four-week crash course in Lao at the Defense Language Institute in Monterey, California.

I did so-so at Camp Peary. Didn't have my heart in it, I told myself. But in Monterey I was at the top of my class.

Twenty-four hours after the graduation ceremony, on November 26, 1971, I found myself flying out across the Golden Gate from Travis Air Force Base, in Fairfield, California.

Several rest-stops and thirty-six hours later, I landed at a familiar hellhole called Tan Son Nhat Airport in Saigon, Vietnam.

After enduring a twenty-minute VC mortar barrage that crept across the airfield and stopped a mere hundred meters short of my petrified, piss-smelling Braniff 707, I transferred to the Air America C-47 which flew me through a fluster of popping Kalashnikovs to that woeful stain on the map where I found myself now.

As directed, I spoke to no one at the air base and stepped outside the gates the moment I cleared customs.

I flagged down a three-wheeled motorcycle taxi, with a

metal roof, called a *"tuk-tuk."* And we roared off in a mass of other *tuk-tuks,* bicycles, motorbikes, pint-sized pickup trucks and decrepit, smoke-spewing buses into a steaming, teeming, palm-fringed, little tropical city constructed almost entirely of blackened, mold-encrusted concrete.

On our way down Sala Klang Road, I saw open-air markets, religious shops with great laughing Buddhas in their windows and dark mysterious places with no signs outside that I assumed to be opium dens, whorehouses, or two-in-one establishments.

I saw tribal women in native garb just down from the hills, and river fishermen with buckets of carp suspended on poles across their backs.

And everywhere I saw soldiers and airmen—American, Australian, Thai, Lao and Hmong—with bargirls on their arms.

At the downtown headquarters of Air-Sea Supply, on Klang Meung Road, a tiny, grinning doorman ushered me into a large, modern office, with Thai secretaries tapping away at typewriters in their cubicles.

I introduced myself to the comely young receptionist as Michael Rafferty and said I had an appointment with Chief Executive Officer George Reynolds.

She made a phone call, smiled prettily, and directed me to the stairway.

"Third floor," she said, in a clipped British-Asian accent. "First office on your left. Please knock before you enter."

As I was about to lift my fist to knock, a loud military-sounding voice magically summoned me within.

Expecting some big, burly, first-sergeant-looking dude, I was surprised when a skinny, balding, pinch-faced little middle-aged man, in a tropical linen suit came forward, firmly shook my hand and said, "Hey, I was expecting you. Have a seat, man."

His rough informal manner, I decided, as he fidgeted into the chair behind his desk, was an attempt to compensate for a rather bland visual representation.

"Okay, trooper, you're not going to have much to do with me after today. My job is to orientate you and see that you're comfortable."

The first word I had to learn here, he said, was "deniability." Since Laos was a neutral nation, and the United States had signed a UN agreement to that effect, our military mission in the country did not exist. For that reason, I was never to utter the letters "CIA" aloud. Instead, I was to call it "the Firm," and I should only refer to The Firm's cross-border Thai-Lao operation by its radio call sign, "Sky."

Sky's focus was on northern Laos. Ninety percent of the war went on there, with the North Vietnamese pitted against Sky's Hmong guerrilla allies. The NVA had 70,000 troops against Sky's 30,000, but it did not have Air America to lift it over the mud, so it couldn't do much in the rainy season. As soon as the dry season hit, though, the NVA advanced, gobbling up a little more territory each year, even though the USAF had already dumped more ordnance on Laos than it had dropped in all of World War II and Korea.

"Okay, enough said about Sky and their ops," Reynolds said. "We're a separate, smaller and more specialized unit. Our code name is Apple, and we go about things in a different way. We are a secret within a secret. We operate against all the rules of warfare, and we make it work."

Most Sky agents lived in the garden suburbs of Nakhon Phanom, he said, where they had homes and families, nannies, gardeners, and maids. They commuted back and forth, on Air America, to Long Tieng, their in-country base of operations, every few days, and they let their Hmong auxiliaries pretty much run things for themselves.

Apple officers, on the other hand, lived with their tribal allies, the Khmu, in the highest, most inaccessible mountains of the north. They concentrated on long-range covert ops rather than set piece air and artillery-backed engagements like Sky. They got a week's R & R after two or three months in the field if they were lucky.

"Excuse me, sir," I said, when he paused for a second. "I wonder if it's too late to apply for a job at Sky."

I was serious, but Reynolds chose to take it as a joke, and he laughed long and hard.

"'Fraid not, trooper. Somebody already volunteered your ass, and it's a done deal."

"Whew, maybe it wasn't too smart to take up with that G-2 lady after all."

"Maybe not. Ha ha. I think I heard of that lady before. Major Duval, right? Well, you know what I told other people in your place? I give 'em a quote from Dante's *Inferno:*

> *'Do not be afraid.*
> *Our fate cannot be taken from us.*
> *It is a gift.'*

Reynolds went on to tell me that I was going to be working

for a man named Jimmy Love, who was Apple's commander in northern Laos.

"Is that his real name, or a radio code name?"

"The latter. His real name is Joachim Liebermann. No one can pronounce it, so we sort of loosely translated it. He's of Ruthenian Jewish origin, from what I hear. And don't ask me where Ruthenia is."

"It's in the Carpathian Mountains of Eastern Europe, I believe, probably part of the Soviet Union or Romania now."

"Whatever."

Reynolds said that Jimmy Love was an "independent operator" with more than twenty-five years of experience in Laos.

He parachuted into Indochina with the OSS in World War II, hooked up with Ho Chi Minh and fought with him against the Japanese until the end.

He was intimately acquainted with all the old political and military players in Vietnam and Laos, whatever their political affiliations. He had fought with or against all of them at one time or another, through all the ups and downs, all the twists and turns since the war, and he was universally respected, if not loved.

Jimmy Love had been running his lone-wolf operation in northern Laos for many years, since long before the war in Vietnam, so the Firm let him go his own way.

He had as little to do with Sky as possible, except to share the services of Air America, and to back them up when "they get their asses into deep doo-doo."

Jimmy operated in the Golden Triangle area where Laos,

Thailand, Burma, Vietnam, and China ran together, Reynolds said, and what he had up there was "an enormously complicated state of affairs," especially where the native population of Laos was concerned.

It was not just a political or military problem.

There was also a clash of cultures.

It was much like the American frontier in the 1800s.

The Lao Lum were relatively prosperous lowland peasants who spoke the national language and supported the Royal Laotian Government.

The Lao Theung—what the French had called the "*Montagnards*", and the Americans called "Yards" or "Indigs"— were the primitive mountain tribes, each with its own unique language and culture. And like American Indians they had been at each other's throats from time immemorial.

The lowlanders discriminated against all the Indigs, regardless of tribal affiliation, and called them *Ling*, an impolite form of "monkeys." For that reason, the tribes agreed on one thing: their support of the Pathet Lao.

The exception that proved the rule was a minority of the Hmong and Khmu tribes, whom the Firm paid off with rice and certain mercantile concessions.

To make things even more complicated, some of the mountain tribes found it profitable to shift their allegiances from time to time, to maneuver for temporary advantages, and to stick it to their perceived competitors whenever they got a chance.

The Firm's mission in the region was to compel the North Vietnamese Army to commit more supplies and manpower to Laos, and less to the war in South Vietnam.

The specific role of Jimmy's Khmu guerillas was to harass the enemy to his east and help prevent attacks on Sky's main base to his south.

Jimmy's headquarters firebase was in the Namptha Mountains, near a village called Thavay.

Laos was the size of the UK, Reynolds said, but it had a population about the size of the Bronx, most of it concentrated in the lowlands along the Mekong River. Thavay was in the least populated province of all.

Jimmy's HQ was built at the top of a river bluff about five kilometers from the village. The Laotians called it Kuany Phu, "Banana Mountain," but Jimmy called it "Firebase Juliet."

It was manned by one oversized company with an HQ Section, a Security Section, and three Main Force Platoons.

Jimmy and his executive officer, a French national working for the Firm, managed the HQ Section.

Thai mercenaries and a token force of Royal Laotian Army ran the Security Section. Three American combat veterans led the Main Force Platoons. Each platoon had three ten-man squads of Khmu riflemen commanded by native sergeants. Each squad had two "tiger-teams" led by native corporals.

For special missions, Jimmy called in the USAF from Udon Thani, in Thailand, or Danang over in Vietnam. For really heavy stuff, he called in the B-52s from Guam.

Jimmy named his companies and platoons in a peculiar manner, Reynolds said.

Instead of "Company A," as traditional in the US Army, he had "Love Company." Instead of "First, Second and Third Platoons," he had "Canarsie, Red Hook and Gowanus Platoons."

"Why does he name them like that?" I asked.

"Guess."

"He's from Brooklyn?"

"Nobody ever said Jimmy had a frail ego."

"And we're called 'Love Company,' and our radio call sign is 'Apple,' as in 'The Big Apple?'"

"Now you got the idea."

"Which platoon do I get?"

"You'll lead Canarsie Platoon."

"Okay, can you fill me in now on what I'll be doing with my platoon?"

"First, you'll be getting them in shape for field ops. Then, you'll take 'em out to harass old Uncle Ho and Papa Lao."

"Who's 'Papa Lao'?"

"NATO radio code for Pathet Lao is 'Papa Lima.' For some reason, it's evolved into Papa Lao. Just like Viet Cong has evolved from 'Victor Charlie' into Chuck, or Charlie, or Mr. Charles. Individual Pathet Lao soldiers are called 'Gomers.'"

"Why Gomers?"

"Well, Jimmy tagged them with that, way back when. But . . . have you ever read the bible?"

"Nope."

"Gomer was a Galatian Jew who lived a thousand years."

"Meaning?"

"Meaning your average Pathet Lao, like his opposing Royal Laotian Army man, is so timid in battle he'll probably live forever. The NVA and the Firm just keep 'em around for window dressing."

"I see. Now, if you don't mind me asking, sir, who am I

gonna be replacing?"

"Tucker Johnson."

"Who's he?"

"A thirty-year-old Abo from Australian Special Forces."

"A what?"

"You heard me."

"Damn, sir, in Vietnam, it seemed like nearly every boonie rat was a smart-ass, nineteen-year-old from the inner city or a pimple-faced hillbilly from the Great Smoky Mountains. It was rare to find an NCO from north of the Mason-Dixon Line, and now here you are talking about Frenchmen, Australian Aborigines, Ruthenian Jews..."

"Yeah, well, what you're going to find out about us, Zack, is that we are not at all what you'd find in Vietnam, or even over at Sky, which is mostly asshole Ivy Leaguers. Jimmy has attracted an amazingly diverse bunch, and I think you're gonna find that to be a tremendous advantage. Our problem here in Southeast Asia, in my opinion, is that no one dares to think out of the box. Jimmy celebrates diversity and creative thinking."

"So, what happened to him?"

"Who?"

"The Australian Abo."

"KIA."

"How long have my fellow platoon leaders been around?"

"Let's see. One of them got here about three months ago. The other has been around a couple of months longer."

"And they also replaced KIA's, I take it?"

"I ... uh ... afraid so."

"I thought you said the Gomers were useless in battle."

"They are, generally. It's the Goomers you've got to worry about."

"Who the fuck are the Goomers?"

"That's what we call the NVA in Laos, don't ask me why. Anyway, they're all over the place. They occupy more than half the country now, maybe two thirds."

"I see," I said, and came within an ace of turning around and walking out the door.

Perhaps gauging my reaction, Reynolds changed the subject.

"Despite certain disadvantages," he said, "this job really does have some pluses, compared to service in Vietnam."

"Oh yeah? And what are those?"

"Well, for one thing you get paid a hell of a lot more. For another, you'll never be interrogated about suspicious deaths in the field. And no matter what you do, you will never be brought up on charges of 'conduct unbecoming of an officer.'"

"Well, that's a real comfort, isn't it?"

"Affirmative," he said, ignoring my sarcasm. "Up there at Firebase Juliet, my friend, you may find it to be exactly that."

After Reynolds had filled me in on various other technical aspects of my job, he smiled and brought up a more pleasant subject.

"While you're here in Nakhon Phanom, you'll be staying at the Queen's Park Hotel. You are a tourist from Los Angeles. You're registered as Michael Rafferty, so use that passport. I'm glad you traveled light because you'll find all the tropical gear you need in your hotel room. We checked to see we had the right size. So just tuk-tuk on over there, make yourself at home, and grab some Z's, if you're so inclined.

"They've got a swimming pool. It's a bit mildewed around the edges. One of my friends claims it gave him an eye, ear, nose, and throat infection. And we won't even talk about the size of the mosquitoes. But it's the best you'll find in these parts.

"Jimmy is down here right now with a couple of his people for a little R & R. Like a lot of old soldiers, he tends to overindulge when he hits town. But you'll never find a better field commander. Even our competitors over at Sky say, 'The man's got hang.'"

"What's that mean?"

"In Lao, the word 'hang' means 'a man who stays and fights.' And it kind of stuck with us English speakers for obvious reasons."

"Okay, I think I'm starting to get the 'hang' of it."

Reynolds forced a companionable laugh.

"Now, if you feel the need of female companionship, before Jimmy rolls out of whatever girly bar he happens to be in, just let me know. I'll send someone over. But don't even think about going out looking for strange stuff.

"Do not let these people fool you, man. They're all smiles. But we're right across the river from Laos, and they've got spies everywhere. Mata Haris of every size, shape, and color. From Thai People's Liberation Army to Red Chinese. Pathet Lao to Viet Cong. Khmer Rouge to Ho Chi Minh Incorporated. Got it?"

"Oh yeah? Then what about Jimmy Love and his bargirls?"

"Hey, you're a newbie. Jimmy's seen it all. No little bar girl is gonna put anything over on Mr. Love. I heard one tried to, a few years back, and you know what he did? He shot her down like a dog, right on the dance floor."

"No way!"

Reynolds sniffed, grinned, and shook his head. "There it is, man."

"Yup," I said, as I had done a thousand times in Nam. "There it is."

"Oh, and one more thing. Jimmy flew down with Kimo Kalani, one of your fellow platoon leaders, and Nittaya Aromdée, his chief medic, and they're staying in your hotel. I doubt they're with Jimmy now. They're in such close-quarters upcountry, you see, they tend to go it alone when they hit town. When you've rested up, you might want to hook up with them. Let 'em show you the ropes before Jimmy turns up."

"Sounds good."

"Nittaya is in Room 318, registered under Mae-Ying Meesong, which I know is some kind of arcane local joke. Mae-Ying was a famous Shan warrior-woman up on the Burmese border back in the Fifties. Anyhow, she's a local girl, very young, and quite a number. Been with Jimmy three or four months. Used to be a medical intern, I heard. Studied in Paris."

"And the guy?"

"Kimo's this big Hawaiian dude. He's in Room 320, registered under the name Hale Akala."

"Isn't Haleakala the name of some big volcano on the island of Maui?"

"Whatever. They're always clowning around up there."

"Okay, one last thing. If anyone asks about me at the hotel, what do I tell them?"

"Just tell them you're in the Import-Export business."

"Isn't that kind of suspicious?"

"Maybe, but around here it's just another way of saying, 'Fuck off!'"

CHAPTER FOUR

A Smile to Die For

Despite my misgivings, the Queen's Park Hotel turned out to be perfectly cool, quiet, and comfortable. Six stories high, with a view of the long-tailed boats on the Mekong River, it had an atrium, a splashing fountain and a pair of pretty, smiling, English-speaking receptionists all fitted out in Thai silk.

My room on the top floor was light and airy, furnished in Siamese faux antiques, with framed wall prints featuring salient events in local history and religion.

I had not slept in more than thirty-six hours, so I threw myself on the bed in my clothes and never fluttered an eyelid until late that afternoon when there came a soft, feminine rapping at my door.

Tiptoeing across the room, squinting through the peephole, I spied a tall, striking young Asian woman who appeared to be dressed for the pool in a fluffy, white, hotel kimono.

She was up close to the peephole, and when she heard me

behind the door, she broke into a preparatory grin that could have simply meant that she was a native of Thailand, "The Land of Smiles."

Or maybe it was just the cordial expression one assumes before meeting a business associate for the first time.

When I looked a bit closer, though, I realized that her smile was real. It was genuine, and it lit up the world. It was so stunning, so unique, in fact, that I hesitated to open the door for a moment to analyze why this might be so. Her lips, I noticed, were fuller than a typical American girl's, a shade or two darker than her golden skin. Her upper lip was even plumper than the lower, which gave her the pretty, pouty look that bi-annual Botox injections provide to Hollywood starlets. Her teeth were bright, white, and even, with one imperfection: a slight, saucy gap between the two front ones. As a general impression, her smile was exceptionally wide and confident, and it rose to a pair of perfect little dimples.

She must have been aware of its potent effect, but there was no hint that she wished to exaggerate it. Her expression seemed entirely open and unaffected, as if she were simply delighted at being young, alive, and beautiful.

Recalling Reynolds's word of warning about unauthorized fraternization with the local Mata Haris, I thought for a moment that she was a bit too good to be true.

I was tempted to ignore her, but something in her attitude—an impish, ironic quality, as if she were on the verge of bursting into laughter at any moment—caused me to open the door instead.

"*Suwadeeka*," she said, pressing her hands together, raising them to her dark moist lips while slowly, serenely bowing in the local form of greeting called "*Wai.*"

"*Suwadeekap,*" I replied and bowed in kind, as they'd taught me at the Defense Language Institute.

"Mr. Rafferty?"

"Yes, ma'am."

"Hello, I am Mae-Ying Meesong from Air-Sea Supply," she said.

An unruly strand of dark hair had fallen over one eye while she'd been performing her ritual greeting, so she cocked her head now and blew on it a couple of times, without much success.

"I have come to answer any questions you might have. Do you fancy a swim?"

Despite my lack of travel experience, I'd always had an ear for accents, and I could usually place an American to within a few miles of his home state.

Yet, this girl had a one-of-a-kind accent. It took me a moment to figure it out, but I soon detected three distinct elements: the carefully grammatical British of a Diana Rigg, the throaty Parisian "R" of a Françoise Hardy, and the charming Asian lilt of a Connie Chan.

Since the one factor linking the three was the cinema, I concluded that she had acquired her accent in English from watching films, a not uncommon occurrence in this part of the world.

Wherever she'd acquired the accent, her voice was deep and husky for an Asian girl, and it skipped from amusement to mockery in an instant. Once heard, it was impossible to forget.

"Normally, I'd love to go for a swim," I said, waving her

into the room after my moment of reflection, shutting the door behind her, wondering what she looked like under that kimono. "But Reynolds has pretty much turned me off on it. From what he said, I'm gonna get the Black Plague if I so much as dip a pinky in."

"Oh, you are not going to turn out to be some kind of milquetoast, are you, Mr. Rafferty?" she said, bursting into the laughter she'd been holding back.

Yet, in a beguiling Oriental gesture of feminine decorum, she shut her eyes, bowed her head slightly, and covered her mouth with a long slender hand to hide her amusement.

Though her merriment was at my expense, it sent shivers of pleasure down my spine and compelled me to scrutinize her with an even more meticulous eye than in my peephole impression.

Unlike some Laotian girls, cursed with squat necks, spherical heads, full-moon faces and flat noses, she had been blessed with an elongated neck, a narrow skull, a lovely heart-shaped face and a prominent, curved nose. She wore her long, thick, black hair piled up in a bouffant to accentuate the beauty of her high cheekbones and large, dark cat eyes. Taken along with her noble bearing, the effect, at least in my overheated imagination, was more ancient Egyptian than Asian.

Yet only when it all came together in a characteristic facial expression was I able to gain an impression of her personality. Vulnerable to error due to an instant and immoderate animal attraction, my impression was that she was well-spoken and highly educated, a woman of character, good humor and breeding.

I might have added integrity, but there was something a

little more complicated than total candor in those bright, fierce, intelligent eyes of hers.

In short, she was an intriguing, exotic, young woman with secrets she could tell—but probably would not.

Another thing I noticed about her was this. Even though there was an enormous full-length mirror just across the room from her, she was so poised and self-assured that she—unlike any other woman I had known—never once sought her own image there.

"I mean, considering what you are about to step into upcountry," she was saying when I finally floated back to reality, "a little dirty water is the least of your worries, *na?*"

"Okay, if you must call into question my manhood just to get your way," I said, hiding my momentary distraction with a wink. "Just give me a sec to find a swimsuit, all right?"

"Is Mr. Hale Akela coming?" I asked, as I stepped out of the bathroom a few minutes later wearing a pair of boxer trunks and a t-shirt. "Reynolds said I ought to consult with him too."

"Before I answer your question, I should just like to say that we can dispense with surnames and pseudonyms from now on when we're *en privé*. We mostly go by radio code names anyhow."

"What's Kimo's code name?"

"Lay-Low."

"Why's that?"

"Well, because he is this big, laid-back Polynesian who likes to stay in the shade."

"What do I call you?"

"Okay, I am Nittaya, but since you Americans seem to find it so difficult to pronounce, you can call me Nita, or Doc, if you like. But please do not call me by my radio code name if you value your life."

"What is it?"

"It is *absurdement sexiste,* and I hate it."

"Go on, fess up."

"'Honeybuns,'" she said giggling, and wriggled them a bit to make her point.

"Wow, you don't dig that? Hey, I think it might be right on, you know?"

"And what shall I call you, *Monsieur,* aside from *indiscret et impoli?*"

"I'm Zachary, but you can call me Zack."

"Fine, but what about a code name?"

"I don't know. What do you think?"

"I get to name you? Hooray!" she said, leaping about like a gleeful twelve-year-old. "Where are you from?"

"Los Angeles."

"What part?"

"Hollywood."

"There it is, *na?*"

"How do you figure that?"

"Turn around and look in the mirror."

"Hey, I tell you what," I said, beaming my most camera-friendly grin at her. "If you don't call me 'Hollywood,' I won't call you 'Honeybuns.' Except over the radio. How's that?"

She seemed delighted with the bargain.

"Now, as to your question about Lay-Low, I am afraid he is busy now. We shall probably not be seeing him tonight."

"Out hitting the go-go bars, huh?"

She covered her mouth again to conceal her glee.

"Oh no, not at all! Lay-Low is a devout Catholic, and he is . . . *strictement fidèle* to his wife in Hawaii. In fact, I suspect he is with his confessor, Father Coquelot, at the Holy Apostolic Mission, as we speak."

"Don't you find it kind of weird that this guy is so devout? I mean, given what he does and all."

"Uh-huh, but from what he tells me, he is pretty normal for a Hawaiian boy. Your *farang* missionaries got to his village back in the nineteenth century, he says. And his people, despite their warlike traditions, have been disciples of Jesus, Maria, Jehovah, the Holy Ghost and all your many sainted martyrs ever since."

"I take it you find our Western religions a bit puerile, open to parody," I said, still bantering with her as we rode down in the elevator.

"Oh, you have me wrong there," she said over her shoulder, as we stepped out into the atrium and headed for the pool. "I am a Theravada Buddhist, and the Lord Buddha teaches that there are infinite paths to enlightenment."

"Hey now, that's one mellow religion you got there, lady. In my country, we got fifty brands of Baptists battling to the death over the meaning of one line of scripture. And we won't even talk about the Catholics, Mormons and Jews."

"The difference is that Buddhism is not a religion," she said, in a chanting, *Metta Sutta* tone that I found enthralling. "It makes no pretenses of being other than one of many humble ways."

At poolside, we found a pair of lounge chairs and pulled them up close.

She threw off her kimono, dove into the pool, and started

doing butterfly laps before I could get more than a glance at her bikini-clad body.

A native pool staffer, had one been standing by, would have been popeyed in shock at her action, so common for a young woman in the United States. That's because, in Southeast Asia at the time, it was social suicide for young ladies to appear in public wearing any sort of Western bathing costume, and a bikini was quite beyond the pale.

In Vietnam, for instance, I had seen the most hardened bargirls and prostitutes frolicking in the surf at Phan Thiet Beach fully clothed, like perfect Victorian ladies.

As I am sure she calculated, her 'improper' behavior inflamed me past enduring, so I flung off my t-shirt and dove in after her.

I found her to be a remarkably strong swimmer, a match for even this California surfer dude.

After half an hour racing each other, splashing water, and giggling like children, we swam to the edge of the pool and started to lift ourselves out.

Partway up, with our arms straining against our weight, we paused for a second as if by mutual consent to give each other a quick once over.

Me, all tan, and buff from months of combat training.

Nittaya, with her flawless golden skin and curvaceous bod, her long, straight, black hair streaming down and her breasts swelling out of her pink bikini top.

Then our eyes locked, we stopped laughing, and there was a *Click!*

We both heard it, and it was so implausibly loud and clear that we burst out laughing and leaned our slick shoulders together as if we had known each other forever.

Once we'd managed to extricate ourselves from our state of enchantment, we lay back in our lounge chairs, shared a joint that she pulled from her kimono pocket, and continued our conversation while blowing smoke rings at the sky.

We spoke easily, like old friends, giggling for the feeblest excuses.

Yet to my torment (and secret titillation), she never failed to hide her beautiful, laughing mouth with her hand.

"It is better we talk here," she whispered, scooting her lounge chair up closer to me. "I mean, if we have anything serious to say. For all we know, the rooms may be bugged."

"I was warned of that," I said, smelling her wet skin warmed by the sun, ogling her breasts, belly, and legs.

Noting my fixation, she laid her head back, smiled, and basked in the warmth of the sun and my mute adoration.

I noticed that she wore a ragged, old, leather thong around her neck, with an antique, bronze, Buddha's head hanging between her breasts.

"Tell me something, Nittaya. Why do you wear that around your neck?"

"Why not?"

"I'd expect a woman like you to be wearing something a little more chic. You know what I mean?"

"Well, I think you may find some other surprising things about me, if you know me long enough."

"I don't doubt that."

"But for some reason I find myself willing to indulge your rude, *farang* curiosity. My Great-Aunt, Celèste, gave me this when I was a young girl. She said it was to keep me safe from harm. It's worked pretty well so far, so I see no reason to toss it out."

"Okay, I see. Now one more question, if you don't mind. How come you're so goddamn athletic?"

"I have always been that way. Do not ask me why. I was a gymnast at my *Lycée,* and at university in Paris, I was on the swimming team."

"Really? Okay, tell me something else. Why are you the only Asian girl I've ever met who wears a bikini in public?"

"Come on, Zack! I studied in France for seven years. *France,* where the bikini was *invented!* And besides . . ."

"What?"

She smiled and reached out to touch my arm.

"When you get to know me better, you will find that I am not like other Asian girls."

"Why not?"

"I have become somewhat decadent and European."

"How? I mean aside from running around half-naked in a bikini?"

"Well, how about this? In 1967, on my annual summer trip home from Paris, I backpacked from Europe to India with all the hippies on the Great Grass Road. And a year later I was right in the middle of *les Eventments de Mai.*"

"All right, I know what the Great Grass Road is, but what are 'The Events of May?'" I asked with a touch of pique.

I'd fallen for her exotic air, and this news of Europe and hippies was not altogether welcome.

"*Mon Dieu,* where have you been?" she said, raising her

hand and slapping my arm in the same spot she'd been stroking a moment before. "You never heard of the student revolt of May 1968? I mean, we took over the entire city of Paris for two weeks!"

"Well, lemme see. Oh yeah, in May 1968 I was in basic training at Fort Ord, California, with my drill sergeant kicking my ass twenty-four hours a day, so I didn't have much time to be reading newspapers about frolicking French students."

She smiled up at me, caressing the place where she'd just slapped me, causing the hairs on my forearm to bristle and stiffen.

"Then, *peut-être*," she said, tilting her head, raising an index finger, "your ignorance can be forgiven."

At this point, a waiter came out, his eyes popping at the sight of Nittaya's bikini, and nervously asked if we'd like anything to drink.

She ordered us a cold bottle of *Pouilly Fuissé* and some vegetable rolls.

We wolfed down the rolls and finished the wine in a flash. She ordered some more, we smoked another joint, and soon we were feeling no pain.

As it turned out, we did not get much business talk done that afternoon.

What we did—we told each other our life stories.

Only later would I learn that we had both fudged a bit.

In her case, maybe more than a bit.

I volunteered to tell my sad tale first. In a blatant attempt to garner her sympathy, I put on a brave face and trotted out the tired, old shtick I had pulled on every desirable chick I ever met.

Portraying my deprived childhood and youth as a tragi-comedy, laughing at all my foibles and defeats, I told of my abandonment on the streets of Hollywood. The series of dreadful foster homes I had endured. The six years I spent working my way through college in a succession of deadbeat jobs. My narrow escapes from annihilation, in the jungles of Vietnam.

And it seemed to work on her just as it had on all the rest. Like a charm.

Her eyes welled up. Her long, dark, lids drooped down. Her heavy, black lashes flickered, ensnaring teardrops as they fell. She looked up at the sky, sniffled, and shook her head.

Then, drawing a corner of her soft, full mouth down in a sweet little gesture of girlish compassion, she tenderly stroked the back of my hand.

When it was her turn, Nittaya painted a far rosier picture than I had. At the same time, she hinted at certain shadowy secrets she might reveal when we were better acquainted.

She came from a bourgeois family of mixed Lao, Thai and Chinese ancestry, she said. She was raised in Vientiane, the capital city of Laos. Her parents, Analu and Yada Aromdée, were both still alive, and she had an older, married sister named Kalama who was now pregnant with her second child. All her immediate family was anti-Communist and supported the Royalist government. Yet oddly, her father's black sheep, younger brother, Vong Aromdée, had been a Pathet Lao commander, and an avowed enemy of Jimmy Love, until his recent death in a US bombing raid.

"Not to be bragging or anything," she said, returning to a more pleasant tack, "but I am pretty fluent in five languages."

In addition to her native Lao, she had learned Thai from her mother, who was born in Bangkok, and Mandarin Chinese from her maternal grandmother. She acquired French at the *Lycée Française* in Vientiane and from her father, who had worked for the French Colonial Administration. She got her English from a succession of British nannies.

Both her parents were medical specialists—her mother an obstetrician and her father a heart surgeon—they had met at Bumrungrad International Hospital in Bangkok, where they practiced medicine at the time.

Without thinking about it very much, Nittaya had "followed in their footsteps."

She studied in Paris at the *Université de Paris' Faculté de Médicine* and went on to an internship at Bangkok International Hospital.

She dropped out after her first year of internship when she felt her country was in danger of being overrun by the communists and felt obliged to do what she could to prevent it.

She met Jimmy Love at her family home in Vientiane. Jimmy and her *papá* were old friends, although their connection was rather mysterious. Probably something political, she thought.

"I was fascinated when I met Jimmy," she said, "because he was famous in our part of the world and sort of . . . bigger than life."

"Could you tell me more about Jimmy? I mean, Reynolds wasn't too specific."

"Sure, if you have all day."

"Is it that long a story?"

"Even longer. But I shall try to make it short. At the Firm,

Jimmy is a very controversial character. Some people call him "an insubordinate but lovable old rascal." And it is true that Jimmy can be witty, charming, and funny when he is in the mood. Others said he is "ruthless, unscrupulous, and corrupt," and there are indeed times when he cuts some ethical corners. Still others say he is an obnoxious, incompetent, womanizing old drunk. In this perhaps, they are overdoing it—at least about the incompetent part—because only his very worst enemies question his record of success.

"What no one disputes is that Jimmy has one of the hugest egos in creation. For example, most landing sites in Laos are named for their height in meters or their location. Lima Site 622 is located on a mountaintop six hundred and twenty-two meters tall. Firebase Bang is built on Mount Bang. Yet Jimmy calls his headquarters camp, Lima Site 5520, or alternatively, Firebase Juliet.

"At first, nobody could figure out why because there was no mountain in Laos that high, nor was there any mountain called Juliet. Then one day someone happened to look at Jimmy's service records and discovered that he was born on 5/5/20. After that, they remembered that Juliet was NATO radio code for the letter "J." Jimmy's mighty, ego-boosting effort came to naught, however, when everybody ended up calling the place, 'The Patch.'

"Why'd they call it that?"

"Shorthand for 'The Poppy Patch.'

"I still don't ..."

"Didn't Reynolds mention anything to you about the price Jimmy has to pay to keep the Khmu on his side?"

"No, what price?"

"Well, aside from feeding them with rice and C-Rations and a large daily dose of rice wine and *lau-lau,* our local firewater, he lets them grow opium poppies, just as they have always done. The difference now is that he gets Air America to fly it to market for them, which increases their profits a hundred times over."

"How does he get away with that?"

"He gives the generals who run our country 'a piece of the action' to keep them quiet, and his bosses at the Firm just tend to wink at his transgressions."

"What I don't get, Nittaya, is why you were attracted to a shady kind of deal like this. I mean, you just don't seem like the type."

"Well, I had heard so much about Jimmy's incredible exploits that I thought he was our only hope. I knew his native troops had suffered many casualties. As a medical professional, I felt obliged to do what I could to help. So, I joined up with Jimmy four months ago, much to the chagrin of my father. Recently, though, I have had some second thoughts."

"And why's that?"

"Jimmy does not think the Firm's strategy is working very well in Laos. 'Look,' he says, 'it all comes down to this. In war, you fight for what you love. The people here are fighting for their homes, their families, and their country. Us Americans, what are we fighting for?'"

"I see what he means. But he left off the one good reason to love our mission here."

"*Oh, la la,* I think I see dollar signs in your eyes."

"You know about that?"

"Of course. How do you think I get paid?"

"Well, as far as I'm concerned, if anything ever deserved my devotion, that Swiss bank account is it."

"You are one cynical man."

"No, a realistic one."

"And how might that be?"

"What I've found in life, money out-trumps love every time."

"You never loved anyone?"

"Never. I mean, I've played around, but . . . What about you?"

"Once . . . I thought."

"Were you right?"

"No, I was dead wrong."

"But it didn't make you a cynic like me, I take it."

"Nothing could make me a cynic. I am an optimist by nature. As Buddha said, *'A good person finds delight in this world and the next.'* And if you are really good, we believe, you can even choose your next life, choose the person you want to be with. So, the way I see it, life is beautiful, and I intend to live all my lives to the fullest."

"Lucky you."

"Oh, for God's sake! Stop feeling sorry for yourself, Zack. Has no one ever told you how tedious it can get?"

"Sorry."

"Just shut up please and let me finish what I was talking about, *na?*"

"What were you talking about? I forget."

"About Jimmy and the reasons why he no longer believes—"

"Oh, right."

"'The Khmu believe in me, Jimmy Love,' he says, 'not in their national leaders. When I am gone, the Royal Laotian Government will be dead as a dodo, and guess who will be taking over?"'

"So, he believes a communist victory is inevitable."

"Yes, that is what he said to me."

"Then tell me something. Why is he still here, risking his neck, your neck, and mine?"

"I am not sure, but I can think of some good reasons. To begin with, he has lived here so long he has kind of 'gone native,' as you say. His wife and children are Khmu. He is a devout Buddhist, absolutely devoted to his native soldiers, their families and to his Laotian guru, a monk named Loa Nyindi. He spends all his money on the tribe. He dreams of getting UN refugee status for them and moving them all to the USA someday.

"Also, he has been here so long, and he has invested so much of himself, if he gave up the fight, he would not know what to do with himself. If they retired him to Florida, he would probably put a bullet in his head within a year.

"Jimmy is a 'war junky,' as you say. When he is in the heat of battle, he forgets everything else."

"Okay, but what about you, Nittaya? Why're you still here? You don't sound like any kind of militant anti-communist to me."

"Good question. Actually, I can see some good in both capitalism and socialism. But as a Buddhist I am afraid of what the communists will do to our way of life."

She tried hard to project sincerity when she outlined her motives for continuing the fight despite her doubts, but I was still not altogether convinced.

Though I expected a certain degree of selflessness from a trained physician, I also presumed that a woman of Nittaya's intelligence, sensitivity and character would require more compelling reasons to risk her life in combat, especially alongside an eccentric, old soldier like Jimmy Love.

Yet, I decided not to pursue the matter any further. I would save it for a more private and opportune time in the future, I told myself, perhaps when we were lying naked together on the banks of an idyllic mountain river.

To change the subject, I asked what her duties were at the Patch.

"*Complexe et multiforme,*" she said, after a moment of hesitation. "I am Jimmy's head translator, his private secretary and his *intermédiaire* with the locals. I run the local primary school. I prowl through the area as a kind of 'barefoot doctor,' on the lookout for illness and injury. I am in charge of Jimmy's aid station and train his native medics. I am his chief combat medic, and—"

"Wait a minute. You're really a combat medic?"

"What is so shocking about that? What are you, a *porc machiste*?"

"What's that?"

"How do you say? Male chauvinist pig."

"Hey, now wait just a fucking second here!"

"Let me tell you something, Zacky-boy, women can do anything men can do, and usually better."

"And that includes combat?"

"If need be. Some of our fiercest enemies are the 'Tiger Women' in the NVA and Pathet Lao."

"I'll believe that when I see it."

"Oh, you will see it. I can promise you that."

"All right, so how much combat have you seen, Nittaya?"

"Well, actually, none, yet. I mean, Jimmy promised my father I would only work as a doctor and I would not be involved in combat. Otherwise, *mon père, tu vois,* he never would have allowed me to come. Now Jimmy says he is willing to 'fudge' on his promise, if we ever have a mission that is clearly a 'cakewalk.' By the way, can you tell me what 'fudge' means other than candy? And can you explain what a 'cakewalk mission' is?"

"Anything else you do at the base?" I managed, after I had expounded at length on the topics of 'fudge' and 'cakewalk' and thus disentangled myself from the web she had so effortlessly spun around me.

"I am . . . I suppose you could say . . ."

At this point, Nittaya paused again and indicated with a shrug, a shake of her head, and a flash of those starry, midnight eyes that she was perhaps Jimmy's half-reluctant, occasional mistress as well.

She was just finishing her story when a thunderstorm suddenly rolled in, with spectacular displays of lightning and a deluge of warm rainwater. We jumped up together and ran for the shelter of the hotel portico.

Though we were already sopping wet, and it made little difference, I held her kimono over our heads with one arm and hugged her slippery body to mine with the other, as if to protect her from the elements.

Just short of the portico, I tossed the heavy sodden kimono aside and pulled her under a big frangipani tree with fragrant, white flowers.

Glancing behind her to confirm that we were safe from prying eyes, I slid my hands round her sleek golden-brown hips. After a moment of what seemed like rather perfunctory hesitation, she slipped her arms around my neck, smiled enticingly, and shut her eyes.

As good as naked, we pressed our drenched swimsuits together.

She opened her mouth.

I swallowed her moan.

A torrent of rainwater pelted our heads and shoulders and ran down our bodies. The water and we were one. And we lost it. It gushed down our legs and soaked into the muddy leaves beneath our feet.

When at last we came up for air, I laughed aloud. "Now, *that* is what I call a *kiss!*"

In reply, she just smiled, shook her head, and patted the tip of my nose with her pinky finger. "Maybe it was a bit more than that, *na?*"

"Have you been eating something sweet?"

"Why do you ask?"

"Your mouth tasted of ambrosia."

"Do you even know what ambrosia is?"

"Not really. The nectar of the gods?" I said, attempting to guide her back into the hotel and up to my room. "I just thought it might be a classy way to describe how delicious you taste."

"Actually, I had a bite of *phi-mi khmn,* just before I met you."

"What's that?"

"A dessert made of oranges and flaked coconut," she said, turning me around and aiming us back toward the pool. "But you know what? I think you have earned your nickname, Mr. Hollywood."

"And you've earned yours, Miss Honeybuns."

"Comme tu es méchant!"

"Uh-uh, no way! I'm a sweetheart when you get to know me."

"That remains to be seen. I believe you can turn a bit *ting-tong* when overheated."

"Which means?"

"*Ting-tong* is a Thai term. It means crazy, coo-coo, wacky-wacky, *absolument fou* in your pursuit of pleasure. Now let us get back in the water and rinse ourselves off before we cause a *scandale* around here, you naughty boy."

"You know what, Nittaya?" I said, when we reached the edge of the pool and perched for a dive. "I never could figure out what guys meant when they called some girl a 'fox.'"

"Et alors?"

"Now I know."

She laughed and smacked me on the shoulder. "I am a fox? Well, you are a great, hairy, panda bear!"

Then she dove in, rolled on her back, and spread her arms.

Floating, with her long, black hair lifting, fanning and coiling about her head, she smiled up at me.

We say that life is short; and it is. Yet, when I conjure up that picture now, fifty years later, there is no way I can accept the outrageous notion that you, Nittaya Aromdée, this water nymph before me, so ripe and juicy and garden-fresh, might have already withered and grown old.

CHAPTER FIVE

Jimmy Love

A few minutes after we had settled back in our deck chairs, the biggest, most ferocious-looking Doberman Pinscher I'd ever seen popped out the door from the lobby, salivating and straining at his leash.

A large, drunken *farang* of late middle age staggered out behind him, chomping on some dirty, black substance that appeared to be a plug of tobacco or betel. Dressed for combat in a camouflage tiger suit, web belt and jungle boots, he was lugging a holstered Berretta, a sawed-off M16, with a collapsible stock, a long, serrated, commando knife, and a pair of fragmentation grenades attached to the upper pockets of his faded bush jacket.

Considering his state of advanced inebriation, and the fact that he seemed to be teetering in our general direction, I found the hoary old trooper and his monstrous dog a bit troubling.

I had expected Jimmy Love to surprise me with his appearance. Considering his original name, Joachim Liebermann, and his

Ruthenian antecedents, I'd even gone so far as to imagine him as a swarthy, little Jew with big, mournful eyes, a hooked nose, a small, pursed mouth and a quivery, nervous aspect.

Imagine my astonishment, therefore, when I was confronted with precisely what I might have imagined had I not been predisposed for a surprise: This huge skin-headed, scar-faced, granite-jawed Hell's Angels type with fierce, beetle brows, indigo eyes, and a grey walrus mustache.

"*Oy, shikse,* wheyabin?" he bellowed in the accent of a Borscht Belt comedian as he swayed above us, his alcohol breath curdling the air in a three-foot circle around him.

Despite the dog's vicious appearance, he seemed to know Nittaya quite well, and he laid his head on her naked thighs to be petted. She did so with a frozen smile, murmuring, "Nice doggie, nice Dybbuk," running the tips of her fingers over the short bristly fur on his neck in a gesture of counterfeit affection that I found obvious, but Jimmy seemed not to notice. Instead, he laid the dog's leash in her hand, casually spat his quid out on the poolside tile, and plopped down beside her, causing her deck chair to sag and strain.

"So wuz up, wuz up?" he said, letting his head fall on her shoulder, shutting his eyes, providing me with the opportunity to give him another once-over. A dribble of brown stained his hanging mustache. A big, gold earring dangled from his left lobe.

Yet despite his aging biker look, I decided the man did seem to possess a sort of rough-hewn charisma. Perhaps it was only the triumphant, celebratory manner of the old warrior, the authentic touch of his worn and well-used armaments. Or maybe, it had something to do with his animal alter-ego, the savage-looking Dybbuk.

Whatever the case, I found that he had triggered a kind of shrinking within me. Especially when I recalled that in Jewish folklore, a Dybbuk is a demon, one that enters the body of a living person and controls its behavior.

"So wha yuz up to?"

"Oh, not too much, Jimmy," Nittaya said, smiling convincingly, giving him a peck on his rough, stubbled cheek while she shoved Dybbuk's wet lapping tongue off her slick thighs. "How was your R & R?"

"Well, lemme see, fus' I check in wit' da wife and kids. Ya know? Ketchup on tings?" he said, blinking torpidly and raising his head to meet our eyes.

Until that moment, I had supposed he was making a stupid drunken joke with the accent, but now I grasped that he spoke an authentic but archaic form of Yiddish-inflected Brooklynese.

With my ear for language, I discovered the key to understanding it only a few moments later. First, Jimmy was unable to pronounce the "th" sound in "this" and "that," rendering it instead as *"dis"* and *"dat."* Second, he pronounced the words "call," "talk" and "walk" in an inimitable manner that cannot properly be transcribed as the usual *"coawl," "toawk"* and *"woawk."* Third, he always pronounced the subject pronoun "you" in its plural form as *"yuz."* Fourth, he ended virtually every sentence with the question *"Ya know?"* Fifth, he tended to run words together as in the following approximations:

"WeahyaBIN?"

"TagidEEZY!"

"DonevenTINKaboudit!"

"WaddayaTOAWKINabout?"

"FuGIDaboudit!"

Okay, I thought, easy enough. Later though, when I attempted to render his odd speech patterns in my journal, I chose to paraphrase them in Standard American to spare myself the tedium of literal transcription.

"Jimmy has a family here in Nakhon Phanom," Nittaya said. "How many kids have you and Kai got now, *Paw-Paw?*"

"Hey, lemme think," he said, flashing a big snaggle-toothed grin. "Not sure I can count that high."

"So, after a little 'quality time' with the family, what did you get up to, you old *dinky-dau?*"

"Hullo? You *know* what I did."

"Got banged and bonged over at Mama Tootka's, *na?*"

"There it is."

"Ain't R & R without a little 'down-time,' is it, trooper?" Nittaya said, her attempt at idiomatic military jargon sounding more than a little odd in her exotic, slightly singsong inflection.

Jimmy raised his head off her shoulder, yawned and shook his head as if he had just awakened from a long night's sleep.

"So lemme ask you something, doll. Who's the goy-boy?"

"Your new man, Jimbo. Just arrived from Travis. Agent Zachary Ogle, radio code name 'Hollywood,' otherwise known as plain old Zack."

I reached out to shake his hand. "Pleasure to meet you."

Ignoring my hand, Jimmy flashed from Nittaya to me and back again.

"So whadaya say, *Bubeleh?* Call for some more *getrinks?* Suss out the newbie?"

The *Mazel Tovs* went on for hours. Despite what he'd said, Jimmy seemed uninterested in hearing my story, even my tales of combat in Vietnam.

He monopolized the conversation, recounting one war story after the other in his Damon Runyonavich accent. After a while, his stories all tended to run together.

Having taken an instant dislike to Mr. Love, I tuned out his monologue for the most part, but there was one tale that stuck in my mind.

The story was that for years Jimmy had rewarded his fighters 5000 Kip in Lao money (about fifty cents) for each enemy ear they brought in. Once, when the US Ambassador in Vientiane questioned his Body Counts, Jimmy walked into his office, emptied a big burlap sack full of dried human ears on his desk, and said, "Hullo? Is this proof enough for yuz, or not?"

Despite the ambassador's subsequent displeasure, Jimmy kept up with the policy until one day he saw a little boy with no ears and asked how he'd lost them.

"So, when the kid tells me his old man cut off his ears for the dollar reward, I says, 'Forget about it,' you know?"

The extraordinary thing about this story, and all the others he told, was the way he told it. It was like he was delivering stand-up comedy lines, and he laughed uproariously when he told of the little boy with no ears, just as he'd laughed at all his other tragic tales.

Later, after Jimmy had drunk enough Mekong Whiskey with Tiger Beer chasers to lay another man under the table, Nittaya called an end to the evening and asked me to help get the boss and his pooch up to bed.

I half-expected her to come rapping at my door again after we tucked them in.

But no such luck.

At breakfast in the hotel café the next morning, Jimmy seemed amazingly chipper, considering what he'd consumed the night before.

Kimo showed up at our table, and he turned out to be exactly as Nittaya had described him. A big, black, happy Hawaiian dude who was short on conversation but long on beatific grins. Like Jimmy, he seemed to take great pleasure in playing up his antecedents, and he went so far as to greet everyone with *"Aloha."* He even said *"Mahalo"* to our comely Thai waitress when we got up to leave, though I noticed he left no tip.

Maybe that was his Christian side at work.

"You cheap Charlie!" she yelled at him as he departed. "Number Ten GI!"

He just smiled benignly back at her.

After breakfast, the four of us, accompanied by our mascot, Dybbuk, strolled over to Sky Special Ops Supply, a dull corrugated metal building reminiscent of a World War II Quonset Hut, and lined up for new equipment—boonie hats, tiger suits, flak vests, jungle boots, rucksacks, ponchos, web gear, ammunition belts, Walther PPF Pistols with suppressors, CAR15 automatic rifles and long, commando knives, with serrated blades.

Then we walked over to a battered Air America chopper —what we used to call "slicks" in Nam—that was already warming up.

Whap-whap-whap.

"Awright. Firebase Juliet? It's two hundred clicks up-country, you know?" Jimmy announced for my benefit as we clambered aboard the shuddering machine.

His tone was rough and caustic, soldierly, but there was a kind of rap behind it, an undercurrent of Yiddish-inflected jive.

"We got a sunny day. Usually takes about an hour. But today? We make a little side trip. Do some recky-teck.'"

He sniffed and pointed in my direction.

"Aerial Recon to you, Shake n' Bake. So just sit back, relax, and enjoy the flight."

While Jimmy chatted with the Aussie pilot up front, and Dybbuk lay at his feet, Nittaya and I headed toward a pile of rice sacks stenciled "MAMA TOOTKA'S BEST."

I had learned from Nittaya that Mama Tootka was the proprietress of a notorious dope den and house of prostitution in Nakhon Phanom, so I wondered aloud whether the stenciled notice referred to the sacks' present contents, or what would fill them on the return flight.

"Hey, lemme tell you something, *Bubkes*," said Jimmy Love in an unkind tone, causing Dybbuk to growl in companionable disapprobation. "I'm gonna say it one time, and one time only. Out in the *Feldt*, you know, I value your observations, okay? But here in town you mind your own fucking business. Got it?"

"Yes, *sir!*" I said, and—hating myself—came within an ace of saluting the old, skin-headed Brooklynoid.

The interior of the slick was stripped to its metal skeleton. There were no seats except for those occupied by a pair of Thai machine gunners, sitting on the either side behind big mounted M60s, with hundreds of rounds in ammo belts at their feet.

As the pilot chattered flight-speak into the radio, *"Roger, Northstar, this is G-45 Southwind . . . copy that . . . over,"* we lifted off in a cloud of dust and circled over the airfield to gain altitude.

We did this, Nittaya said, to avoid the squalid, little shantytown at the edge of the base. Although most of its residents were employed in one way or another in servicing the needs of the soldiers, airmen and covert operatives stationed nearby, it was about twenty percent Thai People's Liberation Army and sometimes erupted in AK-47 fire.

We attained our cruising height of 3000 feet, turned north, and followed the course of the mile-wide Mekong.

To our left: the endless rice paddies of Thailand, stretching smooth and flat to the western horizon. To our right: the mountains of Laos, the Annamites, some so tall that their ridgelines ran to dwarf pines rather than jungle.

We left the Mekong when it swung west, followed its tributary, the Ngiap River, northward, and soon we entered a region of limestone bluffs called "karsts" which rose like giant watchtowers hundreds of feet high.

The terrain was all a deep green except for the rocky, grey karsts and the river, which was a dark, cocoa brown, laden with scummy, fallen trees and the litter of a primitive, pastoral society (including the occasional dead bloated body of an elephant or water buffalo).

As we flew our northerly course, I could see row upon row of meandering east-west ridgelines before us, stretching all the way into China. The mountains were all pristine natural forest, with the occasional slash and burn of Stone Age agriculture.

The only visible habitations were tiny, riverside *villes* that appeared every fifty klicks or so at the bottom of remote valleys.

Jimmy stood up front in the cockpit doorway, hanging over the Australian rotor-head, shouting war tales into his ears, and laughing at his own clever turns of phrase.

Lay-Low sat alone in the mid-section, swinging his jungle boots out the breezy, open door, lost in his own placid thoughts or prayers and ignoring the jumpy, young, Thai machine-gunner beside him.

Nittaya and I lay propped up in back on Mama Tootka's rice sacks.

The sacks were destined for the homes of Jimmy's Khmu fighters and their families, she said, where (just as I had guessed) they would promptly be emptied into giant, clay, rice jars and reloaded with raw opium to be airlifted out on the return flight.

The noise inside the rattling old helo was beyond loud; it was thunderous, earsplitting, deafening.

No longer in danger of being overheard, Nittaya and I leaned in close to each other and censored nothing.

"Was Jimmy jealous that we were getting on so well?"

"Jimmy is not the jealous type. In fact, he is quite the opposite. Kind of an old Beatnik, *na*? 'Do your own thing, Baby,' he says. 'Let it all hang out.'"

"Was he alright last night?"

"Of course. Once I got him to bed, he was 'out like a light,' as you say."

"You tuck yourself in beside him?"

"Now look who is *jaloux!*"

"Just asking," I said, sulky as a love-struck teenager.

"To tell the truth, I never sleep with Jimmy when he is

drunk, which is just about every night. I cannot stand his breath, his *basso profondo* snoring, or the shrunken enemy heads he keeps in jars beside his bed. Not to mention the *grenade à fragmentation* he has tucked under his pillow. What if he had a nightmare? You know what I mean?"

"What about the fact that he's old enough to be your father? How does that set with you?"

"Quite frankly, that is not among the many things that bother me about him."

"Why not?"

"Hey Mr. Slick, I thought you said you spent a year in Vietnam. Do you know nothing of Asian ladies?"

"Not nearly enough, apparently. Why don't you enlighten me?"

"All right, if I really must," she said in a mock pedantic tone, and treated me to a lengthy and detailed psychological explication.

The first thing I had to learn, she said, was about Confucian upbringing, which taught respect for learning, reverence for age and submission to authority. Another clue to Asian female behavior was that, in their cultures, the father was still usually a remote figure who rarely spoke to his children, except to scold them. And in most Asian nations, girls were far less valued than boys. This had profound effects on daughters, who tended to look for dominant male or father figures in adulthood.

Some people thought of the man with a girlfriend his daughter's age as little more than a pervert, a pedophile. What they did not realize was that the attraction was probably mutual.

As for the Oriental woman's attraction to white men, she

said, the explanation was that in Asia subtle variations in skin tone, eye shape, and height were of great importance. Asian ladies avoided direct sunlight and carried parasols not to avoid skin cancer, but to avert a darkening of the face and arms because ivory skin had long been associated with the *"Hi-So,"* the upper reaches of society, and dusky or dark skin with the *"Lo-So"* or peasantry.

The same with the shape of the eye: Manga comic book characters had wide Western eyes, so thousands of Asian women went through painful cosmetic surgery every year because slanted, slit-like eyes with smooth unfolded lids were *déclassé*, while the rounded eyes and folded lids of Europeans were 'cool' and fashionable. In the same way, tallness was desirable, while shortness was the opposite.

In the Orient, then, white was right, as evidenced by the popular cinema. Western movie stars were much more in vogue than native ones.

Thus, in the company of Asian women, the Occidental male, especially the older one, often found himself much appreciated. And Jimmy Love was no exception.

"I see," I said, when she was done, although I didn't. Not really. Not at least until I was a sixty-six-year-old screenwriter and started dating a twenty-five-year-old masseuse from Hollywood's Thai Town. "So, have you made any commitments yet?"

"Commitments? That is such a silly American concept!"

I jerked my head at Jimmy Love, who was still wilting the ears of the poor, patient Aussie pilot.

"So, you're not going to spend the rest of your life with that old fart?"

She laughed and covered her mouth with her hand, teasing me past endurance.

"Life . . . and Love . . . They are such uncertain terms in these times, *na?*"

We left the Ngiap River when it swung east, then continued north over a high, pine-covered ridge and flew over a broad yellow and brown plateau that Nittaya called *"La Plaine des Jarres."*

When I asked why, she said thousands of giant megalithic sandstone jars were scattered all over the plain, some of them dating from 500 BC.

"In any other country they would be declared a protected environment," she said, pointing to the hundreds of water-filled craters that crowded the plain from border to border. "But here in our poor Laos, they are the site of some of the worst fighting in the war, and hundreds have been destroyed by bombs and artillery."

We flew northward over the central area of the plateau and she pointed out a large, military base and airfield. "That is Long Tieng, where the Hmong and their Sky handlers are based."

Then she pointed over a range of hazy hills to the east to another, smaller plateau. "That is Vieng Xai, where the NVA and Pathet Lao are based."

After crossing the Plain of Jars, the Huey abruptly descended and made for the gorge of the Sikhav River, causing Nittaya to fall into my lap.

She took her time recovering, and I felt her breasts pressing against my thighs. She affected a look of pop-eyed astonishment when she noticed the bulge she had generated and shook her finger at me as she rose back to a sitting position.

Sikhav means 'white' in Lao. The pilots followed the sun-spackled rapids of the white river northward, swinging gloriously round its bends at no more than two hundred feet.

Banana trees and narrow rice fields lined its shores. Tiny *villes*, with thatch and bamboo hootches, clung to the soggy, riverside foothills. Towering, limestone buttes rose above, with filmy fingers of morning mist—what the French called *crachins*—wrapped around their bottle-green jungle flanks like ghostly grey vapors on a horror movie set. Sparkling streams and waterfalls plummeted from the deep defiles between the mountains. Far above, rainclouds were beginning to swell and soar and coalesce.

"That is Banana Mountain over there," Nittaya said, pointing toward a broad butte on the west side of the river. "You cannot see the Patch from here, but it is right up at the top. It used to be a Khmu village. They built it up there to be safe from their enemies. It's where Jimmy's wife, Kai, is from. In fact, she still has a sister and brother there."

"What's this little side trip he's taking us on? You figured it out yet?"

"Oh, I have an idea, and I do not like it one bit. See that rice bag at his feet?"

"Yeah. What's in it?"

"Unless I miss my guess, it is human heads."

"What? You're dicking with me!"

"No, really. *Ching-ching.* He caught a couple of spies last week. The punishment for spying is decapitation. So, he cut their heads off and made his Khmus toss pebbles at them to prove their loyalty. They are so *superstitieux!* They believe anyone in league with the traitors who strikes them in the head will suffer the same fate."

"Are you superstitious too?"

"Why do you ask?"

"Oh, just a guess."

"One you developed in Vietnam, *na?*"

"Right. They believe in all kinds of crazy shit. Those wispy, little ghosts that flit around at night after a battle? They call them '*pratas.*' The minute there's a sighting, they *di-di* outta there quicker than pale ale turns to piss."

"Well, assuming you are talking about *la bière*, the answer to your question is yes. We *Laotiens* are no different from *les Vietnamiens, les Thaïlandais, ou les Cambodgiens*, for that matter. I mean, absolutely everyone in this part of the world, from prince to peasant, from the most effete intellectuals to the most committed revolutionaries, believes in the supernatural."

"Why?"

She grinned.

"Because we have lots of ghosts hereabouts."

"You're shittin' me."

"Not at all. I mean, there are *fantômes, spectres, esprits* and lost souls all around us. The most common type is what we call '*phi.*' They are the living dead. You can find them in humans, animals, trees, and rocks. In the jungle, along the river, in our houses and up there in the mountain mists. They even talk through the mouths of monkeys, water buffaloes and elephants. Give yourself a month and I guarantee you will see one too.

"But nobody who is in harmony with himself should fear the *phi.* They only torment people who are against life. They are mischievous and disobedient, like you and me. They are the spirits within us that want to be free."

"Get outta here!" I said, imitating Jimmy's Brooklynese.

"Really, *ching-ching*, mark my words. Jimmy used to be just as skeptical as you, until one night he found one hanging from the rafters in his bunker, half bat and half human!"

"*Alright, okay, you win . . .*" I sang, in the style of Tony Bennett, raising my hands in surrender.

"Oh, what a pushover you are, *Farang!*"

"Only when I want to be."

"You want me to push you over?"

"Yes, and preferably in some soft sand by the riverbank when no one's looking."

"*Ooh la la, monsieur,* you are such an incorrigible *paillard!*"

"What's a *paillard*?"

"A libertine, a debauchee."

"So, you think that's all I am?"

"Until I have *preuve incontestable* to the contrary."

"Okay, but if you could just bring yourself to restrain that caustic wit of yours for a second, Nittaya, would you just answer me one question? If those really are human heads, what exactly does Mr. Love propose to do with them?"

"He is going to drop them on the Pathet Lao base at Gneu Mat to spook them, to haunt them. Also, Jimmy is a show-off. Maybe he is doing this to impress you, the new man, with his *sang-froid*."

"Put the fear of God into me, huh?"

"Something like that."

"That's not very Buddhist of him, is it?"

"Not really. To tell you the truth, Jimmy is more on an astral, psychedelic plane than on a religious one, if you know what I mean."

"Well, lemme tell you something. If he's trying to space me out, he's doing a pretty good job of it."

Sixty klicks up the river, shortly before we reached Gneu Mat, I spotted a kilometer-wide band of pulverized red earth snaking across the southeastern horizon, scarring the pristine green of jungle and mountains for miles on end. Before I even had a chance to ask, Nittaya anticipated me with one word that said it all.

"B-52s."

As we approached our destination, Jimmy directed his Aussie rotor-head to come around a bend in the river fast and low, right over the center of the *ville*. Then he ordered his Thai machine gunners to open up with a little "Recon by Fire."

Ignoring the spent shell casings that were clanging around him, and the AK-47 rounds which had begun pinging into our fuselage, Jimmy pulled two dark, slit-eyed, broad-nosed human heads from the burlap sack by their long, lank, black hair.

While his passengers looked on in horror, he swung one and then another out the doorway and released them, aiming for a low, wooden building banked with sandbags from which a crowd of peasants including women, children, and Pathet Lao guerillas in faded blue uniforms were fleeing in all directions.

"Bombs away!" he thundered,

And as spent shell casings clattered to the floor, and AK-47 rounds continued to ping against the fuselage, Jimmy threw his head back, bared his teeth, thrust his clenched fists and pelvis back and forth in a lewd dance, and hee-hawed like an ass.

There was puff of smoke below, and an RPG streaked toward the helicopter, trailing smoke.

"RPG!" I hollered. "Five o'clock!"

The pilot veered hard left, aiming for a gap in the bluff ahead, and Jimmy nearly got tipped out the door.

The RPG missed the chopper by a few feet, exploded against the wall of the bluff, and shrapnel peppered the fuselage.

A moment later, when the pilot found an opening in the wall of bluffs, he veered sharply to the left, ducked into a water gap, and soon the pinging stopped.

But we weren't out of trouble yet.

The gorge was so narrow, so winding and precipitous that the rotor chopped vegetation off the chasm walls like a lawn mower. Some of it spun onto our fuselage with a loud thwack, setting my poor chickenshit heart all aflutter.

"Bounced 'em both right up on old my old amigo Kham's *schtoop!*" Jimmy exulted, ignoring the sunlight pouring through innumerable bullet holes in the fuselage. "And hey, I wanna tell you. I hit a bull's-eye, you know? Caused a real *plotz* in there. You wanna bet?"

"Oh yes, Jimbo, I am sure you did!" Nittaya shouted, playing to his vanity, as we came to the end of the deep ravine and turned eastward into a long, uninhabited, jungle valley.

"Kham is our local Papa Lao," she explained for my benefit. "And the really odd thing is—he and Jimmy used to be friends and fellow shadow soldiers, until Kham switched sides. And they still get a 'big bang,' if you will forgive the pun, out of playing tricks on each other. No telling what Kham will do now to pay

Jimmy back."

Just then another RPG flared up from the jungle, exploded nearby, and one of the machine gunners got laced across the middle. His safety belt blew away, and he flew out the door into space.

The chopper started to shudder; smoke poured out the engine compartment and we started to lose altitude.

"Mayday, mayday!" The pilot shrieked. "Papa 3, Big Mother Five Foxtrot. We are hit and going down. Five klicks due north of Ban Lou, six aboard. Extract, extract!"

I flung Nittaya back on the rice bags, covered her with my body, and we locked eyes in fear.

Jimmy strapped himself in up front and wrapped Dybbuk's leash around his arm.

The helicopter flew into a narrow canyon, hit a shallow stream, skimmed along it, striking rocks, and trees. Its fractured rotors flew off in different directions and it screeched to a halt at the jungle's edge.

Up front, the Aussie pilot lay dead in his seat, covered with glass, impaled by a sharp tree limb.

I nodded tensely at Nittaya, who clung to me like a child.

"Okay," I said. "Okay. We made it. Now let's get out of here!"

I grabbed her rucksack with one hand, her arm with the other, and helped her out of the flaming wreckage.

The others, including Dybbuk, emerged with only minor injuries, but as we raced for the cover of the jungle, the chopper exploded behind us, knocking us to the ground, peppering us with debris, and a great plume of smoke surged skyward.

A few minutes later, as we scurried up through the jungle,

Dybbuk started to sniff and whine, and Jimmy motioned for us all to stop and listen.

Laotian voices and barking hounds sounded behind us.

Jimmy unsnapped Dybbuk's leash, pointed down the hill, and shouted, "Go get 'em, Boy! Kill, kill!

Next, we heard gunshots, shouting, and barking, which receded as we hastened up the jungle hill.

At sunset, we reached a ridgeline covered with elephant grass. We stopped to listen for sounds of pursuit and heard excited Lao voices below us.

Just then, a big, Jolly Green Giant helicopter thundered in overhead, and Jimmy popped smoke to mark a tentative LZ. But the chopper started receiving automatic weapons fire from down the hill and veered off.

It swung around again, this time coming in fast and low.

Jimmy tossed out two more smoke grenades.

The Sikorsky roared in and landed behind the billowing wall of smoke.

A two-man Security Team jumped out and waved us toward them.

Small arms fire rained in from behind us as we raced for the chopper, heads low, while the security team sprayed the tree line with suppressive fire.

We all scrambled aboard.

The helo lifted off and banked sharply, while automatic weapons fire sounded below.

"Hey, wait a fucking minute!" Jimmy hollered and glared at the pilot. "My dog!"

The Latino pilot looked at him like he might be loco.

"We gotta go find my dog!" Jimmy screamed. "No fucking way do we go home without my dog! No fucking way."

He gestured to the pilot to turn back.

Reluctantly, he obeyed, and a few moments later the chopper descended to a clearing, where Dybbuk barked and capered, miraculously unhurt, sniffing at the dead body of a little, short-haired, native dog.

Jimmy jumped down, whistled at Dybbuk, beckoned for him to run for the chopper, and he obeyed instantaneously.

Once they were both safely aboard, the pilot powered up and climbed skyward.

A half hour later, we rounded a sharp bend in a heavy downpour and saw the tiny riverside settlement of Thavay strung out along the banks.

The chopper suddenly veered 180 degrees to the right, tipping halfway over, sending me into Nittaya's lap for a change (I took my time recovering as well).

Then it powered up the side of the western bluff, blew through the ghostly *crachins* that clung to its slopes, and stormed over the dripping trees at its crest, causing them to bend and quake and shed wet leaves.

I caught a glimpse of the firebase when the Huey dipped its tail to slow its approach and flared over the wet and muddy LZ.

A mucky, brick-red scar on the green, high jungle scenery of mountain and valley, the Patch seemed at first sight to be nothing more than a poor, Montagnard *ville*, surrounded by terraced poppy fields.

A dozen or more water-filled, mortar craters lay scattered across its damp surface, evidence that the place was not as secure as Reynolds had implied.

The only thing remotely picturesque about it was a little pond filled with water lilies that spilled over a cliff in misty chutes and vaporized about halfway down.

Just as we were about to set down, I heard a tremendous *"kaboom!"* that echoed off the surrounding mountains.

The pilot lifted off again and swooped back over the lip of the cliff in a panic, nearly bringing up my breakfast.

But it did nothing to faze Jimmy.

He got on the horn and shouted, "Blue Leader to Apple. Tell that *schmo* to belay his fucking arty practice *now*. Or I'll stick his head so far down the latrine, he'll have to tuck it up his *tusch* to see the light of day!"

"So, this is the famous, unassailable Firebase Juliet?" I said to Nittaya, when Jimmy was finally able to call off the artillery practice and the Huey bounced down amid a herd of slick rooting piglets.

"This is it," she said, laughing, leaping from the chopper into the rain and mud, splashing her boots and cargo pants, scattering piglets every which way. "Home sweet home!"

"Home it may be," I said, as I jumped after her with all my gear, "but sweet it ain't."

Yet the beautiful, warlike Nittaya, splashing across the muddy field after Jimmy Love, with her assault rifle slung casually over her shoulder, did not appear to hear what I said.

Just then, a throng of cheering Khmus with flares and lanterns raced across the field to surround Jimmy and bedeck him with flowers, hollering "Jeemy, Jeemy, Jeemy!" at the tops of their lungs.

That night, squatting over the trench latrine on the edge of the jungle, inhaling the lush aromatic vapors of yellow equatorial flux in light rain, enticing with my pale and nude hindquarters the amorous attentions of a hundred love-struck mosquitoes, I could have sworn I saw one of Nittaya's *phi* flitting about the trees above my head. Young and beautiful, she was wearing a filmy, white gown. And she was so real, I thought I might be hallucinating.

"The best cure for our peculiar local brand of dysentery is this right here," said Nittaya, appearing from behind some nearby shrubbery shortly after I'd wiped my rear end and swabbed my hands with Army-issue, anti-bacterial sanitizer. "Here, try some now," she said, and handed me a lump of a puckered black and yellow substance.

"What is it?" I said, yanking my pants up in embarrassment.

"Raw opium, but do not be alarmed. I prescribe it all the time. You bite into it, chew on it for a while, swallow the juice, and then spit it out. By morning, you will be feeling number one. Jimmy chews it all the time, like just about everyone else at the Patch. Swears it keeps the *phanyad* off him."

"What's the *phanyad*?"

"You want the medical term or the vernacular?"

"The vernacular will do."

"The shits. An occupational hazard up here, even when you put Halizone in the water, as you just found out. But, hey, do not let it get you down, trooper. I mean, what does the lotus flower, the symbol of Our Lord Buddha, spring from?"

"I don't know. Why don't you tell me?"

"From the filth and mud!"

"No shit?" I said, but she ignored my attempt at humor.

I popped her plug into my mouth. Its texture, I found, was like chewing tobacco. It tasted like licorice and was not at all disagreeable. I concentrated my attention on following Doc Nittaya's orders, but when I finally spat out the residue, I was disappointed to find that she had already disappeared into the night.

In the morning, I wondered if she had been there at all.

The only evidence to the contrary was that I was purged of the *phanyad* and still feeling mellow yellow.

CHAPTER SIX

Firebase Juliet

The rain let up the next day, so Jimmy had a teenage Khmu kid come over and roust me out of my rack at 0700 with orders to attend him immediately.

His command post was just down the way from the BOQ bunker where I had spent the night. As I ducked through the CP entrance and went down the steps to the rough wooden floor, the first thing I saw when my eyes got used to the darkness was a fifty-five-gallon, aviation gas drum filled with water and what looked like an immersion heater—Jimmy's bath, apparently.

To my left was a gun rack lined with assault rifles, grenade launchers and a couple of sawed-off shotguns. On a lower one, I saw boxes of ammunition, ammo belts, binoculars, and other kinds of military equipment.

On my right, there was a table with a radio, a propane camp stove, a stack of C-Rat cartons and a flickering Coleman lantern.

Next on my right came a pair of large, metal, wall lockers,

with Buddhist and pseudo-Buddhist paperback books by Alan Watts, D.T. Suzuki, Jack Kerouac, and Alan Ginsberg stacked neatly on top.

Then a pair of cargo chests and a raised platform with an Asian-style bed mat complete with neatly folded blankets.

My impression was that none of this was Jimmy's work. A feminine hand was evident.

At the far end of the long room, some steps led down to a cellar bunker from which rose the sound of a pair of male voices, one raised in anger.

"Goddamnit, you ever pull that arty trick again and I'll . . ."

"Hello?" I said tentatively.

"*Oy, Boychick,* we're on our way up!" Jimmy hollered, and emerged, followed by a little, squinty-eyed, pockmarked, Asian man of about thirty, with extraordinarily long and thin arms. He was sporting a camouflage tiger suit with a bright red sweat scarf and an inscrutable Royal Thai Army insignia on his epaulette. Plastered across his hollow-cheeked face, he wore the wavering, insincere grin of a chastened boy.

"Hollywood, this is Captain Chankul, radio code name, 'Spiderman.' Heads up our Thai artillery and security contingent. Gonna give you the VIP tour today."

After introductions, the captain led me out of the command post and directly across the ridge to its western perimeter, for he proposed to take me on a "methodical, clockwise tour of the base," starting at West Defensive Bunker Number 5.

On the way, he made great efforts to get over his discomfort over Jimmy's harangue. Since I knew from my service in Nam that the worst shame in the world for an Asian man is to be chastened by a *farang* in front of another *farang*, I did my best to put him at ease.

The captain's English was rudimentary at best, but we had little trouble understanding each other, at least when it came to technical talk.

We spoke in Lao, which Thais of the eastern Issan regions speak as a native dialect. I noticed that he addressed me as "*Vao*," which means "Sir," although technically he outranked me. I thought nothing of it at the time, but now I suppose it must have been one of the privileges of being a white man.

Captain Changul conducted me around the base from end to end, explaining everything in detail. When he was done, I had a complete picture of its structure and functions.

If it came to anything personal, though, it was a different matter. Although the captain made effusive attempts to gratify me, the new *farang* on base, he exuded the kind of oily evasion and instinctive distrust that I had found in ARVN officers in Vietnam. Like them, he seemed to make great efforts to hide who he really was.

What I learned that day on my tour was that Firebase Juliet sprawled from north to south over the crest of a mostly flat and treeless ridgeline separating the valleys of the Et and Sikhav Rivers.

Peanut-shaped, humped and rounded at either end, flat and skinny in the middle, it was 500 meters long, 100 meters wide across the middle, and 200 meters wide at its extremities.

The western side, with its spring and pond and waterfall, spilled over a high, limestone cliff to the wild Sikhav River three hundred and fifty meters below, while its eastern slope quickly turned to jungle and more gently descended to the slow, meandering Et River and the village of Thavay.

The low, rounded hill at the north end of the base housed Captain Chankul and his Thai mercenaries, who were responsible for the mortars, howitzers and defensive bunkers that constituted the Patch's protective shield. They lived a bachelor life in fortified barracks and worked in eight-hour shifts twenty-four hours a day.

The Khmu tribesmen lived on the hill at the south end of the Patch in a village of forty thatch and bamboo longhouses built on stilts. Inside, each house was divided into two large sections, one for the men and the other for the women and their many children.

In the women's section, there was a circular mud-brick fireplace where they did their cooking.

The men's section had painted buffalo skulls and ancient crossbows hanging on the walls.

There were animal pens tucked under the houses, but all save the domesticated rabbits roamed free.

I saw chickens, ducks, pigs, goats, ponies, water buffaloes and even a baby elephant feeding on the grassy fringes of the village.

The houses ran up the terraced hillside in four neatly parallel lines. At the top of the hill, there was a tribal longhouse and a small temple with carved upward-soaring roofs, which must have been the nucleus of the original Khmu village.

The longhouse now served as a school for the Khmu children, the captain said. Doctor Nittaya and her assistant teacher, an educated Khmu named Vora, ran it. It opened every day at 0830.

Seated on the steps of the temple, I saw a fat, bald, happy, young monk in saffron robes, grinning at a group of ragged schoolchildren who were offering him tidbit specials of sticky rice balls, ant eggs, bee larvae, and mango cheese.

When I asked who he was, the captain replied that his name was Loa Nyindi, which I knew meant "The Laughing Monk."

"Why do they call him that?"

"Look at him. He is always laughing. Life is a cosmic joke, he says. So why not have fun while it lasts?"

"Is he the one Jimmy calls his guru?" I asked, and when the captain replied in the affirmative, I said in English, "Uh-huh, it figures." My tone of voice was cynical, smart-ass GI, but it went right past him.

The base's headquarters, communications center, medical aid station, central mess hall, BOQ, ammunition dump, resupply area and a small barrack reserved for the token Royal Laotian Army presence were located on the flat middle part of the ridge. The buildings were low dugout bunkers with timber and tarpaper roofs, protected on all sides, including the roof, with piled-up rice sacks filled with dirt.

The large command post where Jimmy lived and held court bristled with antennas, and sported a flagpole with a long, red, three-elephant Royal Laotian banner flapping in the wind.

The aid station, where Doc Nittaya lived with her medics, had a big Red Cross painted on the roof.

The BOQ, where I had just spent the night, bore no discernible identifying marks whatever.

The LZ and helipad, located just below the southern hump, seemed quite busy for such a remote firebase, with Air America choppers and STOLs (Short Take-Off and Landing planes) flying in every hour or so to deliver supplies and troops returning from R & R or deployments to other bases.

A dirt road ran from one end of the ridge to the other and connected with the path that led down to the Et River and village. It was lined with tiny fruit and vegetable stalls featuring such exotic treats as pawpaw, rambutan, durian, bamboo shoots, custard apples, water-lily stems, castor beans, tofu, and tamarind jam.

There was even a butcher's stall with an array of pork, duck, chicken, river fish and fried insects.

In the bright, hot daylight, the dusty road swarmed with buffalo-drawn carts, shaggy little Himalayan ponies burdened with food and ammunition, and a colorful assortment of pedestrians.

There were Thai mercenaries wearing tiger suits, with bright unit scarves. Royal Laotian Army soldiers dressed like French Foreign Legionnaires in kepis and blue berets. Teenage tribal soldiers dressed in ragged, motley clothing and tire-tread sandals. Gaunt, old, Khmu women arrayed in bright, gaudy traditional garb. Lowland peasants in conical straw hats and black pajamas. Droves of scrawny, little, naked children. Plump, prosperous Lao Chinese tradesmen in pith helmets and white tropical gear. Big, bearded, longhaired, Air America crew members in boot jeans and bush jackets with bandanas wrapped around their heads.

The entire military contingent, apart from the Air America men, lived on base, Captain Changul said, but the vendors up from the village had to be gone by nightfall.

The base perimeter was ringed with electronic sensors,

listening posts, trip flares, claymore mines, concertina wire, firing trenches and defensive bunkers with interlocking fields-of-fire.

Just outside the northern perimeter, a trash dump teemed with skinny children and old women rooting for edible garbage and used clothing. According to Captain Changul, the dump was crawling with enormous rats, which the children trapped and sold as food to the Khmu tribesmen, who served them as a delicacy.

A few yards beyond the western perimeter, on a green terraced hillside, two lines of young, singing, Khmu women, with their colorful skirts hiked up over their slender brown thighs, were working in a waist-high field of blue and white opium poppies still wet from the dew.

The first line collected sap from the green stems and patted it into balls.

The second line wrapped it in banana leaves.

Both groups smiled and looked up as we passed by, but they never ceased their shrill, purling mantra to the capricious *phi,* praying that the fickle spirits desist from their pursuit of freedom and pleasure only long enough to assure a bountiful harvest.

The last stop on our circuit was at the far southern fringe of the firebase, where a junkyard strewn with rusted-out, connex containers, busted military hardware, and three wrecked helicopters blighted the landscape.

"So whadaya think?" Jimmy asked when I saw him later that day out at the helipad, as he prepared to lift off for an inspection of one of his other firebases.

"A formidable redoubt, if manned properly."

"Any suggestions?"

"Yes, sir. If I were you, I would limit access to the base by so many outsiders. In Nam, we figured that about thirty percent of the people who hung around our bases were VC informers. And I would think twice about relying a hundred percent on your Thai security contingent. I'd mix it up a bit; maybe put some Khmu on your perimeter defense, as well."

"Why's that?"

"Some of your Thai troops in the trenches and bunkers were smoking pot. I could smell it. Several of them appeared to be nodding off. Only one of your Listening Posts was manned. I asked about Recon Patrols and was told you didn't have one out today. One of your trip flares went off down the mountain and no one batted an eye. They said it was an animal, and it happened all the time. And yet, most of your off-duty Khmu were just sitting outside their hootches drinking rice beer, puffing at opium bongs, and gambling, so why not put 'em to work?"

"Hmmm," he said, spitting a stream of opium sap onto the packed red clay and turning to mount his waiting Huey. "I'll have to think about this, you know?"

A few days later, however, I noticed that he'd halfheartedly tried to implement my advice. He made no attempt to thank me and told every officer on base that it was his idea to "beef things up around here, cut the comings and goings of locals." Yet you could not call him a liar. He was so blinded by his own self-importance that he believed it himself.

After my first couple of weeks at the Patch, I began to feel surprisingly self-assured. And this despite the daytime heat, the nighttime chill and damp, the snakes, leeches, and bugs, the smelly, dirt-floor hootch that I shared with my smoking and spitting fellow bachelor officers, and the fact that I was the Cherry, the Shake 'n Bake, the FNG (Fucking New Guy).

I achieved this miracle of self-confidence by observing Nittaya and following to the letter her astute advice on how to succeed. She had imparted it to me in our rickety, old, bullet-punctured slick on the way back from Jimmy's head-rolling exercise in Gneu Mat.

Above all, she said, I must hold my natural fear at bay by concentrating on my duties sixteen hours a day, pondering my likely fate as little as possible, and affecting *"une attitude dégagé"* in even the most "spine-chilling" situations.

I must also acquaint myself with my fellow bachelor officers, she said, and divine which of them might be helpful and which a hindrance, which a friend and which a foe, and use both for my own ends.

To simplify my task, she provided me with a brief personal appraisal of each of them, which I found invaluable as I came to know them over the following days and weeks.

Despite his impeccably Aryan name and his radio call sign "Kraut," Jimmy's executive officer, Kurt Dietrich, was the clever, soft-spoken, little, Jewish-looking guy I had once imagined Jimmy might be.

Born and raised in East Berlin, he had defected to the French Zone in 1948, and promptly joined the Foreign Legion. He worked his way up through the ranks, became a French citizen, saw action in Algeria, and came out to Indochina to fight the Viet Minh in 1962 as a captain. Captured after the French defeat at Dien Bien Phu in 1964, he spent months in a prison camp.

After the armistice, he worked at the French Embassy in Saigon, "in some sort of intelligence capacity."

The Firm recruited him as soon as he retired from the Foreign Legion in 1968; they had need of a man with his experience in the region.

Since both Kurt and Jimmy had German surnames, everyone had thought maybe they were long-lost cousins or something, even though they didn't look much alike. But there was no relation, and they fraternized not at all, except on military business.

It had something to do with their opposite temperaments, Nittaya said, and then added, "You see, Jimmy is the straightest man I know, sexually speaking. But to be frank, Kurt is a bit bent."

"Bent?"

"He is ambi-everything."

"Meaning?"

"He will have intercourse with anything that moves."

"Wow, I feel for our poor little piglets."

"I never thought about that, but you may be right."

"Typical Frenchman, huh?"

"Actually, Zack, that is a 'bum rap,' as you say. Most of the Frenchmen I know are perfect gentlemen. The only true animals I have met are the American mercenaries."

"Oh yeah? And what about me?"

"That remains to be seen."

"Hey!"

At this point, Nittaya jerked up her chin, raised her hands in a Gallic gesture signifying "Enough of this nonsense," and continued her portrayal of my fellow BOQ officers.

Gowanus Platoon leader Kimo "Lay-Low" Kalani believed we are all in God's hands, she said. He never seemed to worry about anything, least of all about his own death on the field of battle. He had volunteered for the mission in Laos after spending two tours in Vietnam because—as he said without a trace of humor—he was "doing the Lord's work by opposing godless Communism."

Later, as I got to know Lay-Low, I found him to be just as simple, easy-going, and charitable as Nittaya had said he would be. Honest and hardworking, he was a good soldier who loved nothing more than lending a hand to assist his fellow officers and their native fighters.

I asked him one time what he thought his future might hold. He said that he dreamt of nothing more than completing his duty in Laos, returning to his beloved wife and three kids in Waimanalo, getting a job with the state highway department, bodysurfing at Makapuu every evening after work, and drinking Primo Beer with his fellow *Mokes* at the Kailua Chicken Shack on Saturday nights.

Although he might project a sunny, thoughtless, Island Boy image, and would strum his ukulele for us if prevailed upon, he was in fact quite well-educated, with a BA in Engineering from the University of Hawaii.

Agent Billy-Don Hargis, radio code name "Cracker," leader of Red Hook Platoon, was a skinny, little, towheaded, trash-talking redneck from the Ozark Mountains of Arkansas. His favorite activity in the whole world was pulling a square of tobacco from his cargo pants pocket, cutting a chunk off with his serrated dagger, plunking it into his mouth, chewing it up, and then spewing it out in evil smelling streams regardless of where they landed. He played non-stop Country & Western full volume on his tape recorder, and poked relentless fun at my fondness for Simon & Garfunkel and Creedence Clearwater Revival.

"I don't take to no one who don't look like me or my own kinfolk," he said in his croaky, little voice, soon after we first met—and it was hard to tell whether he was joking or not. "That includes in descendin' order Yankees, Niggers, Wops, Kikes, Micks, Frogs, Krauts, Spics, Hunkies, Polacks, Gomers, Goomers, gooks, slopes, dinks, zipperheads and Coon Ass Cajuns. But the lowest of the low in my book are Big City Lefties, Bleedin' Heart Libs and Civil Rights Activists."

He also told me—and again I wasn't sure whether he was kidding or not—that he originally volunteered for military service when the local judge in Blue Eye, Arkansas, gave him a choice to join up or spend three years in Little Rock Prison for shooting a black man who'd looked at his sister the wrong way.

A lumberjack's son, Cracker had grown up in the forest and mountains. He was a natural woodsman, a born hunter and an almost infallible marksman. Along with a killer's instinct, he had a kind of sixth sense of when the enemy was nearby. All the Khmus could smell water and people from far off in the jungle. It came naturally to them. But Cracker's gift was different. It was mystic. In fact, it was such a rare talent in combat that he'd made Staff Sergeant in the Green Berets on his second tour, although he was so poorly educated it took all his powers of concentration to read the sports page in the *Stars and Stripes*.

Nittaya had not chosen to tell me much on the Huey about

Tham-Boon Smith, radio code name Boom-Boom, Jimmy's Eurasian communications officer, and I wondered why. Then as soon as we met, Boom-Boom volunteered the information that he had gotten his job through Nittaya. It turned out that he was a friend of her mother's family in Bangkok. He'd known her all his life and was once engaged to her beautiful cousin, Vipada (until she caught him with another woman).

Tall, photogenic, and devil-may-care, the local ladies' beefcake and dreamboat rolled into one, Boom-Boom was an entertainer by vocation. Apparently, he'd inherited his talents from his father, an itinerant English singer and pianist who had met his Thai mother in a jazz club in Bangkok shortly after World War II. They were married fourteen years, just long enough for their son to learn to sing, play the piano and speak the Cockney dialect of his father, before they "dispersed to greener pastures." When Boom-Boom grew up, he spent several years trying to break into Thai cinema as a singer, musician, songwriter and comedian, without much success.

He had asked Nittaya to get him a job with Jimmy, he said, only because he had been a radioman in the Royal Thai Army during his obligatory military service, and he was fresh out of money or prospects.

Originally, he was only going to stay on until Jimmy got an American replacement. Yet, they got on so well that Jimmy upped his salary, cut him into "a li'l side-action wif' poppy production and sales," and prevailed upon him to stay even though he hated "mountains and greenery and all that shite" and was only happy in a place with "a plentitude of pavement."

Later, voicing a suspicion, I asked him the name of the

woman that Vipada had caught him in bed with. And Boom-Boom hemmed and hawed trying to find an answer for so long that I began to suspect that it might be Nittaya. When I asked her whether it was true, she merely sniffed and turned away, as if a reply was beneath her contempt, so I never got an answer to my question.

Perhaps for this reason, I liked Boom-Boom least of all my BOQ roommates in the beginning, though he was even more affable and easygoing than Lay-Low, and surely the least opinionated of the lot.

Another thing I found odd about my hootch-mates was that instead of trying to get along together in our close quarters, they tended—for some perverse reason—to emphasize their differences. This, of course, led to nightly squabbles over just about everything.

The only way we managed to mitigate the seriousness of our differences and avoid an actual blood feud was with an unspoken mutual agreement to couch our arguments in a raw and exaggerated comic vein, and to play our assigned roles as if we were all merely rude young boys in a schoolyard.

On the topic of religion, I was the agnostic, Kurt the atheist and Tham-Boon the Buddhist. Kimo and Billy-Don were the only Christians. Since one was a Catholic and the other a Southern Baptist, however, they rarely agreed about anything.

As for the remainder of our perennial comic arguments, the Kraut and the Cracker came down in favor of the extreme right wing of the Republican Party, unrestrained firepower regardless of civilian casualties, instant execution of all prisoners-of-war, and the inherent superiority of the white race.

Lay-Low and Boom-Boom were left-leaning Social Democrats who strictly adhered to the Geneva Convention as to the rights of prisoners and non-combatants and held the white race to be responsible for most of the ills of the modern world.

Confronted with two extremes, I found myself holding the middle ground, masquerading as the "voice of reason" to keep the peace. In doing so, I often found myself espousing positions that were not at all in my private compendium of beliefs.

For example, I called myself an "Independent" when I had always considered myself a Liberal Democrat. I said that I had learned in Vietnam that in certain cases, odious as it might seem, it was impossible to avoid civilian casualties. I argued that European civilization, while undeniably more advanced than others in certain ways, could also be blamed for the exploitation of other races in Asia, Africa, and the Americas.

When dealing with our superior officers at the Patch, Nittaya counseled me again to follow her example.

"You must read their very different character traits," she said. "You must predict what they want in advance and convince them that you are a hard-working, enthusiastic and imaginative subordinate dedicated to advancing their separate goals."

Jimmy's goal was simply to have his ego stroked, and to be constantly reassured that his premonition of death in battle was false. So, I applauded his genius as a military commander at every opportunity. I assured him (jokingly) that he was basically impervious to bullets. I aided and abetted his self-love ad nauseam. I commended his faith in Buddha and the spiritual wisdom of his laughing guru-monk, Loa Nyindi. I praised the beauty and housekeeping acumen of *Poo-Ying*, his young, native, servant girl, but not too much. I applauded his beloved pet, Dybbuk, at every opportunity, although I neither liked nor trusted the mutt very much. In this case, the feeling was mutual because Dybbuk was a one-man-dog. The Khmus kept a distance from him as well, for someone had disclosed the supernatural connotations of the word "Dybbuk."

In the Kraut's case, things were perhaps even more complicated. Where Jimmy was big and brash, yet riddled with obvious yet rather appealing self-doubts, Kurt was quiet and self-effacing, but harbored no doubts as to his superiority. Where Jimmy seemed to adhere to the philosophy that "the self-taught are the best taught," and guided me by indirection, Kurt was a nitpicker, a control freak, and extraordinarily vindictive when crossed.

With Jimmy, I always knew where I stood; but with Kurt, I never knew because he was underhanded by nature and adept at hiding his feelings.

Jimmy got over his noisy flare-ups in a minute, but Kurt never forgot a slight, and rarely allowed himself even the faintest self-doubt.

The key to Kurt's character, I knew, lay in what he was hiding. I had taken Nittaya's innuendos about his sexual life with a grain of salt, until I spied him one moonlit night down by the pond, bathing with a pair of pubescent Khmus, one a boy and the other a girl. He saw me catch him in the act and stared at me as if he wanted to kill me. Within a week or two, though, when he noticed I hadn't ratted him out, his attitude improved, and from then on, I had little trouble with him.

Still, there was something about the Kraut, other than his

gnarly amphibian side, that I did not trust. For one thing, he could not help displaying a certain distaste for my person. At first, I thought it was because I'm a normal heterosexual male. Then I noticed he felt the same about Nittaya. When I asked her why she said, "It's a long story," and I couldn't get much more out of her.

Despite all their differences, Nittaya handled our two bosses the same way, so again I took my cue from her. I jumped at all their commands and strove to anticipate in advance anything and everything that might please them.

It was quite easy for me. The "Po' boy" routine I used on women rarely worked with men, so I had learned very early in life to use the "tough and loyal subordinate" routine on the male sex, and it rarely failed. I had done the same with my hated LT in Vietnam and with my detested dorm supervisor in Los Padrinos Juvenile Hall.

Fortunately, both Jimmy and Kurt were so self-involved that they never seemed to have a clue that it was all smoke and mirrors.

Drilled by Kurt and Jimmy and putting my experience as a squad leader in Vietnam to good use, I quickly achieved the seemingly insuperable task of mastering the organizational skills and field craft required to run a thirty-man platoon of primitive native fighters in a mountainous jungle environment infested with enemies.

CHAPTER SEVEN

The Fish Goddess

My one real problem at the Patch was with Nittaya. Ever since we arrived, she had been all business. The sexy, insouciant girl I had known in Nakhon Phanom had suddenly transmogrified into the coolly professional Doctor Nittaya Aromdée, her starry-eyed gaze replaced by the resolute squint of a medical specialist. Working night and day as Jimmy's medic, factotum, and translator, she possessed almost no leisure time.

The only interval she spared for me was at the firing range, where we went twice a week to practice together with pistols and assault rifles.

Nittaya was an excellent shot, in the prone, kneeling, standing and off-hand positions, and she consistently beat me at blasting old clay jars or smacking the center of ten-ring targets from a hundred meters out.

When I asked her where she had learned to shoot like that, she said, "My father taught me the basics, and Jimmy did the finishing touches."

"Got any tips for me?"

"Sure," she said. "First of all, you do not maintain your weapons properly. Clean them once a day. With your CAR15, your hand/foot placement and body alignment are way off. And with your Walther PPK, you are anticipating the recoil. Do not fight it, Zack, or you are going to jerk it off target. Now let me show you what I mean."

With Nittaya's expert help, my shooting improved to the extent that I could expect to win about one in five of the bets we placed, but I never reached her level of marksmanship.

Unfortunately, I can be such an asshole macho at times that I got touchy with her about it, and it came between us.

What I'm saying, I guess, is that although we got along well enough, there was no more of that magical rapport we had shared at poolside back in Nakhon Phanom.

When I confronted her with the issue, one rare evening when we found ourselves alone outside her aid station bunker, I found her unreceptive.

"Shhhhh! Not so loud!"

"Why'd you flirt with me back in Thailand? Why'd you give me the cold shoulder when we got here?"

She put me off by shushing me with her forefinger and inviting me to follow her down into her lantern-lit aid station bunker. I found it to be quite large, rectangular, and very bright and clean.

Its floors were of polished teak wood. Its whitewashed metal walls, pillars and ceiling were made of heavy mahogany logs and deconstructed ammunition crates held together with generous dabs of industrial tar.

Eight neatly made-up military cots—two of them occupied by sleeping female medics—stood at right angles against one wall.

A futon bed on a raised dais lay against the other, with a large waxed-cloth antique wall-hanging of a meditating monk suspended above it.

A small, bronze, Buddhist altar on an overturned grenade crate sat next to it, with rice and water offerings and flickering incense candles on either side.

There was a drug dispensary at the west end of the bunker, and an operating room at the east end.

Numéro Deux of Eric Satie's *Les Trois Gymnopèdies* was playing softly on a tape deck somewhere in the background.

The impression was one of cleanliness, orderliness, and Asian grace, with few pretensions. It seemed surprisingly mature and refined, a pleasing contrast to the dirty, cluttered BOQ where I lived. And it flatly contradicted the impression of wild, flighty disorder that Nittaya had conveyed when we first met.

"Wow!" I said, whispering in deference to her sleeping medics. "Nice place you got here."

"Ah," she replied, with a little self-deprecating laugh that had all the weight of thoughtless self-confidence behind it, "but I have so little to work with here."

"Hey, is there somewhere we can talk alone?"

"In the dispensary, if you promise it is just going to be talk."

"Don't you think that's a bit much to ask? I mean . . ."

She shut the dispensary door behind us.

"Listen, Zack, I want to make something perfectly clear. It is absolutely impossible for us to *batifoler* here on the base."

"What's that mean?"

"Flirt, frisk, frolic."

Sniffing the air, intoxicated by her scent—an earthy, exotic combination of ambergris and musk—I made a grab for her.

"And why not?"

She fended me off with her hands. "Because it is a small world, *na*? And a lady who plays around is fair game in tribal society. If I do what you want, I shall not be able to perform my job. I shall be in danger of getting pawed at any moment. Why do you think I go through this *charade* with Jimmy Love?"

"What charade?"

"Pretending that I am his *maîtresse*."

"Wait a minute. What are you saying? You mean you're *not* his mistress? Lemme tell you, you coulda fooled *me*."

Nittaya gripped my arm and fixed her eyes on me to impress me with her sincerity.

"I am not, and I never have been, Zack. Poo-Ying is his mistress here at the Patch. The truth is, I have only had one real lover in my life, and he is dead."

"Wait a minute. Why would Jimmy want to play that game? What's in it for him?"

"It was part of our deal from the beginning. He desperately needed a competent medic, and he was willing to agree to anything to get one. After my father finally gave his consent, I told Jimmy privately that I would not join him without a clear understanding between us. We could pretend to the Khmus that I was his property, to keep them off my back. But in private he was to keep his hands to himself."

"I believe you," I said, although I didn't. Not completely. "But if we keep up like this, I'm bound fall into doubt. I mean, when are we ever gonna be alone together?"

"We shall have to wait for our next R & R."

"When's that?"

"Maybe five or six weeks."

"I can't wait that long."

"Oh yes, you can," she said, and rose on her tiptoes, ran her hands over my face and searched my eyes, as if asking permission. Then she pressed her body to me, drew me down to her lips and kissed me as no one had ever kissed me before, not even at the Queen's Park Hotel.

For an instant, I could feel this other and opposite human organism, this yin to my yang, open her body and soul to render us a harmonious whole.

Then it was over.

I had never been one to examine myself until then. Not even in my private journals. I had guarded my emotions and rarely allowed myself to become overwrought about anything or anyone. After that kiss, though, everything changed. For the first time in my life, I felt something. I mean, really *felt*. It hijacked all my waking thoughts and my dream life as well, and I prayed that it was not an illusion.

Later, as I considered the meaning of all this in my journal, I decided that it could only be one thing, "that four-letter word I never permitted myself to utter before."

When I say, "prayed," of course, I use the term loosely. I had never been a member of a religious denomination. I'd only gone to church under duress, when one or another of my foster parents happened to be religious. Yet, I was pious in my own way, and the transcendent qualities of that kiss in the aid station had forcefully reminded of it. The fact is, I had worshipped at the altar of my own personal deity since I was eleven years old.

I remember very clearly how I came to see the light. I was living with an obese and half-blind Nicaraguan widow named Mrs. Leticia Abelar on Santa Monica Boulevard, right across the street from the Hollywood Forever Cemetery.

Since my monthly Welfare Department allotment was Mrs. Abelar's major source of income, and I made it a point to be just as quiet, self-effacing, and polite as I had been with all my other foster parents, she never found an excuse to be unkind. Despite her Latina background, she was never much for hugging and kissing, but she always left me food stamps so I could run out to the supermarket and get what I wanted to eat, if I cooked it up myself.

Mrs. Abelar was a secret drinker. She started up with her TV and her Gallo jug wine every day about noon and passed out every evening not long after I got home from school and did my homework.

So, I was left to my own devises.

Which suited me fine.

So, one Sunday morning I woke to the ringing of the magnificent bells at Saint John the Apostle Episcopal Church. Like everything else in Hollywood, their sonorous peeling was a bit overblown and derivative—an electronic amplification of the bell tones in the 1944 film *A Canterbury Tale*.

Yet as a native of the place, I found their very excessiveness inspiring, evocative of the far away and hard-to-imagine.

In the past few weeks, I had been seeking, in my own childish, fumbling sort of way, an understanding of the spiritual nature of the universe. And the sound of those great bells reminded me of my self-imposed, yet seemingly impossible mission.

What made it so hard for me was the fact that unlike my schoolmates, who had Catholic, Protestant or Jewish parents to lay things out for them as infallible truth, I had no one to indoctrinate me.

I had always yearned to identify some solid underpinning to reality, but I knew I would eventually have to come up with any answers by myself.

In our science textbook at Vine Street Elementary School, we were studying mammals and non-mammals, and we had learned that only mammals like humans and monkeys kept their babies with them until they were fully-grown. Non-mammals such as fish just laid their eggs and left them to mature on their own.

So, lying there in bed that Sunday, diligently seeking answers to the mystery of existence, I conceived of this divine being named Pisces the Fish Goddess. Another name I had for her was "MOU, Mistress of the Universe." Although Mou was a sea-breather and therefore technically a fish, she was shaped like a beautiful woman, a mermaid.

It was she who created our world and all others.

She did it like this.

She had an endless supply of eggs. Don't ask where they came from. I never got that far in my imaginings. Anyway, she swam endlessly and gracefully through the universe, dropping her spawn behind her as she went.

She loved every one of her eggs, and she gave each of them its own unique name. For some reason, she had a special fondness for one called "Earth." She made it a little more perfect than any of her other worlds; she laid it in an especially propitious place in the universe called The Solar System, and she filled it with beautiful living beings, including some especially inventive ones that she called "humans."

It broke her heart to leave Earth behind, but she was a fish after all, and had to move on to lay her eggs in other places. So, she swam off, leaving us behind, with these words, "I will see you no more, but I have left you with a beautiful, perfect world. It is yours to enjoy or destroy at your pleasure, for I have bequeathed you the gift of free will."

I became deeply attached to Mou, but not in a passionate or fanatical way. In place of religious ecstasy, she gave me a feeling of peace, of letting go, of floating in the amniotic sea of space. I never tried to proselytize to other children or my foster parents. She was mine and mine alone. I offered her nightly prayers of devotion, but I never asked for her help because I knew she was gone forever. Her absence did nothing to weaken my dedication to her. On the contrary, it made me love her even more.

In woodshop class at Hollywood High School, I even carved a little, eight-inch, pinewood image of her, part woman and part fish, and varnished her so she would stand the test of time.

I was devoted to her right up into my twenties, especially in times of stress. I worshipped her long after I had discovered her rather pathetic Electra-like traits in my Psychology 101 class at LA State.

I kept her close to me always, right alongside my journals. I took her with me to Vietnam and Laos and carried her around in my rucksack.

And I must confess that even now, at my advanced age, I sometimes catch myself picking her up from the bedside table where I keep her and mindlessly mouthing a prayer of adoration to her while rubbing her smooth varnished body with my thumbs.

I have loved one woman all my life, and been married to another, yet Mou the Fish Goddess, is the only woman who has always been mine, and mine alone.

CHAPTER EIGHT

The Good Luck Charm

Despite all my little letdowns and regrets, I worked hard in those first weeks to whip my mostly teenaged native fighters into an effective combat team. After all, it was my life at stake here, along with theirs.

To achieve my objective, I knew I had to earn their trust, if not their affection. So, I practiced humping heavy loads up steep inclines in afternoon heat to increase my stamina and carrying power to match my men's. I diligently labored to improve my Lao language skills and absorb my fighters' folkways. I had their tattoo artist do a coiled king cobra around my right arm, just like theirs. I learned to stomach their diet of chicken feet, puppy dog, jungle cat, snake, wild pig liver and fermented rice beer. I bravely sampled their special holiday treat of deep fried "water bug," a high protein supplement better known as cockroach.

Once, when I had drunk far too much, I even followed the lead of my tribal language interpreter, Vora, by plucking an enormous rice bug out of the air, biting off the soft gooey part, gobbling it down and allowing the hard front body section to fly away into the night.

My greatest accomplishment was when I prevailed upon Jimmy to bribe the Thai supply officer at Nakhon Phanom to fly in some M16's, some castoff Thai combat boots and uniforms to replace my men's old M14's and ragged tribal clothing.

I tried to get them some flak vests as well, but as Jimmy said, "Hullo? They barely got enough for us. And these Indigs? They should care? They're expendable, you know?"

Nevertheless, the Khmus were so appreciative of my efforts that when it came time for me to start training them for serious combat, they sent Gee, the platoon's chief tracker, to explain to me that they already knew much of what I proposed to teach them, because their previous commander, Tucker Johnson, had rigorously drilled them for months. And they volunteered to prove it.

The next day, I took them out to the firing range, and they demonstrated beyond a doubt that they already knew that accurate, automatic weapons fire should be contained to three to five round bursts.

Then they proved that they could reload their weapons in the prescribed four seconds, and pump out ten rounds a minute with a grenade launcher.

When I took them out to the jungle the following day, they showed me that they knew all about hand signals, forest combat formations and setting up ambushes.

Their most impressive performance came when they executed an Immediate Action Drill that would have sent a Special Forces sergeant into ecstasies.

Then Gee taught me some things I did not know. Like how to exploit shadows in the jungle, to stay in the shade at all costs, to bypass even tiny sunbeams. How to cautiously survey the ground before us, looking for trip wires suspended a few inches above the jungle floor, or a section of black claymore wire trailing off through rotting leaves, or the telltale indentations of a punji pit. How to keep my senses attuned to every possible danger including the crack of a twig, the rustle of leaves brushed by a hand or the smell of Vietnamese cooking. He also advised me to dress all of my point and tail men in Gomer uniforms and give them AK-47's, to give us the element of surprise if we came upon the enemy suddenly.

In Southeast Asia, there is a ubiquitous and time-honored tradition called "pok-time." It's a siesta period during the hottest part of the day when everyone tucks himself under a banana tree for a couple of hours. Yet the Khmus had made pok-time an art, an all-consuming pursuit of perfect bliss. Sipping *lau-lau*, smoking bongs, watching their women husk rice, fetch water, cook stew and cultivate their vegetable gardens and poppy fields, with babies slung over their backs and half-grown children clinging to their skirts, they laid around half the day in various forms of undress.

Although I heartily disapproved of the practice, and had already registered my concerns with Jimmy Love, I said nothing more on the subject when he allowed his troops to fall back into their habitual lassitude. As in all my life situations, I desired nothing more than to simply get along with everybody, with a minimum of fuss or bother.

Khmu women all wore elaborate costumes. Each clan's tribal rig-out differed from others according to an intricate scheme of color and pattern. Yet all the costumes apparently required a tasseled skullcap, a puffy white blouse, a dark tasseled vest, a long brightly-colored skirt and hemp sandals.

Although some of the girls were quite saucy and pretty, I chose to resist their charms because I was still hopelessly enamored with Doc Nittaya and I worried that word might get back to her if I succumbed to temptation.

No other men at the Patch—except Lay-Low—seemed concerned about indiscretions, and the woods on the fringes of the base were alive with coupling bodies every night.

Boom-Boom was our uncontested champion in the sexual arena. Kurt was our captain of kink. Jimmy, as Lord of the Manor, enjoyed all the rights and privileges of *noblesse oblige,* and he indulged himself fully, to the extent of his aging capabilities, especially with his dark and delicious Poo-Ying.

Our troops all belonged to the Khmu tribe, but they had split into several different regional clans. Like a large and tumultuous family, they had often been antagonistic in the past and usually only came together to face a common enemy.

I had three native sergeants in my platoon, Dara, Keo, and Vora, each from a different clan. The shortest, darkest, toughest, and most senior of the three was the First Sergeant, Dara. Staff Sergeant Keo was taller, slimmer, and lighter in color, and he had a smile for everyone. The tallest, lightest, and most educated of the three, Sergeant First Class Vora, who was also my official Khmu language interpreter, was for some reason the lowest in rank.

At first, I encountered some resentment from my non-commissioned officers, especially from the eldest, Dara, who was jealous of my lighter-colored and better-educated interpreter, Vora. But I used my gifts for language, invention, humor, and counterfeit *bonhomie* (I encouraged them all to call me *"Capitain Hollywood"*) to maintain a rapport with them.

The problem was that they had little rapport with the members of other clans. I did what I could to bring them together, but I was fighting age-old customs and prejudices, so it was an uphill battle all the way.

Nevertheless, after a few weeks of daily training, I felt that I was at least beginning to mold them into an effective fighting unit, with each clan acting in concert with the others to their mutual advantage.

No one in my platoon, including my "interpreter," could speak a word of English, but I taught them to shout "Hoo-Ah!" when they were dismissed, just like Army Rangers. It seemed to delight them, and to improve their cohesion as a unit, so I taught them some GI slang from Vietnam: "Beat feet" for move out. "Fucked up" for wounded. "Zapped" for killed. "Bird Dog" for observation plane. "Infil" and "exfil" for deployment and extraction by chopper.

I taught them by rote. Being illiterate, they could learn no other way. And they couldn't pronounce anything worth a shit. They said *"beefee"* for beat feet, *"fugaa"* for fucked up, *"budo"* for Bird Dog. But I bent my pronunciation to conform to theirs to a certain extent, and we had a lot of laughs learning together.

The worst of their gaffes was a result of the Asian tendency to confuse the letters "L" and "R". They did all right with "To me!—*Toomi!*" and "Saddle up!—*Saduwaa!*" But much to my chagrin "Lock 'n load!" became "*Rock-a-road!*" and "Let's rock 'n roll!" became "*Rez lock-a-loll!*"

After Lay-Low and Cracker had grown tired of laughing at my Canarsie Platoon's antics, they began to see a method to my madness. They started doing the same with their platoons, and soon the whole company had its own little homegrown military pidgin.

When Jimmy heard about it, he called it a "miracle of innovation, you know?" and praised me to the stars, but Kurt did not seem so happy about it. On the contrary, he looked a bit ruffled and hurt, as if he wished he had thought of it first.

When Jimmy was off base, out visiting his other units in more northerly parts, us officers usually ate our C-Rations while squatting over ammo crates on the dirt floor of our BOQ.

Sometimes, if we were lucky, our delectable Doctor Nittaya would grace us with her presence and tip a cup of *lau-lau* with us, or have a whiff or two of grass, but she refused our C-Rats with a sniff of disdain.

Other times—perhaps at Jimmy's instigation—our bunker door would open soundlessly, announcing with a whiff of incense the appearance of the rotund, saffron-clad monk, Loa Nyindi.

Grinning beatifically, he would descend our normally squeaky stairway without a sound, as if soaring an inch or two above it. Then he would float blimp-like around the room, bestowing *wais* and *Suwadeekaps* upon each of us in turn.

Next, he would squat cross-legged in the center of our dirt floor, close his eyes, and chant "*Nammo tassa bhagavato arahato samma*—Honor to Him, the Blessed one, the Worthy One" for half an hour or more, cracking up occasionally, as if it were the funniest thing in the world.

Then he would turn to Boom-Boom, the only other Buddhist in the bunker, and ask him if he had any need for spiritual comfort.

Boom-Boom, taking a clue from his master, would laughingly reply in Lao, "Yes, oh holy one, I seek to know the meaning of life."

Each visit, the question was the same, but the Laughing Monk's response was always different. I took the trouble to write his words of wisdom down in my journal after every session, and here is some of what he said:

Think lightly of yourself, and deeply on the world.
Letting go is not the end; it is the beginning.
No need to reach for the stars; they are already floating
   inside you.
All the flowers of tomorrow are in the seeds of today.
If you are too busy to laugh, you are too busy.
There is no way to happiness; happiness is the way.
A man is not where he is, but where he loves.

As I read this now in my tattered old journal, many years later, I do see some wisdom in what the plump, young Laughing Monk said, but at the time I could not make head or tail of it, even when Nittaya tried to explain it to me.

There was only one thing about Loa Nyindi that I found truly remarkable. At the end of each session, when he glided back up the stairs in his saffron robe, he never failed to leave an aura of peace behind him, and it would be hours before we were at each other's throats again.

Every time Jimmy came back from his visits to his northern firebases, there was a nightly ritual that never varied. We called it "Chop-Chop at HQ" and we all looked forward to it because we were sick to death of sitting in our hootch every night bitching at each other while eating canned and packaged Army rations.

When Jimmy was on base, he paid an old Chinese lady named Xuě Xiāo to pack a bunch of fresh fruit, meat, and vegetables from Thavay on her pony and stay over to prepare spicy and delicious Lao, Thai, and Chinese dinners for us in the cookhouse behind his HQ. Jimmy's lissome house servant, Poo-Ying, served us with deep bows and gracious smiles.

In the cellar of the HQ bunker, he had a larder stacked with cases of beer, whiskey, and *lau-lau,* along with burlap sacks full of local-grown cannabis and opium, all of which he encouraged us to enjoy at our leisure.

Most nights, Loa Nyindi was there. At Jimmy's request, he often summoned a native country band. Bearing outlandish-looking flutes, lutes, fiddles, bamboo mouth organs, gongs, drums, cymbals and unnamable brass instruments, they trekked up the trail from Thavay for an after-dinner serenade of the unearthly local *Lam Luang* music.

Sometimes, the Laughing Monk even prevailed upon Nittaya and Poo-Ying to dress themselves in tribal garb with bells round their ankles and perform a slow, smiley, head-bobbing dance in time to the wailing of the band.

Other times, if Nittaya had imbibed enough *lau-lau,* Jimmy would coax her to stand up in front of the band and sing.

Arrayed in her colorful tribal dress, looking like some antique Asian doll, swaying her hips to the music, she would warble one of her high-pitched and unutterably foreign *Khaplam Wai* folksongs as the band shrilled and quavered behind her.

At such times, while marveling at her extraordinary flair and beauty, I would briefly consider another notion: Although we derived from incontestably alien places, and Nittaya was more exotic to me than anyone I'd ever met, she had somehow transcended the vast differences between our worlds to ensnare not only me, but virtually every other *farang* at the Patch.

Yet I never went too far with this line of thought, as I recall. It was still the age of the Beatles, after all, and I was inclined to just *"Let it be, let it be, let it be. There will be an answer, let it be."*

Payback time for our nighttime festivities came when Jimmy dismissed the band and held court at the head of the table till the wee hours of the morning.

Proposing toast after toast, he rarely permitted anyone except his laughing guru to say a word except *"Mazel Tov!"* or *"Chaiyo!"* which is a Southeast Asian attempt to pronounce the English "Cheers!"

At such times, it seemed clear to me that Jimmy was a lost soul, a man engaged in a marathon of self-indulgence, a frantic attempt to hold his terror at bay and puzzle out a meaning to his existence with the aid of booze, bombast, and Oriental mumbo-jumbo.

On the other hand, I once heard him say that he drank to excess for the same reason he went into battle, "to see how close I can get to the edge." And I believed there was some truth in that as well.

Whatever the case, it quickly became apparent to me that Jimmy's alcoholism was the result of a narcissistic personality disorder. His self-importance and grandiosity, his disdain for social norms and his search for spiritual solace revealed a desperate need to fill an emotional vacuum inside him.

With time, I came to believe that Jimmy, despite all the transcendent teachings of his guru, feared not only death, but also life—ordinary human existence.

One of the ways that he tried to hold this fear at bay, I would come to learn, was to forget everything in the heat of battle and fall prey to a bloodlust that led him to take outrageous risks.

If Jimmy's mental problem caused him to take risks with his own life, so be it; but I did not feel at all happy about him risking my life, or Nittaya's.

Another part of the "Chop-Chop at HQ" ritual was an after-dinner poker game in which Jimmy always cheated but never won. Boom-Boom and Loa Nyindi were usually the big winners, with stacks of coins piled up in front of them and happy grins on their faces, and I often wondered how they managed it. Were they simply more skillful than Jimmy? Or were they simply better cheats? If they were cheaters, what was in it for them since Lao Kip coins were virtually worthless? Only Buddha knew the answer.

On the rare occasions during these ritual dinners when our commander permitted two-way conversation, the Laughing Monk would instantly detect bad vibes in the air and glide off into the night.

Then Jimmy and Tham-Boon would engage Kurt and Billy-Don in a war of words that was so timeworn that their perennial audience of four could voice their opposing arguments by heart.

Basically, Jimmy and Boom-Boom were as anti-war as Jane Fonda, while the Kraut and Cracker were as pro-war as Mississippi VFW leader, Jefferson Davis Browne.

As I remember it now, their back and forth went something like this.

"How can you and Boom-Boom say you're anti-war, Jimmy, when you're out here fighting it every day?" Kurt would ask, in his oddly high-pitched accent, and then append a phrase we could all recite by rote. "I mean, you take cynicism to a new high. It just shows that you've never lived under a totalitarian regime, as I have."

"Or lived under a money-grubbin', pro-nigger Yankee regime, like we done in the South," Cracker would put in, and only half in jest.

"If you'd lived under such an inflexible regime," the Kraut would conclude, "you'd rather die than submit."

"What're you talkin' about?" Jimmy would say, his Brooklyn accent becoming more pronounced as he drank. "I'm fightin' to buy time for my Khmus. You know? And nothin' else. What'd old Mao say? 'The guerrilla is the fish, and the folk is the water?' Hullo? Our water is all dried up, you *schlumps!*"

"Oh yeah?" Cracker would say. "Then how 'bout our boys up here at the Patch? Don't they support our asses no more?"

"Course they do," Jimmy would say. Then he'd laugh. "Keep 'em in booze, bong and bootie long enough, they'll support the *tayvl* incarnate."

"See? See what I mean?" the Kraut would say. "What do you call that if it's not cynicism?"

"Realism!" Jimmy would yell.

"Fatalism!" Nittaya would shout.

"Nihilism!" I would holler, and everybody would laugh.

Then Boom-Boom would put up his hand as if to stop the ruckus and say, "Cor' blimey, it ain't none of that. Trouble wif' this war, you bloody Yanks are sissy-maids. Put the shoe on the other foot, put *you* out in the jungle wif' bare feet and no air cover, eaten up by insects, napalmed and cluster fucked wif' B-52s every night, you'd surrender in 'alf a bleedin' hour. And these li'l dinks, they been at it for twenty years."

One night in my eighth week at the compound, when the old argument began to drag, Nittaya prevailed upon Jimmy to prep us for the coming operation.

"About ten days from now, you know? When I got you *pischers* ready to start *schlogen* it out with Papa Lao again," he said, swallowing another quarter bottle of Mekong Whiskey and washing it down with a Tiger Beer, "we're gonna initiate an operation. Code name? 'Fortunate Dragon.' Target? Gneu Mat. And we are gonna come down upon old Kham's traitorous *tukhes* like all the fiends of hell."

"And we're going to do this all by ourselves?" the Kraut said, not bothering to disguise his skepticism.

"Sorry to disappoint you, Kurt. I know you like to throw out the 'no-can-do's' and *'Je ne sais quois.'* But the US Air Force, in its wisdom, says the place is 'of insufficient strategic importance' for a B-52 bombing raid. So, we gotta hump it like the old days. One good thing? I got slicks. I got air cover. I got a SOG Team working with us. Case you don't know, Newbie? SOG is short for a *bindl* of bad *mutter-schtuppers* in a super-secret covert ops unit stationed in Nam. What does SOG mean? Who knows? Who cares? It's a weasel word anyway. I call 'em 'Sons of God.'

"Now in this operation, hullo? Surprise is where it's at. Zero prep bombing. The LZ? Out of sight and sound. The other side of a mountain. Nine klicks north of the target. We send in a three-man recon team, you know? Make sure there's no lost gooks. No water buffalo wandering the LZ. Then we infil by chopper.

"The Sons of God—nine black ops and forty of their little Indigs—they insert eight klicks east of the target. Their code name: 'Hammer.' Ours? 'Anvil.'"

"So, this is your 'cakewalk,' Jimmy?" Nittaya said, grinning with excitement.

"Hey, what'd I say, *Bubeleh*? It's skate duty. Slack City. Or I wouldn't let you near it, you know? So, anyway, both teams infil at 0200. Converge on target at 0530. Who're we up against? One Gomer battalion. Five to one odds. But hey, old Davey Baskerville—runs a Bird Dog out of NP—you know what he says? They're conscripts. Country *bubkes* in tire tread sandals. And *oy* do we got a surprise for them! When we show up? They're still gonna be tucked away in their *schlofen* holes."

Puffing at an opium pipe that Poo-Ying stoked and re-stoked every few minutes, chugging bottles of Tiger Beer and biffing the empties into a trashcan ten feet across the bunker without missing a shot, Jimmy narrated this as if it were the most ordinary excursion, like maybe we were all going backpacking for the weekend.

Yet, I felt an electric shock run through my body, a jolt of fear that nearly rolled me off my ammo crate.

Only Nittaya, sitting there listening calmly, nodding her head in affirmation from time to time, prevented me from running for the jungle.

Later, when I caught her alone outside her aid station, I said, "But that time Jimmy threw the heads down on Kham at Gneu Mat, wasn't that kind of telegraphing this attack?"

Before replying, she took the time to flick back a lock of hair with her hand and blow a last unruly tuft out of the way with her breath.

"Oh, Jimmy would tell you just the opposite. He would say those cut-off heads spooked them so much they will be too scared to fight. You see, Mr. Love relies on his 'tribal instincts' to fight his enemies. He believes they are infallible."

"And you agree?"

"Sometimes, I must say, his intuitions are quite uncanny."

"And this time?"

"This time?" She folded her hands, raised them to her mouth, and extended her index fingers upward in the shape of a steeple. "Maybe you should wear this, na?"

She reached in her medic's bag, pulled out a colorful cloth bracelet composed of twenty-eight knots, the Buddhist equivalent of a St. Christopher's medal, and tied it around my wrist.

She made me hold it up, looked at it quizzically for a moment, turning my wrist in her hand. Then, shaking her head as if unsatisfied, she reached behind her neck, untied her leather thong with the bronze Buddha head, and pulled it from under her tunic.

"What's this for?" I asked as she tied it around my neck.

"A little extra insurance."

"But what about you?"

"What about me?"

"You said it's kept you safe ever since your great-aunt..."

"That is correct, but I have a feeling you are going to need it this time more than I do," she said, tucking it under my bush jacket.

"Nittaya, this..." I said choking up. "I swear this is..."

"Oh shush," she said, touching a finger to my lips. "And remember, you must never wear it outside your clothes. It has got to be touching your skin. Otherwise, it will not work."

CHAPTER NINE

The Good Witch

Early on the evening of Operation Fortunate Dragon, Jimmy called us into the Command Post and informed us that he wanted "every swinging *schlong* out on the LZ at 1900 on the dot."

"And does that include those of us not so endowed, sir?" Nittaya said with a little *blink-blink* smile of affected innocence.

"Affirmative!" Jimmy slurred. He was already too far gone in drink to see the humor in her response.

As it turned out, our chief wanted nothing more than to gather us all out on the LZ, around an enormous campfire, and treat us to a native sendoff party—called *phou* in Lao—presided over by himself and his guru, the Laughing Monk. It was supposed to be a time when the mountain *phi* flit about and bestow harmony upon everyone who participates.

Once we had feasted upon old Xuě Xiāo's barbecued terrier, scup soup, stuffed frog, carp roe and stir-fried amaranth, with hyacinth beans and flower cabbage, Jimmy had Poo-Ying pass out paper cups of rice wine and Mekong Whiskey.

"Hullo? Don't be shy. Step right up!" he shouted. "We got liquor up the yin-yang here. *Mazel tov!*"

Then he demanded that each of us sing a song from our native place. He started things off with a rousing, wedding song in Ruthenian Yiddish.

The Kraut sang the *"Marseillaise"* and *"Deutschland Über Alles,"* each in a perfectly authentic accent.

Cracker sang *"Dixie."*

Lay-Low sang *"Blue Hawaii,"* accompanying himself on the ukulele.

I sang *"California Girls."*

Loa Nyindi sang *"Prajulamanee, A Prayer to Buddha,"* and commended our fleeting lives to the Gautama's discretion.

Boom-Boom entertained us with several uncannily accurate renditions of songs from the film *"Anna and the King of Siam."*

Poo-Ying sang a weirdly high-pitched folksong from Southern Laos called *Leuk-Leuk.*

When Nittaya's turn came, she bravely informed her loud and drunken commander that if he proposed to make every single one of the three hundred people here sing a song from his or her native place, we would all be here until dawn and have to scrub the mission.

Thereupon, without securing his permission, she raised her hands like a conductor at the Met and led all the partygoers in an emotional rendering of *Pheng Xat Lao*, the national anthem of Laos, followed by a rousing American "Hoo-Ah!"

At that point, my interpreter Vora stood up before the crowd, raised his hands for quiet, and asked leave to speak.

Not so much for his light color and unusual height, but for his ability to read, write and teach, Vora was one of the most respected of the native fighters.

So, no one objected when he began to address the crowd in a loud but careful Lao that all could hear and understand.

"We call you *'paw-paw'* in our language," he said, turning to face Jimmy Love, who was starting to sag a bit by now and had to be propped up by his guru and Doc Nittaya, "because you are indeed like a father to us. You have led us into battle without fear. You have carried our wounded to safety. You have slept with us in the jungle. Every one of us would die for you, as you would die for us. We are your sons and warriors. Our women are your wives and daughters. And we will follow you to the gates of hell and beyond. Hoo-Ah!"

Everyone cheered wildly at the end of the speech except for Vora's jealous rival, Dara.

After loudly protesting that he did not deserve such praise, and bemoaning his tendency to tempt fate, Jimmy entrusted his soul to Buddha, cried like a baby, passed out, and had to be carried into his rack at HQ. All of which, Nittaya assured me later, was *"comme d'habitude,"* and no one would be particularly surprised when he rose from the dead in a few hours.

Just as she had predicted, Jimmy was "up and at 'em" by 0100 in the morning, seemingly unaffected by his carousing of only a few hours before, and he quite capably supervised his native fighters in their ritualistic pre-battle routine of applying black camouflage sticks to each other's faces and strapping on the battle gear determined by our mission.

When we had saddled up to our leader's satisfaction, and

he had made us all chug one last liter of launch site water to conserve our canteen water, he marched us out to the pitch-black helipad and formed us into lines to await the arrival of the nine unmarked slicks that would serve as our air transport.

We could hear them echoing up the deep river valley minutes before they arrived, *whap-whap-whap,* and the noise became earsplitting when they came roaring over the edge of the cliff and hovered for landing. The wind from their rotor blades whistled down on us, raising a choking cloud of dust.

I boarded the fourth helicopter to lift off with one of my squads, but Nittaya stayed close to Jimmy and Boom-Boom in the last one to launch.

As our chopper veered out over the river valley and gained altitude, I swung my legs out the door beside one of the Thai machine gunners as I had seen Lay-Low do. I wanted my Khmus to perceive their leader as relaxed and in control. Yet I was scared shitless, and for an instant, I wished myself a million miles away.

Then I thought of Nittaya. I knew she was as tough as any man in the company, but I chose to think of her as too frail and fragile and female to be out here flying through the night toward a brutal firefight. If she had to be on the mission, then I wanted to be with her.

Flapping along in three-chopper wedge formations at an altitude of a hundred meters, following the contours of the land, we skirted the northern slopes of the Phou Dendin Mountains until we reached a small, grassy valley called Na Nhia, just on the other side of a range of tall jungle hills from our destination at Gneu Mat.

I had seen not a single light, not a single sign of human

habitation during the entire fifty-klick flight. There was no moon, and a million stars in the shimmering night sky provided the only light.

After receiving a radio message that our Special Forces recon team from Nakhon Phanom had found the LZ clear of enemies and animals wild and domestic, our pilot broke formation. He banked sharply and we went spiraling downward, falling so swiftly through the darkness that it was like being in an elevator with a broken cable.

My ears popped, plugged up, then popped again, and my heart came up almost literally into my mouth.

Swift as it was, our descent seemed to last forever. The only way I knew we had reached earth was when the rotor blades changed pitch and the chopper flared its nose to hover a meter above the Landing Zone.

My squad and I jumped into utter darkness, into a storm of dust and thudded into waist-high saw grass with all the weight of our rucksacks and field gear whamming down on our shoulders.

True to its name, the grass was sharp-edged and cut like a paper burn when I hit it wrong with my hand.

Even before I'd hollered *"Toomi!"* and got my platoon headed for the tree line, our three Hueys had rumbled off into the darkness and another formation was landing.

After all the choppers had departed and Jimmy had formed us up at the tree line, he whispered from behind us in a comic Montagnard accent, *"Hokay, twoopers, rez rock-a-roe! Rez kirr a Commie fo' Christ!"*

Cracker hooted. "But you ain't even a Christian, Jimmy!"

"Awright awready! So, let's kill a Commie for The Great

Fahklempt in the Sky!"

And so, we marched off into the darkness, giggling sotto voce at our leader's antics.

We went single file, with Cracker's boys on point, mine on slack, and Lay-Low's as tail.

Jimmy marched with Cracker.

Kurt did rear guard with Red Hook Platoon.

Nittaya walked just ahead of me in the slack platoon.

"I can't tell you how happy this makes me, Doc."

"What?"

"That you're with me now."

"And why is that," she whispered over her shoulder in French, "*mon cher Capitain?*"

"Because I've come to regard you not only as the girl of my dreams, but also as my guide."

"You mean like a blind man's dog?"

"Yes, what would I do in this wilderness without a bitch like you to accompany me?"

"I thought I was supposed to be a fox, *na?*"

"All right, have it your way. A vixen then."

"Oh, what a sweet thing to say! You become more loveable all the time, *Khun Farang*. How can a girl possibly resist you?"

"And not only that," I said, switching to English. "You're my good luck charm, my walking, talking talisman."

"Wow!"

"Mojo even mightier than the bronze Buddha you hung around my neck."

She laughed under her breath. "I believe that might be a compliment, if I could only figure out what 'mojo' means."

"Mojo is magic, *juju*."

"So now you want to make me a witch?"

"You already *are* a witch, Nittaya, as you know very well."

"Hmm, then at least I hope I am a *good* witch."

"Yes, well, that remains to be seen," I said, and we fell silent as we contemplated the several layers of underlying meaning in our ostensibly jocular conversation.

With the aid of his compass, his starlight scope, his Khmu point man and his faithful Dybbuk, Jimmy was able to make his way along a predetermined azimuth through the jungle, skirting six-foot anthills, waking colonies of chattering gibbons and spider monkeys and bevies of screeching parrots on the way. He found the rope bridge he was looking for, the one that led to the mountain defile, on his first try, infusing everyone with such exhilarating self-confidence that he had to stop and pass the word to "shut the fuck *up!*"

Chastened, Love Company set off silently down the narrow meandering trail in the darkness, each fighter following the shadow of the one ahead of him.

The jungle around us now was triple canopy, what the grunts in Nam had called "Old Mother Green the Killing Machine." The lowest layer was mostly shrubs and giant ferns. The second layer was palms and tropical trees about as high as those that line a typical suburban street. The canopy layer consisted of immensely tall teak and mahogany, rivaling the redwoods of California in girth.

There was a special feeling in that kind of jungle, one that I was familiar with from Nam. With the wind shut out by the mountains and encroaching vegetation, the air was close and humid, thick with the smells of flowering plants.

After the monkeys and birds had ascertained that their invaders meant them no harm and had fallen silent again, there was only the sound of buzzing mosquitoes, croaking tree frogs, bamboo rattling on bamboo and the cursing of a little lizard that made a repetitive noise exactly like the English expletive *"Fuck you, fuck you, fuck you!"*

To me, the rainforest had always felt more than a little claustrophobic; I sweated like a pig though the night air was mild.

The reward for my travails was that I could groove behind the fragrant yet unseen proximity of my darkling love.

By 0500, when we glimpsed the first smudge of purple in the eastern sky, the canyon had broadened into a narrow, grassy valley. The jungle had receded to the flanks of the mountains and, according to my map, the swift-running Gneu River lay just over the next rise.

It was then that Dybbuk started to bark, and Cracker reported to Jimmy that he was spotting fresh signs of the enemy.

"Hullo? What're you talkin' about?"

"Fresh smothered cookin' fires, spider holes that look like someone just up and left," Cracker said, while my tracker Gee nodded in agreement beside him. "And Bata Boot prints, not Gomer sandals."

"I smell Uncle Ho, not Papa Lao," Gee put in. *"Nuoc Mam* fish sauce from Haiphong. And he right nearby."

Then we heard firing off to the northeast, and a flare went up in the sky over the same location.

Trouble was—it was way too soon.

Neither the Sons of God nor we were in position yet, and we were not supposed to commence firing until exactly 0530.

After glassing the valley ahead of us, and the mountains above us, Jimmy stopped the column and called his officers, his radioman and medic up for a little conference.

"This sucks, you know?" he rasped, gesturing angrily toward the firing. "It's all *fercockt*."

"Yes sir," we agreed. "It truly is."

"Some traitorous *mutter-schtupper* let the cat out of the bag," he said. "It's my fault. I listened to you, Doc. Did the prep talk a fucking week in advance. We got a mole among us, people. There's a world of trouble waitin' for us, just a few meters up the trail. So, what do we do?"

He shrugged and raised his hands.

"We fold up. You know? Funk out. Call in some Air. Beat feet for the LZ. Establish a perimeter and dust off. Hop back to the Patch and un-ass. Flush out the spy and lop off his *kop*. Then we stick it up on the flagpole and throw stones at it."

"What about the Sons of God?" Lay-Low wanted to know.

Jimmy snorted. "Hey, they're pros, *bruderman*. They know an ambush when they see it. And they got their own little air force. Before you can sing *'Bei Mir Bist Du Shayn'* they'll be over the hump and back in Nam. So, let's about fuckin' face, and boogie outta here."

Yet even before we got back to our platoons, one of our tiger-team leaders—a cheerful, little, native corporal named Yim—tripped over a catgut fish line tied to a tree root. It snapped with a pinging sound that we could all hear. Yim looked down at his feet and his eyes went big and round. Then it blew.

"When the dust cleared, his body was lying dead on the ground and his legs lay entwined high in the limbs of a longan tree." At least, that's how I recorded it later in my journal.

I don't remember the scene now, and I admit that I sometimes dramatized the hellish and unreal scenes I witnessed in order to give them form and structure and thereby make sense of them.

Anyway, Papa Lao or Uncle Ho or whoever it was must have taken Yim's spectacular exit as an auspicious sign because he opened up from the western heights a moment later.

It happened so quick; I was too surprised to be scared.

One moment I was watching the sky grow pink and the shadows retreat. The next moment Jimmy was yelling, "Incoming!"

Mortar rounds started bursting up the trail, getting closer by the second. Rockets streaked over our heads. Green tracer rounds floated down from the heights and started pinging into rocks beside the trail, then humming off into the distance.

Then I thought about Nittaya. She had stayed behind with Gowanus Platoon to get fresh orders from Jimmy. I turned and saw her caught out in the open with Cracker, and I freaked because I thought she'd buy it right there before my eyes.

Enveloped in a firestorm of tracer rounds, Cracker died like the second lead in a war movie, jerking and dancing and taking long seconds to spin into the elephant grass.

Yet Nittaya seemed immune to the gunfire. It was like that big Red Cross she'd painted on her backpack was somehow sacred. Like the Goomers and Gomers had suddenly begun observing the niceties of civilized warfare for the first time in twenty years.

Marveling at her extraordinary karma, at her seeming

immunity to red-hot flying lead, I returned my attention to my men.

I ordered them to retreat the way we had come, into the protection of the narrow canyon and the triple-canopy jungle. I warned them not to return fire. We still had the benefit of semi-darkness, and I did not want muzzle flashes to give our position away.

Apparently, everyone else in Love Company had the same idea, so we all hauled ass for cover.

Every few steps, though, someone would get hit and fall on the trail. One of his fellow tribesmen would stop to help him, and everyone else would try to hurdle the two of them or dodge around them.

But it didn't work that way.

We tripped and fell. We got hung up in the thick underbrush by the side of the trail. We started bunching up in mini-traffic jams, and the fighters at the rear of the column were stopped cold, perfect targets for our enemies.

Then an order came up the line from Jimmy.

"Leave the mortally wounded behind. Aid only the walking wounded."

The Khmus obeyed him to the letter, slitting the throats of their hopeless cases without a flicker of apparent remorse, dragging the others behind them.

Finally, we made it to the tree line.

Jimmy had Canarsie and Red Hook Platoons deploy across the trail at the edge of the jungle with their grenade launchers, machineguns and assault rifles pointing back the way we'd come, and he had Gowanus Platoon lay down a welcome mat of claymore mines.

Meanwhile, the enemy commander (presumably Jimmy's old *kamerad* Kham) sent three companies of NVA down the mountain and up the narrow valley.

He left his Pathet Lao contingent on the ridge to bombard us with mortars and rockets.

Ahead, I could see harmless-looking twinkles of light that were, in reality, the muzzle flashes of automatic weapons. I saw their green tracers crisscrossing with our red tracers in the sky above no-man's-land.

I heard a sound like a popping bottle cap, then a *whoosh*, and I saw a rocket propelled grenade streaking toward me, leaving a sparkler trail behind it. It seemed to come very slowly at first, and yet it was on me so fast I had no time to duck. Luckily, it went right over my head and tore into the jungle behind me.

Next, a bunch of little yellow fellows in jungle green pith helmets, Goomer uniforms and canvas Bata Boots suddenly rose to their feet and came marching through the tall grass, firing as they came.

Now they were sprinting up the gentle incline, ducking, weaving, and falling. One of them, taller, bulkier, and lighter-colored than the rest, was wearing a Spetsnaz camouflage uniform and a Ruski flak vest and appeared to be a Soviet Bloc advisor.

What truly astounded me was that some of the soldiers in the vanguard, though dressed in the same uniforms as the others, were women.

Out of nowhere, an enemy soldier, a peasant girl with a round face, a bad complexion and squinty eyes, appeared above me with a Kalashnikov at her hip.

She had stretched her mouth so wide in a battle cry that I could see her tonsils, her gold fillings, and the spittle forming on her tongue. We were so close I could smell the smoke-fire scent of her uniform, the stink of her unwashed female parts, her fishy breath.

Through all the clamor of war, I could not hear her voice, but I could see by the fiery glare in her black eyes that she was utterly fearless.

She despised me, and everything I represented.

She would kill me without a qualm.

I had an advantage over her because I'd suddenly risen up out of the tall grass and was already aiming at her, while she was moving rapidly and had been surprised by my appearance before her.

Yet out of some obscure and antiquated scruple, I hesitated to fire upon her for an instant because she was so young, no more than teenager, and a member of the "weaker sex."

Which very nearly proved my undoing.

That instant's hesitation resulted in the two of us firing simultaneously. She hit me smack in the heart; I hit her in the same place, and we both would have died had it not been for the flak vest I wore.

As it was, I blasted a little round black hole through her breast and a big one out her back.

And she hit me so hard in the ribcage that her seven-millimeter AK-47 round dug a deep trough in my flak vest, knocked the breath clean out of me, and blew me back on my ass.

The girl soldier took another step, then wilted upon me,

clutching at my arm as if I might help ease her pain.

Just before her eyes rolled up in death, I felt her sniffle against my shoulder, once, twice, like a small hurt child.

Sheltering behind her thin, little body as she bled out, I fired short bursts of automatic fire at her more cautious male comrades whom I could now see creeping and crawling toward me through the elephant grass.

Meanwhile Boom-Boom had called in air cover, and soon I could hear Cobra attack helicopters and A-1 Super Spads circling above.

They couldn't chance blitzing the valley because we were so closely entwined with our enemies, so they turned their attention to the Gomer artillery on the mountain above the battle.

The Spads were prop-driven, World War II vintage, but they were as big as B-17s and carried more weight. I could hear them roaring overhead, blasting the enemy above with napalm and 500-pound bombs.

The sounds of battle grew louder.

AK-47s went *crick-crack-crack!*

M-16s went *dut-dut, dut-dut!*

Commie machineguns went *chut-chut-chut!*

Jimmy's went *bap-bap-bap!*

Mortars and rockets went *whomp, thump, bam!*

Then there were the curses flung at the enemy.

The howls of agony.

Pleas to God and Buddha.

Cries for Mama in different languages.

When the dinks had first started firing at us, I'd felt a burst of adrenaline and sensed everything acutely. The burning heat.

My parched throat. My tongue like old leather. The sting of sweat in my eyes. My panting breath. The hot gun in my hand. The weight of my ruck and all its gear pressing me down.

Adrenaline only lasted so long, though.

By now, I was nearly deaf from all the noise, and everything started to sound like it was coming from far away.

My eyes had grown bleary from all the smoke and fire, which only added to my sensation of peculiar unreality.

I began to feel like another person, like some remote observer looking down upon this reluctant shadow warrior sheltering behind the body of a zapped little Asian girl.

At the climax of the battle, when all the furies of hell seemed to storm and fume about me and I saw my interpreter, Vora, vaporize into tiny red droplets before my eyes, and I should have been petrified with fright—I felt very distant from worldly cares. I had no time for such minor considerations as instant death.

I fired my weapon into the approaching waves of Goomers, until it was so hot it warped and jammed up.

I picked up the girl's AK-47 and mowed down another wave, only to see yet another rise behind them.

I felt nothing.

I was numb.

And when we finally got the order to retreat, I had absolutely no preference between heaven and hell.

Lay-Low's platoon pulled out first, quickly followed by mine.

Kurt led the retreating forces. Nittaya and Boom-Boom accompanied him as medic and radioman.

Jimmy stayed behind with Dybbuk and the late Cracker's platoon, which assumed the role of "tail-end Charlie," covering our retreat.

No one questioned the decision, so typically Jimmy, yet so totally unlike other senior officers, who preferred to maintain an "objective distance" from the battle.

Everyone knew why he'd chosen Gowanus Platoon to accompany him in his heroics. It was his spoiled favorite. This was not because of its stellar performance, but for a strictly sentimental reason.

Jimmy was born and raised on the Gowanus Canal in Brooklyn.

As we ran for our lives through the jungle, rocket propelled grenades whizzed over our heads. Mortars exploded. Ricochets hummed about us, kicking up dirt, smacking into the trunks of trees, blasting off twigs and branches. Yet the thick jungle canopy absorbed so much noise that it wasn't as loud as one might have expected.

Then we hit a patch of jungle that was already aflame from rocket and mortar fire. Blasted trees lay in burning piles. Dead men from Red Hook Platoon lay entwined amongst the flaming logs, the smell of their barbecued flesh filling the air.

Apparently, the enemy mortar and rocket teams were moving along the western ridge above us, keeping pace with our retreat.

By this time, about halfway back to the LZ and in the full light of day, I was so exhausted I felt I might flop down and just expire in the fiery ashes.

A rocket exploded just behind us and my tail gunner came running toward me, trying to hold his bloody entrails in with his hand. Just as he reached me, he collapsed in a pile of glowing red ashes. His flesh started sizzling, smelling of grilled innards.

But we kept going, going.

Every few steps forward, someone else would fall, whether from wounds, exhaustion, or smoke inhalation I didn't know.

If they were still alive and moderately functional, my men and I simply picked them up and dragged them forward.

If they were not, we left them where they fell.

And always there was the NVA just behind us.

We caught glimpses of reflected metal moving through the underbrush.

We heard footsteps crackling over dry leaves.

When they crept up too close for comfort, we'd wheel as one and mow a few more down with our assault rifles. Or we'd throw a frag grenade up high to burst over their heads because we knew we could kill more of them that way.

Parched with thirst, I dipped my canteen in a little creek we crossed while still moving. I loved the purling sound it made. I could almost taste the water. I paused for an instant, braving the fire overhead to drink it down.

Not even the wild buffalo dung I spotted upstream could spoil my enjoyment as I slogged ahead.

When we finally reached the LZ that afternoon and were able to count our losses, we discovered that we had lost over a third of our number, and nearly all of us were wounded in one way or another.

I got clipped in the thigh and didn't even realize it till I felt blood sloshing around in my boot.

We survivors crawled out of the jungle and lay exhausted in the grass, while Doc Nittaya and her native medics came around to tend our wounds.

She cleaned and bound mine in what seemed like seconds, injected me with something, and was on to the next wounded man, before I could even coax a smile out of her. Yet, I was so happy to see her alive and among the few unwounded that I didn't even bother to grumble or complain.

Our bodies cried for sleep, but we knew the Goomers were right behind us.

Kurt formed us into a perimeter just inside the edge of the jungle and told us in his odd accent to "take a breezer." But our breather didn't last long because within minutes we could hear them creeping up on us again.

Boom-Boom contacted the 0-2 Bird Dog that was directing the air battle above us, impressing him in rapid Cockney that we were in "a world of 'urt."

A few minutes later, a couple of Cobras came skipping over the jungle canopy, one of which got Boom-Boom on the horn.

"Anvil 4-2, Red Team Leader. Mark your Lima Zulu with smoke. Over."

"Roger that, Red Team Leader," Boom-Boom replied, and Kurt had Lay-Low throw out a phosphorous grenade we called a "Willy Pete." He'd been a star pitcher at Windward High School in Hawaii, so it went a long way indeed. When it exploded, it sent up a mushroom cloud that rose above the tallest trees.

"I have smoke!" Boom-Boom hollered into the radio. "Confirm?"

"Roger, Anvil 4-2, I got it in sight. Over and out."

The Cobras fired 20 mm cannons, smoke rockets and tear gas bomblets to hide us from the pounding of the enemy and spoil their aim.

Next in was a pair of fat, green and brown Super Spads that left bright, metal, napalm canisters flipping through the air behind them.

When the napalm hit, I could see Goomers dancing in the fire.

Then it sucked all the air and sound out of the world.

I got smacked in the face by the mother of all winds, so hot it felt like every hair on my head had burnt off.

A flight of sleek F-4 Phantoms showed up next. They'd had a slow day over Nam and were itching to get rid of their 500-pound bombs and fire off their M61 rotary cannons.

Best of all, our Bird Dog was able to call in a Magic Dragon with Gatling guns that could chop down jungle like wheat in a field.

Over the next fifteen or twenty minutes they plastered everything on the other side of the smoke signal with so much ordnance that it set the jungle on fire again.

How anyone could live through that inferno, I didn't know. But live they did.

And they came crawling up on our perimeter, laying down a wall of fire. They were so close I could see their eyeballs rimmed with smoke like kohl and the gunships dared not hit us again for fear of friendly casualties.

It was then that Kurt directed the Bird Dog circling above us to call down fire upon our own position.

"Everyzing but napalm," he said, for which I was eternally grateful.

As for Jimmy, Dybbuk, and his men, I heard later that after all his claymores and most of his grenades ran out, he ordered the rear guard to slowly fall back.

When the platoon had lost nearly half its number and was in danger of being overrun, Jimmy picked up the machinegun of a fallen fighter. He motioned for anyone who was carrying an M60 ammo belt to drop it beside him and run like hell for the LZ.

With twenty belts of ammo piled around him, and a pair of teenage native volunteers named Havika and Akamu to help him feed the machinegun, and the fearless Dybbuk as moral support, Jimmy was able to hold off the entire attacking force, although little, sixteen-year-old Havika was killed in the action and both he and Akamu were wounded.

When they had fired off all their ammo, killing dozens of the enemy and pinning most of the rest down, Jimmy and Akamu abandoned the M60, picked up their assault rifles and sprinted up the trail.

Instead of following the retreating platoons, as the enemy might have expected, they veered off into the thick jungle on the right side of the trail.

As the pursuing soldiers rushed past, Jimmy and Akamu stepped out and mowed them down from behind on full automatic.

When they'd again run out of ammunition, they dropped their useless rifles, faded back into the jungle, and made for the eastern ridgeline four hundred meters above.

Akamu led the way. Born and raised in the region, he knew a secret path to the top.

Jimmy, limping from a leg wound and using a fallen branch as a crutch, followed him.

At the top, Jimmy sent Dybbuk back down the mountain

with orders to "Kill, kill! their pursuers while he searched the sky for a helicopter.

All the way up the ridge, he had heard choppers coming and going, but now that he needed one, they were nowhere to be found.

At last, he could hear a flight of slicks coming in from the west, obviously bound for the LZ to pick up his troops. He set off a smoke grenade, flashed a mirror toward them, and one of them peeled off to investigate.

Jimmy had Akamu lay out their last few mini claymores to cover their withdrawal, and they raced for a bald spot on the ridge.

Jimmy called out for Dybbuk, but he never appeared, and no one ever saw him again.

The Huey came down fast, taking so much fire from the fringe of jungle that the pilot decided to hover at twenty meters and let down a couple of rope extraction rigs rather than risk a landing.

When the ropes came down, Jimmy strapped Akamu in one yoke and himself in the other and signaled the chopper to go, go, go!

The pilot got the message, and away they flew, while AK-47 tracers streaked the sky around them.

Just when it looked like they'd been righteously saved, an RPG hit the chopper in the cockpit.

It suddenly dove over the far side of the ridgeline, trailing fire, and smoke, jerking Jimmy and Akamu along like a pair of fish on a line.

The crewmember hoisting them up waved a mordant

goodbye and cut their ropes.

They fell ten meters to earth and rolled thirty meters down the western side of the ridge, till they got caught in a dense thicket of ferns and exposed roots.

The chopper spun four hundred meters into the valley below and exploded in a ball of flame.

When Jimmy came to, he reached out for Akamu and discovered that he had broken his neck and was already attracting flies and fire ants.

He could hear the enemy soldiers beating the bush all around him, but without their tracker dogs to sniff his trail they seemed to have lost him.

He waited for night and slinked back up to the ridgeline. The going was easy, he found, because the ridge was rocky and mostly barren.

He followed it cautiously till he judged he was four or five klicks north of the chopper wreck, which was sure to attract the enemy like flies to dead meat.

Then he dropped down into the valley, crossed it in the darkest part of the night, and set off westward, dragging his left leg.

Two days later, at the top of another ridge, he managed to attract the attention of a passing Bird Dog with his mirror.

The Bird Dog called in a slick, which extracted him with a rope rig without incident.

Sixty hours after he had launched Operation Fortunate Dragon, Jimmy was lying in bed with an IV in his arm and his leg in a sling at the Royal Thai Army Hospital in Nakhon Phanom, still fuming about the traitor in his ranks and bemoaning the loss of his valiant Dybbuk.

Meanwhile, back at the LZ, Kurt had bought us some time by unleashing a tornado of aerial weaponry on Love Company and its interlocked enemy.

I was so numb by then that all I remember is the horrible ripping sound of the rockets followed immediately by a whoof of hot air that singed my eyebrows and kept blowing the hat off my head.

In the end, the air attack killed more of them than us, so Kurt felt confident enough to call the Hueys in for the exfil. As they made their approach, though, one of the choppers got hit by an RPG and exploded while another one took so much fire it had to turn around and run for its base.

The remaining six choppers pulled up again to wait for some more air cover. Luckily, a new flock of Cobras and Super Spads had flown in, and we still had the Magic Dragon lurking about.

In the eight or ten minutes it took for our enemies to recover from this third assault upon their ranks, the slicks swooped in three at a time to exfil our asses as quickly as possible.

We loaded the wounded and Doc Nittaya in the first two choppers, then what was left of Red Hook Platoon in the other, along with our executive officer (who ridiculed Jimmy's notions of "going down with the *sheep*").

What was left of my platoon and Lay-Low's hung behind to await the next exfil.

By the time the last three choppers landed, the firing from our perimeter had picked up considerably. In an act of foolhardy Christian charity, for which I'll feel indebted till the day I die, the big happy-go-lucky Hawaiian volunteered to hold the line with his Red Hook Platoon while I exfiled Canarsie. I signaled the third slick to lift off and await Lay-Low's platoon.

I rushed my remaining men aboard the second chopper and it prepared to lift off.

I intended to stay behind with two of my men, First Sergeant Dara and Tracker Gee, cover Red Hook Platoon while they ran to safety, and exfil in the third and last chopper now hovering a couple of hundred meters overhead.

But my plan proved impossible to execute because the enemy, now consisting of both NVA and Pathet Lao, rose up from three sides of our perimeter, overran Red Hook Platoon's defenses, and raced for us across the grass.

The door gunners fired their fifties at them non-stop, and the chopper overhead opened up as well, but that only slowed them down a bit.

Crammed full of fighters, taking fire from every direction, the Huey started to lift off while the three of us were still holding off our attackers.

Even though we had all been wounded again in this last foray, we leapt for our lives and just managed to cling to the edge of the doorway of the rising chopper.

As bullets pinged into the fuselage, whistled through one open doorway and out the other, and Dara got stitched with machinegun fire and fell back in the grass, the helo hovered a few feet above the ground, straining to gain altitude.

"That's it! Get 'em off!" the pilot shrieked. "I can't take any more weight!"

"Let 'em in!" I heard Boom-Boom yell.

"Negative! Negative! Tell 'em to jump off or we'll never make it over the mountains!"

"Let 'em in, you bugger, or I s'll blow your bleedin' brains out!" Boom-Boom screamed in Cockney, and pulled his pistol out, an act of insubordination for which I shall forever be thankful.

With no choice, the pilot let our platoon-mates hoist Gee and me aboard and pile on top of them.

"Anyone who's still got a grenade," I hollered in Lao, "throw it out!"

Four grenades sailed out the door. Three of them exploded midst our attackers, buying us the few seconds we need to lift off.

The Huey dipped its nose and lumbered off down the valley, trailing smoke, pursued by a tempest of machine gun and rocket fire.

Inside, it reeked of pissed pants, but when I felt the cool air whooshing about my wet legs, I thought we might live after all.

Unable to gain more than a few feet in altitude, the chopper just kept whap-whapping along until we began to think we had pulled off a miracle.

Then about five or six klicks from the extraction site, we looked ahead and nearly lost it. There before us, rising steeply out of the jungle floor, was a razorback ridgeline enshrouded in mist.

Throwing up his hands in frustration, the pilot put the bird down in a grassy open space in the jungle.

By luck, we had a little Filipino kicker-mechanic along with us. Apparently, he was on some sort of familiarization ride, but when the pilot ordered him out to check the damage, he shook his head in refusal and seemed petrified with fear.

Aided by Gee, I grabbed him by the scuff of the neck and literally kicked him off the aircraft.

Faced with no choice, he set to work, and within a few minutes, by some marvel of mechanical science, or through the collective efforts of the several deities to whom we prayed, he was able to put out the fire in the engine and patch up the leaking gas hose that was causing the problem.

Slowly, tentatively, we lifted off again.

The pilot circled back a click or two and poured it on. We gained altitude, and for a moment, it looked like we might squeak by.

Brushing the tops of the tallest teak and mahogany trees, we slipped over the ridgeline, looked out upon the vast and beautiful tableau of jungle and mountain, and heaved a great simultaneous sigh that needed no translation.

By now, it was twilight. The valleys before us were purple and orange; the tall, karst buttes and rolling ridges had turned gray and dull green in the lengthening shadows.

To us, it was a vision of heaven.

Then we hit a downdraft.

The pilot hadn't the power to lift us out, and we spun toward the forest in slow motion, our prop wash thrashing the outer branches, blowing a furrow through the leaves.

Holding our breaths, we heard the tops of trees scraping our metal bottom.

Then we seemed to settle midst the tallest limbs.

Our rotors caught, snapped off, and spun away, chopping wood into kindling, scattering leaves and vines, making a fearful racket, scaring birds and monkeys into flight.

Yet mercifully, the dense canopy of the jungle enveloped us in its coiling, green tentacles and prevented us from crashing.

Instead, we felt ourselves sinking, sinking, then dropping a bit and sinking again.

It was such an unexpected sensation that we were not at all afraid. It was like some silly, new ride at a state fair carnival. I think we just felt curious about what was going to happen next. We even laughed at a couple of stomach-turning lurches, as I recall.

Then we came to an abrupt halt ten meters off the floor of the jungle.

Hanging there akimbo, like a bug caught in a giant web, we held our breaths again for at least a quarter of an hour before our flying machine slipped and slid and swiveled to a gentle rest on Mother Earth—upside down.

I raised Nittaya's bronze Buddha to my mouth and kissed it passionately.

By some miracle, the chopper's radio was still working, so the pilot cranked it up and got Sky HQ on the horn.

We marched down the hill to a lightly forested area.

My Khmus pulled out their long, Kachin machetes, and in thirty minutes, we had an LZ.

An hour later, a "Jolly Green Giant" appeared in the sky above us, and I shot off a flare to attract its attention.

By eight o'clock that night, we were in triage at the Royal Thai Army Hospital in Nakhon Phanom.

"So much for Jimmy's 'cakewalk,'" I said when Doc Nittaya, all freshly bathed and radiantly beautiful in crisp white medical scrubs came around to tend my wounds. "I guess those lopped-off heads of his didn't do their job."

She aimed one of most dazzling smiles at me and ran her fingers through my hair.

"No, I suppose not, but we shall never even hint at that to our glorious leader, shall we?"

A deputation of Jimmy's CIA masters flew out from Washington while he was still in the hospital. With no regard for his serious wounds, they gathered round his bed and produced an in-house document that called him to account for the "military disaster" at Gneu Mat. They accused him of "negligence" in allowing a spy to ferret out his battle plans. They charged him with "incompetence" for placing his company in an "indefensible position" and allowing it to be ambushed by "a vastly larger enemy force." They warned him that any further "blunders" of that order would result in his dismissal.

The answer as to why they didn't fire him on the spot, or why Jimmy was never frightened they might, lay in something they had always known but had neglected out of self-interest to reveal to the public, or to their own Communist-obsessed superiors in government.

Jimmy's mission in Laos, and indeed the entire United States' mission in Southeast Asia, had been doomed from the start. General Douglas MacArthur had put it best when he said, "Never get into a ground war in Asia." Now that the specter of defeat was showing its face, and Nixon was struggling frantically to find some way out, the Firm could find no one other than Jimmy to stay and fight a hopeless, useless, immoral war.

Notwithstanding our commander's "failings," however, Love

Company destroyed more than two enemy companies that day, nearly two hundred and fifty main force NVA and Pathet Lao soldiers, at a cost of fifty-six KIA.

True, we suffered numerous wounded, and a casualty rate of more than ninety percent, but our achievements would become legendary in the arcane world of Covert Ops, as would the action we engaged in on March 16, 1971, which would forever be known as "The Battle of Gneu Mat."

In recent years, "Posttraumatic Stress Disorder" has been much in the news, and it is incontestable that returning combat vets often suffer from flashbacks, nightmares, sleeplessness, hyper-vigilance and unprovoked attacks of anger.

Yet few have chosen to speak of an altogether more common post-battle syndrome, the mindless exultation common to soldiers who have lately experienced those two most primitive of human emotions, bloodlust, and terror or have miraculously survived a near-death experience.

As a combat veteran myself, I can say that I've experienced both of the above, the latter far more intensely than the former.

In the days following the Battle of Gneu Mat, my overstimulated brain was awash in that kind of savage elation. I felt in some way exalted by the totality, the immediacy, the intensified sense of awareness in this most primeval of all experiences.

Disremembering my horrific encounters in the Vietnam War, and my resentment toward Major Duval for "seducing" me again into combat, I now felt almost disappointed at the possibility that I might never know this wild and ferocious rapture again.

The feeling was so intense that I refused to register the moans of the amputees in my hospital ward, the whimpering, begging, and crying of the mortally wounded, or the odor of infected stomach wounds and overfilled bedpans. I sealed it from my consciousness, and it has remained so until now, nearly fifty years later.

It's a form of self-protection, I guess.

My time in the hospital also marked a sea change in my opinion of my commander, Jimmy Love.

Deluded I may have been, but I remember feeling that his unmatched bravery, selflessness, and tactical prowess diminished his immense character flaws to virtual insignificance. Bedridden as I was, swathed in blood-seeping compresses and dressings, groaning in pain, spaced on painkillers, I felt the germ of admiration I felt for Jimmy Love swiftly mutate into the mindless adulation of his tribal warriors.

CHAPTER TEN

The Lady of The Moon

In the hospital, Nittaya's public attitude toward me abruptly changed.

I could only guess why.

Maybe she was just worried about my injuries.

For whatever reason, she tended me like a doting wife or mother, cooing over me to the point where the staff complained, and all the other wounded fighters burned with envy.

"What am I, chopped liver?" Jimmy fumed. "This *schmuck* got somethin' I ain't?"

"How about youth and good looks?" Nittaya said, but he did not reply with his usual self-deprecatory humor.

Under my physician's tender loving care, I recovered remarkably fast. She discharged me from the hospital while Jimmy Love and many of our other fighters were still in the Intensive Care Unit. Better yet, she got me a room right next to hers in the Bachelor Officers' Quarters.

One night, I met her in the hospital cafeteria when she was just coming off her twelve-hour shift in the ICU ward. Her bouffant was straggly, hanging over her little pointed ears. Her eyelids were drooping with fatigue. Her lipstick had smeared, and she was still in her soiled doctor's scrubs.

Yet to me she never looked more desirable. I was fixated especially on her neck tendons, the hollow at her throat, and the delicate wings of her collarbones framed by her pale V-cut blue smock.

So, what did I do? Of course. What I always did with girls. I tried to arouse her sympathy.

While we sat sharing a Krong Thip cigarette and a bowl of rambutan fruit, I told her the tragi-comic story of how my US Army commander, Major Duval, had seduced me into combat against all my most fervent wishes.

"But you know," I said when I'd finished my tale, "sometimes bad shit leads to good. I mean, if it hadn't been for the major, I wouldn't have met you."

"I suppose then we have more in common than we thought."

"How's that?"

"Well, we both got into this through misguided love, and yet maybe—like you say—it turned out for the better."

Then she told me the equally tragi-comic tale of her affair with a young, Vietnamese student named Nguyen Ly. They had met at university in Paris, she said, backpacked together across "The Great Grass Road" to Asia and intended to marry one day. Then he'd been killed in a random Viet Cong bombing while visiting his family in Saigon, and his senseless death left her incensed against the communists.

"Maybe that is one of the reasons I agreed to work with Jimmy at the Patch," she said, "to avenge his death in some way, *na?*"

"Could be, Nittaya. But it sounds a little far-fetched, don't you think? And I've got another question for you. How come it's suddenly okay to hang out together?"

Instead of replying, she took my hands in hers and looked me in the eye.

"I adore the way you pronounce my name, Zack, in your California surfer accent. And I love the way your tough GI talk is so often in opposition to your inner sensitivity. Like you are half-afraid someone is going to call you a sissy-boy, *na?*"

"And I love the slightly mocking tone you always take with me, Nittaya, even when you're giving me some kind of backhanded compliment."

"And why is that?"

"Because it tells me that I amuse you, even when you're evading my questions. And what's love without amusement?"

"Yes, amusement is nice. But to tell the truth, *mon cher,* I think of love as something a little more substantial than that. I mean, how about friendship? Shared interests? A mental as well as a physical bond?"

"Sounds good to me."

"You have never thought about it much, though, have you?"

"Not really. Whenever I thought of love before, I never got much beyond the throbbing part."

"Typical man."

"I'm still young. I can learn."

"And I am to be your teacher?"

"Why not?"

"When do you want to start your course of instruction?"

"How about tonight?"

"All right, but we take it slowly at first, *na?* I mean, we would not want to pop any of those stitches of yours, would we?"

"Uh-uh, no way, we sure wouldn't want to do anything like that. But actually, step-by-step is okay with me."

"Really? *Ching-ching?*"

"Uh-huh. You know why? Because all my life it's been one '*Wham-Bam, thank you ma'am!*' after another. I want this one to mean something."

"Are you just saying that to please me?"

"Yes, but it also happens to be the truth."

"I have no idea why, but I believe you," she said, pinning me with her orbs.

Without another word, she took my hand and led me out of the hospital and into the town, making for the river.

A bright and silvery quarter moon had risen halfway up the sky, and it filtered through the leaves of the street-side tamarind trees to mark little shivery patches on the blacktop and gravel. The air was full of the smell of charred wood from *al fresco* kitchens. Moths and gnats swarmed about the external lights of cafes and restaurants. Nightjars flew in and out of the picture, their wings blocking and freeing light. Bats shot through like suppressed pistol rounds.

Down at the Mekong, Nittaya spread her shawl on a patch of riverside grass, and we sat there in the evening cool for the longest time, hand in hand, gazing up at the dry season moon and stars, swatting at mosquitoes, saying nothing.

"Do you know what we call a smiling moon like that in

Lao?" she said at last.

"I'm afraid they didn't go in much for romance or poetry where I learned Lao."

"We call her 'The Lady of the Moon.' When we are children, we offer her presents to show her how happy she makes us. When we grow up, we do the same thing—to show our appreciation for the lover she sent us."

"Did you offer her something for me?"

"No. We are not lovers . . . yet," she said, and let her head fall on my shoulder.

I ran a hand around her hip and bottom, marveling at how soft she was, and how sweet she still smelled after a long day's work in an unpleasant place.

"Tell me something, Zack, what do you honestly believe in?" she said, looking out over the river to the shadowy mountains of Laos and the starry sky beyond. "I mean, what *did* you believe in before you met me?"

"What makes you think I believe in you?"

She raised her head from my shoulder and made as if to get up. "Whatever."

I grabbed her by the arm and dragged her back down to face me. "I mean, it's possible to love a woman, to be madly, helplessly in love, but still not be sure of her. You know what I mean?"

"Maybe, but then . . . what *do* you believe in?"

"Well, I never had much instruction in moral questions, so I never developed much more than a hazy notion of right and wrong. Unless you count what was pounded into me at Juvenile Hall."

"That is so different from me, Zack. I have always held to very concrete ideas of what is right and what is wrong."

"I figured that."

"So, you still have not told me . . ."

"Hey, I've learned from hard-earned experience to believe in only one thing, and I think if you really apply yourself you can probably guess what it is."

"Yourself?"

"Yup, and maybe my alter-ego, a little wooden statue of a made-up goddess that I carved as a kid and carry around in my ruck."

"That is *so* sad," she said, snuggling up to me, sniffing at the hair that showed at the open neck of my bush jacket. "Yet so enchanting. So 'Zack.'"

"Okay, what do *you* believe in?"

"Oh, lots of things. I believe in my country, my people. But most of all I believe in that little spark of the divine that exists in certain rare human beings."

"How do know it when you see it?"

"By the love in his eyes."

"You actually believe that love is divine?"

"Oh yes I do, with all my heart."

I pulled her up and kissed her then. Tasted her. Breathed her. Held her tight.

"So, what do you see in my eyes right now."

"What I always believed in."

"Really?"

"Yes. And what do you see in mine?"

"I'm still not sure yet."

"Listen, Zack," she said, and locked those dark, glittery, up-slanting orbs upon mine in an expression of almost manic intensity. "You can ask me anything right now. I mean absolutely *anything,* and I swear on the graves of my ancestors I will tell you the truth."

"You know, I don't think I'm ready for that yet, Nittaya," I said, and went on to speak of other, more commonplace things.

CHAPTER ELEVEN

Fire and Water

Nittaya had the next couple of days off; her first break in over a month. So, the next morning she tipped a kitchen lady thirty baht to pack us a lunch, and we hiked to a secret river beach she knew, on the way to the Dhamma Thakra Temple.

There, we just lay on a straw mat all day in our bathing suits, under a big, shady, mango tree, swatting flies, falling asleep now and then with our balled-up clothes for pillows, saying little of importance, except what we could see in the other's eyes.

An hour after lunch, she said she wanted to go for a swim. I made as if to follow her, but she said it was far too soon; my wounds were still healing, and they would surely become infected in the mucky Mekong.

Then she dove in, spectacular in her bikini, and swam halfway to Laos.

The current swept her downstream a klick or two, and I limped after her along the shore. Splashing in the shallows to keep my bare feet from burning on the sand, I worried irrationally that the river might carry her away and I might never see her again.

When at last we connected downriver and humped back to our bathing spot, we spotted a pair of dirty, little, underfed, Thai urchins running up the levee with all our things.

Nittaya chased them down, and when I caught up, I helped her wrestle them to the ground.

They kicked, they bit, they screamed and cursed us while we laughingly deprived them of their booty.

We had taken so much pleasure in the chase that we tipped them thirty baht before we booted them off down the trail.

Back at our beach, I got Nittaya to read from a little volume of Jacques Prévert's poetry that she had carried along in her newly recovered handbag. And she chose this poem:

Une orange sur la table
Ta robe sur le tapis
Et toi dans mon lit
Doux présent du présent
Fraîcheur de la nuit
Chaleur de ma vie.

An orange on the table
Your dress on the carpet
And you in my bed
Sweet present of the present
Coolness of the night
Warmth of my life.

"Thank you, Nittaya," I said. "That is so beautiful."

Lying back on the mat, she stretched her arms out behind her and raised her knees.

"Poetry is my one, big, soft spot. I really do not know how I could live without it."

"I didn't know that! It's mine too. What else is there I don't know about you?"

"Oh, more than you could ever imagine. But one thing I will confess is that I have kept a diary where I write all my most secret thoughts, ever since I was ten years old."

"Me too. But I started at twelve, and I have literary pretensions, so I call it a 'journal.'"

"As a 'literary man,' then, I imagine you take all kinds of liberties with the truth, *na?*"

"I have been known to fictionalize at times, yes. But, hey, with your 'poetic sensibilities,' don't you sometimes find yourself doing the same?"

"I may enjoy reading poetry and literature, but as a scientist, a doctor of medicine, I consider it my duty to make accurate observations of the world around me, and to examine even my strongest emotions dispassionately—at least after the fact."

"Wow, I tell you what. I'll show you mine if you show me yours."

She laughed and slapped me on my unwounded right thigh.

"Never! Oh, never, never, never! I have hidden it away where no one can ever find it!"

We were nearly naked, hip to hip in our swimsuits, and the sun was hot on our bodies, even filtered through the leaves of our mango tree.

"You know what?"

"No, what?"

"Devil or angel, I'll love you forever," I said, but she just looked up at me with a drowsy pok-time smile.

All that day, I had this sense of mindless, childlike happiness, a pleasure in the smallest things.

The sunlight in her hair.

Her hazy afternoon eyes.

The way she looked at me.

On our way back to the hospital that evening, in our tank-tops, Bermuda shorts and flip-flops, with the sun sinking into the endless rice fields of Thailand and the mountains of Laos already falling into night, I spoke of colors, of how each human being had a special one.

"I'm red. That's clear. And you're blue, no?"

Nittaya stopped and hesitated to reply, as if I had caught her by surprise.

She turned and squinted up at me, her nose crinkled like a kitten's.

Gnats were flying around her head. Our long walk had caused her to perspire. The sweat coiled down through the dark whorl of hair at her temples; it swept in rivulets over her high brown cheekbones and dropped off her chin. I smelled her heated body. I savored it.

"Uh . . . yes," she said at last. "We are like fire and water, *na?*"

"And you know what I'd like to do right now?

"No, what?"

"I'd like to just . . . drown in you."

"Don't talk so fast," she said. "You might just get your wish."

CHAPTER TWELVE

The House of Sand

The next day at our river beach, I recall, we made a little house of sand near the water's edge.

"If it falls down the next time a boat makes waves," I said, "that means we're not going to last; but if it stays up, that means we'll be together forever."

When the next long-tailed boat sailed by and the ripples started lapping at our house, it looked like it might fall. But we set to work helping each other to shore it up, and it stood against everything the river threw at it.

We made a wall, a garden, a path, a terrace for the sun.

Then Nittaya broke off two little sticks, set them in the garden and said, very softly, "This is you, and this is me, *na?*"

I looked at her in a certain way, and she said, "Oh, right!"

She broke off another, smaller stick.

"This is a half-grown one; he is the boy."

Then she got a tiny, tiny stick, and put it next to the other three.

"This is the baby; she is a little girl," she said, and when she looked up at me, I thought we might both die of bliss.

A bit later, when we had awakened from our love trance, I said, "What are their names gonna be then? Will they be English or Lao?"

"Why not meet somewhere halfway, *na?*"

"Alright, we both speak French . . ."

"How about *Tristan* for the boy and *Cybèle* for the girl?"

"Perfect."

"And they will not be the last," she said rapturously. "There shall be a whole great brood of them running wild and naked, under the redwood trees of California. All of them with romantic French names. I can just see them now!"

Yet later that afternoon, on the way back to the hospital, Nittaya succumbed again to the niggling constraints of reality.

She halted abruptly in the path and turned to look up at me as if she were preparing to deliver some important announcement.

"It is not just our cultural differences," she said, *a propos* of nothing. "It would probably never last between us in any case. Love is such a fragile emotion, Zack. It can die in a second with a word, a look, a smell. Mostly, it just dies slowly over the years. So, why should we inflict ourselves with *illusions romantiques* when we are doomed to fail even if we run off to some Atlantis-by-the-Sea and try to live happily ever after?"

A sudden breeze swept over the levee, blowing plastic bags, paper sacks and rice-candy wrappers.

Across the dirt pathway, above her shoulder, I could see a pair of black and yellow sunbirds sitting on the limb of a flowering

Mai Saw tree, with red and yellow blossoms.

Somewhere in the distance, back the way we had come, a water buffalo bawled, and a bull elephant trumpeted.

In the bamboo shantytown ahead, I could hear dogs barking, pigs grunting, children playing games in the dirt road, a fisherman marketing his catch, a baker's girl hawking her wares.

"You have no clue as to who I really am," Nittaya was saying. "I mean, if I had not studied medicine, I think I might have made a pretty good actress. Under everything, I feel so needy—like an orphan. Like you, Zack. I feel this compulsion to surround myself with allies, to be what everyone wants me to be, to make everyone like me. In Paris, I played at being French. At the university, I played at being a student activist. On the Great Grass Road, I played at being a hippy. With my old boyfriend, Nguyen Ly, I played at being an intellectual. With my father, I played at being a dutiful daughter."

"Okay, so tell me. Who's the real Nittaya under all that?"

"You want the truth? Sometimes I do not know myself."

"So, who is this girl with me right now?"

"I am not sure yet. But tell me something. Who is the real Zack under all the load of *merde* you pack on your back?"

"There's only one way to find out."

"How is that?"

"Ask."

"Okay, I tell you what," she said, starting to walk again. "We already told each other the whitewashed versions of our lives, so . . . we have another couple of kilometers to go. Let us get down to the . . . how do you say?"

"The nitty-gritty?"

"Yes, who goes first?"

"Let's flip for it."

I lost and told her some rather tame stories about being "seduced and abused" by a few of my foster mothers in Hollywood.

When I finished, she scolded me about "pulling punches," so I finally came up with something meatier. I fictionalized it somewhat, as is my way, but it was true in all but a few embellishments.

"I'm not sure how old I was at the time," I said, "but I was very little, and I saw a face looking down at me. It's a very young and pretty woman with long, shiny, platinum blond hair, big blue eyes and a turned-up nose, and she's bending over me, smiling. This is my mommy's face, I know, and it fills me with a sense of shivery happiness and well-being.

"So, I'm out playing with my mommy on the grass behind our apartment building on Beachwood Avenue in Hollywood when I hear someone call her name.

"'Kristina, phone! It's your agent, I think.'

"'Back in a second, hon,' says Mommy, in her kind of singsong Minnesota Swedish accent, and she runs into the building.

"As soon as she's gone, I see this dark, round, kind of distorted face above me.

"Someone is bending over me again, but it's not my mommy. It's a young, Mexican boy about twelve and he's smiling, but his smile is not pleasant at all.

"I know this kid. I've seen him at the park. His name is Leo, but everyone calls him 'Feo Leo,' which means 'Ugly Leo' in Spanish.

"Later, I'll find out that he's one of the homeless, illegal alien boys 'employed' by Tom Willis, the pedophile who runs a mortuary and ambulance service next door to my mother's apartment building.

"'Come, come, come with me,' says Feo Leo.

"Then he takes me up in his arms and runs across the yard, out the back gate, down the alley, into the rear gate of the mortuary and through the squeaky door of the tool shed.

"All the time, I'm screaming my guts out. 'No, no, I want my mommy!'

"Inside the shed, there's a bright shaft of light that streams down through a crack in the wooden shingles. I can see spider webs, old broken tools, and a greasy workbench. The place smells of must, oily sand, and pigeon shit.

"Still smiling, Feo Leo lays me out on the workbench. He shakes his head and puts a finger to his lips when I kick my feet and cry out.

"Then he slides a hand into his pants pocket and out comes this switchblade knife.

"I'm looking up at him, with my eyes popping out of my head, and I see the smile fade from his face.

"Quick as a snake, he reaches down with his other hand and clutches me by the throat.

"'Don't move,' he whispers, and he flips the knife open and cuts through the front of my pants.

"Now he's doing something to me with the knife, something that hurts more than anything, something that makes me scream in terror, something that'll wake me up screaming for the rest of my life.

"'I'm gonna make you a little girl like me,' he says in his Mexican accent, looking me straight in the eye, ignoring my shrieks of pain.

"My body goes into spasms. My heart seems to burst out of my chest. Just as everything starts to go black, my mommy bursts through the door. She slams it open with a big bang. The dust and light swirl around in a kind of slow-motion cloud. Howling like a banshee, hair flying, eyes as big as eggs, mouth wide open, she grabs a broken broomstick from beside the door and whirls on Feo Leo, who's cowering and whimpering in the corner. Then she starts jabbing at him with the sharp end of the broomstick. Right in the face. Right in the eye. Right in the ass.

"'Oh my God, my God, my God!' I can hear my mommy screaming, still screaming, even now.

"She scoops me up in her arms, races across the yard, up the back steps of the mortuary, through the back door, and flings open the door to Tom Willis' office.

"Tom is this big, fat, old, nearsighted man. He's sitting at his desk in a black mourning suit and a green visor cap, under an adjustable reading lamp. Bent over a stack of bills and receipts, he's scrutinizing them from an inch away with his magnifying glass. There's an empty lunch tray lying beside him on the floor.

"'Look! Look at this, you fucking pervert!' my mother shrieks, kicking the lunch tray and dishes against the wall.

"She holds me out over Tom's desk, and right up into his face, turning me this way and that, flinging blood all over his white shirt and papers. And she starts wailing at the top of her lungs, 'Look, look what your bugger-boy has done!'

"'Where is that little, spic sonofabitch?' Tom hollers, but I can see that there's not a trace of remorse in his face. 'I'm gonna have his *ass* for this!'

"Next thing I know, we're in one of Tom's ambulances with the siren wailing. We pull up in front of the ER at Hollywood Presbyterian Hospital. A nurse carries me into the operating room.

"Then something happens to me that I contrive to forget, to grow scar tissue over . . . A year or so later, my mom's giving me a bath. 'Mommy,' I say, 'what's this mark I got on me down here on my sack?'

"'Why, honey, that's the seam where God sewed you together when he made you.'

"'And how come I got three eggs, one big one and two small ones, not two the same size, like other boys?'

"'Because, honey, God loved you so much He wanted to give you a little something extra,' she says, and I choose to believe her.

"But in my heart—and down lower—I always knew . . ."

After I finished my story, Nittaya smiled and patted me on the arm.

"You know, Zack, although I have not had the pleasure yet, I get a feeling your mother may have been right."

I beamed at her then like I'd never heard anything better in my life.

And I probably hadn't.

"Okay, now it's your turn."

"All right," she said. "When I was barely seventeen, my parents sent me off to France to study. During my first week in Paris, I decided to take a shortcut one night across the Luxembourg

Garden, which was in my Left Bank neighborhood. I knew it was stupid, but I have always been a bit of a daredevil and I liked to take chances. When I was halfway across the park, three young Arabs jumped out of the bushes.

"They put a knife to my throat, threw me down on the ground, and raped me one by one.

"I was so terrified that all I could do was say, 'Do anything you want; just please do not kill me!'

"The weird thing was that on some insane level, I enjoyed it, or at least my body did, because when the last Arab climbed on, I had an orgasm.

"When they had done with me, they spit on me, called me 'saloppe,' and 'sale pute' and left me lying half-naked on the grass.

"Only after they had gone did the full impact hit me. Only then did I start whimpering, crying, and worrying about disease.

"Finally, I put myself together and ran out of the park. In my room at the dormitory, I spent hours bathing myself in hygienic soap and hot water, but I told no one.

"Later, when I did not show any signs of venereal disease, I neglected to go for an examination, even though I knew I ought to.

"My chemistry professor at the *Université de Paris* was a flamboyant, middle-aged bachelor named Pierre Archambaut. All the girls in class were mad about him, and I was no exception.

"One weekend he invited all his students out to his country home in Normandy. On the first night, he came into my room and crawled into bed with me. He was about to make love with me when I said, 'Maybe you will not want to when I make my confession.'

"After he listened to my story about the rape, he said, 'you did nothing wrong, *ma chere,* so there is nothing to confess. I shall take you in for a physical exam next week.'

"He slept chastely beside me, and on Sunday night he drove me home with the rest of his students.

"The next week, I passed the physical exam and became my professor's sex toy. By 'sex toy,' I mean that very soon I came to understand that he was twisted in some way. After our second night together, he started bringing a little doctor's bag along, full of all kinds of whips, clamps, and chains. And for a while, I found it rather exciting, you know, but soon it just started to get boring, and I broke it off.

"Wait. No. That is a lie. The truth is, I was afraid I might grow to like his perversions . . . as punishment."

"Punishment for what?"

"For what my father did to me. I have always felt a little guilty about it. Like it might somehow be my fault."

"What'd he do to you?"

"He started coming into my bed at night when I was eleven and he kept it up until I was fourteen, when I told my mother—who of course did not believe me.

"What I remember now, with the most bitterness, is what he said to justify his actions. 'I made you,' he said, 'so I can do anything I want with you.'"

"Were there . . . any lasting effects?"

"Yes," she said, leaning her head on my shoulder as we walked, avoiding my eyes. "I think there were. I mean, part of me has always yearned for true love, tender affection, a sweet guy like you, a happy, little family of my own. But there is this other part . . . This other tiny part of me that wants to relive the perversion I suffered as a child. Do not ask me why, Zack. It comes to me in these horrid dreams and sometimes I feel *so* bad about it."

"Shhh, it's nothing we can't work through together," I said, kissing the top of her head, breathing in the scent of her hair, and I wanted quite desperately for it to be true.

That night, we hitched a ride in an Air Force jeep into Nakhon Phanom to find a room, a place far from prying military eyes where we could be truly alone at last. We looked everywhere, but there was a Thai political convention in town, so the place was packed.

On the verge of giving up, we tried one, last, little, working-class, boarding house, and after a bit of bribery they let us in.

Our room was little more than a rooftop shack, but there were potted fruit trees and tropical flowers all around it, and a view of the moonlit Mekong across the flat cluttered rooftops of Nakhon Phanom.

Inside, we found that it was spare but clean, with a polished teakwood floor, hanging plants in the windows, and a single bug-buzzing bulb for light. A long, filmy, white, mosquito net hug from a bolt in the ceiling and flared out over the hard, double floor mat that served as a bed.

Yet, we only had time to give it a cursory glance. As soon as the door clicked shut behind us, there was a tremendous explosion. It lit up the sky, shook the floor under our feet, and scared the living shit out of us.

We rushed back out outside, looked over the parapet toward the river, and saw the Sala Klang Royal Thai Navy Base in flames.

Later, we would learn that the Thai People's Liberation Army had done the job, with help from traitorous naval personnel on the inside.

At the time, we could only guess.

I remember we stood there with our mouths hanging open, too surprised to exclaim, watching the ammunition dump and supply depots blow, and police, fire engines and Thai Army units arriving.

I went, "Wow! In-fucking-credible!"

Yet Nittaya turned strangely calm, and after a few minutes she took my hand and led me back inside.

The instant we were in the door, "our things floated away as in a dream," as I had it later in my journal, and while the fire continued to rage, illuminating our room like flickering night-light in an old silent film, "our mouths found each other like fire and water."

When at last we paused to draw breath, Nittaya leaned back in my arms—dark-eyed, musky, and full-breasted. "What ... what do you want from me, Zack?"

"Everything."

"Yes, yes," she said, and swept back the wispy, mosquito net, fell back on the sleeping mat, and pulled me down toward her.

"Wait, wait a second."

"Oh, please, ..." she begged, stretching like a cat on the sheet, twisting and turning in frustration.

"Wait," I said again and held fast on my knees a moment to contemplate her image before me on the bed.

I saw her as a classic nude, a *Naked Maja* or *Reclining Venus*. Raven hair flying about her face. Midnight eyes aslant, half-shut.

Nose flaring. Lips swollen from my kiss. Pulse beating in the hollow of her throat. And those delicate winged collarbones. Those full, dark breasts and taut, purple nipples, rising and falling with each shallow breath. The curve of her hips. The roundness of her belly. The dark dip of her navel. The fine, black down on the fringes of her *chatte délicate*. And those long, lithe, earth-yellow thighs and legs. Those long, narrow feet kicking out at the mat in hunger and vexation.

"Wait, I want to freeze this picture in my mind forever."

Taking a deep breath, as if at the end of all patience, she sighed, shook her head, and waggled her hands at me.

"All right, Zack, but in return for my forbearance I want you to promise me something."

"What's that?"

"When you finally manage to defrost that mental refrigerator of yours, you will not suddenly thaw out like some saber-toothed tiger frozen in the ice for ten thousand years and attack me with your claws out. You will make love to me with *gentillesse et tendresse*."

"I never dreamed of doing it any other way."

"Oh, I love you," she said, when I finally abandoned my image of her to embrace her more tangible and succulent parts.

She was only slightly moist at first, but when I kissed her there, she magically wetted, and I could taste her on my tongue. She spread her legs, raised her hips off the mat to meet my mouth, and started to pant and moan. I spread her labia with my fingers and licked her clitoris, until it swelled and hardened. Softly, slowly, I ran a finger inside her. A bit faster, a bit harder and I had it all the way down past the little crook at her wellspring.

Now I had her bucking and humping by instinct.

She grabbed me by the hair and ground my face into her, growling like a leopard cat.

She came so hard she bubbled over, oozed out to glisten on hair and thighs.

Then she collapsed, her breasts heaving up and down, her sated, female smell wafting up to meet my dripping nose. And I breathed it in, relishing its elusive, uniquely Asian aroma, which I described later in my journal as "sliced dragon fruit laid out in the morning sun."

After Nittaya recovered her breath, she threw back her head and heaved with laughter.

"And . . . and . . . and you have not even fucked me yet!"

A few moments later, when I had recharged her libido sufficiently, and she lay open at last to the immense erection I'd developed during our lengthy foreplay, she cried out, as if astonished by the notion, "Oh, yes, I really do love you, I think!"

In the end, things turned out even hotter than we had intended.

Nittaya's love was like that fire at the naval base. It burned all night, no matter how hard I poured it on.

Yet, we never lacked for *tendresse*.

After each round of lovemaking, we lay warmly, wetly intermingled, like breeding invertebrates.

In the morning, we found that our blended juices had dried and glued us together, and we were breathing perfectly in tune with each other, like a single being.

"Wow," I said as we finally started to melt apart. "I always thought couples were exaggerating when they said, 'We are one.'"

"I did too," she said laughing, and lay her soft, little face on my hard, woolly chest. "And you know, usually when you wait a long time for something that you want bad, you are a bit disappointed when you finally obtain it, *na?* But last night..."

"It was even better than we imagined," I said, inhaling that unique human fragrance of Nittaya and Zachary entwined. "The only problem is—how can anything that good ever happen again?"

"You know what the Laughing Monk says?" she said, cupping my face in her hands, smiling down at me. "*Every happy moment lasts forever.*"

"I don't know about that, but I do know one thing. All my life I've felt alone. And now I don't."

"Yes. I suppose it is simply chemistry, you know? No one can explain the why of it. Our minds click. Our bodies fit. And I feel so ... so *safe* with you."

"I don't feel altogether safe with you," I said, twisting my hands in her hair, drawing her down for another kiss. Then I laughed and whispered in her ear. "But hey, I'm a soldier, right? Danger only adds to the excitement."

She said nothing in reply, and suddenly we both grew very solemn.

"I adore you, Nittaya, but I have absolutely no idea where we're going," I said, and cupped her cheeks to pull her back and search the dark and limitless swirl of her eyes.

"You think I do?" she said and started to cry.

CHAPTER THIRTEEN

Without a Trace

It was two months after The Battle of Gneu Mat. The more lightly wounded of our men had recovered. New tribal recruits, several of them defectors from Pathet Lao units, had replaced the dead and severely wounded.

Jimmy himself was "in the pinkus," he said.

So, two weeks after he was released from hospital, he had all the fully recovered and able-bodied members of his unit helicoptered back to the Patch. For some reason, he flew all his officers back with him in the same Jolly Green Giant.

On our way up the Mekong River Valley, he introduced us to his two new platoon leaders.

"Hullo? Listen up, ladies. I want you to meet our FNG's!" he shouted above the din of the chopper, pointing to the stocky, pug-faced, little Latino who had been ogling Nittaya ever since he climbed aboard. "Meet Agent Alfonso Garcia, from Pueblo, Colorado!

"And Agent Brian Barksdale, from Waco, Texas!" he roared, indicating the lanky, cowboy type who'd isolated himself in the rear as soon as we lifted off and hadn't said a word or cracked a grin since.

"*Oy, boychiks*, what'd they call you over in Nam?" he hollered, whipping his shaven head back and forth from one to the other. "Hey, we should care? You know? Up at the Patch, we do our own code names."

He pointed at the ugly, little Mexican and said, "You're Valentino." He pointed at the tall, close-mouthed cowboy and said, "You're Walky-Talky."

Honeybuns, Boom-Boom, and I suppressed our titters only with the greatest difficulty. The Kraut kept his own counsel, as usual.

Immediately after we landed, Nittaya made it her priority to plod off through the dry season dust and lend comfort to some of the new widows whose families she'd treated in the past. She had me tag along with her as moral support.

There was one birdy, little sixteen-year-old Khmu girl named Nok, whose child Nittaya had recently managed to bring into the world despite a trying breech-birth delivery.

Her seventeen-year-old husband, Liko, unlike most of his fellow tribesmen, had been extraordinarily helpful and positive, never shirking in even the most bloody and painful moments. During their lengthy ordeal, the three of them established a bond.

Afterwards, Nittaya had looked in on them and their thriving baby girl as often as she found the time. They had gotten so close, in fact, that they'd taken to addressing her with the honorific *"Pi Nittaya,"* meaning "Big Sister Nittaya." She called them "Little Brother and Little Sister," which are terms of the deepest affection.

She'd had to amputate Little Brother's right foot after the Battle of Gneu Mat. She tended him with loving care and assured him that he would recover, get fitted with a state-of-the-art prosthesis, and return to his wife and family as good as new. Then only a few days ago he had succumbed to an exotic amoebic infection that seemed impervious to antibiotics.

Now it was her duty to inform Nok that her husband was dead. It was clearly one of the most difficult moments of her life. What made it worse, I think, was that Little Sister took it so calmly, rocking the baby at her breast as if she were unable to process the meaning of the news.

Going out the door, Nittaya tried to maintain a stoic face, but there was no hiding her emotion from me.

I put my arm around her and said, "Hey, take it easy now," but she tore away from me and ran out into a sudden, torrential rainstorm, of a kind quite uncommon this early in the year.

I raced after her, ripped my bush jacket off and held it over her head, burbling, "Hey baby, baby, baby!" But she was oblivious.

She ran into the aid station, clomped down the stairs into the brightly lit bunker, sullying its usually pristine floors, with her muddy boot-prints. She pushed past her medics, paying no heed to their wide-eyed looks of shock and dismay, slammed the door to the dispensary in my face, and locked herself inside.

I could hear her throw herself down and start wailing and beating her fists and feet against the wooden floor-planks like a little girl.

I banged on the door for what seemed like hours, but she would not let me in.

That night, Jimmy sent his native top sergeant around to the BOQ with a note:

> All active-duty personnel save those engaged in perimeter defense are ordered to muster on the LZ at exactly 1900. The assembly is obligatory, of grave importance, and no excuses will be accepted.

When the sergeant left, I ran across to the aid station bunker and shouted the news through the dispensary door.

"So, come on out of there, Nittaya, right now!"

I heard her moving around inside and I could see through the crack under the door that she had lit her kerosene lamp.

When I heard the lock turn, I pushed inside and found her hiding behind the door, stark naked. She was breathing hard, and her eyes had dilated to an unnatural size and brilliance. I was on the verge of voicing my concern when she hushed me with her hand, shoved the door shut behind me, and relocked it.

The instant we were alone, she spun me around and whispered, "Have you ever heard of *Nari Mængmum*?"

"No, what's that?"

"She is the most dreaded ghost in Laos. She glides along in the jungle at night. She ensnares her foolish quarry in the web of her beauty. She is famous because her prey finds such pleasure in her body that he cannot stop mating, even though he knows that at the instant of insemination he will die."

"So, you see yourself as Spider Woman, and me as . . .?"

Nittaya pinned me with her eyes.

"Yes, I want to suck the life out of you."

"Be my guest," I started to say, but even before I could get the words out, she had jumped me, bowled me over backwards, whipped me out, thrust me inside her, and was humping me like a wild animal, hammering my tailbone into the floorboards with each desperate thrust.

Shrieking, howling, gabbling in unknown tongues, frightening her staff in the next room into petrified silence, she kept banging at me long after I'd died inside her.

"Wow, girl," I said when she had done with me, trying for macho levity when what I really felt was a childlike wonder, "how you ever gonna top *that?*"

"I may not have to," she said, and I chose not to ask what she meant.

As directed, we assembled with the rest of Love Company at 1900 hours. Then we stood out on the LZ a good fifteen minutes in rain and mud and darkness waiting for our oddball commander to appear.

"Hey, dude!" I hollered at Boom-Boom, who was our unofficial weatherman at the Patch. "What's with all the rain? I thought this was supposed to be the dry season."

"Accordin' to the radio, it's the arse-end of a bloody great typhoon. Blew in off the Sea of China."

"It gonna be around a while?"

"Well, it sor' of bumped up against the mountains, they say. So, it's got no proper place to go, you see? Could be wif' us two or three days, mate."

Once we were thoroughly drenched, Jimmy staggered across the soggy parade ground, bearing a Buddhist ritual lantern in his hand.

The Laotians watched his progress in fear and fascination, for each swing of the lantern lit and unlit his craggy face, his droopy grey mustache, his glossy dome in a kind of glimmering chiaroscuro, like an image of the walking dead.

He had not seen fit to bring Loa Nyindi along with him, and this only added to their trepidation. The only time Jimmy left his guru behind was when he had bad news, as the Laughing Monk refused to tolerate bad vibes.

"Ten-shun!"

After letting us all soak for another minute or two, he beckoned Nittaya to his side and launched into a long, drunken speech full of digressions, which she attempted to translate into Lao.

In a brief introduction, he commended "the majority" of us on the sacrifices we had made, the deaths and injuries we'd sustained without complaint, and our sterling virtues of bravery and loyalty.

Then he took on a more serious tone. He spoke of treachery, of disloyalty, of the traitors in our midst who had caused the terrible casualties we had suffered.

As a dramatic touch, he'd stuck two automatic pistols in his belt, cross-draw style, which he patted from time to time to emphasize his words.

"Corporal Kahoku and Private Lilo," he shouted when he had concluded his meandering diatribe, pointing them out in the ranks of my platoon, "step forward!"

Two of my youngest and bravest fighters, both recently wounded, seemed shocked and bewildered, but stepped out of the ranks as directed and stood before him.

"On your knees, traitors! Eyes to the ground!"

Baffled by his accusation, they looked to Nittaya for clarification, but when she seemed just as flummoxed, they made no protest and obeyed his command.

"Confess, you little *schlekts!*" Jimmy screamed, showering them with spittle. Then he whipped his pistols out and pressed the muzzles between their eyes. "'Fess up right now. Or you know what? I blow off your fuckin' *kops!*"

Nittaya translated his words as accurately as possible, including the Yiddish she'd learned at his figurative knee, but they seemed to have no idea what sin they ought to accept blame for, and looked at each other quizzically, as if the other might have some clue as to why their esteemed leader was so incensed.

"Hullo? Talk to me! Any objections? No? So, I'll waste the little scumbags right now," Jimmy said, which Nittaya dutifully translated. Yet since the word "scumbags" was untranslatable into Lao, she substituted the foreign word "condoms," which made no sense at all.

At this point, I stepped forward. As commander of their platoon, I felt it my duty to address their accuser.

"Permission to speak, sir!"

"Granted."

"If you don't mind, sir, could you please tell us on what grounds you suspect Corporal Kahoku and Private Lilo? They're two of my best men."

"Awright awready. You want it? You got it. They got family

in the Pathet Lao."

"Excuse me, sir, but is that the extent of your evidence against them? I mean, from what I've heard, there are more or less constant connections between our men and their families on the other side. Whether it's just to say hello or something else I don't know, but—"

Before Jimmy could answer the question, Kurt shouted from the ranks in English. "Is that it, Jimmy? You can't find any better scapegoats for your own *débâcle?*"

"Whaaa? You gonna question my authority now?" Jimmy hollered back at him, but there was a flinching, a shrinking in his tone that could not be mistaken.

"I don't question your authority," Kurt said, stepping out to confront him over the heads of the cowering native boys. "I question your rush to judgment. But maybe we should discuss this in private, instead of out here before the ranks."

In answer, Jimmy merely shrugged, stuck his guns back in his belt, and motioned for his two young "scapegoats" to rise and be off.

A few moments later, we officers were all standing before his desk/dinner table in the command post bunker, dripping rain on his floor. Little Poo-Ying was hovering over the miniature gas stove behind him, preparing tea and rice cakes.

"Wha? You callin' me a liar?" Jimmy said, pointing across his desk at Kurt.

"Come off it, man, you know exactly what I'm talking about!"

"I think I know what Kurt is referring to, Jimmy," Nittaya said, taking a deep breath. "I told you once, but maybe you forgot, *na?* I had a relative fighting for the other side, too. He is dead now, but, but . . ."

"And who," Kurt went on, "who was it that wanted a prep of the operation a week in advance?"

"It was me," she admitted, "but I only voiced something that everyone wanted to . . ."

"So, if we're talking about degrees of possible culpability, Jimmy, why don't you threaten to shoot Doc Nittaya?

"Right, exactly," Kurt said when Jimmy seemed at a loss for words. "When it comes to your little Honeybuns, you're like those monkeys on Hollywood's sweat scarf, aren't you? 'Hear no evil, see no evil, speak no evil?'"

"Get outta here!"

"Please, hear me out, Jimmy. I have just received some important intelligence. And it might shed some light on this issue of moles and infiltrators."

At that point, Kurt asked if he might bring forth a witness.

Something in his tone, and his veiled glance at Nittaya, warned me that this "witness" might be offering testimony that could prove hostile to her.

Jimmy shrugged. "Whatever. You know?"

Kurt called outside and a pretty, light-skinned, young Lao girl stepped down into the bunker. She was dressed in an immaculate French-style uniform complete with polished black combat boots and a jaunty blue beret, and she was smiling eagerly. After she had performed her *wai* to Jimmy, she hesitated a moment, as if gathering herself to convey intelligence of the utmost importance.

Meanwhile, she was regarding Nittaya as if she were food for tonight's dinner feast, and Nittaya's eyes had gone wide, so there was little mystery as to what was coming next.

"This is Corporal Alana Racha," Kurt said. "Radio code name 'Queenie.' She's one of the Pathet Lao defectors we've recently taken on. Corporal Racha, can you please tell us what you just told me on our way over here from the LZ?"

"Yes sir," she said in passable English. "Year ago, I study at Vientiane University. Big sister, she make me join Pathet Lao. We attack American radar base. Sister die. I get hit bad. Doctor Nittaya Aromdée, she standing right here. She Pathet Lao medical cadre. She operate on me at NVA aid station. Run away and leave me to die when Americans come."

The revelation was so shocking that all Jimmy, Tham-Boon, and I could do was gape at the accused with our mouths hanging open.

Yet Nittaya coolly turned to Jimmy and said, "I am going to have to talk to you in private now, sir. There is something the Firm has designated 'Top Secret' about the current state of affairs. I have been ordered to divulge it only to you, and only in an emergency situation such as this."

Like nearly everyone else in the bunker, I guessed that this was simply a ploy to buy time, but Jimmy just shook his bald pate, squinted up his eyes and stroked his biker's mustache, as he often did when baffled, befuddled, or bemused.

Holding my breath, I found myself praying that he was drunk enough to bite.

"You know what?" he said at last. "Everybody out!"

"*Gross Got!*" said Kurt. "Will you not at least . . ."

"*Aus!*"

"Well, what about *her*, then?" Kurt said, angrily gesturing at Poo-Ying, who had shrunk into a corner and appeared to be making no plans to depart.

"Hullo? What're you talkin' about? She's barely seventeen years old. Can't even read or write her own *zhargon*. And English? You wanna get her to scrub the shithouse? You gotta use sign language."

"But . . ."

"Hey! I'm gonna suspect someone? How 'bout Herr Dietrich? I mean, *oy*, where you from? East Berlin? Maybe you're some longtime Commie plant. You know? Just waitin' for the word?"

"Why, how dare you!"

"Out, goddamnit! All of yuz, outta here! And I don't wanna hear you *schnupen* around the doorway neither."

Nittaya and I only had an instant to make eye contact before I left the room, and I detected a plea for understanding.

I should have felt angry with her, I guess, but I just raised a brow and shook my head in mild exasperation, as if to say, "See? I always knew there was something you were hiding from me."

I walked over to the aid station bunker and waited up for her, hoping to get a chance to talk, but she never showed up.

The next morning, when Kurt appeared at headquarters, he asked the guard if anyone had passed through the door during the night.

The guard said no, but when Kurt stepped down inside the bunker, he found Jimmy lying dead in his rack.

Poo-Ying was gagged, tied hand and foot to a chair, and beaten brutally about the face.

Later, when we checked our perimeter defenses, we found a bunker full of dead Thai mercenaries, a marked path through our minefield, and a hitherto unknown deer trail that led down the western cliff to the Sikhav River.

And you, my love?

Big surprise.

You had disappeared without a trace.

Part II

CHAPTER FOURTEEN

In Black and White

On the morning of January 13, 2020, a fat, bald, old monk stops at a teakwood staff cottage on the grounds of a hospital in the ancient capital of Laos. He is wearing a clean, new, saffron robe, flip-flop sandals with peace signs imprinted on them, and he's smiling as if at some long-cherished private joke.

A dignified lady of about his own age stands waiting for him at her garden gate. Tall and stately, with her long greying hair swept up in a bouffant, and still dramatically beautiful, the lady bows and offers the monk a cup of green jasmine tea and a bowl of rice cakes that she has prepared.

After the customary *"wai"* and a brief benediction, the monk takes the tea and drinks it in a gulp.

Then after sharing a wink and a grin with her, as if recollecting some mildly scandalous mutual memory of their long-ago youth, he turns to go.

"What, no pearls of wisdom today, Loa Nyindi?"

"Oh," the monk says, as if he has forgotten his usual practice, yet conveying in the same breath that he has not forgotten at all, that he merely savors the trivial earthly vanity of having his distinction as a transcendental guide reaffirmed.

He then reaches within the folds of his robe and pulls out a crumpled rice candy wrapper, on the back of which he has scrawled something in a tiny yet careful hand.

He proffers it to the lady with an amused parody of beatitude, and they perform another *wai*.

"*Suwadeeka.*"

"*Suwadeekap.*"

Without further ado, the Laughing Monk turns, starts finger-nibbling at his bowl, and ambles up the tree-lined avenue toward a nearby tourist hotel called *La Residence Phou Vao*.

The lady unfolds the wrapper and reads:

Peace is found within, not without.
You only lose what you cling to.
A fearless heart is free of desire.

She continues to stand at her gate, gazing at tendrils of morning mist leaching from tucks and pleats in the green jungle hills across the valley. A waft of wind off the nearby Mekong River rattles the leaves of the silk tree in her narrow street-side garden, puffs at the thin, cotton, heat-drapes in her doorway, flutters her long, wispy, white kimono. She breathes in deeply, savoring the cool, misty, morning air, the scent of violets, dog roses and lilacs. In another hour, when the air heats up, the cicadas will commence their monotonous chirruping. Yet for now, her only serenade is that of the wood-swallows and fairy bluebirds flitting about overhead.

A few moments later, a young postman on a rickety three-wheeled bicycle arrives in front of the cottage. He hands the lady several letters, one of which is air mail express, with a foreign stamp. The letter is addressed as follows:

Madame Nittaya Aromdée, MD,

Director, Department of Surgery,

Residence 12, Vietnam-Laos

Friendship Hospital,

Avenue Sakkaline 9/217,

Luang Prabang,

People's Republic of Laos

Glancing at the return address, Doctor Aromdée seems to falter for a moment. She raises a hand to her narrow breast and inhales deeply, as if in shock or pain.

She turns, crosses the garden, steps lightly onto the veranda, and brushes past the heat drapes in her doorway.

Slipping off her sandals just inside, she pads across the polished wooden floor in her bare feet, pivots in a corner, lowers herself onto a straw mat, and spreads her kimono about her as she descends.

She folds her legs in the Lotus Position, straightens her back, and rests her hands on her knees as if preparing for meditation.

After a few moments of breathing exercises, she contains the trembling of her hands, opens the letter, and reads the unfamiliar English.

She is not as surprised by the words as she might have been, had the Laughing Monk not forewarned her.

December 16, 2020

Dearest Nittaya:

All these years, and I never knew whether you were alive or dead. I don't know where to begin. Please don't be angry, but our granddaughter, Katay, whose existence I never imagined, has put me in touch with you. Apparently, she was snooping around your cottage one afternoon when you were at the hospital and she discovered a trove of diaries and photos in your bamboo chest. Without bothering to ask your permission, she took it upon herself to find me on the internet and send me a couple of purloined photographs.

Doctor Aromdée makes a great effort to continue reading the letter. Recalling the Laughing Monk's words of wisdom, she even pauses for a moment to do her breathing exercises again.

Yet when a photo falls out of the envelope, one of herself as a young woman in combat gear standing with a big, grinning, American soldier beside the open door of a camouflaged helicopter, she finds that she can no longer focus her eyes on individual words.

Still seated erectly, with her legs folded and her hands lying placidly on her knees, she "zones out," as one said in her youth.

Her mind flies away into the past, and it all comes back to her, from first to last, not in the vivid jungle colors one might expect, but in the grainy, artful black and white of a cinematic style known in her youth as *"La Nouvelle Vague."*

CHAPTER FIFTEEN

Bam!

There is a saying in French. *Le temps dévore toutes choses, même de mémoire, ce qui est son dessert.* I am not sure where it comes from, but it means, "Time devours all things, even memory, which is its dessert."

Yet for me, it is exactly the opposite. I recall the events of the late 1960s and early 1970s in microscopic detail, with the aid of my diaries of the time, but I sometimes find it hard to remember what I did yesterday.

When young people of my granddaughter's cyber-obsessed generation see doddering seventy-somethings such as me, especially here in staidly Buddhist and Communist Laos, they probably cannot even imagine that I belong to the most unconstrained, uninhibited—not to say wild and wanton— generation since the height of the Roman Empire.

We—at least those of us educated in Europe and America— were the "Youth Quake," the "Forever Young," the generation of "Sex, Drugs, and Rock and Roll." We refused to trust anyone over the age of thirty, and we changed absolutely everything. Che Guevara was our hero, and he was imprinted on all our t-shirts. You name it: fashion, music, education, women's rights, personal freedom, politics, warfare. We had a revolution to cover it.

So, to enliven my 1967 summer vacation from the *Université de Paris, Faculté de Médicine,* and to delay my annual visit to my home in tradition-bound Laos where I sometimes felt uncomfortably suspended between two worlds, I decided to make my way overland on "The Great Grass Road" from Europe to Southeast Asia.

It may sound an altogether rash and imprudent journey for a young woman nowadays, when the entire region is ablaze with murderous sectarian warfare, but I assure you that it was not in my day.

Well, perhaps it was a bit unusual for an Asian girl of twenty-one, but after five years in Paris, I was feeling more than a little European.

The Great Grass Road was frequented by penniless hippies and students from Western Europe and North America united in their pursuit of absolute freedom through travel, adventure, free love, mind altering medicaments and the "transcendent perceptions" of certain exotic spiritual exercises extolled by the Beatles and other idols of our generation.

Since we moved fast and met few natives other than truck drivers and the occasional threadbare guru, I doubt that we gained few insights into their authentic cultures and beliefs, but we did see a lot of scenery, and I must say we thoroughly enjoyed ourselves.

At any one time, there were thousands of us on the road, of both sexes, and we ran into each other in trains, buses, youth hostels, and standing on the outskirts of desolate villages hitching rides on long-haul trucks.

Unfortunately, however, the Middle East of the time had yet to enter the New Age. It was therefore imperative that a young woman find a male traveling companion.

Since I was—if I may be so bold—an attractive young woman, I had to choose my travel mates with care. The first was a sweet-natured but rather fey and insipid Spaniard named Ignazio de Molina whom I had met at the *Faculté de Médicine*.

The distance from Paris to Istanbul is approximately two thousand kilometers, and we made it in seven days. Ignazio was only going as far as Turkey, so when we parted I had to choose another travel mate.

Luckily, the bunk opposite mine in the Istanbul youth hostel was occupied by a big, buff, barb-haired, Austrian lesbian named (astonishingly enough) Eva Braun. Although neither of us spoke more than a few words of the other's language, we established an immediate rapport, made a commitment to travel to India together, and neither of us ever regretted it.

What I liked about Eva was that she kept her mouth shut, never whined, or complained, and shared what she had. She kept a blackjack in her pocket and was not afraid to use it. And she never tried to push herself on me in bed.

We made it from Istanbul to Teheran—eighteen hundred kilometers over rough roads—in only eight days. A fortnight later and we had crossed the Great Salt Desert and the Sefid Kuh

Mountains and found ourselves in Kabul, Afghanistan, which at the time looked positively biblical. Another week and we were over the Khyber Pass, across the plains of the Indus River, and standing in line outside the Grand Trunk Road customs booth on the India-Pakistan border.

And it was there that we ran into our first glitch on the entire trip. Well, that is, apart from the lecherous, Islamic truck drivers we had to deal with on an almost daily basis.

For some reason, the Indian authorities refused to allow me in without a transit visa. When I enquired where I might obtain one, they informed me that the only consulate in Pakistan capable of issuing an Indian visa to a Laotian national was in Karachi, nine hundred kilometers to the south. From there, I learned, I could book passage to Bombay by sea.

I complained and made veiled accusations of racism (why was a visa required of me and not for my white friend?), but I did not really make much of a fuss.

Actually, the news did not particularly disappoint me. I had already come nine thousand kilometers from Paris, after all, most of it over rough roads, so what was another few hundred kilometers?

Besides, I had long since learned that I could count on every detour in my travels to provide me with marvelous new adventures.

I bade *auf wiedersehen* to big Eva, who unexpectedly cried in my arms and pressed her Vienna address upon me, and turned to re-cross the no-man's-land between the Indian and Pakistani borders. Escorted by a pair of turbaned, Sikh soldiers, I made my way along the tall fence that lined the road, until I saw a young man leaning on the Indian side of the wire, smiling at me.

After weeks in the Middle East, I had grown used to desert sand, dun-drab hills, dusty camels and donkeys, and grimy-robed denizens. Now, from out of nowhere, comes this tall, dark, handsome, Asian man, a double for the great Hong Kong cinema star Wang-Yu in *The One-Armed Swordsman*, yet packing a *farang* rucksack like my own that he had slung jauntily over his shoulder.

"*Excusez moi,*" he said in French. "*Mais d'ou venez-vous, Mademoiselle?*"

"Well, just now I am coming from Paris," I said, stopping in my tracks, winking at my grinning, indulgent, military escorts. "But eventually I hope to wind up at my parents' home in Vientiane."

"Forgive my impertinence, but you do not look very Laotian to me."

"That is because my mother is from Bangkok, of mixed Thai and Chinese blood."

"Then perhaps we are cousins. My mother is half-Chinese as well."

I laughed. "As the number of Chinese in the world is now approaching one billion, that is highly unlikely. But since you seem to be such a nice young man, I am willing to give you the benefit of the doubt."

"*Merci, Mademoiselle, vous êtes très aimable.*"

"*De rien, Monsieur.* And where are you coming from just now?"

"From Brussels, but my homeland is just across the eastern border from yours."

"There is only one country to the east of Laos. And Vietnam is not a very pleasant place to be just now, I have heard."

"That is precisely the reason why I have chosen to return," he said, and then quickly changed the subject. "I saw you at the border post and I followed you here. Your *détachment*, your *insouciance* is what impressed me. Anyone else would have been bitterly disappointed and caused a big row, but you simply kissed your girlfriend goodbye and . . ."

"She is just a friend, a hitchhiking mate."

"Well, anyway, you seemed so philosophical about it all."

By then, I had approached the fence, with the blessing of my guards, and I was hanging on the wire, with my hands close to his.

"I was intrigued by your backpack," he said, "your well-traveled air. Have you actually hitched the whole way?"

"Well, not exactly. I have a bit of money from *mon père, tu vois?* So, I do not have to *auto-stop* all the time. If I cannot get a ride, I can always take a bus."

Now my military escorts were starting to get restless. Realizing that time was short, the young man and I glommed onto every word, peered deeply into the other's eyes, and tried to size each other up in the few moments that we had left.

There could be no question but that it was instant, and it was reciprocal. Doubly compelling was the time element, the fence separating us, and the fact that we might never see each other again.

Now my escorts were tugging at my sleeve, and the young man and I were suddenly almost desperate. We actually groped for each other's hands through the fence and came within an inch of kissing.

"Where are you headed next?"

"Karachi, and then on to Bombay, I hope."

"I shall drop you a line in care of American Express in both places, okay?" he said breathlessly, as the Sikhs started to lead me away. "Let's travel across India together; what do you say?"

"Yes, I think that might be fun!"

"What is your name?" he shouted after me.

"Nittaya Aromdée! What is yours?"

"Nguyen Ly!" he screamed, rattling the fence wire in his excitement. "How do you spell your last name?"

I spelled it out for him as loudly as I could, but I was not sure he got it, for by then we were quite a distance off.

Of course, that only made it even more romantic. So, all the way to Karachi on the train, down along the scorched plains of the Indus River Valley, I went over and over our meeting in my mind.

Handsome though he might have been, Nguyen was so Asian in appearance that he looked totally out of character in his backpacker garb of red sweatband, Strawberry Fields Forever t-shirt, cut-off jeans and hiking boots. How long had it been since I had seen a young Asian man like him? His black shoulder length hair was so thick and heavy that it bounced up and down every time he nodded his head. With his golden skin, his beautiful up-slanting eyes, broad nose, flimsy goatee and full, sensual mouth, he looked like a time traveler, like he had just stepped off a bas-relief from an eleventh century Vietnamese pagoda.

"Are you some kind of artist?" I had asked him at one point; but I was merely flattering him, for what he really looked like was a male artist's model from the Lý Dynasty.

"I am a classical pianist," he replied, speaking quickly, urgently, yet enunciating every word very precisely. "I just finished six years of *hautes études* at the *Consérvatoire de Bruxelles*."

Yet there was something very sensible and practical about him as well. Those backpacking clothes. And his handshake, so firm and dry.

In Karachi, I expected nothing, and therefore I was especially delighted to find a note from Nguyen awaiting me at American Express. Like all the notes I received, from all the people I knew, I stuck it in the appropriate page of my diary. I have kept it there all these many years, and I have it before me now:

Chere Mademoiselle Aromdée:

> *Vive cette entreprise capitaliste décadent, American Express, qui permet la réunification de gens sympas comme nous!* Long live that decadent, capitalist, enterprise, American Express, which permits the reunification of such nice people as us! Nittaya, it occurs to me that you know nothing about me, nothing of my likes, dislikes, personal tastes. I love late Renaissance, Orlandus, Lassus, Palestrine, and German Baroque. In this century: Stravinsky, Prokofieff, Bartok, Hindemith. I also love traveling, and I absorb everything, enough to last a lifetime! I love our people of Asia who toil the land. I hate the ones who exploit and murder them, and although I am no soldier, I

have resolved to commit my life to their struggle. Why can I not just come out and say what is in my heart? I cannot stop thinking about you, Nittaya. Do you feel the same way about me? Yet how can it be? We only met for a moment.

Je 't'embrasse,
Nguyen

I fired off an answer to Nguyen expressing like sentiments. With more than slight exaggeration, I told him of the socialist views I had developed through the overwhelming influence of my classmates at the *Université de Paris*, and of my resolve to turn my back on my life of privilege and do whatever I could to alleviate the suffering of the desperately poor peasants of my country. I asked him to meet me in Bombay, at American Express, at a specific hour in a week's time.

At the Port of Karachi, I booked deck passage on the Indian ship *Sabarmati*, bound for Bombay via the Rann of Kutch. In Bombay, I checked into a cut-rate, Salvation Army hostel in the port district, near Fort Point and the Gateway to India.

My room was dorm-style, a bargain at ten rupees a night. I bedded amid lean and braless young female backpackers like myself from every corner of Western Europe and North America.

Two mornings later, I hurried to American Express at Church Gate, and there was Nguyen standing just inside the door. He was so excited that he nearly danced across the marble floor to greet me; and the perfunctory buss on either cheek that was *de rigueur* became a lingering kiss that set the middle-aged, *farang* patrons to gaping. He smelled so good that I could have lived in his hair.

We strolled hand-in-hand to an English tea shop near St. George's Church, chatting in French and laughing about absolutely nothing, seated ourselves at a corner wicker table, ordered a pot of Earl Grey, with milk, honey, butter and scones, and put our heads together.

"I imagined so many things," he said, fixing those deep dark eyes upon me, entwining his long, cool, pianist's fingers in mine. "I built it up in my mind to such an extent that it's like this whole great edifice that I am afraid is top-heavy and will soon just collapse and come tumbling down on top of me."

"I know exactly what you mean."

"It happened the first instant I saw you. I do not know how, but I knew immediately that you were the one. It was like *un coup de foudre, tu vois?* It just hit me. But afterwards, on the way here, I could not trust my instincts, and I started to doubt, to tell myself what a silly fool I was."

"I had no doubts at all," I said, lying through my teeth. "But I hear you."

"So now?"

"So now we just see what happens, *na?*"

"Right."

"To tell you the truth, I think I need some time to sort this all out in my mind," I said. "You know what I mean? Now that I have seen you, *je perdre la tête, tu sais?* I am freaking out. Feel my heart. You see? Maybe we should just call it a day."

"What?"

"Go home to our hotels and reflect. Put our thoughts in

order. Write each other a letter explaining how we feel. Meet tomorrow and exchange them. *Qu'est-ce que t'en penses?"*

"Of course." He smiled sweetly, squeezing my hand. *"Votre souhait est mon désir, Mademoiselle."*

"But first I want to ask you something. In the lobby of the Salvation Army Hostel there is an old baby grand, the bequeathal of an Anglo-Indian lady. It is not perfectly in tune, but I should like you to play it for me. Just one piece. Whatever you like. Would you do that for me?"

"Avec plaisir, ma chere."

So, we went back to Fort Point. Nguyen played Bartok's Piano Sonata on the rickety piano, and I had never heard anything so beautiful in my life.

The next morning, when I woke up, I packed my rucksack, went downstairs, and left Nguyen a note in French at the reception desk.

> *J'ai quitté Bombay. Comprends-moi. Je suis trop embrouillé pour commencé.* I have quit Bombay. Understand me, please. I am too embroiled to commence. You see, it is not that easy—a dream constructed over years. *Est-ce la joie ou la terreur?* Will you create me or destroy me *en m'emprégnant de ta virilité?* Give me some time. I shall meet you in Calcutta on 25 June. I shall leave a note at that horrid, capitalistic American Express.
>
> *C'est moi,*
> *Nittaya*

Why had I written that note? Was it really because I suffered from such poetic fears of making love with him? Of course not. It was because I had awakened that morning with that occupational hazard of all South Asian budget travelers of the time, crab lice, which I had acquired alone in my bed at the Salvation Army Hostel. I could hardly make love to him in that state, could I?

After a visit to the local pharmacist, a close cropping of the *mons veneris*, a dose of Pyrinate A-200, and a train ride across India, with brief stops in Agra, Delhi, and Benares, I arrived in Calcutta on the appointed date and checked into the Sikh Temple, near Bara Bazaar.

Like all Sikh Temples everywhere, it had a generous open-door policy for foreign backpackers. I took a quick, cold shower in the stall in the courtyard, changed into a tank top and a miniskirt, checked my rucksack in the beadle's office, and hastened toward American Express on Strand Road for my third meeting with Nguyen.

"Do I love you, or just the idea of you?" I kept asking myself on the way, my heart and mind racing in unison. "Am I deceiving myself out of loneliness? Once I obtain your love, will I value it less?"

Just as I was walking into American Express, his rickshaw pulled up in front.

"Nittaya!" he shouted, and I dashed back down the stairs two at a time to throw myself in his arms.

"Oh, but you leave me weak," I gasped, and let my knees give way.

Yet *his* knees crumpled that night in our hotel before we ever made love.

"Be good to me, Nittaya Aromdée," he said, weeping, clasping his arms about my naked loins, pressing his face to me.

I raised him up and kissed his tears away, but I wondered for the first time whether I could trust his sincerity, for some of his gestures and actions seemed affected, even melodramatic. He was so wound up in his own emotions that he did not seem aware of my separate existence. Not even enough to notice my newly sprouted *Mont de Vènus.* And it struck me then that there was something important about Nguyen that I had not learned yet, something I might not like.

I wanted the first night to be so perfect, to fit all the romantic scenarios that sustained me across India. I wanted soft colors, a melting into the rhythm of love. But Nguyen wanted to talk nasty. He wanted to tie me up and spank me. Lost in his own pleasure, he did not look at me when we made love. His eyes rolled back in his head, and he saw nothing. It was as if he was doing it with himself; and when he really got hot, it was not like he was making love at all but having some kind of epileptic fit or spasm.

Although this might be exciting to a casual lover, it frightened and disillusioned a poetic and rather soulful young girl like me, who had centered all her dreams on her ideal man.

Yet, I hated only the nights. Our days were golden. We awakened happily in the mornings and tramped about, seeing the sights, smooching, and giggling like a pair of honeymooners.

We took a plane to Burma a few days later. After a peek at the Golden Temple of Rangoon, it was on to Bangkok for tours of the Floating Market, the Royal Palace, the Temple of the Sleeping Buddha and obligatory visits to my mother's family in

Thong Lo, where I introduced Nguyen as my "fiancé." We played up his Chinese blood, which pleased them immensely, for Thais are prejudiced in favor of the lighter yellow skin and proverbial business acumen of their neighbors to the north.

A week later, we hopped a bus for Cambodia. The country was frantically preparing for a visit from Jackie Kennedy, America's current "worldwide ambassador of goodwill."

When Nguyen heard about it, he said, "Too bad we missed the bitch when we hit her husband in Texas."

I pretended to agree, though I really did not have much against the woman and had once rather admired her. The truth is—what little anti-Americanism I felt was merely of the jingoistic kind fashionable among European students of the time. "Those gross, crass Americans," we all said, and yet we idolized Bob Dylan and Joan Baez and went out to watch every Hollywood film we could find.

Yet I suppose this is *sans importance*, for at that moment in time I probably would have agreed to pretty much anything Nguyen said.

It was the selfless surrender of a woman in love. A less romantic but more scientifically accurate description of my syndrome would be to say that it was a primal urge, the libidinous, young female's irresistible impulse to submit to the alpha male's permeation and dominion.

Yet even now, with all my medical experience, all my conceptual data on the quirks and kinks of humankind, all my feminist principles, I still remember with pleasure one incandescent moment.

I am standing above Nguyen on a grassy hillside in Angkor

Wat. The crumbling, mysterious temple of Phnom Bakhenga is directly behind me. Two great, walled terraces fall away before me, grey with tropical years, their images reflected in a vast lily-covered moat. With his camera in hand, he is looking up at me, smiling as sweetly and innocently as a little boy. About to snap my picture, which I still have tucked away in my diary, he exclaims, as if it has just occurred to him, *"Mais comme tu es belle!"*

Next day, we rode the six kilometers from our hotel in Siem Reap to Ankhor Wat in a pedicab, and the leisurely pace suited us perfectly.

The smell of jasmine and fresh, new leaves wafted over us in the humid air. We sniffed the air. We turned to sniff each other.

Sniffing, like rubbing noses among the Eskimos, is a mode of expressing affection predating the custom of kissing, which we Asians acquired from our European overlords. Yet I must say, our choice to sniff rather than kiss at that moment had nothing to do with anti-Imperialism.

Later, we found a hidden arbor, to the rear of the bulbous temple of Banteay Kdei, and lay together on the ancient pitted volcanic floor supine, not touching, staring for long minutes at the writhing, slithering, entwined, black, banyan roots that held up the crumbling stone ceiling.

"Mon Dieu, Nguyen! How do they do it?"

"Je n'ai aucune idée. I am a lover and an artist, not an engineer."

"A lover, you say? Then prove it."

We made love on the temple floor, and I told him I wanted it to go on forever. Nguyen responded with all his heart, and I saw pure, uncomplicated love in his eyes. He kissed the bronze Buddha head I wore round my neck and said, "For you, *ma chere*, I am even willing to give up my devout Epicureanism."

So lost were we in our state of bliss that we barely noticed the rough volcanic stone that chaffed my bottom and cut his knees until they bled. Even when we saw a caretaker peeping down at us through the banyan limbs, we merely laughed him away.

Everything was perfect, until we went to bed at night.

It was not that it was unexciting. Nguyen was a frenzied and fearless lover, always interested in novelties; and absolutely nothing was off-limits or taboo. He wanted his rectum licked. He wanted to stick plantains up my vagina. He wanted to seduce me in a foot of moonless Mekong River mud with crocodiles nosing about. He wanted to do it in hotel corridors, the back seats of taxis, outdoor movie theaters and anywhere else where there was a good chance of getting caught.

The Lord Buddha knows I was no prude. It was the 1960s, after all, but I just could not "get my head around it" with him. I hated to admit to double-standards, yet the truth was—I was a bit old-fashioned when it came to the man I wanted to be my husband.

In sum, Nguyen was everything I had dreaded all my life, everything I had secretly desired. He thrilled me beyond words, yet he scared the wits out of me. I wanted romance, and he gave me fever. He tasted better than anything; but he tasted, ultimately, of my own ruin.

He confessed to me that a representative of the North Vietnamese government had recruited him in Brussels. He was to return to Saigon and use his wealthy family's connections to acquire a position in the South Vietnamese government, preferably in counterespionage, or intelligence.

He was to become a spy, and he wanted me to do likewise in Laos. Through his handler in Saigon, he would put me in touch with the Pathet Lao.

I said it would not be necessary. He asked me why, and I told him that my Uncle Vong, the black sheep of my family, was already a commander in the Pathet Lao.

"Wow!" he said in English. "Someday, we might be comrades in arms!"

We spent Cambodian Independence Day in Phnom Phen. There was a big party in the dining room of the *Hotel Indochine*, with a Thai rock band, free Dim Sum, and a seemingly endless supply of champagne.

We told all the French tourists we met that we were on our honeymoon. They called us *Monsieur et Madame Ly*, and we were madly in love.

Not knowing how unused to spirits Nguyen was, I let him drink too much champagne. He seemed perfectly normal, having a wonderful time, until it hit him. He suddenly went all red in the face and turned into a comic Asian drunk. Burping and hiccupping, he leapt onto the bandstand, elbowed the lead guitarist aside, sang a lewd, French song off key, did an outrageous Bump & Grind, and passed out in my arms.

As I dragged him up the stairs toward our room, everyone—European and Asian—stood up to clap and cheer, *"Bravo, Monsieur et Madame Ly!"*

The instant we got in the door, though, Nguyen vomited all

over the bed and passed out. I bathed him, cleaned up the mess, and watched over him, marveling at his youthful Lý Dynasty beauty, the innocence of his breathing, wondering where he would take me.

Then he woke up, still drunk, but in a confessional mood. He told me of all his sexual adventures, including the ones in India while I was out of touch. A plump and prosperous Anglo-Indian businesswoman of fifty-five. A married German couple. A teenage Canadian backpacker boy...

"Any sodomy with animals?" I asked. *"Pas de pédophilie, nécrophilie?"*

"Do not get fresh with me. I just want to be open with you."

"Save it for your fellow freaks," I said, and he did not take kindly to that at all. In fact, he spat in my face and rubbed it in hard with the heel of his hand.

Next morning, Nguyen went out to a hush-hush meeting with some secret local operative of the Viet Cong, so I had breakfast in the hotel dining room alone. Presently, a ruggedly handsome, middle-aged Frenchman, with a beautifully blond Van Dyke beard, came up and asked if he could sit at my table.

"Avec plaisir," I said, and we spent the morning chatting.

His name was Paul Godard. He was a medical doctor working for an NGO in Cambodia, and he had done his pre-med course at the *Université de Paris*. It even turned out that we had mutual left-leaning acquaintances in Paris.

To make a brief story even briefer, we ended up in his room. I cannot say precisely why. It was not simply that he was attractive. I suppose it was my response to Nguyen's brutality of the night before, and a desire to find out if all men were like him.

I spent the day with Paul. He was not a passionate lover. His attentions seemed rather halting and unsure, as if he felt self-conscious about possessing a woman young enough to be his daughter. Yet, he reconfirmed my faith in the male sex.

It was not until late that night that I condescended to grace Nguyen with my presence.

"I have something to tell you," I said, grimly, when I finally walked into our room.

"If it's about Yellow Beard, save your breath. I already guessed."

"But how? . . ."

"I saw him staring at you yesterday morning at breakfast."

"Listen, Nguyen. You hurt me more than anyone ever did before. I needed someone mature enough to understand me."

After I had vented my feelings, I suddenly found myself changing my tone with him. I took his hand and put it to my cheek. I looked deeply into his eyes and said, "You don't hate me, do you, Nguyen?"

"No, not really," he said, but I could see in his face that he was hiding his true feelings.

We slept on opposite sides of the bed.

The next morning was to be our last together before he set out for Saigon, and I for Vientiane.

It had dawned grey and rainy, so we went out to a French coffee house on the Quai Sisowath called *La Muse*.

It was cold inside with the air conditioning, and *La Muse*, with its Classical European music playing softly in the background, its wooden floors and walls and its windows overlooking the Mekong River, was just what we were looking for.

The fragrant teak wood of our corner held us in, contained us, as if it were our own squirrels' nest, and we had gathered all our nuts within.

We sipped coffee and drew on our cigarettes, listening to Rachmaninoff.

Smoke curled round us.

Music encircled us.

The grey rain outside pressed to get in.

"I love the woody quality of this old building, don't you?"

"Yes, nature is just round the corner, it seems."

"How do you feel about me now, Nguyen?"

He paused to draw on his cigarette and blow smoke out the side of his mouth.

"I still love you, Nittaya. But it is remote now. I do not need it anymore."

Later we visited the Ounalome Temple and sat cross-legged on straw mats that were damp with humidity.

Incense filled the air.

Not far from us, a pretty girl was kneeling before a large, Buddhist altar, bowing, crying and praying intensely; I could only imagine what kind of Cambodian sorrow had got to her.

Probably something to do with a man, I thought.

Nguyen sat on his knees beside me, his eyes far away, and I felt the weight of the huge wooden pillars all round us.

The atmosphere inside was still and hot, somehow weighty, and expectant.

The windows glowed white from the sun behind clouds.

"I thought I was *enceinte*," I said, as we left the temple. This was another exaggeration, if not an outright lie. Actually, I had only been a few days late. "That is why I did what I did. I hated you for getting me that way, for cutting my life short, for chaining me down with your bizarre *insécurités et predilections* and your naïve political aspirations."

"And now?"

"I don't hate you, Nguyen; I just got my period this morning!" I said, quite gaily, lighting up a cigarette.

When night fell, and our time of departure neared, we stopped at a noodle shop in the Kandal Market and had Khmer Water Spinach Soup to fortify us against our "moment of truth," or parting, or whatever it turned out to be.

Later, over some palm wine, I pulled out a French translation of "Proverbs of Hell," by William Blake, which I happened to be reading, and read the following quote to Nguyen. I read it as if it had just come to me spontaneously, but I had already thought it out very carefully—a fact that did not escape him for an instant:

You never know what is enough
until you know what is more than enough.

He laughed, and then pointed to another quote a few pages on in the same book:

The road of excess
leads to the palace of wisdom.

And we both had a little giggle about that as well.

Walking toward the taxi stand, we seemed to be feeling great. We were actually capering in the street. And I found myself—

for some reason that I could not fathom—to be tremendously excited.

In the Phnom Phen Airport lounge, we stopped to say goodbye, before we went our separate ways. Having suddenly reverted to traditional Asian morays, we refrained from kissing in public.

"Nittaya," he said, "there is something I want to give you."

I returned his smile and nodded, half-expecting a parting gift.

"Something to repay you for everything you have given me. Something you really deserve."

"What is it, Nguyen?"

"This!" he said and, drawing back his long pianist's hand as far as it would go, he swung with all his might and slapped me across the face.

My head snapped back.

I staggered with the impact.

A sensation of intense pain spread across my cheek and jaw. I shook my head in disbelief.

Meanwhile, all the airline passengers stopped to stare, seemingly spellbound by this lovers' quarrel unfolding before them.

When I opened my eyes and looked at him, I could see cruelty, bewilderment, and perhaps a tiny bit of regret.

Then he disappeared into the crowd.

"Bam, did he hit me!" I said to myself as I tucked into an empty ladies' room to assess and repair the damage before my plane took off. "Bam, did I deserve it!" I said aloud, laughing into the mirror at my injured face, at the inextricably mixed feelings it revealed. "Bam!"

CHAPTER SIXTEEN

Revolution, I Love You

Despite the violence of our parting in Phnom Phen, Nguyen and I maintained an intermittent contact over the next couple of years, care of his family home in Cholon, Saigon.

In July 1969, I even sent him an article from the *Renovateur de Vientiane* announcing my graduation with honors from the *Faculté de Médecine* in Paris.

Then in October 1969, when I was doing my internship at Bangkok International Hospital, he suddenly appeared at my door one evening to ask me out to dinner.

He was as handsome as ever, although he had aged about the eyes, which seemed a bit troubled. He had cropped his hair short, and he wore a conventional linen suit, with a French straw hat. I also noticed something spiteful in the shape of his mouth.

He asked me if I was involved with anyone and I told him a fib. I am not sure why. I said that I was engaged to a Thai-Eurasian entertainer named Tham-Boon "Boom-Boom" Smith.

Yet the truth was I had only had one drunken fling with him in a wine cellar at his engagement party (Yes, I admit the truth; in my misspent Sixties youth, I could sometimes be quite shockingly *louche*). To make things worse, Boom-Boom's fiancée, my cousin Vipada, caught us in the act. Despite her fiery initial reaction, however, she readily forgave me soon after (in fact, she thanked me profusely), when she hooked the Hi-So son of Thai Stock Exchange President, Arak Aimoad, to whom she is still happily married despite his several mistresses.

"So, you have no objections to marrying a social parasite?" Nguyen was saying, in his insufferably self-righteous tone.

"Oh, spare me, Nguyen!" I said. "You are not going to get all 'holier than thou' on me, are you? After all the kinky tricks you pulled on me? And besides, I have evolved into a revolutionist all on my own."

"And how may I ask did that occur? You seemed quite the political *dilettante* when you were with me. Giving lip service to the revolution, without doing anything particular about it."

"Yes," I said, "but I have evolved since then."

Originally, I told him, I had joined the revolution not for socialistic reasons but for the sheer joy of rebellion. I thought I was the equal of any man, and I wanted to prove it. At that time, I scorned conventional communism. It was too stodgy and set in its ways for me. Like most young people of our generation, I had gone through a prolonged period of adolescence. As adolescents, we sometimes had an overwhelming desire to toss a rock through a window, just to prove that we were tough enough, cool enough to do it. I had probably fallen into politics simply because it was the thing to do in Paris at the time. For a while in 1968, during and after *les Eventments de Mai*, I had worked as an organizer for Danny the Red and his happy band of student anarchists and feminist activists, and I had never felt more ecstatic in my life than when I was marching shoulder to shoulder with them down the Champs-Élysées waving flags that read:

BOREDOM IS COUNTERREVOLUTIONARY!
WORKERS OF THE WORLD, ENJOY!
REVOLUTION, I LOVE YOU!

Then a group of French Colonial medical students like me, Africans, Arabs, Asians and Pacific Islanders, asked if I might like to do some volunteer work with them in the working-class suburbs of Paris. I said yes simply because I did not think I could endure their scorn or ridicule if I refused.

Once I got to the *banlieux,* though, and observed at first hand the plight of the poor black and Arab immigrants there, and the prejudice they endured, I felt appalled at their ill treatment.

At the same time, I saw how the immigrant men abused their women in some ways worse than their oppressors treated them. This brought back certain buried memories of how my father had ill-treated my mother and me when I was a child, and recollections of the patriarchal society of traditional Laos, a culture that treated women—even educated women—as little more than chattel. There were no women in the Royal Laotian Army, but the Pathet Lao had dozens of female warriors, "Tiger Women," some of whom had attained nearly mythical status among the peasantry.

That is what set me on my inevitable course. It was not

ideology but personal observation and experience that led me to become a socialist and feminist.

Then a bit later, I told Nguyen, I came under the influence of a marvelous professor at the *Université de Paris,* Madame Agnès de Sauvebelle-Bouchet.

Although she was a majestically beautiful woman, born into the highest aristocracy, she had renounced it all to join the revolution. In the Thirties, she had gone to prison for her beliefs; in the Forties she was forced into exile, and she was now a Communist Party member in *L'Assemblée National.*

When she learned something of my life, she had me read the biographies of Zhang Shenfu, the radical feminist and communist revolutionary of the 1920s, and of Bao Yu, the fierce, Malaysian woman who was one of the leaders of the armed anti-British insurrection there in the 1950s.

However, it was the biography of Pao Sy, the Pathet Lao Tiger Woman who had died fighting the Royal Laotian Army in the early 1960s, that was my inspiration. I remembered her words with the kind of reverence we Laotians normally reserve for our ancestors.

"A woman's reason to fight in the revolution," she said, "is to destroy the corrupt dictatorship, to end the exploitation of the poor and indigenous, to create a more just society for our children, and to obtain gender justice in our lifetime."

In this way, Madame de Sauvebelle-Bouchet convinced me that the New Left was merely a passing phase, a happy gang of hippies and fun-seekers that would not last more than a year or two. The student movement could achieve no lasting good for the proletariat, she said, and even less for the coming worldwide socialist revolution. Only communism could successfully oppose the capitalists and imperialists and meet that supreme challenge. If I wanted to become a true social revolutionary, she said, I must develop an almost religious faith in the righteousness of the cause. Like a medieval saint, I must rise above the normal weaknesses of humankind, suppressing all my doubts, denying even my friends and family to serve the goals of the revolution. Most importantly, I must renounce my infatuation with decadent European political and intellectual vogues. I must arm myself with whatever skills and talents I had acquired at home and abroad, return to my country, contact its true revolutionaries, and fight for *la justice social* in my own unique way.

"Very impressive," Nguyen sneered when I finished explaining my political transition, and I could not imagine any reason other than jealousy as to why he felt obliged to voice such disdain for my conversion to his own principles. "Maybe now I can convince you to work for us."

"I am afraid not. I have decided to follow Professor de Sauvebelle-Bouchet's advice."

"Return to your country?"

"Yes."

"In what capacity, if I might ask?"

"Sorry, I am not at liberty to say."

"Perhaps you will infiltrate the opposition, like me?"

"As I say . . ."

"I know, I know," he said impatiently.

"Now," I said, "what about your career as a pianist?"

"That is over. I am a full-time employee of the Ministry of Foreign Affairs in Saigon now."

"What do you do there?"

"I work in the Public Relations Department."

"Any good spying there?"

"Sorry, but I'm not at liberty to say."

"*Touché!* But what happened to your other career, Nguyen, your music? You were such a marvelous, classical pianist."

"You want the truth? I simply was not good enough. You know what Saint Thomas Aquinas said? *'Only three things are needed for beauty: wholeness, harmony, radiance.'* The consensus seemed to be that I had not enough of the latter, even for a backwater like Saigon."

After dinner, I half-expected that we would simply kiss goodbye, but he wanted to know if I was up for a stroll along the Petchaburi Canal.

Down on the quay, with the water gushing below us, and the lights of Bangkok playing on its eddying surface, and the barges and ferryboats floating by, we mellowed toward each other despite the tension that we had felt all evening. We even walked along hand in hand for a while, just like old times.

Then, almost before either of us realized it, "*a quickly extinguished fire is quickly reignited,*" as the French say, we found ourselves pressed up against a stone wall under the Sukhumvit 55 Bridge, kissing passionately, tearing at each other's clothes, heedless of passersby. I bit his lips. He bit my nipples through my blouse. I found bare skin under his shirt and dug into his back with my nails. He pulled off his suit coat, wrapped it round us and jerked up my skirt. I dropped my knickers round my ankles and kicked them over the bank.

And right there, under the bridge, with gawking pedestrians

strolling by, I unbuttoned him, dragged him out into the night air, and plunged him inside me, both of us moaning and crying out and muttering garbled words. Just as he was about to erupt, I pulled him out, fell to my knees, and fellated him as I am sure he had never been fellated before, licking the sperm that spouted across my hungry lips.

"Oh, I feel so humiliated!" I cried when we were done.

Although there were several conflicting emotions running through me at the time, I must admit that humiliation was not one of them. Nevertheless, I took the opportunity to race up the stairs to Thanon Petchaburi and disappear into the night.

Yet, the very next day, we were at it again in his hotel.

Perhaps to make up for the violent passions of the night before, or as a parting gift, we made love sweetly and gently this time, the way I had always wanted.

"The weird thing is—none of it was real, was it?" he said, as I was leaving.

"*Mait dit donc, Nguyen!* The whole thing was a childish illusion, a passing fancy, a holiday romance. '*Le temps des lilas et le temps des roses ne reviendra plus.*'"

He jerked his head toward our unmade bed. "So, what is all *this* about?"

I gazed up at him tenderly, holding his hands in mine. "It is about memories. A fleeting past that we shared. The impermanence of all things. *La désillusion inévitable de l'amour.* It is about growing up and saying goodbye."

A month or two later, Nguyen sent me a letter from Saigon, expressing in conventional terms his delight at seeing me again and his hope that we might meet again.

I sent him an equally conventional reply and was astonished when the letter was returned to me with a stamped postal note in Vietnamese, French, and English:

Người nhận đã chết, trả , lại cho người gửi
Destinateur décédé, retourner à l'expéditeur
Addressee deceased, return to sender

I sent another letter to his address, enquiring of his parents as to the circumstances of his death, but received no reply.

I had no idea whether the enemy had shot him as a spy or one of our own had inadvertently blown him up in a street bomb attack. Nevertheless, I decided that ultimate responsibility for his death should rightly be borne by the American Imperialists and their South Vietnamese lackeys who had caused the war in the first place.

At the time of my meeting with Nguyen in Bangkok, I had not been nearly so clear about my future as a revolutionist as I had implied, and I certainly harbored no illusions about the communists.

Despite Professor de Sauvebelle-Bouchet's advice to commit myself to the Party with an almost religious faith, I knew enough modern history to understand that what the anti-communists said was not all lies and fabrications. I knew that Party members often employed unjust and brutal methods in their quest for power, and once having attained it, they used the same methods to stay in power.

Yet, Nguyen's death changed the direction of my thinking. I decided that the situation in Laos was too critical, and the peril to its people too grave, to permit myself any more qualms or doubts. It was a question of either black or white. I could let no half tones enter the picture.

Plagued by an enormous and seemingly insurmountable gulf between the rich and the poor, and an endemic corruption in the public sphere that would prevent any change by democratic means, Laos was desperately in need of a new and more fair-minded order.

I had no illusions about bringing about some sort of "classless society" in my own lifetime. Nevertheless, I came to see that I had to do whatever I could to alleviate the suffering of my people. I would do it not only for them, but also for my own self-esteem as a doctor, a healer of the ills of my fellow Laotians.

So, when I left the hospital for Laos that year on what was supposed to be a brief holiday to celebrate *Bun Pha Wet*, the Birth of Buddha, I had no intention of coming back.

Thus, strange as it may seem, my unloved lover furnished me with yet another motive in my gravitation toward active revolution.

It is difficult for me to explain now, except in this way: It was as though Nguyen had indeed become the husband of my dreams, and I must therefore avenge his death.

In time, it became like my own brand of Buddhism; I believed in it, and indeed devoted myself to it, without questioning it too much.

Later, I would find that many of my comrades had joined the armed struggle for similarly offbeat and arbitrary reasons.

CHAPTER SEVENTEEN

Uncle Vong

To understand me, and the life I have chosen, you must understand my family history. Let me begin with a time in the early 1920s when two brothers were born in Vientiane, Laos. Their names were Analu and Vong Armodée, and they came from an old and respected family of bourgeois professionals.

They lived in style, spoke French at home, attended the Catholic Church and the *Lyceé Française,* and were groomed for a higher education in France.

Since the brothers were so close in age, their mother had raised them as twins, dressing them in the same white, tropical shirts, shorts, and knee stockings.

Yet they could not have been more different.

The elder, Analu was slight, near-sighted, pale yellow in coloring and rather sickly as a youth. He wore thick, horn-rimmed glasses, and although he was not particularly ugly, he was a rather ordinary looking Asian man of his era. Quiet, unemotional, humorless, and law-abiding, intent on his studies and on getting ahead in the French Colonial system, he was favored by his Francophone teachers but had few Laotian friends and displayed little interest in the opposite sex. When he completed his studies at the *Lycée* in 1937, he went abroad to study at the *Université de Montpellier's Faculté de Médicine*, where again he excelled. Luckily, World War II did not interrupt his studies because his university was in the Languedoc-Roussillon region of France, which came under the jurisdiction of the collaborationist Vichy regime.

After the war, he returned to Asia and accepted a position as staff doctor at Bumrungrad International Hospital in Bangkok. Since Thai and Lao are similar languages, perhaps more akin even than Spanish and Portuguese, he adjusted quickly and soon met a plain-faced female intern from an old and distinguished Buddhist family named Yada Wattana. As a rational decision, rather than as an act of love, they decided to marry and start a family. To pacify Analu's family, Yada converted to Catholicism, but secretly retained her Buddhist faith. Analu got a job at the new Charles De Gaulle Hospital in Vientiane, Laos. They moved there, and my sister Kalama was born that same year. A year later, I came into the world.

Throughout his life, my father was a staunch conservative, a devout Catholic, and a devotee of the status quo, whatever it might be at the time. If I had to name his two greatest faults, I would say he lacked imagination and empathy for others, which I consider grave defects for a Doctor of Medicine. For much of his life he was a Royalist, and worshiped Crown Prince Boun Oum as a minor deity. This was not as odd as it sounds nowadays; in fact, much of Vientiane's Catholic upper crust believed the same.

Due to their extreme disparities in temperament, my father was forever in conflict with his younger brother, Vong. I do not believe it is an exaggeration to describe their feelings for each other as mutual loathing. The one characteristic the two brothers had in common was unusual intelligence, and their greatest difference lay in the way they employed that intelligence.

Vong Aromdée was tall, dark, well-built, and handsome. Unlike his elder brother, he excelled at every sport he tried, including swimming, tennis, and soccer. Fiery and fun loving, impetuous, and highly imaginative, he was a born rebel. At the *Lycée* he attended with his brother, he neglected his studies to lead an anti-colonialist and anti-Catholic student movement called *Avanti Popolo*, which he held in sway as much by his wicked wit as by his lectures on Marxian dialectical materialism. Although his teachers despised him, he was immensely popular among the student body, and the girls buzzed about him like fruit flies to sliced mango with sticky-rice.

Due to his bad marks, he was held back in school and did not matriculate until 1939. The war had started in Europe, so there was no question of him going off to study at a French university. For a time, Vong worked half-heartedly with his grandfather in his import-export business.

In 1941, however, when the traitorous Vichy government invited Japan to station its troops in Indochina, he traveled to northern Cochin where he joined a native, communist, resistance army that would later be called the Viet Minh.

Notably valorous in the battle against Japanese Imperialism, Vong quickly rose in rank and by the time of the Japanese surrender in 1945, he had risen to the rank of captain and commanded a company of Viet Minh.

In that capacity, he helped wage a low-intensity guerrilla war against the French colonialist powers, until the Battle of Dien Bien Phu, in 1954, which ended in a bitter defeat for the French forces, and the colonial power's exodus from Indochina. Even more significantly, perhaps, it put to rest the legend of Western invincibility and ushered in a new era of anti-colonialist struggles all over the world.

In 1960, at the direction of North Vietnamese General Giap, to whom he still owed his first allegiance, Vong established Group 959 in Vieng Xai, a Laotian village near the North Vietnamese border. It soon became a major military hub for the supply, training, and support of the communist movement in Laos, the Pathet Lao, and so it remained for the next thirteen years.

Although my father hated his younger brother with a passion that political, religious, and temperamental differences could not fully explain, it was easy for me to contact my Uncle Vong when I decided to do so in mid-1970.

I did it through my mother.

She and her dashing brother-in-law had met many times at family gatherings when he was in Vientiane during truces between the Communists, Neutralists and Royalists, and they had maintained correspondence throughout the years despite her husband's disapproval.

This was not uncommon in Laos at the time. Family ties were sacrosanct and superseded even the most diverse political affiliations. Still, their communication was so scandalous to some in our vast, rumormongering family that they went so far as to accuse them of conceiving a child together.

It happened, they said, while Yada's husband was attending a three-month period of medical retraining in France and Vong was in town on a mission to negotiate another brief truce between our contending political factions.

As evidence, they offered three "facts." First, I was born a suspiciously short time—eight months—after my father returned from abroad. Second, neither of my parents was particularly attractive and I resembled my dark-skinned, good-looking Uncle Vong to an almost uncanny extent. Third, my mother was a "secret communist" because her family, the Wattanas, had been vocal, left-wing members of the Thai parliament since its very inception.

Perhaps needless to say, the Thai side of my family called their Laotian in-laws "congenital liars."

At the time, I could not have said who was right, but I did have certain suspicions, mostly based on the breathless way my mother uttered the name *Vong Aromdée* in the French she had taken great trouble to learn, and on my uncle's reputation as a "lady's man."

To make a long story short, when my holiday ended in May 1970, I allowed my father to assume that I was returning to Bangkok to resume my training as an intern. Then I connived with my mother to book a bus ticket to Xam Nua, in remote Kham Muan Province, near the village where Uncle Vong had his headquarters.

I arranged my trip easily enough. Strange as it may seem, travel, mail and commerce went on virtually unimpeded throughout most of the Laotian Civil Conflict. Riverboats sailed up and down the Mekong, bearing freight and passengers. Buses ran from one end of the country to the other on the old, French Colonial, highway system, halting now and then at roadblocks to pay a transit tax to one faction or another, be it Royalist, Neutralist or Pathet Lao.

With all the stops and inspections, my two-hundred-kilometer journey to the north was long and tedious (at least for a native Lao bored with the endless repetition of jungle ridges and rice-growing river valleys).

There were only three worthy sights along the way: The Mysterious Standing Stone of Hintang, the Pagoda of Ban Muong Vaen, and the Plain of Jars.

My bus crossed over into Kham Muan Province thirty-six hours after my departure. I probably could have gone just as fast on horseback.

According to the old, French roadmap I carried, the province was shaped like the head of an open-mouthed dragon. For some reason known only to the departed colonial rulers of Indochina, the beast had nibbled about fifty kilometers into North Vietnam.

Kham Muan's principal municipality and its seat of government, Xam Nua, was in the center of the province, in the high valley of the Xam River, and appeared to be only about twenty kilometers from the Vietnamese border in every direction but west.

When my bus finally crawled over the 2000-meter Xa Ngoa Mountains and wound down into the valley, I found Xam Nua to be a shabby village, encircled by soggy, mud-colored, rice paddies, steaming bomb craters from a recent American air attack and misty, pine-clad karsts, with anti-aircraft emplacements dug into their sheer inclines.

It was grey and icy cold when I arrived. Everyone—including male and female NVA and Pathet Lao soldiers in uniform, local citizens and tribesmen down from the mountains—walked round bundled in makeshift shawls, tattered blankets and burlap sacks, scrunching up their shoulders as if surprised at this sudden and brief onslaught of winter that descended upon them for a month or so each year. This included me; I was dressed for a much warmer climate and had not thought to bring a jacket along.

Happily, it was easy to find Uncle Vong. All I had to do was utter his name and the ragged, hungry-looking townspeople went all big-eyed and pointed me on my way as if frightened of reprisals. His headquarters was a cave, they said, in a hillside above the village of Vieng Xai, about three kilometers east of town on the old, French Highway 6. When I asked an elderly Party cadre about the condition of the road, he proudly informed me that the local authorities kept it in excellent repair, despite repeated US bombings, and it ran all the way to Hanoi, one hundred kilometers away.

I refused a ride on the *tuk-tuk* that served as the one taxi in the province, for I had planned my entrance onto my uncle's revolutionary stage as one of stouthearted, soldierly confidence and self-reliance.

I hiked the three kilometers out of town with my old, French rucksack bouncing on my back. I scrambled up Vieng Xai Hill in my Swiss mountaineering boots past a bivouacked platoon of battle-hardened NVA to a pair of scruffy, young, Pathet Lao guards at the mouth of the cave.

When challenged, I shouted my name at them in what I

thought to be a properly brusque military manner and flashed my *Carte d'Identité National* to prove it.

One of them pretended to scan it (clearly, he could not read) and waved me past. The other one accompanied me into the mouth of the cave and up to the desk of the duty officer, a tall, handsome, Vietnamese officer in the uniform of an NVA commissar.

Glancing at him, preparing a little speech about my need to see Colonel Aromdée on a special assignment, I found myself looking into the intelligent, conniving eyes of Nguyen Ly, apparently newly arisen from the grave.

He threw himself back in his chair and laughed aloud when he saw me start in fear and shock.

"But . . . but . . ."

"Not to worry, love," he said in French, still laughing. "Reports of my death have been greatly exaggerated. I assure you that I am still mostly flesh and bone. We shall talk later, *non?* Meanwhile, Colonel Aromdée is awaiting your arrival."

Then switching to brusque, poorly pronounced Lao, he addressed the young man who had accompanied me.

"Private Nong, show the comrade to the command post. And make it quick."

I was so stunned by the meeting that for a few seconds I took no notice of my environs as Private Nong led me deeper into the cave.

I mean, silly though I may have been, I had joined the revolution in revenge for my unloved ex-lover's supposed noble death at the hands of the American bandits. And now, suddenly he turns up, hale and hearty, in all his snotty and pretentious reality.

I swear, on some level I felt cheated and even a bit offended by his magical resurrection because it exposed my romantic gesture to be just as pathetic and farcical as I had always suspected it to be. I was not at all looking forward to meeting Nguyen again on a daily basis and could not imagine which of my many transgressions had impelled the fates to inflict me so.

When I was finally able to register my surroundings again, I was astonished for the second time in as many minutes. I had often thought of my uncle's cave in the past, and I had envisaged it as a dark and narrow Paleolithic environment, but as we stepped more deeply into its interior, its size staggered me.

At least twenty meters in height, it had been carved out of the native limestone in precise and orderly dimensions. Its rooms and corridors were perfectly rectangular. Its walls ran up in a true perpendicular to the roof. Its several stories of living and office space were connected by spiraling wooden staircases. Its central lobby or atrium was broad and spacious, full of canvas-covered supplies of food, weapons, and ammunition.

What surprised me most, perhaps, was how well-equipped the cave was. Bright, transformer-generated electric light flooded all but the most remote corners. An efficient air-conditioning unit expelled stale air and cooking smells. The smooth, wood plank floors were swept and polished. The field kitchen and medical clinic were spotlessly clean, equipped with running water piped up from the river. The single largest space, the barracks, was lined with hundreds of sleeping mats, each with a perfectly folded futon cover. Only the roof of the cave, when visible, displayed the rough, rocky, stalactite-festooned surface I had imagined.

I had not seen Uncle Vong since I was a teenager, when I'd had a frightful crush on him, complete with sexual fantasies. Clearly, it was a reaction against my father, an impulse toward any man his opposite. It may have even been a primal instinct to inject a little fire and blood into the family tree.

Whatever the case, Uncle Vong had been a perfect gentleman about it. He had deflected my all too obvious infatuation by laughing and slapping me on the back all the time, inviting me to soccer games and one-on-one tennis matches that he always contrived to lose, and genially treating me as one of the boys.

Now, as I was conducted past the military clerks and cubicles and tapping typewriters of his headquarters toward his little, earthen, cubbyhole office at the end, I asked myself what Vong might look like now, what I should expect.

In the years since I saw my uncle last, my father had aged into a prematurely old man, with a bent back, sagging cheeks, grey hair and a bald spot on his crown. Therefore, when at last I found myself standing before my uncle's desk, I was astonished by how little he seemed to have changed. And this despite the grievous wounds of war he so obviously bore, including a wooden hand swathed in a leather glove and a scar that ran across his cheek from his chin to his right ear.

Hooting gleefully, he leapt up like a man twenty years his junior to clap me to his NVA uniform jacket.

"*Mon Dieu*, Nittaya, look at you! All grown up now, and a doctor of medicine too, I hear!"

I grinned back at him as he held me at a distance to regard me more closely.

"Well, almost, Uncle Vong. I just quit my internship."

"But you were in your last year, *ma chere!*" he said, seeming to take an ironic pleasure in his own avuncular patter. "I mean, I heard your mother's version of the story, and I still cannot figure out why you did it."

As I prepared my answer to his question, which I had carefully rehearsed on the bus ride, my thoughts were deflected for an instant by something I had either forgotten or stuck away somewhere at the back of my mind.

My uncle and I shared a truly remarkable resemblance in both looks and personality. It was not just his lively, spirited presence, or his dry wit, or the shape of his head or his obsidian eyes, with sparking flecks of gold in them. It was the way he cracked a grin out of the side of his mouth. The way he waved his hands around when he talked. The way he laughed from the belly up. I mean, when I was up close to him, with my neck resting on his shoulder, and I got a whiff of him, I swear we even smelled the same—like green jasmine tea and mango pudding.

'Uh, well," I replied at last, and then I blushed at the blatant transparency of my prepared answer even before I delivered it. "Actually, I felt a need to do my part in bringing justice to the people of Laos."

"I see," he said, but he did not seem altogether convinced.

"I mean, things have reached such a critical state in this country, Uncle Vong, that I felt I could not wait another minute," I said, trying to pick up the pace, to impress him with my sincerity. "I can finish my internship after the war. But right now, action is called for, and I believe, really, truly, that everyone must do his or her part."

"And so that is what has brought you here to me?" he said, guiding me to a seat close to his desk chair.

Yes. I . . . uh . . . I could not think of anyone better than you to help me in pursuing my aim."

"You sure it had not anything to do with Commissar Junior Grade Nguyen Ly?"

"What? No! I had no idea he was here. I thought he was dead. And I certainly had no notion that he had become a political officer in the NVA."

"I see. Well, that pretty much coincides with what he told me when he arrived. He said that he faked his death when he defected to the NVA to avoid repercussions to his family in Saigon. He said he specifically requested duty in Laos because he once had a very dear Laotian friend. Then he asked me if I was any relation to you. I told him yes, and he said you were the friend he was referring to. Of course, I guessed it might have been something more than that. Am I right?"

"Yes, but it's over now, Uncle Vong; I swear to you."

"If you say so, I believe it. You were always honest with me, Nittaya, and you never minced words. So, I can tell you that it is fortunate that you and Commissar Junior Grade Nguyen Ly are now only friends and comrades. The reason I say so is that we enforce a strict non-fraternization rule between the sexes here. Our troops are one fifth female. You can imagine what would ensue with five hundred sex-starved soldiers fighting over one hundred lonely girls living in a cave. We would be back to the Cro-Magnon Age quicker than you could recite such good Marxist phrases as 'Use-Value versus Exchange-Value.'"

"Thank you, Uncle Vong, and I promise to live up to your

trust in me."

"Marvelous," he said, laughing indulgently. "Now, my dear, aside from your general desire to be helpful in liberating the masses, did you have anything more specific in mind?"

"I should be willing to do almost anything to help, but I thought the best spot for me might be some place where I could use my medical skills to the best advantage."

Stroking his chin, my uncle took a more serious turn. "Well, I know we're going to be able to use your skills in one way or another. But before we talk about that, I think I had better explain how things work here. *D'accord?*"

"*Oui, d'accord, mon oncle,*" I said, and after that we spoke only French, perhaps to avoid unwanted listeners.

"To begin with, I must treat you exactly as I treat everyone else in my battalion. There can be no sign of favoritism, no hint of nepotism. If anything, I shall have to come down even harder on you than I do with the rest, simply to avoid jealousy and gossip. What this means in practice is that you will see little of me, and I will not be able to intercede on your behalf if you have any problems with your supervising officers, including Commissar Junior Grade Nguyen Ly. Do you understand, Nittaya?"

"*Bien sûr, mon oncle!*"

"Good. Now to begin with, I am the commander of all NVA and Pathet Lao forces in Kham Muan Province. Our mission is to work together to keep the province free of foreign aggressors, and to mount combat operations against their Hmong, Mung and Khmu tribal lackeys in the region. In doing so, we sometimes sustain serious casualties, both among our soldiers and the civilian population, mostly due to aerial bombardment.

"Eventually, I want you to employ your skills as a medical doctor. But before you can do that, we must follow official protocol, which states that 'all who join our struggle must start at the bottom and work their way upward as quickly as their skills and talents permit.' That is the bad news. The good news is that there is no sexual bias. You will therefore rise in the hierarchy just as fast as any man."

And so it went. I checked into the underground female barracks that same day. After lunch in the cafeteria, where I was handed a rice bowl and fished for my pork and vegetables from the common pot, I was issued an olive drab uniform with a sun helmet, a sleeping mat, a blanket and a small shelf for my meager clothing.

That evening, I attended the obligatory lecture on Marxist-Leninist theory delivered in Vietnamese by none other than Commissar Junior Grade Nguyen Ly and translated into Lao by a pimply teenage boy.

Nguyen winked and leered at me, but he made no attempt to speak to me afterwards, so I assumed that my uncle had spoken to him on the non-fraternization issue as well.

After a fitful night—I had nightmares of being entombed under tons of earth—I started sweeping and polishing floors and cleaning latrines the next morning.

A week later, my supervisor, a female sergeant in the Pathet Lao, indicated her approval of my work ethic and positive attitude, so I was moved up to the laundry room. Now I could attend the Communist singing and dancing sessions that followed Commissar Junior Grade Nguyen Ly's required nightly lecture. I also had twice-weekly, target training sessions, with

Soviet-Russian assault rifles and handguns.

A week scrubbing uniforms and I was sent to the kitchen to wash dishes and mop more floors, from which I graduated to food service and preparation. Then it was on to the medical clinic, where I worked the midnight shift as a cleaning lady.

When I was set to rise to a position as nursing assistant, my commanding officer, a middle-aged NVA cadre, recommended me as a prospective Party member. After a month's probationary period, the Communist Party of Laos accepted me as a full-fledged member, which included immediate admission into the Pathet Lao.

As a Party member, I was now qualified to ascend to the rank of ward nurse. A few perfunctory days in that capacity and I became an operating room nurse. Another week and I became a Doctor of Internal Medicine.

The whole process had taken no more than three months, which indicated how desperate they were for medical professionals. I might proudly add that within those same three months I had earned a Marksman 1st Class award in both the side arm and assault rifle categories.

Nguyen and I kept our distance from each other, delivering perfunctory, comradely smiles at each other when we happened to meet while performing our duties.

I was perfectly content with this and let him know so. Yet I feared that Nguyen was not satisfied, for he never failed to convey with a significant look his intention to flout the colonel's orders and confront me at some expedient time in the future.

What really astounded me about Nguyen at this time was the change in his personality. The classical musician, the backpacker, the European-educated intellectual I had met on the Great Grass Road was long gone, replaced by a stern, stiff-backed, party functionary of the most insipid type.

In short, for the first time I began to see my ex-lover for just the man he really was—a flawed, weak-minded, vindictive character who pretended to be strong, just and caring. He was not successful in his pretense because he could not quite convince himself, let alone others.

Not long after I was certified as a doctor, I received orders to travel to the far north of Laos, to Po Khoa Chay, where our Kolo tribal allies were suffering a severe outbreak of dengue fever. I chose a pair of young medics and an experienced nurse named Lae Martel to accompany me.

Lae and I had become friends shortly after I arrived at Vieng Xai because we had a lot in common. We were both attractive, mixed-blood Asians of about the same age; we were taller and fuller-figured than the average Asian girl, and we had a kind of foreign appearance that made the local people look at us askance. I mean, Lae had *blue eyes!* Her father had been a French soldier; her mother was Lao and Chinese. She had been educated at Thammasat University in Thailand, and she had even worked for a time at Bangkok International Hospital. She spoke French, English, Lao, and Thai. Like me, she was far more worldly and sophisticated than the other medical staff, who were of mostly Vietnamese peasant stock and sometimes viewed us as effete interlopers from the upper classes who were not to be entirely trusted.

We were even similar in how we had come to the revolutionary struggle. Lae had met her doctor lover at the hospital where she worked; he had convinced her to come join the revolution with him, and then he had promptly expired in an American bombing raid. She had even stayed on to avenge his death even though they had parted several weeks before his death.

"Why did you split up?" I asked her one evening in the operating room after we had just performed an appendectomy together.

Removing her rubber gloves and tossing them into the recycling container, in the single swift gesture of a practiced professional, Lae waited until she was standing over the sink, washing her hands with anti-bacterial soap, before replying.

"Nittaya, if you really put your mind to it," she said over her shoulder, "I think maybe you can guess."

"You had an affair with my uncle," I said, moving up beside her to wash my hands as well.

"*Et voila!*"

"I guess those non-fraternization rules do not apply to the top dog then, do they?"

Lae giggled, covered her mouth with her hand, and wriggled her saucy bottom in her pale blue, medical scrubs.

"No challenge, no sacrifice is too great for our honored leader."

Then we both fell out laughing, smacking faucet water at each other like a pair of gleeful ten-year-olds.

For all these reasons, it quickly became apparent that Lae and I were blood sisters. Neither of us had ever had a female friend like this before. A friend with whom we had total rapport. A friend we could tell absolutely anything.

So, we packed our medical equipment and, accompanied by

our teenage medics, traveled on an NVA military convoy north on Highway 1A, the new Chinese road to Yunnan. We got off at the Nam Hou River Bridge, thirty kilometers short of the border, engaged a sampan, and poled up the river in a westward direction for two days to the tiny Kolo village.

When we arrived, Lae and I found a large portion of the adult population and nearly all the children infected. Our first task was to stabilize our patients through oral rehydration, intravenous fluids, and blood transfusions. Our next was to determine the cause of the epidemic, and that was not hard to find at all. There was standing water everywhere, and it was alive with dengue-bearing mosquitoes.

We pressed the healthy Kolos into work parties and set them to spraying insecticide and filling in water holes all around the village. We even had them fill in their water well and replace it with a pipe and pump that my uncle had provided us with.

Within a few weeks, things were looking up. The children were running about again, playing games, the women were tending their fields, and the men were out hunting and fishing.

After persuading the Kolos to keep their village water-free and advising them that it might be better if they moved their bamboo huts to higher, drier ground for their slash and burn agriculture, we left with their sincere thanks, and their promise that they were at the disposal of Papa Lao, whenever he needed them.

Riding back to our base, standing up in a dusty, rickety truck bed full of NVA soldiers, Lae and I spoke of what we had accomplished at the Kolo village, and of our deep sense of satisfaction at our achievement.

"You know," I said, "I felt much happier up there in the mountains, living in the rough, treating the Kolos, curing them, and showing them how to better their lives, than I ever felt in the cave."

"Really?" Lae giggled, covering her mouth with her hand. "Well, much as I take pride in what we achieved, dear doctor, I cannot wait to get my little butt back home!"

"That is because you and your little butt have got something to look forward to," I said, shaking my finger at her, "you naughty girl."

Then I confessed to her that I had felt perfectly delighted to put some distance between myself and my dreary, dogmatic ex-lover.

"Yes," she said, sniffing, shaking her head, gazing languidly over the railing at an archetypical Asian scene.

A pretty, half-naked, little girl lay astride a long-horned water buffalo, in the middle of a flooded rice field. Arms hugging its slick flank, an ear pressed to its hairy hump, she was smiling at us ecstatically, as if she wanted us to know just how much she loved her great hairy, black beast.

"Yes," Lae said again, inhaling deeply of the fecund upcountry air. "I must admit that I find your Commissar Junior Grade Nguyen Ly a bit tiresome as well. And I often wonder what you ever saw in him."

"It is what I keep asking myself. Maybe it just had to do with new sights and sounds, new adventures every day. Travel can be romantic, you know? It can turn your head."

Three days after we returned to Vieng Xai, Lae and I were ordered to accompany our unit on its next military operation, an attack on a radar-navigational station that supported US air operations in North Vietnam and northern Laos.

Colonel Aromdée considered the mission so critical that he had Commissar Junior Grade Nguyen Ly make a special presentation to our medical team.

"The station in question is located twenty kilometers southeast of our present position," Nguyen said, in the painfully didactic tones he had acquired at the commissar's school he attended in Hanoi. "The American bandits constructed it in the year 1966. It has been active at that site since that point in time. Its staff consists of twelve Central Intelligence Agency operatives and ten military technicians. It is defended by a force of a hundred Thai and Hmong mercenaries."

We had never attacked it before, Nguyen said, because it was built in a virtually impregnable position, at the top of a five-hundred-meter karst, with perpendicular walls called Phou Phiaton. It had no need for land supply because it could rely on helicopters. The station was extremely dangerous because it possessed a sophisticated guidance system with an effective range of 300 kilometers. It could direct American air bandits to targets anywhere in northern Laos and Vietnam, night or day. In the four years since the installation of the station, Colonel Aromdée had worked tirelessly to find a way to neutralize it, and some months back he had decided on a sapper attack.

With that in mind, he had conducted a prolonged secret reconnaissance of the target, including the locations of approach routes, listening posts, detonation devices, perimeter wire fences, trenches and machinegun bunkers. Then he performed several live assault rehearsals on a mockup of Phou Phiaton that he had built on a nearby karst.

It was at this time that he plotted his supporting mortar and artillery concentrations, trained his sappers to climb the mountain with ropes, and estimated the time required to overrun the base, destroy it, kill its defenders, and escape before being attacked by air bandits.

In recent weeks, the colonel had built camouflaged roads into the area strong enough to bear heavy military vehicles. His soldiers had ascended the peaks surrounding Phou Phiaton and placed heavy artillery and antiaircraft weapons there. Most importantly, he had stationed his tribal allies—the Kolo and Hani—in positions to thwart any attack on his northern and southern flanks.

"Although the colonel is confident of victory, he has warned that the operation will be difficult and hazardous," Nguyen said. "We therefore anticipate heavy casualties. However, if we succeed in our attack, we shall significantly reduce the number of daily bombings that cause such devastation to the regions of northern Laos and Vietnam.

"Your team will consist of two surgeons, one internist, seven battlefield medics, ten nurses, and a dozen assistants. You and all your medical equipment will be transported to the field of operations by truck. Once you arrive, you will set up your field hospital in a limestone cavern at the base of the mountain. You will have everything unloaded and functioning perfectly within twenty-four hours. Those are your orders. No exceptions permitted. Do you understand, comrades?"

"Yes, Comrade Commissar!" we all shouted, as required, and then he was gone, but not without conveying a little self-satisfied smirk in my direction.

To honor our vow to the commissar, we loaded our trucks with swift and easy delivery in mind. We negotiated the artfully camouflaged road into the mountains without mishap. As soon as we arrived at our cave, we worked like demons to unload all our equipment and organize our field hospital.

Within an hour, we had set up our generator, strung up electrical wiring and were furnished with light and power. We ran a pipe down to the creek, got a pump working, and *voilà* we had running water. Laboring all night, we set up a field kitchen, an emergency room with a triage center, an operating room, an intensive care unit with intravenous drips and monitoring machines, a pharmaceutical dispensary and a convalescent ward.

Our superior, NVA Chief Surgeon Dong, had designated me as a battlefield wounds specialist, and Lae as surgical nurse.

An enthusiastic but physically disabled Party man who hobbled about on two canes, Dong arrived at the aid station the morning after our arrival.

After complimenting us on our progress, he said, "Pass the word; the weatherman says there will be low clouds and fog tonight. The American bandits will not know what hit them. And even if they have time to call in air support, they will not be able to tell one mountain from another."

The first wave of sappers was composed entirely of dedicated young volunteers, many of them women, who made less noise when climbing or moving through foliage. They carried automatic weapons, RPGs, grenades, and satchel charges. They wore nothing but leaves in their hair and olive-green undershorts and covered their entire bodies with grease and charcoal to make them invisible. They strapped their weapons and explosive charges to their bodies to minimize noise as they crawled up the leafy slope and hung coiled climbing ropes and pitons round their necks. Thus attired, the women—many of them young, shapely, and pretty—were truly a remarkable sight.

That night, a few hours before the scheduled 2 a.m. attack, they lined up outside our aid station and we gave each of them a generous dose of the herb *Má Huáng,* a powerful stimulant used in traditional Chinese medicine from which the drug *Ephedrine* is derived. We assured them that it would sharpen their reflexes and render them impervious to fear. I had full confidence in its effects because I had taken some myself and felt like a goddess of war.

Thus fortified, our sappers spent hours creeping and climbing into position at the rim of the karst, and then "laying dog," as we said, awaiting the signal to attack.

We in the medical aid station killed time by whispering meaningless nonsense to each other, and nervously checking and rechecking our medical equipment.

At 1:30 a.m., our first wave of sappers was only fifty meters outside the concertina wire in the defensive perimeter. Just as predicted, a thick blanket of fog had enveloped the entire area.

At 2:00 a.m., our mortar and artillery barrage commenced, firing at prearranged and calibrated targets with deadly accuracy, catching the defenders completely by surprise. The noise as the mortar rounds whooshed off and exploded on the karst was so loud, echoing up and down the surrounding mountains and valleys, that I could imagine how terrifying it must sound in the target zone.

By 2:15 a.m., when the mortars and artillery stopped firing, our first wave of sappers had neutralized the defensive trip flares and claymore mines, crept through the first two concertina barriers, and were nearly over the third.

Now they were blowing holes in the third barrier with bamboo torpedoes or running over them on rush mats they had thrown down across the coils.

The roar of our sappers' rocket-propelled grenades, satchel charges and torpedoes created the impression that the artillery was still firing, so the Thai and Hmong mercenaries on the perimeter mostly stayed hunkered in their bunkers, too scared to pop up and see what was happening.

As soon as the sappers had slipped by the outer bunkers and penetrated the firebase, a second wave of older and more conventionally armed NVA troops led by Commissar Nguyen Ly (may Buddha forgive me, but I imagined some fortuitous trip-mine neutralizing the swinging source of his arrogance) made an assault from the other side of the perimeter.

The few enemy defensive forces that were not hiding in bunkers were compelled to fight off their attackers from their front and rear at the same time. Confused and frightened by the notion that they were surrounded and had little hope of survival, the mercenaries quickly lost energy and focus. They crawled out of their bunkers with their hands in the air, crying for mercy. We had orders to take no prisoners, for speed was of the essence, and enemy soldiers would only hinder our escape, so we shot them down like dogs.

At 0600, the CIA radar base at Phou Phiaton was a smoking ruin, never to see service again in the war, and our fighters had rappelled back down the karst.

The fog and clouds were holding, and though we could hear American jets and helicopters whizzing and clattering overhead, they dared not fire their rockets or drop their bombs out of fear of hitting their own men.

Our casualties had been light, with only five confirmed KIA. We lowered our dozen wounded (including Commissar Nguyen Ly, winged on the inner thigh, only four regretful centimeters from the wellspring of his insufferable self-importance) down the cliff by a system of ropes, pulleys, and bamboo baskets, and they received medical treatment in remarkably short order.

The most serious case that Lae and I treated was a "tiger woman." One of the few Pathet Laos in the attacking force, she had been hit by friendly fire during our initial artillery barrage.

She was an attractive, well-spoken, young girl from a middle-class, Vientiane family and her name—I shall never forget it—was Alana Racha.

A part of her right buttock had been blown off by shrapnel, and her entire leg and foot were punctured by hundreds of large and small wounds. To make it worse, sand, mud and shrapnel were embedded in every perforation.

After injecting her with the only painkiller we had available (a not altogether successful Chinese rip-off of the American brand Demoral), Lae cleaned the girl's major wounds and I sewed them up. Then we did our best to treat her other wounds, but it was not easy because there were so many rips, tears, and holes in her.

I could not just amputate the leg as I might have done in other circumstances because it was Pathet Lao policy to save the limbs of soldiers at all costs so they might fight again. Therefore, we had to painstakingly locate each puncture wound and remove all the infectious debris. Using a scalpel and tweezers, taking care to avoid digging into blood vessels and nerves, we prodded and poked the poor girl, until we had dug out every grain of sand, mud, and shrapnel.

We worked at her for four hours straight, all through the attack, demolition, and withdrawal phases of the operation, because we had to disinfect her wounds continuously during the process. In the end, Lae and I took enormous pride in having removed all the foreign bodies from her leg, cleaning and stitching them up when necessary, and bandaging them artfully to staunch the blood and drain them simultaneously.

We took greater pride when she regained consciousness and seemed to be responding to our blood transfusions. She even managed a wink and a smile of thanks to the both of us. She was such a pretty girl that one could almost call her beautiful.

Lae and I felt so good about her later, when we were finally allowed a rest break, that we whooped, whacked each other on the back, and gave each other high fives, like a pair of victorious soccer players.

Then, just when we were on the verge of pulling out, all hell broke loose. Our Hani tribal allies, whom we had relied on to hold our southern flanks, had suddenly turned on their NVA military advisors. Murdering them in cold blood, they allowed our Khmu enemies, led by the infamous CIA operative Jimmy Love, to march through their lines without opposition.

The Khmu came streaming up the Xam River Valley and attacked us without warning, just when we were celebrating our victory. Since we had relied on our Hani allies, we had a light defensive perimeter. It was manned by Pathet Lao troops, who were nowhere near as battle-ready as the NVA, so the Khmu irregulars overran it in a matter of minutes.

The first thing I knew about it was when someone started screaming outside the cave, "The Khmu are here! The Khmu are here!" Then Chief Surgeon Dong shouted, "Abandon the cave now; run for the trucks; leave everyone except ambulatory patients!"

So, Lae and I were obliged to meet the eyes of our brave and beautiful patient, Alana Racha, and confess to her that we were leaving her behind. To soften the blow, we told her that the Americans rarely killed Pathet Lao prisoners. Instead, they tried to convert them to their cause. But we were blowing wind, and Alana knew it. So, when I swept the hair from her lovely dark brow the last time, and Lae wiped the tears from her eyes with the edge of her coverlet, we broke down as well.

Alana grabbed our hands hard in hers as we turned to go and gazed up at us with bright, feverish eyes. "You are Buddhists. So, you know."

"Know what?"

"You will have to pay someday."

"Pay for what?"

"For leaving me like this!"

We tore our hands from her hot, sweaty grip and ran for the mouth of the cave.

"I swear you will both come back as insects," she screamed after us. "Earthworms! Green mold under a rock!"

We made it to our transport area despite intense machinegun

fire and I managed to load all my ambulatory patients including Nguyen on the first truck to leave. Lae followed with the second.

Pursued by rocket and mortar blasts, my Vietnamese driver geared off down the camouflaged roadway as fast as his belching, smoking Chinese truck would go. Several times, we were bracketed by mortar and rocket fire, and we missed getting pulverized by a hairsbreadth.

Yet I was mostly oblivious to the danger, I recall. I had what the Americans called "the thousand-yard stare."

I neglected Nguyen, who kept leering at me, gesturing that he wanted me to re-bandage the scratch on his inner thigh and maybe tickle the stiff that had risen in his pants as well.

Instead, I replayed young Alana Racha's final words in my mind again and again, especially the "green mold under a rock" part.

Therefore, as we reached Vieng Xai and looked back down the road, I felt paralyzed by fear, but not particularly astonished, when it appeared empty of traffic.

Later in the day, as more of our troops straggled in on foot, I learned that the American bandits had targeted Lae's truck with a 60-millimeter mortar shell, despite its large and clearly marked red crosses, and blew it into tiny pieces.

In the days that followed, everyone in the medical unit kept asking, "Why did the Hani betray us?"

Some of my colleagues believed that the Hani had little choice in the matter. Their NVA advisors were few, and the Khmu were many.

Commissar Junior Grade Nguyen Ly said, "They betrayed us out of simple greed. They were offered opium and Yankee dollars and could not resist the temptation."

As for myself, I did not really care why the Hani betrayed us. I heaped all the blame on one person, Mr. Jimmy Love, the murderer of my dearest friend.

While it was true that we had destroyed the radar station on Phou Phiaton, we had overestimated the effects of our victory. The Americans simply increased the number of their spy plane missions, set about constructing a new radar station on another karst, and soon they were bombarding us again, with renewed ferocity.

Anyone who has endured a B-52 attack will tell you that it is like the end of the world. Even when it is a thousand meters off down the valley. Even when you are in a cave dug into the mountain. I shall never forget the feeling. First, there is this blinding light. Then a sound like a meteor crashing to earth from outer space. You are struck blind. Your eardrums burst. The earth rumbles like no earthquake you have ever known and shakes you right off your feet. The rock walls of the cave tremble and seem about to dissolve into dust. Stalactites fall like spears from the ceiling.

Despite my nightmares of being buried alive under a mountain of rock, and despite my profound sorrow over the death of my best friend Lae, I remained on duty in the headquarters hospital at Vieng Xai Cave.

Rebuffing the daily advances of our zealous Commissar Junior Grade on grounds of "non-fraternization," I quickly rose in the medical hierarchy to combat surgeon. I had advanced from toilet cleaner to the top of the heap in a matter of only five months.

This sounds like an extraordinarily rapid advancement, and there were whispers among the staff that I owed it to the fact that I was the commander's niece, but it was not the case. Due to unremitting aerial bombardment, and intermittent attacks by American led indigenous forces, the attrition rate among our soldiers and staff was so high that I am confident that I would have made Pathet Lao Surgeon General before the war ended.

But that was not in the cards.

Late one night, my uncle summoned me to his earthen cubbyhole command post in the deepest recesses of the cave. Favoring me with one of his cinematic smiles, he enquired of my health and praised my success as a front-line medic. Then he made it a point to commend me on my successful resistance to the blandishments of my ex-lover.

"How do you know about that, Uncle Vong?"

He laughed. "Come on, Nittaya. Nothing in the cave gets past me. Surely you knew that."

"No, I did not, but I do now."

"Anyway, I hope you have not become discouraged by our setback at Phou Phiaton. I mean, after all, we did what we set out to do. We just did not anticipate the cost."

"Non, mon oncle, je ne suis pas découragé."

"Brave words for a young girl, but I . . ."

"Merci," I said before he could finish. "I want you to know that I am in this with you to the end, Uncle Vong. Whatever it takes."

"I believe you. And I can assure you that things will again turn in our favor."

"This is your own personal opinion?"

"Yes."

"Nothing to do with official Party dogma?"

"Absolutely not!" he said, banging the table to impress me with his sincerity. "I anticipate a total victory within a year or two. American public opinion has turned against the war. They have already pulled more than half their troops out of Vietnam and their ARVN allies are collapsing from within."

"This is a fact?"

"You can read it in any newspaper in the Western world."

"Unfortunately, my subscription to *Le Monde* has run out," I said, stifling a grin. "And we do not get many newspapers up here, in any case, other than Party organs."

"Well, let me offer you some more concrete evidence then. The Americans might have turned our Hani allies against us, but some of the other tribes have sniffed the way the wind is blowing. And they have started defecting to us. There is a Mung tribal leader named Kham, for instance. He has just come over to us with an entire battalion. Five hundred well-disciplined, American-trained fighters."

"Voilà de bonnes nouvelles!"

"Yes, it is good news. Which brings me to my next point. I have an assignment for you, *ma chere.*"

"A medical assignment?"

"Not really. Or only in part. It has to do with gathering intelligence for our new ally, Kham."

"What kind of intelligence?"

"From the other side."

"The other side of what?"

"From our enemies."

"You mean to say I am going to be some kind of Mata Hari?"

"If you want to put it that way. But I am sure you will achieve far better results."

"What makes you think I shall be any good at it?"

"Mais dit donc, Nittaya! Who could be better than you? You, a French-educated doctor of medicine from an old and respected family of staunchly conservative Royalists."

"Whatever you say, *mon oncle.* I only hope I can repay your faith in me."

"I have no doubt that you can. But I want you to be careful. Your mother would never forgive me if anything happened to you."

I grinned and winked at him.

"Dear Uncle, what place in the entire world could be more dangerous than where we sit right now?"

"Yes, you may have something there. And maybe there is an added plus as well."

"And what is that?"

"You can lose that silly ex-boyfriend of yours!" he said, and we laughed long and loud together.

Forgetting ourselves, pounding the desk in glee, not caring about eavesdroppers, we became father and daughter at last.

CHAPTER EIGHTEEN

The Poppy Patch

Thirty-nine hours after my departure from Vieng Xai, I reached Vientiane's Central Bus Station and took a *tuk-tuk* home to the Rue du Puits.

In our capital city, the rich and poor often live cheek by jowl, and that was the case with my family.

We had a rambling, three-story, French Colonial *grande maison* surrounded by a high, glass-encrusted wall that encompassed a manicured garden of enormous shade trees, grassy nooks and meandering walks. We even had a swimming pool, a summerhouse and a rose arbor.

Yet, when my driver left me off at 66 Rue du Puits, I had to push through a throng of ragged, child beggars, ratty pedestrians and pushcart vendors loudly hawking everything from hot pork to barbecued fish to cold *Bière Lao*.

A tourist might have found the tangle and clutter colorful and amusing, but my long road down from Kham Muan Province had been even rougher than the first time I went. I had slept not at all, and I was two days into my period. I felt dirty and physically exhausted. All I dreamed of was a nice, hot shower and twelve hours of sleep, so I must say I was a bit brusque and un-socialist in pushing through our teeming neighbors and up to our front gate. Attempting a smile, I thrust a few kip into the dirty outstretched hands of two especially persistent street urchins, then shouted at our big turbaned gatekeeper, Rajpal, to let me in.

Bowing, smiling in welcome, speaking to me in Hindi-accented English, he welcomed me home, grabbed the rucksack off my shoulder, and accompanied me across the garden to the veranda.

"Mam'zelle is home!" he shouted at the top of his lungs, battering at our vast mahogany front door as if this were the most glorious of occasions. "Mam'zelle is home!"

Our plump parlor maid, Gladi, took her time opening the door, and she was not her usual garrulous self when she greeted me.

"And how is my father?" I asked, as custom demanded, after I had acknowledged her *wai*.

"He is out of town," she said, her face impassive. "Another of his medical conferences."

"*Et Maman?*"

"Your mother is not well."

"*Qu'est-ce qu'il y a?*"

"As soon as she read the headlines in this morning's paper, she called the hospital to cancel all her appointments and took to her bed."

"What do the headlines say?"

She led me into the foyer and handed me a copy of *Le Renovateur.*

"Here, read it for yourself, *mam'zelle.*"

I read it, but it was a while before I could assimilate it.

UNE BOMBE ÉNORME
DÉTRUIT UNE GROTTE DE SIÈGE PATHET LAO
AUCUN SURVIVANTS APPARENTES
SE RÉJOUIT DU GOVERNEMENT LAOTIAN
ET L'AMBASSADE AMÉRICAINE

BUNKER BUSTER BOMB OBLITERATES
PATHET LAO HEADQUARTERS CAVE
NO APPARENT SURVIVORS
LAOTIAN GOVERNMENT
AND AMERICAN EMBASSY REJOICE

It was a good while before I could accept the evidence of my own eyes and absorb its meaning. Whether this was due to fatigue or a simple refusal to confront reality, I do not know.

When it finally sank in, my first reaction was a profound sigh of relief, because I had exited that cave only fifteen hours before the American air bandits blew it to hell.

Then a moment later, I felt the deepest shame and remorse. Here I was reveling in my own miraculous survival when my cherished Uncle Vong, my ex-fiancé Nguyen, whom I had once dearly loved, and all my comrades had just been vaporized. When that struck me, I collapsed and fell into a fit of weeping that went on until Gladi grabbed me by the arm, lifted me up off the floor, and walked me into the bathroom.

"Refresh yourself, *mam'zelle*. I shall go to your mother and tell her you are here and well."

Lying naked on the shower floor in the fetal position, pelted with water so hot that each drop seemed to burn a hole in my skin, dripping warm menstrual blood down the drain, I felt my sentiments of guilt (I had wished Nguyen dead a couple of times!) and sadness transmogrify into something far more potent.

If I had ever had any doubts before as to my role as a double agent, they were gone now.

Forty minutes later, all showered, shampooed and turned out in a long nightgown that Gladi had found, I finally went up the stairs to my mother's room.

Though Gladi had told her I was home, and thus very much alive, she cried out in shock when she saw me, as if she had seen a ghost.

I sat down beside her on the bed and wrapped my arms round her thin, little body, reassuring her with my freshly bathed scent that I was one hundred percent flesh and blood. I smiled into her slit-like Chinese eyes, her yellow moon face. I shook my head at her, touched her nose with my finger, and eventually got her to laugh through her tears.

"I thought I had sent you to die there with Vong," she said, and ran her hands through my damp, heavy hair.

"Thank Buddha that *Papá* is not here now, watching us cry over his black sheep brother."

"Oh, he might surprise you."

"And how is that?"

"You may find that he mourns Vong, in his own way."

"I sincerely doubt it," I said. It was important to maintain my father as a villain in my mind. It would help me to do all I had to do. "In his heart he knows . . ."

"What?"

"That what everyone suspects about you and Uncle Vong is my . . ."

She put a finger to my lips.

"No, I have a right to know."

"Vong never told you?"

"Never. But now that he is gone . . . You do not have to go into details, *Maman*. Just a straight yes or no will do."

My mother tried then. I could see the effort in her eyes, but she could not bring herself to confess it. Just as she could neither accept nor admit what had gone on between my father and me when I was a little girl.

"I shall take your silence as a yes," I said.

When my father came home, he mentioned nothing about his brother's death. Yet, he did attend a memorial service in his honor and seemed genuinely moved. Whether it was an act or not, I could not say, but I got the feeling that he and the rest of his family were secretly relieved that the prodigal son had now been laid safely to rest.

When we returned home after the service, I asked to speak to my father in private on a matter of the greatest importance. He showed me into his study without touching me and did not offer me a seat.

He had never touched me once since I told my mother what he did to me. He had barely spoken to me, and he never failed to turn down his thin little mouth in a frown when he saw me, as if he could barely tolerate my iniquitous presence.

I wondered then—as I had often wondered—what he told his sour-faced, effeminate confessor, Père d'Artois, about our unnatural liaison. I felt a nasty little suspicion that he had portrayed me, his eleven-year-old daughter, as the evil one, the temptress, the abuser of a sacred trust.

"Mon père," I said in the formal French he preferred, while standing before his desk like a supplicant. "I must tell you that I have quit my medical internship in Bangkok."

"And why, may I ask?" he said, raising his chin and narrowing his eyes at me, which was his closest approximation to an emotion.

"Because I felt my country needed me in the fight against communism," I said, and when he eased the frown a bit and sat back in his desk chair, I took it as a sign of approval. "So, I was wondering, *mon père,"* could you ask your old friend, Monsieur Love, if he needs a qualified medical professional at one of his bases?"

"I will think it over," he said, without altering his expression, which was about as close to an affirmation as he was capable.

Then without another word, he motioned me out of the room.

"Why in Buddha's name did he swallow my story so easily?" I wondered as I went out the door and up the stairs.

Alone in my bedroom, I thought it over for a while and came to the revolting conclusion that on some level my father might not object too much to putting me in danger. A devout Catholic who attended daily Mass, he surely must have felt my presence as a constant living reminder of his own depraved and sinful nature.

A fortnight later, Jimmy came to dinner, and despite my animosity toward him, we hit it off immediately. I mean genuinely so. If we had not been fighting on opposite sides, if I had not detested him for ending my dear friend Lae's young life at Phou Phiaton, I might have liked him a lot.

He was funny and over-the-top. He was full of bombast but allayed it with a kind of humorous self-deprecation. He was a marvelous storyteller and had an infectious laugh. Oddly enough, he and Vong had a lot in common. They were both great and charismatic leaders. They were both foolishly brave. They were both devoted to their soldiers and their families. They were both womanizers, and they both had a great sense of humor.

Their biggest difference was in how they perceived their missions. Jimmy felt riddled with self-doubts, uncertain about his mission in Laos, and feared death in battle. Vong was utterly fearless and had no doubts of any kind. They were both giants. Of the two, though, I would say that Vong was the greater. His was the bigger soul.

A few days after Jimmy's visit to my home, I flew up to the Patch on an Air America "Twin-Pak." Jimmy welcomed me at the Landing Zone like a long-lost niece and showed me round the firebase in person.

When we reached my aid station and clinic, I found that Jimmy had gone out of his way to equip it with all the modern medical marvels of the US Army, and I was much impressed.

Afterwards, he invited me to dinner in his private dining room, introduced me to his all-purpose maid, Poo-Ying, who was small and pretty and looked about sixteen years old.

She served us a delicious meal of papaya salad and a spicy mixture of marinated river fish with herbs and green vegetables and then sat down to eat alongside us.

The three of us got quite tipsy on Jimmy's wine, and we laughed and joked together half the night. When he suggested that it might be fun if we three spent the rest of the night in his bed, I hesitated for a long time, as if battling with my better instincts. Then, after I had teased him almost past endurance, I smiled, shook my head, waggled my finger at him and said, "Yes, if we don't make it a habit, Jimmy." It was worth the sacrifice, I told myself, because it might prove productive from an intelligence point of view.

Although Jimmy's drunken, wheezing fumblings that night left me so cold and dry that I had to resort to surreptitious swipes of my own sputum, I must admit that I was aroused by the breathless voyeurism he displayed while I enjoyed the favors of his soft, sweet, teenage concubine, Poo-Ying.

From then on, I held the great Jimmy Love in the palm of my hand. Rationing our *ménage à trois* to once or twice a month, affecting a sexual conventionalism, a virtuous reluctance that was far from my real nature, I had him panting after my attentions, and I was able to charm him into unwittingly revealing all his military secrets.

With my hardest task behind me, I began to feel quite at home at the Patch. Jimmy's Khmu tribesmen, and his Thai mercenaries, I found, were just as full of flaws and virtues as any other human beings. I doctored them every day. I healed their ills and wounds, delivered their wives' babies, and cured their children of yellow flux and whooping cough. I trained some of them to be combat medics and accepted their heartfelt thanks. I laughed with them in relief when things went well. I cried with them when things went badly. Therefore, I could not help but develop a rapport with them.

I am a doctor, after all. It goes with the territory. It came to the point where I sometimes wondered whether I was making myself feel this way to perpetrate my fraud upon them, or whether my compassion was genuine.

In the end, I could not tell the difference anymore and gave up trying. I found it so hard to maintain my feeling of vengeful wrath against these very ordinary human beings that I wondered how all the great spies of the past had resisted such notions.

The same went for Jimmy. The more I got to know him, the more I worked to cure his viruses, diarrhea, chronic indigestion, high blood pressure, arthritis and gout, the more I tolerated his sexual pawing, and his flaws of self-love, mawkishness, and overdrinking.

It probably had to do with the fact that he genuinely liked me as a person, not simply as a sex object. The only problem we ever had was one time when I talked about my dedication to gender equality.

"Hey, don't get me wrong, *Bubeleh*," he said, and I could tell that he was only half-joking. "I love women, you know? As long as they know their place."

Yet in time, I even trained myself to ignore his casual male chauvinism.

In Kurt Dietrich's case, I was in no danger of complacency. When I first arrived at the Patch, I strove to gain his friendship, as I did everyone else's. After all, what is the role of the Mata Hari, if not to ingratiate herself with the enemy? And for a time, it appeared that Kurt and I might have something in common that I could work with.

He tried hard to conceal his bi-sexual predilections, especially from Jimmy, but one could not really hide anything in the closed world of the Patch. Several of my Khmu patients had mentioned his partiality for "boy-girl-boy love" (which they heartily approved of), so when I got a whiff of this, I let it drop that when I lived in Paris, I used to spend a lot of time at a notorious bisexual hangout on the Left Bank called Chez Bibi.

Kurt appeared to respond favorably to my comment, and soon we were on the road to a friendly relationship. It helped that we were the only *Francophones* at the Patch, and that we both had a genuine interest in the great French poets and writers. We shared the few books we had brought along, and for a time we even held "literary nights" in my dispensary, during which we discussed the *auteurs postmodernes* Roland Barthes and Jacques Derrida and the *Écriture féminine* of Hélène Cixous and Luce Irigaray.

Everything seemed to be going fine, and I was gleaning a decent amount of enemy intelligence from him, when we had a falling out. It was my fault. The first rule of spy-craft is to agree with everything your mark has to say, especially when it has to do with anything political.

I knew that Kurt was a member of the far-right *Front National* and held some reactionary opinions. However, I drank too much Cointreau one night and got so wound up in a literary dispute with him—he called the right-wing surrealist Gérard de Sède's

1967 novel *L'Or de Rennes* "a great work of art" and I called it "a pile of fascist buffalo dung"—that he stomped out of my clinic in a huff.

Then two nights later, he came in complaining of a "head cold." I gave him some aspirin and he was about to leave when suddenly he threw me down on my operating table, pinned my arms, dove at my neck with teeth bared and sucked at my skin like a vampire while thrusting at my lower body through his fatigue pants. He ejaculated in a flash and did not actually penetrate my body, but he left me lying there with such a huge, ugly, red, and purple love-bite that I had to cover it with a scarf for a week.

"This is to remember me by," he said, as he headed out the door.

I briefly considered telling Jimmy what he had done, but I decided against it. "Why roil these rich fishing waters?"

I assumed Kurt might feel grateful to me for keeping his secret, but such was not the case. He did everything he could to make my life difficult.

The only positive aspect of the experience was that it forced me to admit something I had been hiding from myself for a long time.

You see, Kurt was not the only one who had achieved an orgasm that night.

I was not happy to acknowledge this to myself. Yet I was able to ease the shame, guilt, and humiliation I felt with the notion that all the time I was working at the Patch, developing such new "relationships," I was secretly operating under the orders of the opposition.

Impatiently, therefore, I waited for my secret Pathet Lao envoy to manifest his or her existence.

Then one night, Jimmy invited Xuě Xiāo, the old Chinese lady from Tavay, to cook for one of his chow-chow feasts. The next morning as she was preparing to return to the village, she caught me out by the women's latrine. She grabbed my arm, checked to see that no one was listening, and pulled me up close to whisper in my ear.

"Poo-Ying is the one," she said, in a far less peasant accent than the one she affected in Jimmy's outside kitchen. "Tell her everything you find out, and she will deliver it to me. And one more thing. If your knife happens to slip when you are operating on one of these Running Dogs, I am sure that Buddha will forgive a small lapse in your Hippocratic Oath."

After that, every time I had a tidbit of intelligence, I managed to find a way to apprise Poo-Ying of it. She passed it on to old Xuě Xiāo who waltzed down the mountain, delivered it to the Pathet Lao agent in Thavay, who happened to be her cousin, and in no time, it was in Papa Lao's hands. Yet, I always felt a tiny bit *coupable* for betraying my newfound friends, and I certainly did not intend to renounce my Hippocratic Oath.

One great thing about our underground telegraph system was that I was able to enquire through covert channels as to whether Uncle Vong and Nguyen had, by some miracle, survived the bunker buster attack on the headquarters cave in Vieng Xai, and I was overjoyed to finally learn that press reports of casualties had been exaggerated.

There had been more than a dozen survivors, including Uncle Vong and Nguyen. Although they had both been grievously wounded, they were now hospitalized in Hanoi and their doctors predicted at least partial recoveries. I must confess that I was far more concerned about my uncle's recovery, and I recall wishing that whatever wound Nguyen had incurred would teach him some humility.

Up until Xuĕ Xiāo informed me of Poo-Ying's secret role in Jimmy's household, I had underestimated the girl. Like everyone else at the Patch, I took her for granted. She was just Jimmy's number one mistress, his pretty little bit of fluff, and my occasional sexual plaything, and that was it.

Yet, after I received the news that she was a Mata Hari like me, I began to observe her with a more perceptive eye.

She had bobbed, black hair, a round, pretty face, with a broad nose and narrow eyes that crinkled up when she laughed. She seemed a happy, thoughtless, flirtatious girl, and giggled a lot over nothing much. She was not tall, with a tiny waist, plump rounded hips, perky breasts, and nipples that neither Jimmy nor I could get enough of. Her skin was dark, and her bright toothy grin seemed all the whiter by contrast.

The Khmu, given their suspicion of outlanders, usually kept Lowland Laos at arm's distance. A testimony to the girl's charm was the fact that they embraced her as one of their own, just as they had done with me.

Although I thought it unlikely that we had much in common, other than a sensual pleasure in each other's bodies, I made it a point to establish a closer relationship with Poo-Ying, whose real name, I found, was Kaew Soong. The more I got to know her, the more interesting she became, and soon I reached a point where I no longer had to affect a friendly attitude toward her.

What I liked most about her was what she had hidden about herself. She pretended to be a simple country girl, with little or no learning, and no one at the Patch knew any different, when in fact she had been educated at a Catholic girl's school in Muang Khang, in the south of Laos near the Cambodian border. She spoke French, Cambodian, and classical Lao. Her one deficiency was in English. If it had not been for that, she said, the Pathet Lao probably never would have felt the need to call me in.

Like me, Poo-Ying had a love for our Laotian people, felt a great sympathy for their struggles, and had come to the revolution in fits and starts. Both her parents were schoolteachers, communists, and clandestine members of the Pathet Lao. Yet she had little interest in joining the Party until after high school, when she fell in love with a handsome, young, Khmer Rouge soldier named Chan Thou who spent months recovering from a serious war wound in her family home.

It is a familiar story, I know, but it is the truth, and from what I have learned since from other female revolutionaries, it is all too common.

Anyway, Chan Thou found it much easier than her parents to inspire her with revolutionary fervor. At his urging, she began running errands for the Pathet Lao and eavesdropping on conversations in cafes frequented by Royalist government officers. After establishing a proven record of success, the Party accepted her as a member. When her beloved went back to fight in Cambodia, she accepted an important mission from the Pathet Lao.

Because of her beauty, and what her Party boss called "an erotic appeal that oozes from your pores without discernible effort, like the scent of mimosa in the rain," she was elected as the one, perfect, young woman to worm herself into the good graces of the infamous Jimmy Love.

Her parents were such devoted communists that they gave their blessing to the mission even though they were fully aware of exactly what it would entail, and both the Pathet Lao and her parents were immensely pleased at her success.

As for her beloved Chan Thou, he died in battle not long after he returned to Cambodia. He died a virgin. He'd had too much respect for her parents to do anything more in their home than steal an occasional kiss.

Poo-Ying lost her virginity to Jimmy Love.

As the two of us became better acquainted, we found ourselves revealing more and more, until we reached a point where we disclosed our most intimate secrets, our hopes and dreams, our doubts, and fears. We became such good friends that I believed Buddha had sent her to me as a gift to replace my dear departed, Lae Martel.

Oddly enough, our new relationship made us less interested in having sex with each other, and eventually we stopped it altogether, much to Jimmy's chagrin. In explanation, we told him that such things seemed frivolous and unseemly, given our sincere bond of friendship.

Poo-Ying and I discovered something new that we had in common almost every day. For instance, we both claimed to be inspired by revolutionary fervor. Yet in truth, neither of us was as hard-core as our co-conspirator, Xuě Xiāo, and we admitted to each other that the longer we spent working at the Patch, the more torn we were between duty and sentiment.

The revolution was an ideal that we believed in, but our work at the firebase was our daily reality. Although we shared an aversion for most of the *farangs* at the Patch, we found it difficult to dislike the good-natured Khmus and Thais, all of whom we knew to be terribly vulnerable in one way or another.

The heart and root of our guilty feelings, of course, was that we would soon be responsible for placing them in mortal danger.

While we had a true and abiding desire to rid our country of its foreign invaders and change its system of government for good, we sometimes felt seduced by the notion that it might not be worth all the innocent lives it cost. If Jimmy discovered we were spies, we half-believed that his punishment would be just, even though he routinely decapitated traitors and stuck their heads up on poles for the tribesmen to pelt with stones.

"Speaking of which," Poo-Ying said to me once when we were walking the perimeter of the Patch, taking our daily "constitutional" (which was in reality a reconnaissance of current defensive emplacements), "if something does go wrong up here, may the Lord Buddha forfend, and you have to run for your life, let me give you some advice, Nittaya. First, if you find yourself in the command post, there's a secret emergency exit tunnel. Jimmy had it dug out a few years back. Nobody here remembers it, but he told me about it, 'in case we're ever overrun.' So, anyway, let's say you get past the perimeter defenses in one piece. Never take the main eastern trail down to the village and the Et River. They'll catch you and lop off your head before you get halfway down."

"So, what shall I do, attach myself to a *phi* and fly away in the wind?"

"Actually, you may not have to call upon your mystic powers, Nittaya. There's a secret trail down the side of the cliff to the west. It's a rough, deer trail, broken by landslides in places, and it goes down to the Sikhav River, which has lots of really bad rapids. But it's navigable by raft, and there's supposed to be an abandoned village at the halfway point where you might be able to rest up if necessary. I looked the Sikhav River up on the map, and the good thing is that it flows into the Sidoa River, which swings round to the north and west and eventually flows into the Mekong River near Luang Prabang."

"Who told you about all this?"

"Xuě Xiāo and Loa Nyindi."

"Okay, I can see where Xuě Xiāo might know something about all this. But the Laughing Monk?"

"Actually, he's the one who told me about the secret trail."

"How did he know about it?"

"He said an old woodcutter told him."

"And how did he know you might want to run?"

"I asked him, and he said, in that weird *Metta Sutta* voice he uses, *"You are already gone."*

"You think he is on our side?"

"I don't think he's on any side."

"How do you figure that?"

"'There is only one side,' he said, *'the side of life.'"*

"He is not going to tell Jimmy?"

"No."

"Why not?"

"It's only a feeling I have."

"A feeling is not enough."

"In this case, I think it is. I looked into his eyes and I said to myself, 'I would trust this Laughing Monk with my life.'"

"We might have to, someday."

"So have a little faith, Nittaya."

"Right. If only faith were enough."

"I even asked him how to get past the trip flares and detonators round the perimeter. And you know what he said? *When the student is ready, the teacher will appear.*'"

"What is that supposed to mean?"

"I think it means something like, 'Figure it out for yourself.'"

"True words of wisdom. And have you figured it out yet?"

"Yes, with Buddha's help, I think I may have. The trip wires and explosive humps on the western side are obvious in the light of day. We can map them out on our daily walks round the perimeter. Just in case we miss any, we can make it a point to stop at Bunker 5 every day. You know . . . the bunker just above the secret deer trail? We can get to know the Thai mercenaries there. Use our feminine wiles. Win them over with a charm offensive. Milk them of information. It'll probably only take us a few visits before we discover a way through. The hard part will be sneaking out at night and marking the way."

"How are we going to do that?"

"With colored pebbles and little scuffs in the dirt that only we can recognize."

"Fine, I can see a way we could do that. One of us plays 'Lonely Lady' and chats up the night shift in Bunker 5 while the other sneaks out to mark the trail."

"Sounds good. The only problem is we might have to do more than 'chat them up' to keep them occupied."

"I am not so sure of that. They think of us as 'Jimmy's girls.' They will probably be afraid of what he might do to them if he ever catches them in the act."

"I hope you're right. I think I'd rather take my chances out there in the mine field than with three, horny, unwashed Thais on the dirt floor of a bunker."

"Better death than dishonor, *na?*"

"Something like that."

"I feel much the same way."

"So, what're we going to do, flip for it?"

"No, I will take the Thais, if you take the mine field."

Poo-Ying rolled her eyes and laughed.

"So, the mine field is the lesser of two evils, *na?* As my superior, and for the good of the cause, you are willing to . . ."

"If you want to put it that way."

As it happened, though, neither of us had to make the ultimate sacrifice. Poo-Ying marked a way through the minefield without setting one off, and I handled the Thai soldiers without compromising my virtue. This is not to say that either of our tasks was trouble-free. Poo-Ying came within a centimeter of blowing a trip flare, she said, and there were moments in Bunker 5 that I prefer not to recall.

Later, when we had an opportunity to speak of our adventures, we agreed that our previous supposition had been correct. Poo-Ying's ordeal had probably been less disagreeable than mine had been. It was not that my soldiers were any worse than other randy, young, military men. It was the idea that one day I might be compelled to enter Bunker 5, under the guise of friendship, laughing and joking with them as before, and murder them.

CHAPTER NINETEEN

Love Like No Other

Then on my second R & R to Nakhon Phanom I met the inimitable Agent Zachary Ogle, and he could not have caught me at a better time.

At least from his point of view.

From mine it could not have been worse.

Because of my divided loyalties, and the pain and guilt I was suffering, I felt very vulnerable when he arrived at the Queen's Park Hotel. To make things worse, I felt an irresistible attraction to him, an attraction that flew in the face of all my self-professed hatred of everything American. It went beyond the fact that he was charming, ruggedly handsome, had a marvelous body in a bathing suit and wore the kind of bristly military mustache that I liked . . . the kind that scratched . . . just a little.

Part of it might have been a result of my dual personality. While on the one hand I have always been a devoted Buddhist and respected tradition, on the other I have also had a lifelong predisposition for rebellion, for breaking the most hallowed taboos. Like when I was in my third year at the *Lycée* and ran away from home for three days, refusing to divulge to my irate parents where I had been, what I had done, and with whom.

I admit a large share of it was about sex ... the juicy, honeysweet way this big, hairy, grunting American invader turned me to hot, melted butter with no more than a glance.

Nevertheless, and despite the above, the more I came to know Zack, the more he appealed to me as a *person*. If we had not been potential lovers, I told myself, if we had not been mortal enemies, we might have been the best of friends. It is no more difficult to explain than to say it was fun being with each other. We got along quite naturally, right from the start, and without any effort, despite all our many differences.

What I liked most about Zack I think was the fact that besides being a rather poetic soul under all his military bluster, he was a good listener. It was a rare trait among the male sex, I had found. Most men were too wound up in their own desires to be truly concerned with what a woman had to say about herself and her perceptions. In all my life, only my Uncle Vong, Zack, and a couple of gay friends at university had displayed an interest in me that went beyond the obvious.

I remember that Zack fell asleep for a few minutes in the sun, in his lounge chair by the hotel swimming pool. Although I felt sleepy myself, I stayed awake to stare at him as he gently snored. I could not stop looking. There was something in his expression, something that ameliorated the macho effects of his soldier's mustache, his jutting action-hero jaw and cheekbones, his muscular physique. There was a vulnerable quality in his sensitive, full-lipped mouth, in those long, dark lashes hiding those swirly, blue-grey eyes, which spoke of childhood anguish. This is what instantly captured my attention and affection.

Later, he would confess to me that I was not alone, that all the girls he had known felt the same way. I suppose that should have put me off, but it did not in the least. It was the mother in me, I suppose, the mother that all of us pitiable female creatures carry within in us from birth until death. It was also a feeling of rapport, of shared experience, I think, because despite my far more privileged upbringing, I had had my own share of childhood *angoisse*.

Swimming and lounging with him at the hotel pool, I told myself that I was seducing him to use him at some time in the future to further the revolution, but I was fooling myself. One of the first rules of spy-craft is to keep as close to your own personality as possible. Yet, I strove to convince him that I was nothing more than a flirt, a floozy with hot pants. I could not let him get a glimpse of the real me, I thought, because that would be tantamount to giving myself to him. Which would make me a double agent even unto myself.

I therefore held him at bay more out of guilt than policy, during those weeks up at the Patch. The rules of spy-craft might dictate that I tease and tantalize him into submission, into sexual slavery, and use him so, but I simply could not allow myself to stay anywhere near him for long.

I felt so proud of myself when I talked Jimmy into prepping us for the mission at Gneu Mat. I had managed to elicit valuable intelligence, which I swiftly sent off to Papa Lao via Xuě Xiǎo's cousin. Yet as soon as I did, I felt a thunderbolt might strike me dead for my treachery.

When it came time to go off to battle, I sought to accompany the fighters as chief medic not because I was brave and motivated, as Jimmy and everyone else believed. I went for another reason entirely. I felt that by exposing myself to danger I might mitigate the effects of my deception.

If I were to die, it would be a just reward for my perfidy. Of course, to be honest, I hedged my bets by painting enormous red crosses on all my equipment and forewarning the opposite side to avoid firing on my person.

Then at the terrible Battle of Gneu Mat, and later at the Royal Thai Army hospital in Nakhon Phanom, I was able to view at first-hand what I had wrought. Asking myself what possible political objective could be worth all that pain, death, and destruction, I felt something far more serious than my previous shame and remorse. It was more potent even than self-loathing. It was *le dégoût de soi*, and if it continued, I knew, it would lead to my mental and emotional deterioration and collapse.

This was my state of mind when Zack and I came together again at the hospital and became lovers at last.

I forget how many times we had sex, but each time was beautiful in some new way. And with each, I came to desire him more. Unlike Nguyen, Zack gave himself completely to me when we made love. He did not withdraw within his own pleasure. He looked deeply into my soul and adored what he saw there. Even if his perceptions were misguided, I loved him even more for trying.

The time I remember best now, many years later, happened in the bright light of morning.

It was time to leave the little rooftop hotel room where we had spent our first night together and head back to the hospital.

I rose off our sleeping mat, swept up the mosquito net, and padded naked across the room toward my dress and underthings which I had let fall to the floor the night before.

I knew my lover was watching me, so I paused to yawn sleepily and stretch—a carefully calculated stretch that put me up on my toes with my arms raised wide and my hair flung back.

Hearing him start to breathe a little harder, I yawned again. I shook my head from side to side. I let my arms fall and bent over, taking my time to retrieve my things from the floor. I snatched my panties up first, delicately between thumb and forefinger. Very slowly, first one foot then the other, wriggling my hips and bottom, I slid them on. Next came the minidress, a flimsy white cotton thing, perfect for the tropics. I raised it up, slid it over my head, and wriggled again to help it fall. Then I glided barefoot to our sleeping mat, spun around on one foot, shook my shoulders, and said, "Zack, can you zip me up?"

Perhaps needless to say, he did not do as I had asked. Instead, he rose behind me, jerked the dress off my head, flung it across the room, and slid my panties down. Smoldering at his touch, I felt myself wetting, widening. I bent over before him and thought he would enter me then, but he did not.

Instead, he went down on his knees, spread my cheeks and labia to warm his fingers there, setting me to tingling all round my underbody, back to front. Then he chose to pause for an instant before doing what I needed him to do. He was always teasing me like that, holding fire until I begged for it. I hated it. I loved it.

"Now, please, now!" I cried, and he thrust his tongue inside me from behind, lapping at me until I was arching backward, rubbing myself in his face, moaning in a frenzy of desire.

Just when I thought I could take no more, he jumped up, spun me around and kissed me. I tasted me in his saliva, and the tingling sensation now ran all the way up to my breasts and nipples.

Then he threw me down on the mat, shoved my legs over my head, and drove inside me.

He filled me up. He pierced me to the marrow. He melted me down. He made me all new and whole.

"Oh . . . how . . . I . . . *love* you, Zack! I cried when we came, and for long seconds I shuddered uncontrollably, as if an electric impulse were running through me. I had never felt anything like it before and feared I never would again.

Afterwards, lying in bed, ignoring the fact that we were both technically AWOL, we were silly with joy. I kissed and caressed his old wound from childhood, his fresh battle wounds—wounds that I had caused—and cooed over him like my own hurt little child.

When he got up to urinate, I followed and stood behind him. I reached round and aimed him as he spurted a great, bubbling stream into the toilet bowl. He was so big, so strong, yet sometimes so childlike and vulnerable. When he was done, I pressed myself to him from behind, fondling his mutilated scrotum, kissing the rippling muscles on his back. Then I swung round him and squatted to urinate as well. He started to leave, but I stuck a handout to stop him.

"Listen," I said. He laughed as it sizzled in the pot. He

watched while I washed myself with water in the Asian style. "I want you to see."

"But why?"

"I want to be you," I said. "I want you to be me."

Then I swung him round and walked him to the bed, where I licked him all over like a mother cat. I sniffed his dark curly hair, his big ears. He smelled as he always did, of sea brine and sage, although we were a world away from either.

I looked then far, far into his oceanic eyes, and I saw many things, some mutually exclusive. I saw tenderness, love, lust, commitment, and the perverse excitement men feel when they detect in the object of their affections a mystery, a hint that she might not be exactly who she pretends to be.

And I came within a finger's breadth of confessing the truth to you then, my love, running away and starting a happy little family with you in some normal, peaceful place, far from the sound of war.

How different our lives might have been, *na?*

CHAPTER TWENTY

Aping the Apes

On the day before we were to depart from Nakhon Phanom and fly back to the execrable reality of the Patch, Zack and I decided to go on a river excursion.

Accompanied by a group of rapt and religious middle age Buddhists from the affluent suburbs of Bangkok, we took a ferryboat ten kilometers down the Mekong and climbed to the top of the sacred hill of *Pra That Phanom*, where there was a famous shrine and an equally famous troop of tame gibbons.

I considered myself a self-confident, uninhibited, European-educated, medical professional, but on occasion, I recall, I would unaccountably revert to an extreme form of girlish, Asian diffidence. Maybe it was some residue of my staid bourgeois upbringing. Or the fact that people tended to think any Thai or Laotian girl on the arm of an American was a prostitute.

For whatever reason, when we found ourselves in a traditional or religious environment, among crowds of my fellow

Asiatiques, I sometimes became shy and self-effacing, frightened of standing out, and sensitive to the fact that I had a *farang* lover.

To add to my discomfort, I had learned over the weeks we spent together at the hospital that I was not the only one of us burdened with a dual personality. While Zack's dominant nature, I believe, was quiet, reflective, and even a bit intellectual, he could on rare occasions become a loud, obnoxious tease, a typical "asshole GI" on leave. And nothing set his belligerent side off like the coyness and timidity of a quailing, Asian Flower.

For this reason, I was horrified, but not particularly astonished, when on this our last outing together he perversely conceived a plan to bring about what I feared most, and to taunt me past enduring.

"*Mademoiselle?*" he said, as we climbed the spiraling trail toward the shrine, sweltering in the heat and humidity. "Did you know that in English a synonym for the verb 'to imitate' is the verb 'to ape?'"

"No."

"Well, the reason for this is that apes will copy whatever you do. *Tu comprends?*"

"*Tu te moques de moi, pas vrai?*" I warned in the soft, breathy, confidential tone that I reserved for his most profound cultural transgressions. "You are kidding me, *na?*"

"Not at all," he said, as we reached the hilltop, ignoring my veiled, reproachful look. "Just watch!"

Zack swaggered over to where the Thai tourists, each sporting a little sun hat, were snapping pictures in front of the shrine, and feeding peanuts to a great, bearded, male ape who seemed to be the leader of the tribe.

He approached the ape and stuck out his tongue. The ape grinned and followed suit. He thrust his thumbs into his ears and wriggled his fingers, which the ape copied to perfection. He flapped his elbows like a bird, which the ape did as well. He jumped in the air, spun around, and landed just as he was. The ape did too.

By now, all the Thai tourists were slapping their thighs in glee, snapping pictures like mad, while I was hanging back near the tree line, trying to pretend that I had never seen this *farang ting-tong*, this crazy foreigner, in my life.

As his *pièce de résistance*, Zack raised his fists, beat his chest like Tarzan, and issued the ape a noisy invitation to a boxing match. The ape put up his fists as well and beat his chest. For a moment, it looked like they might just go a round or two, Marquis of Queensberry Rules. Then suddenly the ape reverted to his animal instincts. Howling in fury, he leapt upon Zack, wrapped his claws round his throat, and started taking ferocious bites out of the silk monkey scarf he wore round his neck.

Now Zack was not laughing and joking anymore. He was screaming in terror. This of course made the Thai tourists laugh even more, and they crowded each other to get shots of this unprecedented spectacle of the *khun phiw khaw ngo*, the stupid white man, and the ape.

By this time, however, Zack was in a world of hurt, and he could not have cared less.

Spinning on heel, he tore off down the winding trail to the river like a dog with its tail on fire, with the fierce, brown gibbon, whooping in victory, hot on his ass.

Later, safe on the ferryboat, I suppose he expected me to

ignore him and pretend I had never met him before, but I astonished him—and myself as well—by smothering him with affection.

"But why, Zack, why would you ever do such a thing?" I kept marveling, as I bathed and disinfected his wounds in the ladies' rest room and bound them with material from the boat's first aid kit. "I understand nothing about you."

"For the fun of it," he replied at last in English, but it was the asshole GI still talking, trying for bravado, and not quite making it.

"You know, I think you performed this whole ape-show as a test of my love," I said. "You want to assure yourself that my devotion can withstand even your *comportement le plus vulgaire et impie.*"

When he admitted that there may have been a grain of truth in my analysis, I said, "And you know what?"

"What?"

"You somehow pulled it off, you demented bastard. Do not ask me how."

We took the ferryboat back up the Mekong to Nakhon Phanom. There were out-of-season thundershowers all the way, and tears pearled up in my eyes and curled down my cheeks like the rain on our window.

When he asked me why, I said, "Oh, Zack, we get so close, and in a lot of ways we are so similar. Like, I can be a bit of a tease as well, you know. But then I see all our differences, all the cultural baggage we carry round, and it breaks my heart. I mean, how can you possibly learn to live in my world? And how can I learn to live in yours?"

"Come on, Nittaya. The clash of cultures, our differing ways of looking at things, that's what makes us so exciting."

"Promise me, cross your heart, you will never disrespect the Lord Buddha again."

"Hey, I meant no disrespect, girl. I was just monkeying around with the apes."

"Do you not understand, you crass *farang*? Everything in the temple is sacred!"

"Even the apes?"

"Most especially the apes."

"Then I guess you're right. I haven't got the foggiest notion what you're talking about."

"See? You Americans make fun of us. You feel so superior. You come over here and try to impose your values on us, but you make no attempt to appreciate our way of thinking. We are a land of Theravada Buddhists. No matter whether we are Royalists, Neutralists or Communists, we will walk through your minefields and unexploded cluster bombs to worship at the graves of our ancestors. Can you even begin to fathom that?"

"No, I can't, my love. But you know what? I've always been a sucker for the exotic."

"So have I, Zack. But there may come a time when we will both regret it."

The next morning when I left for work, I slipped an envelope under his pillow. Inside was a pair of poems I had written in Classical Lao, on fine, Yuzen paper. I even went to the trouble of translating them into English for him.

MR. AMERICA
"I am me!" says the raindrop
as he falls upon the sea.

LADY NITTAYA
In the other room, through the wall
rodents move. . . . I'm not alone after all.

CHAPTER TWENTY-ONE

Next Lifetime

A day or two later, we flew back to the Patch, where Kurt promptly produced my sexy ex-patient, the turncoat, Alana Racha, to denounce me as a spy.

Luckily, I managed to convince boozy old Jimmy to talk to me in private. He expelled everyone except Poo-Ying from the bunker and I told him an outrageous story about being a triple agent reporting to some vague CIA nabob far above his pay grade.

"Jimmy, if you do not believe me, all you have to do is contact Reynolds," I said, when he seemed hesitant to reply. "He will confirm everything I am saying."

"Awright awready," he said, shrugging his shoulders, raising his hands. "But I can't do that yet."

"Why not?" I asked, though I knew the answer very well.

"That delegation of fact finders from the Firm, you know? The one that wanted to ream me out a new *tutkes*? They took him back to Washington. Want him to appear before the Presidential Advisory Board. Help 'em spin it right for the Senate Intelligence Committee."

"So, lock me up, Jimbo! And wait till he gets back, *na?*"

"What're you talkin' about?"

"You might feel safer that way."

"Get outta here! You're like family, *Bubeleh*."

"You trust me?" I said, my eyes welling up with tears. Even now, I cannot say whether they were crocodile or not.

"Hey, how many times? How many fuckin' times you held my life in your hands? You know? I mean, look at the bullet holes you sewed up. Right? And how 'bout that tapeworm you pulled out of me? You remember that one? How long was it, anyways?"

I wiped my eyes and laughed with relief. "Yes, I do remember, Jimmy. It was thirty centimeters long. And I thank you with all my heart. You cannot know how much I appreciate your faith in me."

He wobbled to his feet, weaving toward his sleeping mat in the corner. "Well, you can start by helping little Poo-Ying here give me a good Thai massage."

"No trouble at all," I said cheerily, heading for the physician's bag that I was never without. "First, I shall administer your nightly sleeping potion, and maybe a little something to assuage that hangover you are bound to have tomorrow. Then we rub you down with some magical Chinese skin cream I bought from Xuě Xiāo. No worries, Jimbo. Poo-Ying and me, we shall ease you right into dreamland."

And so, we did.

Once he was safely asleep, I was about to put him down as I might have done an aged family dog, but at the last instant some Hippocratic scruple, some residue of affection for the old brute, weakened my resolve.

Poo-Ying caught it, and she grabbed my arm and pulled me up close. "I don't like it either, Sister, but it's him or us, and we won't even talk about the revolution."

So, we tucked Jimmy tenderly in his rack and kissed him goodbye. We asked Buddha to ease his way, and to understand that our choice was not our own; it was thrust upon us by events beyond our control. I injected him with a lethal dose of Chlorpromazine, and he went off to live as he had always said he would . . . "in that big PX in the sky."

When Poo-Ying and I had wiped away the last of our tears, I said, "So where is that secret exit tunnel you were telling me about?"

"I'll show you," Poo-Ying said, still sniffling and blowing her nose. "We just raid Jimmy's stores and pack you up with what you need on the trail; and then . . ."

"You are not coming?"

"I'm more useful to the Party here, I think. So, slap me round a bit, draw some blood, gag me, and tie me up. Otherwise, they might suspect I'm in collusion with you."

"It will be my pleasure, Sister."

"Anything for the revolution, *na?*" she said, and we dutifully laughed at our attempt at humor.

"Now we have only one more problem to solve."

"What's that?"

"I cannot even think of leaving without talking to Zack."

"Are you mad?" she said, getting right up in my face. "Stop acting like a bourgeois bitch, with only yourself to consider. I swear, if you blow this now for that American bandit, I'll—"

"I understand where you are coming from, Poo-Ying, but you see . . . love has no country. It's a world in itself."

"You're telling *me* that, of all people?"

"Okay, I ask only one thing," I said at last. "Deliver a message to Zack."

"Right, and then he immediately assumes that I'm in league with you. They chop my head off and stick it up on a pole for the locals to throw stones at."

"No, they will not."

"Why not?"

"Remember? I am going to beat the living shit out of you, leave you bound and gagged. You can tell him I forced you to do it."

"I really shouldn't do this, you know? If our people ever found out . . ."

"Poo-Ying, I will take it with me to the grave. And I am not going to write anything down. I just want you to tell him something for me."

"What do you want to say?"

"Only four words."

"What are they?"

"'See you next lifetime.'"

"All right, if you insist."

"Why the sudden change of heart?"

"Woman to woman? It is just too romantic to resist."

So, while the rain drummed on Jimmy's bunker roof like a

gang of rutting, spider monkeys and my world of love dissolved beneath their splashing feet, I went about the dirty business of making myself scarce.

CHAPTER TWENTY-TWO

Escape

I splashed across the dark and flooded landing zone to Bunker 5. I rose out of the rain like a *phi* and peered in through one of the gun ports. My Thai soldier friends were gathered round a tiny clay lantern, engrossed in a game of cards called "Black Frog, Red Frog."

I knew all three of them quite well by now. Sergeant Jaruk was a tall, dour, married man of thirty, with a pregnant wife and two children in Chiang Mai. Corporal Chaiyos was a handsome, happy-go-lucky, twenty-five-year-old, with a fiancée in Nong Khai. Private Aka was a shy, pimply-faced teenager from Bangkok, with plans to become an electrician's apprentice when his enlistment was up.

I said nothing for a moment, and when they finally registered the arrival of their nocturnal visitor they froze, and their eyes went big and round.

"*Swasdi dek!*" I said with a playful laugh. "Hi, boys!"

When they recognized my voice and overcame their shock, they greeted me with happy, expectant smiles, as if they thought I might have brought them something special to while away their hours of duty.

Still laughing, playing the coquette, I pulled out Jimmy's suppressed Walther PPK, slipped it through the gun port and extended my arm far into the bunker to minimize the coming flashes.

Mutely begging the Laughing Monk's forgiveness for what I was about to do and commending the souls of my all-too-human enemies to Buddha, I whipped off three quick shots.

I fired at them in descending order, from sergeant to private, age to youth, as if the younger ones deserved an instant more of life. Yet in fact, it was a matter of pure practicality, for I shot the nearest ones first.

Thus, Sergeant Jaruk and Corporal Chaiyos died with smiles on their faces, but poor young Private Aka had a moment to grasp the truth, and I shall bear with me to the grave the sad, disappointed look he gave me just before he took the bullet between his eyes.

Impaired by tears, darkness, and rain, yet fearless of death in my pain, I crouched in the shadows for a moment to catch my breath and glance to the left and right.

When I detected no signs of alarm in Bunkers 4 and 6, a hundred meters off through the mist and rain to the right and left, I pulled out Jimmy's wire clippers and groped my way on hands and knees down Poo-Ying's meandering path through the sodden minefield, clipping my way through rolls of concertina wire.

At the edge of the cliff, I paused again to listen for signs of discovery, but tranquility reigned over all the span and breadth of the Patch. I thought perhaps that the entire Thai perimeter force was absorbed in games of Black Frog, Red Frog.

Then it was down the dark and crumbling switchback to the Sikhav River, with Jimmy's penlight stuck in my mouth.

Halfway to the bottom, I slipped, fell, and swung out over the abyss on a vine and the penlight fell into infinity. Swaying back again onto the trail, I regained my foothold and crouched to remove my shoes.

Thereafter I felt my way centimeter by centimeter with my toes and fingers, bridging collapsed segments of the trail by clinging to rocks, vines, and exposed roots.

I coped, as Uncle Vong had taught me, by setting aside my present cares and dangers, letting my consciousness drift toward a brighter future.

In Buddhism, there is no concept of 'sin' as an act of defiance against the authority of a personal god. There are only transgressions against the universal moral code. So, I was never afraid that Buddha would give up on me, or that he might act like some vengeful Jehovah, smite me dead, and send me to burn in hell for my sins. I knew he would lead me on my way toward light and away from darkness, even if it took a thousand lifetimes. And I never doubted for an instant that he was guiding me on my journey.

Part III

CHAPTER TWENTY-THREE

A Letter from the Past

It's a warm and bright, California afternoon in early spring. Zack Ogle, recovered from his recent, mild, heart attack, is on his way home from a nine-hole chicken run at Griffith Park.

He turns northward off busy Franklin Avenue into slow and shady Bronson Canyon Drive. Passing quaint, old, wood-frame houses, along with the occasional Spanish Revival, he guides his little, gunmetal grey Mazda 3 around a curve and into his driveway.

He climbs out from behind the wheel, slams the door behind him and takes a moment to stretch his arms and back. Sniffing the air, he smiles when he catches a whiff of vanilla-nutmeg, a sure sign that his gardenias around the side of the house are healthy and blooming.

He steps to the rear of his car and pops the trunk, hefts his golf bag out, grunting with the effort, feeling his war wounds, and carries it stiffly across his lawn and up his front steps. He sets them down beside his screen door and searches for his keys in the front pocket of his jeans, feeling the arthritis in his fingers as he does. Once he's got his keys out, he opens his screen door, unlocks the front door and sets his clubs just inside the living room.

Then he steps back out to check his mailbox, from which he pulls two letters.

One is a bill from Los Angeles Water & Power.

The other is from Luang Prabang, in the Peoples' Democratic Republic of Laos, dated January 2, 2020.

He rips it open as he walks and stops to read it on his front porch.

Dear Zack:

Yes, Katay is indeed a naughty girl. She found the hidden key to the bamboo trunk where I keep all my treasures. She opened it, pillaged it, discovered my secrets, and had the effrontery to contact you without my permission. Yet I had not the will to punish her for it. Do you know why? Because I was the kind of girl who might well have done the same at her age. And yes, my dearest one, it has been a long time. A lifetime. I am delighted to hear that you still wear that old bronze Buddha round your neck, and that you share my fond memories of our life together . . .

Leaning against the wall of his front porch with one hand

extended, trying to calm the mad thumping of his heart, which his cardiologist has called "arrhythmia," Zack finally gets his breath back.

He carries the letter into the house, steps into his kitchen, and pours himself a glass of foul-tasting Los Angeles tap water. After gulping it down Covert Ops style, as if he might not get another drink for hours, he steps into his parlor, flops on his couch, and takes up the letter again.

But old Hollywood Zack ... he doesn't get far before he chooses to lay it on his chest, cover it with his hands, shut his eyes, and allow its supposed contents to summon half-forgotten events from more than fifty years ago.

And it works!

They come zooming back into his consciousness again in living technicolor.

CHAPTER TWENTY-FOUR

Nadir

A week after the spy's escape, I was exfiled by helicopter, and a day later, flown back to a meeting with Mr. Reynolds in Nakhon Phanom.

Right until the moment I entered his office at Air-Sea Supply, I was expecting the worst—that the Kraut had sent word ahead to cast doubts on my loyalty to the cause. That he would accuse me of an unholy devotion to the Communist spy, Nittaya. That Reynolds would incarcerate my ass in some CIA torture chamber where I would be water-boarded into confessing to trumped up charges of "aiding and abetting" a foreign agent."

As it turned out, though, all my fears were for naught. Desperate for a hero, for any kind of good news to send home in this bad-news war, Reynolds praised my record and recommended me for a Distinguished Intelligence Cross.

In addition, he promoted me—over Kurt's strong objections— to Jimmy Love's position as Apple's upcountry executive officer.

To keep us "out of each other's hair," as he put it, he reassigned Kurt as commander of all Apple firebases in the far north of Laos, with headquarters in Fong Sec, and left me as the sole commander of Firebase Juliet.

After a spell in the Royal Thai Army Hospital to purge my body of parasites, most notably the hookworms I had acquired at the firebase, I was offered a month's convalescent leave. I flew to Bangkok, stayed in a five-star hotel in Sukhumvit, and got "bonged and banged" every night in Soi Cowboy. I even looked up Nittaya's maternal relatives, the Wattanas, in Thong Lo, but they would not take my calls.

When I returned to duty at the Patch, though, I found that I was not as happy as I should have been with my promotion. Even when I discovered Nittaya's personal diary in its hiding place and found that she had loved me, in her own way, just as much as I had loved her. Even when I inherited Jimmy Love's command post bunker and his hot little housemaid, Poo-Ying.

And it wasn't long before my unhappiness turned into something stronger, something that might nowadays be termed "chronic depression" or "post-traumatic stress disorder" but at the time I just thought of as "stuck in a rut."

Poo-Ying picked up on it, and one night when we were in bed, she cupped my face in her hands and whispered a plaintive Lao phrase in my ear: *"Thanmi jang seiyci nan?"*

"What makes you think I'm sad, Poo-Ying?"

"Even the monkeys in the trees know it," she said, smoothing back my hair. "To love your enemy is not bad, *Khun Zack*. The Laughing Monk says it is good."

"If only it was as simple as that."

"You know, when Nittaya ran away, she wanted me to give you a message."

"Why didn't you tell me before?"

"Afraid."

"Of what?"

"Maybe you think I am bad like her."

"What's the message?

"'See you next lifetime,' Nittaya said, and then she cried."

For a while, I took heart from the message. I consulted the Laughing Monk as to its exact meaning in Buddhist terms and found it spiritually soothing. *"Choose the right path in this lifetime,"* he said, *"and you can choose the one you want in the next."*

Yet these and other such scenarios only buoyed me so far, and I quickly reverted to my state of constant, unquenchable yearning.

"Next lifetime" just seemed too long to wait.

I took to drinking and smoking opium. I stopped shaving and bathing. One minute, I was morose and uncommunicative, the next I was talking a streak of nonsense. I struck out at my Khmu troops for no reason and wallowed in self-pity. I couldn't get it up anymore with Poo-Ying. I even turned down the advances of sexy Sergeant Alana Racha, when she came through on R & R, much as I was tempted to repay Kurt's hostility, by screwing his purported mistress.

And most significantly, I let the Patch go to shit. I disregarded my knowledge of a coming enemy attack. I discounted the NVA's proven ability to climb perpendicular cliff faces and penetrate seemingly unassailable defensive barriers. I left my lax security contingent to police itself. I permitted my incompetent platoon leaders, Valentino, Walky-Talky, and the new man, Lisimba Jones, to go their own ways. I lost all the affinity I once had with my Khmu and Thai troops.

It wasn't long before word of my unmilitary conduct reached the ears of my commander, Kurt Dietrich. He wasted no time informing his superior, Mr. Reynolds, who sent me a twelve-word radio message that said it all:

Either shape up or ship out.
I'll give you a month.

At the time, I just laughed and said to myself, "Hey, do me a favor, man. I'd be outta here in a fucking minute!"

Yet from my present perspective, I realize that Reynolds was right to be concerned about my performance; in fact, it was far worse than he imagined. The sad part was that my dereliction of duty would have grave repercussions not only for myself, but for all my military subordinates and their families as well.

It's something I've had to live with ever since.

Two nights before Reynolds' deadline expired, I woke to the wailing sound of a heavy, incoming shell, followed by an explosion. It wasn't particularly loud because the dugout walls and sandbagged roof of the command post bunker muffled all noise from outside.

At first, I thought it might just be the pounding in my head from last evening's drinking binge. Then when I heard several other thumps and booms, and my rack started shaking, and I felt tar and sand roof debris come pattering down on my head,

I decided that Captain Chankul, my eccentric artillery man, was just getting in a little late night fire practice.

So, I stayed tucked in my rack, nursing my hangover, until I heard Boom-Boom in the radio room next door shout into his radio, "Incoming, incoming! Request air support!"

At that point, I figured maybe the Gomers had surreptitiously moved up a mortar or two and were peppering us with a little harassing fire.

"Nothing that can't be handled with some decent arty and air support," I told myself, but I was talking shit; and on some level, I must have known it.

I mean, the war by that time was no longer the farce, the fiasco portrayed in the popular press; it was a catastrophe of monumental proportions, in both Laos and Vietnam.

The NVA had recently destroyed an entire division of ARVN troops on the Bolovan Plateau and shot down nearly a hundred allied aircraft. Nearer by, a pair of NVA battalions had been assaulting the Sky main base at Long Tieng for a week and its Hmong defenders were talking surrender.

On a more personal level, the Laughing Monk had departed the Patch a couple of days before with the words, *"If you don't change direction, you may end up where you're heading."* And Poo-Ying had disappeared that same night without a word.

Still flaked out in my rack, spurning the obvious, I heard something directly over my head. I figured it was only the little gecko that lived in the ceiling beams. Every time it gulped down an insect, it performed a little clicking victory riff.

Yet, when I raised my boozy, bleary-eyed head to listen more attentively, it seemed like something closer to a slithering than a clicking sound, and it was not inside but outside, on the roof.

Telling myself that it was probably just one of the rats that infested the base, I swung my bare feet down onto the wood plank floor and reached for my pistol.

Then the door slammed open above me.

In the instant I had to react, I tried to wrap my mind around one astounding fact. Enemy sappers had infiltrated our firebase, and despite their very loud, preparatory barrage, they had done it without alerting a single perimeter guard.

Struggling to accept the evidence of my own eyes, I was finally able to identify the person standing above me in the doorway, outlined by the firing and explosions behind her, as a young Asian woman. Naked save for a garland of leaves and a pair of jungle-green shorts, she had blackened her slender body with grease and soot. She was holding a grenade, and she seemed to be adjusting her eyes to the darkness to find a target.

I knew better now than to hesitate in deference to her youth and femininity, so I raised my pistol and shot her in the gut. Falling back through the doorway, she managed with her last gasp to fling the grenade into the bunker.

I stood transfixed as it sailed upwards in slow motion, hit the ceiling, landed on the wooden floor with a bang, bounced once, rolled toward me, and stopped at my feet. To say, "it was the longest moment of my life," or "the tension was unbearable," or "my life passed before my eyes" as I waited for it to go off would be to trivialize the experience.

It swallowed my soul.

It erased my past, present and future.

I have never been the same since.

Yet at the same time, another part of my brain was very actively concerned with survival. I remembered that NVA grenades were usually of poor quality; they took three of four seconds to detonate, and sometimes failed to explode at all. I remembered to open my mouth to reduce its concussive effects, as I had learned at Camp Peary. I kicked the grenade across the room, and I turned to find a piece of furniture to shelter behind.

I was in mid-air, vaulting over the fifty-five-gallon, aviation gas drum that we used as a bath, when the grenade exploded. Luckily, it was defective, and the blast was much less destructive than it might have been in that enclosed space.

Still, it riddled the gas drum with shrapnel and caused the bath water to gush out and flood the floor.

It blew me across the room and into the aluminum wall.

I smacked down hard on the file cabinet, rolled off, and tumbled to the floor.

I struggled to rise but fell flat on my face.

I didn't feel any pain, but I couldn't see or hear, and I could not catch my breath because I was breathing in water from the floor.

My ears were buzzing like a plague of locusts, and there seemed to be a bright shining light in the center of my brain.

The light slowly dimmed, and then there was nothing, not even darkness.

When I regained consciousness, I found myself jammed in the prone position between two shattered file cabinets with my head against the wall and my pistol jutting into my crotch. A portion of the heavy roof was teetering overhead, and punctured sandbags were sliding off its splintered edge.

I was in pain, but I could not identify its source. It seemed like it was everywhere at once. I felt blood dripping down my forehead, but I had no idea how serious my wounds were.

The good news was the water had seeped into the cellar and I could breathe.

Then I heard someone jump through the gaping hole in the roof and land beside me.

I shut my eyes and played dead.

Someone else jumped into the bunker, and then I could hear two young men talking. My Vietnamese was rusty from disuse, but I was able to pick up the gist of their talk, which they carried on in normal conversational tones.

"Is he dead, Quang?"

"Looks like it."

"Let's see if he's got anything worth taking."

"Hey, he's an American, Duc!"

"Then you can be sure he's loaded."

"If he's the commander, we are in deep shit."

"Why?"

"We're supposed to take him alive; bring him in for interrogation."

"Too late now," Quang said, and kicked me hard in the ribs. Then he laughed and said in heavily accented English, "You sure you dead, GI?"

And he kicked me again, even harder. I made sure to expel my breath as a dead man would, but not to inhale.

Apparently, I convinced him. He slipped the watch off my wrist. When I felt his hands in my pockets, groping for my wallet, I whipped my pistol out from under my crotch and shot him in the stomach, aiming upward toward his heart.

He crumpled on me, and it hurt like hell, but it turned out to be fortunate because he took the shot that his partner Duc meant for me. Using Quang as a shield, I pumped two rounds into young Duc, and he dropped dead. Neither one of them was over sixteen years old.

I rolled Quang off me, crawled and kicked my way through the smoking, sizzling debris, and threw myself to the side just as half the roof collapsed.

I found Boom-Boom under a burning beam in the radio room and managed to heave it off him by wrapping my hands in an old bush jacket. He was alive. He was even grinning thanks at me.

"Radio's down, mate," he gasped. "I got 'fru once. Called for air. All we can do now is pray this bloody cloud cover lifts."

Then someone from outside tossed in a phosphorous grenade. It went off, filling the entire bunker with blinding white light and sucking the air from our lungs.

Both of us were concussed and bleeding, blind and deaf again, but we managed to slither to the cellar door, fling it open, and throw ourselves down on the muddy dirt floor two meters below.

The entire command post was now like one big clay oven, and we were the peanut noodles. We each grabbed a pistol, an assault rifle, and a tactical vest with ammunition pouches from the rack on the wall. Then we groped our way through wet clay toward Jimmy's emergency exit, the same one Nittaya had used to make her escape the year before. Just as we reached the tunnel, a flaming roof timber crashed down behind us in a storm of sparks.

After crawling in darkness for what seemed an eternity, we emerged near a burning perimeter bunker. We stuck our heads out to gulp some air and have a look around and found the entire base enveloped in a billowing cloud of smoke, with ghostly figures running from bunker to bunker, tossing explosives inside.

All around us lay bloodied bodies in shredded Thai, Khmu, and Laotian uniforms. I looked toward the mercenary barracks and they appeared to be in flames. I turned toward the Khmu village on the other hill and saw a white flag flying from their tribal longhouse. I glanced at the burning BOQ bunker and saw Valentino, the black man Lisimba, and Walky-Talky come walking out with their hands in the air, shrieking, *"Dầu hàng, dầu hàng!* We surrender, we surrender!"

They hadn't gone ten feet before they were cut to ribbons.

Satchel charges, tear gas grenades, RPGs, cluster flares and tracer rounds flashed, banged, thudded, and shook the ground beneath our feet, lighting up the night in red, green, and yellow. Then the ammunition dump went up like a volcanic eruption, blowing us off our feet, showering the entire firebase with flaming debris.

Just as it had begun to settle, the air support that Boom-Boom had called in finally arrived. We could hear them roaring overhead, both jet and propeller-driven, but there was nothing they could do to help. We had no radio to communicate with them. Low cloud cover and enemy anti-aircraft fire prevented them from coming down any lower than a thousand meters. Even if they had managed to get below it all somehow, they would not have risked bombing because there was no way of telling who was who. All they would've seen was a bunch of blurry figures running around in the hazy firelight.

Then we heard excited Vietnamese voices, and we could see another wave of sappers coming over the wire from the west. We dropped to our bellies among the fallen and played dead. The sappers ran right over us, shrieking victory cries.

Once they had disappeared in the direction of the supply depot, we rose to our knees and elbows. Assuring ourselves that the coast was clear for the moment, we snail-walked past the flaming bunker, rolled into the perimeter trench, and landed on a squad of mercenaries crouched in hiding.

"*Pheŭxn!*" Boom-Boom whispered in Thai before they could bring their weapons up. "Friendlies!"

Everyone shut up after that, trying to figure a way out. By now, our enemies had completely overrun the firebase. We had seen what they did to anyone trying to surrender. Since neither attacking nor capitulating was an option, Boom-Boom whispered with his fellow Thais and tried to determine a course of action.

On the point of doing something truly desperate (like running across the minefield in a kick-off-line, praying that the blasts we caused by our deaths would part the concertina wire so that one or two of us might make it over the cliff), we began to hear muffled voices at the other end of our trench.

Unable to determine what language they were speaking, we hunkered down, hoped for the best, and held fire until we could identify them. A few seconds later, we heard footsteps splashing up the muddy floor of the trench. Then we could see naked crouching figures with wreaths in their hair approaching, very cautiously.

"I'm outta here," I whispered to Boom-Boom.

"Where to? Into the bloody air? Ta, mate, it's karma-time."

The soldiers made us for enemies about the same time we made them. The trench was so narrow there was only room for one man to fire at once. So, one Goomer dropped to his knee, allowing a comrade to shoot over his head and create maximum firepower. The Thais followed suit; and all of a sudden, there were four soldiers firing at each other on full automatic. The light and sound effects were like being inside an electrical storm, and in that narrow space there was no way to miss.

Luckily, my self-preservation instincts had kicked in an instant before the shooting started, and I'd thrown myself down on the floor of the trench without firing a shot. The Thais behind me assumed I'd been wounded and commenced firing over my head. Playing dead for the third time that night, I let the bodies pile up on top of me.

It takes time to describe, but it was all over in a couple of seconds. The floor of the trench lay under a choking cloud of gun smoke and I trembled with the effort to prevent a coughing fit when the light-footed sappers came leaping over their fallen comrades to search the bodies above mine.

Smelling of fish sauce, rancid sweat and unclean genitals, they rummaged for rings, watches, wallets, and weapons. They mocked the wounded as "capitalist running dogs," cursed them for killing their comrades, and shot them in the head while they pleaded for mercy.

I lay with the dead for what seemed like hours, and I was surprised to learn that they are by no means silent. I heard them releasing air from their lungs and passing gas from their bowels.

I heard their blood and urine going *plip-plop, plip-plop.* I did not permit myself to feel repelled, however, even when splattered with gore. On the contrary, I forced myself to concentrate on the sounds of the dead to distract my attention from my crushing fear of discovery. I listened so hard that sometimes I believed I could hear the dead men whispering farewells to their loved ones.

When the last of the lithe, young ghouls had departed, I slipped and slopped under the deadweight of slimy carcasses toward a more comfortable and breathable position, and it wasn't long before I found myself staring into the lifeless Eurasian eyes of the late Tham-Boon "Boom-Boom" Smith.

Whispering into what was left of his ear, I praised him as "a Buddhist, a ladies' man, and the world's only Cockney-Celestial." Then I bid him the fond and (only slightly) ironic farewell I knew he would appreciate. I spoke in Lao, in the chanting *Metta Sutta* tone I'd learned from Nittaya. *"May you be flung far from the wheel of existence, dear friend, and ride the emptiness to nirvana."*

I had been running on adrenalin until then, so I was unclear as to how serious my condition was. I knew I had several shrapnel wounds, but I did not know how much blood I'd lost.

Wrapped up with Boom-Boom in a foul embrace that neither of us would have desired in life, I felt myself going into shock. It was a kind of listless sensation, a floating into nothingness. I tried hard to forestall the inevitable, but there came a time when I could no longer concentrate, and I felt myself slipping away.

I must have been unconscious for hours. When I awakened, it was to warm and misty sunlight, and the stench of vacated bowels and rotting corpses. It filled my nose and lungs. It clung to my skin, hair, and clothes. I could no longer recognize the man with whom I lay entwined. Flies and maggots had consumed his eyes. Fat black leeches had fastened themselves to the photogenic face that women had loved. And I'm sure I didn't look much better.

Next thing I knew, something was sprinkling on the bodies above mine. At first, I thought it was rain. Then I decided it must be piss. When it finally overwhelmed the smell of decomposing flesh, I knew it was gasoline, and the impression was strong enough to rouse me from my stupor. I must have thrashed about then because the next thing I recall is the sound of voices, a conversation in Vietnamese that was being conducted somewhere above me.

"Hey, Trong, one of them is moving!"

"Orders are to burn them all, dead or wounded."

"This one is a *farang*."

"No matter. Toss a match in, Bao, and light 'em up."

"Don't you remember? If we find their commander, we're supposed to . . ."

"What makes you think this one is the commander?"

"He's got a bronze Buddha hanging around his neck."

"So what?"

"That's how we're supposed to recognize him."

"A lot of people wear Buddhas around their necks."

"Not *farangs*."

"Why not?"

"They're *Christians*, you stupid shit."

"If you say so."

"Okay, let's pull his smelly ass out and torch the rest of them before they stink up the whole province."

I felt hands grabbing me then, but I slipped from their grip. I flopped back down with the stinking corpses. The pain was so intense that I blacked out again.

I woke up in a little wooden cage somewhere in the jungle. It was night, hot and humid. I could hear a bombing raid somewhere far off in the distance. I was naked. Flies buzzed around me. Leeches and maggots sucked at my wounds. I hurt so bad that the word "painful" cannot begin to describe the feeling. I was all hurt, and nothing else. The floor of the cage was mud, and it was crawling with what felt like worms. I had soiled myself somewhere along the line and smelled of shit, piss, sweat and festering wounds. I wasn't hungry, but I was dying of thirst.

Then a light appeared outside the cage. Someone had a clay lantern. He was swinging it around with one hand.

In the light of the lantern, I saw an Asian man in an NVA officer's uniform. He was leaning over me with his hands resting on his knees, smiling, and gazing down at me fixedly, as if I were of great interest to him. When I was able to bring his face into focus, I found that he was spectacularly handsome and bore an uncanny resemblance to a famous Hong Kong movie star named Wang-Yu whom I'd seen in a couple of Kung-Fu flicks in Vietnam.

"What is your name?" he said in French, still smiling pleasantly.

"Z-Zachary Ogle," I mumbled, almost too feeble to get out the words. "What's yours?"

The young officer laughed at that, slapping his uniform pants in glee, as if it were the funniest thing he'd heard in years.

"*Commissaire Nguyen Ly, à votre service!*"

"P-Pleasure to meet you. Think . . . think I might've heard that name before," I said, which caused him to laugh even more.

"Who do you work for?"

"Air-Sea Supply in Nakhon Phanom, Thailand."

"I see. And what were you doing at Firebase Juliet?"

"Passing through, on a mission for AID."

"And what was that mission?"

"Handing out food to the natives."

"You are not a CIA operative? You were not the commander of the base?"

"No."

"Then why do you suppose you are of such grave interest to Doctor Nittaya Aromdée and her uncle, Colonel Vong Aromdée?"

"No idea."

"You do not know Doctor Aromdée?"

"Never heard of her."

"I do not believe you," he said, and rose to take a step closer.

From the way he hopped forward, I could tell that his leg had been amputated above the knee and he wore a prosthetic device.

When he was standing directly above me, he reached down through the wooden bars, clasped my bronze Buddha head in his fingers, ripped its leather thong off my neck, and put it in his pocket.

"You won't be needing this anymore," he said, then he calmly unbuttoned his uniform trousers, extracted his uncircumcised penis, and pissed on me.

I tried to turn my head and fling up an arm to deflect the stream (pale pink in color and smelling of beetroot), but I was too weak, so I was made to take it in the face.

After he had emptied his bladder and disappeared into the night, I felt no sense of relief, for even degradation offered a diversion from my body's agony. Alone with my pain beyond pain, I prayed for oblivion.

CHAPTER TWENTY-FIVE

Lao Heaven

I woke in a clean, white space with a beautiful young Asian woman in medical scrubs holding my hand, smiling down at me, and I thought I had died and gone to heaven. She said something to me in English, and I realized that she was a figment of my imagination because she could not be who I wanted her to be.

"You do not know how lucky you are," she said, and I realized that I was indeed dead, and my angel was Doctor Nittaya Aromdée.

"That man had no right to piss in my face or take my Buddha head."

"Who did that to you?"

"He said his name was . . . was . . ."

"It would not have been Commissar Nguyen Ly, would it?"

"Yes, maybe he's the one."

"He had no right to . . ."

"He's not your old? . . ."

"He is, Zack."

"But I thought he was . . ."

"Let us focus on the present, *na?*"

"Where am I now?" I said, too tired and happy to feel the least bit of jealousy at the revelation.

"In the Savang Vatthana Hospital in Luang Prabang."

"I thought that was Royalist territory."

"Not anymore."

"So, I guess I'm not dead yet."

"No, but it was 'touch and go' for a while."

"Am I all in one piece?"

"More or less. I had to nip and tuck here and there, but eventually you should be pretty mobile."

"How long before I'm up and about?"

"That depends on whether you follow your physician's orders."

"Whatever you say, Doc."

"In that case I should think you will be walking with crutches in a month or two, and on your own in three or four."

"It's that serious, huh?"

"I am afraid so."

"How can I ever thank you enough?"

"You cannot. You are the sole survivor of all the Laotians, Thais and Americans at Firebase Juliet."

"The base is destroyed?"

"Utterly."

"And the Khmus?"

"They have elected to join us in our struggle."

"And I'm a prisoner of war?"

"Exactly. Until every last American bandit has disappeared from Laos and Vietnam and all your running dogs are either dead or locked up in a re-education camp."

"How long you figure that'll be?"

"Not long at all, *mon cher*," she said, and laughed that marvelous laugh from the belly up that I remembered from all our good times together. "We have them on the run now. Nixon just sent Kissinger to Paris to beg for peace."

Whatever her opinions of my compatriots, Nittaya cared for me as usual in the weeks ahead. Ignoring the hateful stares and hostile comments of the hospital's NVA and Pathet Lao patients and medical cadres, she fussed over me like a loving wife, and I recovered even faster than her prognosis.

On the night of January 29, 1973, she had her orderlies roll my bed into her operating room. When they left, she locked the door behind them, which I found odd. I also noticed that she had liquor on her breath. She wore a big, boozy grin on her face, and none of the usual surgical nurses were in attendance.

"Hey, what's up?"

"We win, you lose, *Farang!* Kissinger just signed the Paris Peace Accords with Le Duc Tho. Now make some room in that bed and let me show you what victory feels like."

Despite her warlike words, she made love to me tenderly, taking care to leave my wounds unharmed. We took no precautions, and when I mentioned it afterwards, she said, "I know exactly what I am doing."

"You do?"

"Yes, I am luteal phase."

"Which means?"

"The mature egg is available for fertilization."

"You want my baby?"

"Could I be any more specific?"

"Why?"

"I do not know," she said, giggling. "Maybe to seal the peace, *na*? I can tell everyone you fired off your gun to celebrate the ceasefire, and our baby, born nine months later, is the result."

"Does love enter into the picture at all?"

"Yes," she said, after considering it for a moment. "But that does not mean I am making any promises."

Yet, despite her declaration of love, and the fun we had in my hospital bed, I recall feeling a tiny bit used afterwards.

No man likes to be called a loser.

When Nittaya had me well enough to hobble around on crutches, Commissar Nguyen Ly clomped into my ward one morning, with a pair of sour-faced military policemen.

"Colonel Aromdée has ordered that you, CIA Agent Zachary Ogle, be summoned for immediate interrogation," he said, as if reading from some official document. Then he turned to his men and said, "Drag him of that bed, handcuff him, chain his ankles, and slip a rope around his neck so we can pull him along smartly."

After kicking and shoving me down the stairs and out of the building, causing me to take a painful tumble or two, the commissar and his men led me up Sakkaline Road like an animal to the slaughter.

It was only a few dozen meters from the hospital to the French Colonial building housing the former *Gendarmerie Royal*, but it was farther than I had traveled in many weeks. Regardless of my rough and inhumane treatment, I was tearful with bliss at being out in the sunlight, among normal, bustling civilians again.

Once inside, however, the commissar shoved me into an empty, windowless room and left me there under bright fluorescent light, without food or drink, for thirty-six hours. I was not permitted to lie down, and every time I started to nod off one of the military policemen assigned to watch over me jerked me awake and badgered me with stupid, hostile questions.

"You number ten GI, *na?* How many Lao you kill?"

Yet, when the colonel finally had me hauled into his office, I found him to be worldly, intelligent, and charming, not at all the dour Communist functionary of lore. His Soviet-style, olive drab tunic and slacks were of a finer quality than the usual. They fit him beautifully, despite the empty left sleeve of his jacket, and appeared to be hand-tailored. He shook hands with me briefly and firmly, looking me straight in the eye, like a perfect continental gentleman, and motioned me to sit in a chair beside his desk.

"Looks like we banged each other up pretty good," he said in French, pointing to the wounds we both so obviously bore. "But the way things are going, maybe we won't have to do much more of it."

"Let's pray the peace holds, *mon colonel.*"

"Yes, let's do, though I have a suspicion we both have certain doubts about the efficacy of prayer," he said, and we shared the cynical laugh of two, battered, old enemies, with a long-disappointed dream of peace. "Perhaps you would like something to eat and drink now, Agent Ogle, before we begin our discussion?"

By this time, it was March 1973, and the United States had fled Southeast Asia yelping, with its tail between its legs. The NVA was not required by the Paris Peace Accords to disengage, so it now controlled most of Vietnam and Laos. It was still advancing on all fronts, and its puppet Pathet Lao was the majority party in the Laotian national government.

The Catch 22 for CIA operatives like me was this: The United States had never disclosed its military presence in Laos, so it could not admit that there were American prisoners in the country.

Since I did not officially exist, my employers at Air-Sea Supply could not demand my repatriation. I had a sneaking suspicion they wouldn't, anyway, even if they could. My three-year contract was about to expire, and I was sure they would be quite content to never hear from me again.

I felt only the mildest twinge of disloyalty, therefore, when I spilled my guts to Colonel Aromdée.

It took sixteen hours, and he taped it all.

When he had milked me of every dirty CIA secret I knew, he thanked me rather warmly, I thought, for my "full disclosure," and appeared convinced that I was telling the truth, holding nothing back.

Thus encouraged, I attempted to convince Colonel Aromdeé that I no longer posed any sort of threat to his government. I pleaded with him to release me from custody, allow me to leave the country and go my own way.

Of course, I did not reveal that my "way" would lead straight to the Swiss bank where I had three years of accrued CIA salary plus interest awaiting me.

When the colonel replied that his people would demand that someone be held accountable for US war crimes in Laos, and that I was the only suspect in custody, I argued that I was an unlikely candidate. "I had been a mere cog in the wheel," I said, "a simple soldier obeying orders, unaware of the full extent of CIA atrocities."

It was a desperate ploy, I knew, and I was not at all surprised when the colonel declared that my excuses were disturbingly like those uttered by Nazi soldiers in World War II.

Without a credible counter argument, I played the only hand I had.

I asked for mercy, one soldier to another.

A measure of the rapport we had established was his comment, "I'll think about it, but I wouldn't get my hopes up, if I were you."

Aside from the above, there was only one rough patch in the interrogation. It came near the end, when Colonel Aromdée asked me to describe my relationship with his niece, Nittaya.

Coloring with embarrassment, I weighed my options before replying. I had promised her to say nothing of our love. If I told him the truth, I risked losing Nittaya forever. If I lied, I risked my life.

"Before you answer," said Colonel Aromdée, taking a severe tone for the first time, "I want you to know that an informant has come forward. He says that you and Nittaya were sexually involved. This is a serious allegation."

I took a deep breath, reconsidered my alternatives, banished all thoughts of fear or panic, and said, "It's true I fell in love with your niece, *mon colonel*. And I asked her to marry me. But she told me that we come from irreconcilably different worlds, and she was already married to the revolution."

He laughed, apparently delighted with my adroit handling of his question. He seemed so pleased that for a moment I even indulged myself in the fantasy that he might someday approve of our match.

"But it is my dream that one day, when the past has receded, that we might . . ." I began, struggling with the words in French.

I hesitated as soon as I saw the colonel's handsome, well-weathered face freeze up and a dangerous glare appear in his eyes. Yet for some perverse (yet all too familiar) reason I persisted in direct opposition to my best interests.

". . . that Nittaya and I might ask your family's permission to marry."

Colonel Aromdée rose from his seat abruptly, nearly knocking over his chair, and started for the door. Halfway there he spun around, pointed a finger at me and said, "That, *jeune homme*, is a most unlikely proposition. However, I might be willing to consider it under two conditions. The first is that Nittaya agrees to accept you. The second is that you agree to give up your United States citizenship, become a Communist, and work as an international voice for the revolution."

"So, you mean you want me to be a turncoat, a propaganda tool, right?" I said, responding instinctively, before I had time to consider the possible repercussions.

Unmoved by the discourteous tenor of my response, the colonel replied mildly. "Yes, I believe that you could prove very useful to our struggle in the next few years."

"Let me ask you a question, *mon colonel*," I said, still unable to moderate my tone. "Would you do it, if the shoe was on the other foot?"

"No, never. I would die first."

"Then you know my answer."

"If I were you, Mr. Ogle, I would reconsider," he said, pulling a recent edition of the *International Herald Tribune* from his briefcase, pointing at the headline.

NEWS OF SUSPECTED TURNCOAT
FEEDS FRENZY OF CIA CRITICS
IN U.S. CONGRESS

I glanced at it for a moment, reading that an alleged CIA operative named Zachary Ogle had been accused of treason for associating with a Pathet Lao agent and purposely leaving the firebase he commanded open to enemy attack.

"How did they get this information?"

"One of my young commissars gave it out," the colonel said, seemingly amused by the story he was about to recount. "He did not seek my approval beforehand. Apparently, he has some sort of private grudge against you, Monsieur Ogle. I was furious at him at first, but I let him off the hook when he convinced me it might play well for us in the world press."

"I see," I said, running frantically through my diminishing options.

I could accept the colonel's offer and live happily ever after with Comrade Nittaya and our little bevy of Young Communists. I could assent and then escape later and tell my masters at the Firm that I had spoken under duress. Or I could refuse categorically and quite possibly face a firing squad.

I came within an inch of hitting the brakes and back-pedaling to some more typically Oglesque choice such as Option One or Option Two. Then, only the Fish Goddess knows why, some scrap of loyalty to my blood tribe, some sentimental attachment to the American Dream, some waiflike need for a spiritual home, conquered my love for Nittaya and myself and caused me to choose the quite probably fatal Option Number 3.

"All right, you have made your bed," the colonel said with a sigh that seemed to contain both a measure of respect and a mild disdain. "Now you must be prepared to lie in it."

He left me alone in the interrogation room without food or water or access to a toilet for another twenty-four hours, until I had collapsed from dehydration.

When at last the door opened, I found myself confronted by a sneering Commissar Nguyen Ly and his two military policemen. They took turns punching me in the face. Then they kicked me to the floor, cuffed my hands behind my back, and dragged me down some stairs to a dark, stony, dungeon-like place full of scrawny, howling, Royalist prisoners packed in threes and fours into cells meant for one man.

I was there a week. I know that because they fed us moldy rice and fetid water once a day. But it felt like forever. My fellow prisoners (and former allies) attacked me, blaming me as an American for their defeat. My wounds got infected again in the filth, and lice infested my hair and clothes.

At a point somewhere beyond despair, I heard my name called. I was lying on the stone floor, unable to rise, when Commissar Nguyen Ly arrived with his two military policemen.

He directed them to grab me under the arms and pull me to my feet. As they dragged me out of the cell, my fellow prisoners kicked and spat at me and called me *"un poltron Américain!"*

Nguyen and his guards manhandled me back down the street to the Savang Vatthana Hospital (which I noticed had been renamed in my absence as *Hôpital de l'Amitié Vietnam-Laos*) and locked me in the prison wing.

A homely, frowning, young nurse, in a Soviet-style medical corps uniform, took charge of me as soon as I staggered in the door. Ushering me roughly down the hall, she shoved me into a big communal shower, ordered me to divest myself of my reeking jail uniform and throw it into the garbage bin. Then she tossed me a rag, some antiseptic soap and a delousing solution and shouted, *"Lavez-vous bien!"*

When I'd scrubbed and scoured myself thoroughly enough to meet her approval, she gave me some hospital pajamas to put on, led me into a room full of Royalists suffering from the effects of prolonged physical and psychological abuse, and chained me to a cot. She hooked me up to some sort of Chinese monitoring device with a saline and antibiotic drip for a couple of days, and thereafter she left me to my own devices.

Five days later, Commissar Nguyen Ly appeared again with the same pair of gruff, military policemen. As they stood guard at the foot of the bed, he approached me, leaned down, and just before un-cuffing my hands from the bedstead he whispered in my ear. "You are lucky to have such powerful friends, Monsieur Ogle, but I would not feel too smug, if I were you. Anything can happen; and it usually does, if you know what I mean."

Then he and his thugs re-cuffed me, escorted me out of the

prison wing and down to the reception room where a tall, thin, refined-looking old Laotian woman wearing the kind of tropical dress fashionable in the French Colonial Era awaited me.

Blanching at my appearance—bare feet, soiled pajamas, untended bandages—she got right up in the commissar's face.

"What have we come to in in this country, to allow such disgraceful treatment of prisoners?"

"It is nothing to what these bandits inflicted upon us," he angrily retorted, un-cuffing my hands from behind my back and shoving me toward her.

"Yes, but we are supposed be better than they are, *na?* This could not be anything personal, could it, *Monsieur le Commissaire?*"

"It is far beyond personal by now, Madame, but why not have a talk with your family, your nephew and grand-niece? They have more detailed information on the subject than I do."

"You may be assured that I shall, at my earliest opportunity. And I would advise you to retain your commendable objectivity on the matter, Monsieur, in the interests of your ... future prospects ... Well, I think you follow my meaning. Thank you for your help, and I shall no longer require your assistance."

Dismissing Nguyen and his cohorts with a toss of the head and a flick of the wrist, the kindly old *grande dame* signed me out at the front desk and helped me downstairs to a long, black, pre-war Citroën almost before I could register that I was free from custody.

Afraid that I might somehow jinx my miraculous escape, or that Nguyen might suddenly change his mind, I asked no questions.

As we drove off down Sakkaline Road, the lady turned to me, flashed a beautiful smile that I found hauntingly familiar, and introduced herself. "Just call me *Tante Cèleste.*"

After all my recent trials, I found the calm of the ancient capital of Laos, with its shady, tree-lined streets, its rough wooden houses and soaring Buddhist temples, utterly unreal.

Monks and merchants, peasants and mountain tribesmen, shopkeepers, and customers, pedicabs and pedestrians, all went about their business as if the world were enjoying a peace that had lasted a hundred years. There were even signs plastered on walls advertising a night of poetry readings and a production of "Waiting for Godot."

In the Khili quarter, on leafy Khem Khong Road, we stopped at a big, old, teakwood house with a lush, tropical garden out front.

Tante Cèleste's driver—a muscular, silent, all-purpose servant and bodyguard named Toom—helped me out of the car and through the front gate.

Intoxicated by the sights, sounds, and smells of the garden, I prevailed upon *Tante Cèleste* to linger a moment, *"Pour me réorienter à la beauté de la nature."*

Pale pink orchids, golden shower trees, purple parrot flowers along the walkway.

Sunbirds and red-tailed swallows singing in the trees.

Monks chanting in the tall, golden temple next door.

The view down the hill to the dramatic confluence of the muddy Mekong and the blue Khan Rivers.

Later, after showing me into her lovely home, which she described as *"l'ancienne maison de la famille Aromdée,"* she handed me a straight razor, some soap, shaving cream and cologne, and directed me to her upstairs bathroom.

"Take off those pajamas, hand them to Toom, and he will burn them in the incinerator," she said in the no-nonsense, take-charge tones of an elder female relative. "Have a nice, long, hot bath and a shave. When you are finished, give me a shout and I shall provide you with a change of clothes."

Refreshed, renewed, and smelling like a rose, fitted out in a set of white, 1930s tennis togs courtesy of *Tante Cèleste's* long dead husband, I dined with her that night on sticky rice and lemongrass chicken, prepared by the multi-talented Toom. We washed it down with a cool and delicious *Chenin Blanc de Gaillac* "fresh from my late husband's spidery old cellar." After a dessert of "inferior local cheese" and mandarin oranges, after a *café express* and a *digestif*, after we had toasted the Paris Peace Accords with an *Armagnac Clos Martin*, *Tante Cèleste* finally got around to explaining how and why she had arranged my release.

"When my niece, Nittaya, found that you had not returned to the hospital, she knew something bad had happened. She went to her uncle, my nephew, Vong Aromdée, and asked him what had become of you. He said you were a threat to the revolution, or some such nonsense, and refused to release you. Nittaya telephoned her mother, Yada. She explained the situation and had her ring Vong. My nephew has never been able to resist Yada—do not ask me why. After equivocating for a few days, he called Nittaya into his office and gave her a choice.

"'Promise to never see that American bandit again and I shall let him go. See him again, and I shall prosecute him as a war criminal and seek the death penalty.'

"Nittaya promised, and she and Vong arranged for me to be the go-between. So here we are, *mon cher*. Nittaya booked passage for you on a riverboat to Chiang Khan, Thailand, which is about two hundred kilometers downstream. It's a three-day trip and it leaves tomorrow morning.

"She has given me some money for you, as well as a boxful of your papers that she dug up at some place called 'Firebase Juliet.' She said she'd left a letter for you inside."

I thanked Madame Aromdée and told her I would always remember her kindness. Then I retired to the room she had given me, which I discovered was full of dated girlish accoutrements and had once belonged to her married daughter.

I opened the metal box and found all my journals intact.

I opened the letter, and it was typically droll and impromptu:

> I read every word you wrote. I know you so well by now, Zachary Ogle, and I love you so much, there were few surprises. Not even Pisces the Fish Goddess. I do not know whether you are aware of this or not, but your "goddess remote from human cares" has a long history, going all the way back to the Epicureans of ancient Greece. The one thing that struck me was how you seemed to have grown more mature in your perceptions and more careful in your language in the past few years. I am sure you had similar revelations when you read my diary. As you will find, I took the liberty to write my feelings in your journal, just as you did in mine. When you

read my scribblings, you will find these closing words: *Bon voyage, mon amour.* I know we will see each other again, whether in this lifetime or the next, whether we be fish, fowl or human. Actually, I think it might be fun if we were reborn as mermaid and merman, *na?*"

> Yours forever,
> Nittaya

I slept not at all that night. I spent the hours trying to figure out some way to meet her. I could hear Toom outside my door the whole time, coughing cigarette smoke and occasionally snoring, so I determined that I was still not altogether trusted. Either that, or Toom worked for two masters.

In the morning, after bidding a fond *adieu* to Madame Aromdée, I briefly considered bailing out of Toom's old Citroën on the way to the river port, tracking Nittaya down somehow, and begging her to run off with me. Yet in the end, I funked out, rationalizing that an escape attempt would probably cost me my life.

I wouldn't be any good to the girl dead, would I?

Toom let me out at a big, rusty, old riverboat, a leftover from French Colonial times called *La Dame du Dragon* that looked as if it might have plied the Mississippi in the time of Mark Twain. I climbed aboard, followed by two hard-looking men in the uniforms of NVA military policemen. Upon closer appraisal, I recognized them as Nguyen Ly's goons.

Distressed by what their appearance portended for my river

voyage, I mounted the rickety gangway on unsteady feet, and presented my ticket to the purser at the top of the gangway with a trembling hand.

Although by no means pacified, I felt my mood improve slightly when a pretty steward's mate escorted me below, and I discovered that Nittaya had booked me a first-class cabin. Not only that, she'd packed a briefcase full of classic left-wing French language reading material (Hugo, Zola, Sartre) and civilian clothes in exactly my right size.

"Damn, what a wife that girl would've made!" I said to myself, and almost burst into tears.

It was hot, humid, and slow going down the chocolate brown Mekong. My old, chug-chugging riverboat stopped at every town along the way to load and unload cargo and passengers, and the riverside scenery of uniformly green jungle, karsts and rice paddies rapidly became monotonous.

It took us twenty-four hours to reach the Ta Deua Ferry Crossing, which by my reckoning was only about fifty klicks downriver, so I thought our three-day timetable was a bit optimistic.

I whiled away most of the hours reading in my cabin, but I noticed that every time I stepped out to take the air or visit the cafeteria, one of Nguyen's thugs was parked outside my door.

Obviously, they were to be my shadows, either to ensure my departure from Laos or to execute some more sinister plot. With that in mind, I locked myself in my cabin every night and never, ever walked the deck alone.

On the morning of the fourth day of our voyage, we pulled up at the Chiang Khan District Boat Station. Unable to resist a mocking, dismissive wink and wave at my two custodians, I bounced down the gangway to Thailand.

Once I'd stepped out onto the cluttered dock, however, and started weaving my way through shipping crates and piled bags of rice, I had to consider the next obstacle in my way.

What was I to say to the Thai customs officials that I could see waiting for me at the end of the dock if they asked for a passport?

After a moment's consideration, I decided to throw myself on their mercy. I would take a mundane approach and claim to be an American tourist or AID worker whose passport had been lost or stolen, or I'd go for something more dramatic and say I was an escaped American prisoner of war. I would ask if I might phone the US Embassy in Thailand and request its assistance.

As it turned out though, all my plotting and planning proved unnecessary. A *tuk-tuk* came putt-putting up to the customs post. A native girl stepped off and greeted the customs officers with a smile. She spoke with them for a moment, laughing and joking, pointing to her ring finger, and handed them an envelope. Then she turned and came running toward me, and I realized that what I had discounted as fantasy was real.

My angel of mercy threw herself in my arms, smothering me with kisses and tearing at my hair. I lifted her off her feet and swung her around until she shrieked that she was going to *"perdre la connaisance!"*

"Is this our Hollywood ending?" I said when I set her down on the damp and half-rotted dock.

"What do you think?"

"Somehow I kind of doubt it," I said, looking over her

shoulder at my two Laotian guards.

I had expected them to be registering some interest in my meeting with their commander's niece, the girl who had sworn that she would never see me again. Yet, in fact, they were just calmly standing at the rail, smoking cigarettes, and watching us recede into the morning mist.

"You are probably right," Nittaya said, leading me past the grinning customs men to her waiting *tuk-tuk*. "So, let us make the best of it while it lasts, *na?*

CHAPTER TWENTY-SIX

Goodbye

There was to be no Hollywood ending, but I really did give it my best shot. I declined to address my deep suspicions about Nittaya's true motivations and intentions. I refused to ask myself several obvious questions. Like why had she broken her word to her uncle? How did she escape his surveillance? What was Nguyen Ly's role in all of this? Why were his thugs so unsurprised at her sudden appearance? What else had she agreed to do to secure my release? Had she and her uncle some further use for me as a propaganda tool? And most importantly, would she come away with me, once I'd played the role that she had contrived for me?

After a three day "honeymoon" at a luxurious spa in the nearby Loei Mountains, during which Nittaya used all her Spider Woman wiles to entice me into a state of mindless euphoria, she smuggled me into Bangkok by mini-bus and found discreet lodgings for us at her cousin Jet Wattana's large, Malibu Modern home in Thong Lo. Jet and his wife were residing in Europe for the year; most of the servants were on furlough, and we had the place to ourselves.

The morning after our arrival, we were sitting out by the pool having breakfast when I leaned across the table at her and said, "Nittaya, I'd like to phone the US Embassy today."

"For what?"

"Well, at some point I'm going to have to try and regularize my status."

"And precisely how to you intend to do that?"

"Oh, I don't know. Maybe apply for a new passport and find out if I have any legal problems."

"Are you mad? You are poison to the CIA. The minute they hear you are in town; your life will not be worth a buffalo turd."

"You got any better ideas?"

"Absolutely. Before you do anything else, I want you to tell your story to the international press."

"Hey, that's only gonna piss 'em off all the more. I mean, I signed a non-disclosure clause."

"Yes, it might make them a bit cross at you, but it will be hard for them to do anything violent because of all the international publicity. The easiest thing for them to do would be nothing and just wait for the story to fade away."

"You really think so, huh?"

"Just leave it to me, baby," she said, jumping up, grabbing me by the hand and leading me into Jet's spacious library.

We spent the next twelve hours concocting a story. To give the story "legs," Nittaya granted me permission to tell most (but by no means all) of our "Romeo and Juliet" story.

It was obvious that she had already given this a lot of thought.

I would not have been surprised to find that she'd consulted her uncle's advice on the matter, or even Nguyen Ly's.

She wanted me to follow a precise narrative line, one that portrayed the Vietnamese and Laotian communist forces as simple, selfless, jungle peasants who through a sense of destiny, unity, and incredibly heroic persistence had defeated the most powerful country on earth.

I made no protest. I admit to being her willing accomplice.

For one thing, my own experience of combat with the communist forces of Southeast Asia had taught me that they were indeed the most powerfully motivated and formidable military force on earth.

For another, I would have sold hot sauce to the devil or ice to the Eskimos to win Nittaya's hand. I was so afraid of losing her that I didn't even try to bargain with her, to trade my political capital for a lifetime commitment.

I was alone in the world.

She was my only family.

I simply could not face the possibility that she might say no.

When, at last, I had polished my story and rehearsed it enough to win my demanding drama coach's reluctant approval, she phoned Dave Larsen, Bangkok bureau chief of the Associated Press. She got through to him quite easily because he was a member of the Thong Lo Tennis Club. She had been introduced to him by another member, the Thai parliamentarian, Sum Wattana, who also happened to be one of her many maternal uncles.

I insisted on standing beside her during the phone call, and

I heard everything they said.

"Hi, Dave, listen, I think I have a story for you."

"Hey, Nittaya, sounds good."

"You have heard of Zachary Ogle, *na?*"

"The CIA guy?"

"Yes."

"Wow, he's pretty hot news right now."

"Well, Mr. Ogle asked me if I knew anyone in the press that he could tell his story to, and I recommended you. He is willing to grant you exclusive rights, on the condition that you keep it secret from the US Embassy, until it goes to press."

"I don't see any reason why not."

"He would also like you to recommend a television reporter, preferably someone from the American Broadcasting Corporation."

"Why them?"

"He thinks they have been more even-handed about the war."

"No problem. I've got just the man for you. His name's Gil Jones, and he's ABC's Bangkok bureau chief."

"All right, Dave. Shall we set up an interview then? Mr. Ogle is in hiding. He has apparently angered the CIA and fears for his life, so it will be best if we do both press and television interviews at the same time."

Dave contacted Gil Jones as soon as he got off the phone. Gil phoned Nittaya, and they set up an interview for that very night. They were to join us with their Thai cameramen at Jet's house, at 2 a.m., to avoid any possibility of unwelcome observers.

"Dave is an old Asia hand," Nittaya said, while prepping me

for the meeting over a take-out supper of stir-fried morning glory, curried fish cakes, fried rice, and a bottle of Jet's *Pinot Blanc.* "He has been here ever since the end of World War II and he knows absolutely everyone. At one time, he and Jimmy Love were great friends, until they had a falling out over some bargirl in Soi Cowboy. Gil is younger and newer on the scene, but he is married to a Cambodian woman and he made a name for himself covering the Vietnam War from Saigon and Phnom Phen. Apparently, he was a close friend and colleague of Errol Flynn's son, Sean, before he died. Both Dave and Gil have been very skeptical about US involvement in Southeast Asia, so they are just the kind of reporters we are looking for."

When they arrived, I found Dave to be a short, stout, engaging man of about sixty, with the beery, raucous good humor of a confirmed expat. He reminded me a bit of Jimmy Love, just as Nittaya had said he would. Gil was decades younger than Dave was, and his exact opposite. Tall, blond, and conventionally good-looking, he was poised, self-assured and telegenic, but he said little and let Dave do most of the talking.

I felt no loyalty to the CIA, and never had, so I had little compunction about telling them my whole story, beginning with my seduction and recruitment by Major Duval at the Presidio and ending with my safe arrival in Thailand after three years in the field.

Following the script that Nittaya and I had devised, I aimed my most disarming smile at their cameras and edited my narrative very carefully to avoid even the slightest hint of unpatriotic behavior. Relying on the fact that there were few live witnesses to contravene my account, I named names and places and described my military experiences in colorful and gripping detail. I provided specific examples from personal observation of the United States' decade-long, military involvement in Laos, and its relentless bombardment of Laotian civilians in contravention to international law.

I spoke of how Nittaya, a highly educated, medical professional from one of Laos' finest families, had chosen to turn her back on a brilliant future to become a spy for the Pathet Lao, to seek justice for her people. I told of how we had fallen in love even though we fought on opposing sides. I related how I became her captive, how she saved my life repeatedly, and how she braved the censure of her superiors to help me escape from Laos, where I faced indictment as a war criminal. I ended up with several appalling, yet irrefutable, statistics that even now, many years later, I find horrifying.

"Between the years 1964 and 1973," I said, "the tiny, impoverished nation of Laos was struck by a B-52 bomber on an average of every eight minutes, twenty-four hours a day. In all, two hundred and sixty million bombs fell. That is fifty-two bombs for every man, woman, and child in Laos, which makes it by far the most heavily bombed nation on earth. About a quarter of those bombs failed to explode, and they continue to inflict hundreds of casualties a year. And I won't even talk about the lasting effects of Agent Orange, which was sprayed from one end of the country to the other. What is most shocking about all this is that such terrible destruction was accomplished in absolute secrecy, and the United States refuses to accept any responsibility for its actions."

When I had finished with my prepared statement, Dave

asked me several very pointed questions, two or three of which I found acutely uncomfortable because they raised doubts about my bravery, constancy, and loyalty. Don't ask me how, but I managed to fend them off or fib my way out of them. Then Gil, who had been virtually silent up until then, said that my account seemed "one-sided," and that American television viewers might find its news of US atrocities "unpalatable."

This could have proven the most difficult question, but I was able to field it quite easily for two good reasons. One was that Nittaya had anticipated it and prepped me for it. The other was that I believed in what I said, so I projected a very convincing sincerity.

"The United States Government has hidden its crimes and misled the American public for years," I said, "and now the day of reckoning has come. Yes, some people might find news of our government's crimes in Laos unpleasant, but it's the truth, so help me God. And eventually they're just going to have to swallow it."

Dave filed his story with AP the next morning. That night, it aired on the ABC Evening News, with Harry Reasoner commenting that "the account you're about to hear from former CIA operative Zachary Ogle seems disturbingly plausible, and the White House's statement of 'no comment' today only adds fuel to the fire."

Nittaya arranged interviews with NBC, CBS, Reuters, and *Agence France Presse* the next day, and within twenty-four hours the story was a worldwide sensation.

A day later, when the story was at its absolute peak, Nittaya decided that it would now be safe for me to either seek asylum in some neutral country or approach the US Embassy and request a passport.

"If you want to go to the US Embassy," she said, as we sat over a papaya salad, Mandarin roast duck and Chang Beer one evening at Jet's kitchen table, "we shall have to get you a good international lawyer to accompany you. Actually, I know of one, an American. My cousin Puy has used him in the past."

"Why do you think I need a lawyer?"

"Are you serious? When you are on the grounds of the embassy, you are at their mercy. They can do anything they want with you. Prevent you from leaving the grounds. Kidnap you. Arrest you as a traitor. Hand you over to the CIA. Or simply refuse to issue you a passport, let the Firm empty your Swiss bank account by some nefarious means, and leave you to 'piss in the wind.'"

"I hear you, Nittaya, but I was born and raised an American. It's not so easy to give up my country, my identity. I'd be willing to do it, though, under one condition. If you agree to come with me, I'll give up everything; I'll go anywhere on earth."

"Will you return with me to Laos?"

"That's my one exception."

"Very funny."

"Okay, why can't we compromise? We'll go someplace that's neither yours nor mine. We'll even speak a neutral language, like French."

"Look, my darling, I can easily imagine us living together in a quaint chalet in some picturesque, mountain suburb of Gèneve, raising little Tristan and Cybèle to be good Swiss citizens. It would be heaven on earth."

"So, what's not to like?"

"I love you with all my heart, Zack, but there are some things more important to me than romance."

I lost it then. I smacked the table with my fist, sending glassware everywhere.

"What things? The Hungry Masses? The People's Revolution? You manipulated me, didn't you? You and your uncle and your old boyfriend."

"You want to know the truth? Yes, I used you. Along with saving your life. But I am not telling you anything you have not known all along. You wanted me to use you, Zack, right from the start. That is who you are."

"Okay, so now that I've performed my little song and dance, what're you gonna do?"

"I really do not know."

"Oh, you know alright."

"Listen, let me tell you, frankly. I do not even believe all this communist crap myself half the time. What I love is my people— my poor, suffering people. They need my help desperately now, and as a doctor of medicine, I just cannot bring myself to leave them."

"See? I don't understand that, Nittaya. And I never will. I mean, there comes a time when you really have to think of yourself. We only have one chance at life."

"I do not believe that, and you know it."

I threw up my hands, smiled, and shook my head in resignation. "I guess no two people could be more different."

"What a pair, huh?"

"We had some wild times, though, didn't we, Nittaya?" I

said, and then rose and headed for our bedroom.

"We did, Zack," she said, following me through the door. "We really did."

"But I'm not going to change, and neither are you."

"Anyway, it was probably just too intense to last."

"Eventually, for sure, we'd have blown up in each other's faces," I said, and started stuffing things into my rucksack, gently waving her aside when she tried to help.

"So, what have we really lost?"

"Nothing."

"We really were something, though," she said, and started to cry. "Weren't we?"

"Never anything like it," I said.

Yet, in truth, I felt as if we were delivering lines from a film, one produced and directed countless times in the past.

We kissed goodbye on the veranda. I held her at arm's length for a moment to get a last look and commit her to memory. She was wearing a long, filmy, white kimono, with nothing underneath, and though her breasts and body were spectacular to behold, I turned my attention to that unique facial aspect which had captured me in the beginning and made her Nittaya Aromdée. Her earth-yellow skin. Her jet-black hair, parted in the middle, hanging over one eye, as usual, and running all the way down her back. Her brows thick and arched high. Her cat eyes. Her nose like an Egyptian queen. Her lips a tiny bit too full and red. The gap between her two front teeth.

As a parting gift, she flashed a smile at me, and despite all she'd been through in the past three years, it still revealed the kind of sauciness I had fallen in love with. She looked years younger than her age. Anyone else with her looks could have been a model, a Thai movie star, a *Hi-So* wife and mother in an upscale suburb of Bangkok with a houseful of servants. But she . . .

"Oh, for fuck's sake!"

"I know, I know, my love," she said, reaching up to wipe a tear from my eye.

"Right," I said, pressing her body to me, smelling her for the last time, a fragrance like no other on this earth.

"Wow, I almost forgot," she said as I turned to go. Reaching into the folds of her robe, she brought forth a new, twenty-eight knot, Buddhist bracelet and slipped it around my wrist. "This is to replace the one I gave you before. It will protect you, just like the last one did."

"And when it wears out?"

"I have this for you," she said tenderly, and handed me the battered bronze Buddha head she had given me before the Battle of Gneu Mat, the one Nguyen Ly had ripped off my neck.

"My God, what'd you have to do to get this back?"

"More than you will ever know," she said, as she fitted it around my neck on a new leather thong. "But if you lose it again, *mon amour*, you will be on your own."

"I'll guard it with my life."

"I know you will."

We waggled our fingers at each other, and I strode off into the night, heading for the long-tail boat station on the Petchaburi Canal. Halfway there, I heard her shout something after me. I'm not sure, but I think it was, *"Prochiane vie!"* Which in English, of course, means "Next Lifetime."

CHAPTER TWENTY-SEVEN

The Aftermath

The Vietnam War and the illicit, American, military involvement in Laos were immensely unpopular in Europe, where the people often treated American dissidents and deserters as heroes.

Such was my case.

A friendly, French-speaking, consular official at the Swiss Embassy granted me asylum, with only a minimum of bother. He presented me with a student visa within days, and he verified that my Geneva bank account was not only untouched but had accrued a great deal of interest.

Within a month, I enrolled in the Comparative Literature program at the *Université de Genève*.

I graduated with a master's degree in June 1977.

By then, the tempest over the AP and ABC exclusive, "The Shadow Warrior and the Mata Hari," was long forgotten, overwhelmed by Watergate and other disasters. Meanwhile, the

American public was trying hard to pretend that their debacle in Southeast Asia had never occurred. That same year, Jimmy Carter offered pardons to the 30,000 draft dodgers, deserters and defectors who had sought asylum abroad, and many of them started to drift back.

In 1978, I got a job teaching English at the *Panthéon-Sorbonne* in Paris.

In 1980, I married Danielle "Dany" Voet, a pretty divorcée of Flemish origin and a colleague of mine in the *Département d'Études Anglais.*

In 1983, I sold a screenplay to the great, French director, Louis Malle. The film was never made, due to financial constraints (it was set in far-off Laos), but it led to several years of work as a "script doctor" to various French directors who needed bits of English dialogue perfected.

In 1985, I gained French citizenship, and Dany and I bought an apartment on the Rue Boissonade in Montparnasse, just around the corner from Hemingway's old hangout, *La Closerie des Lilas.*

Our marriage was collegial rather than passionate. We had no children as a matter of choice. Yet we lived together quite harmoniously, until I retired from the Sorbonne in 2008.

Our divorce was amicable, caused by my *"impulsion irrationnelle"* to apply for a US passport, return to my hometown, and seek my fortune as a scriptwriter.

Like many Europeans of the intellectual elite, Dany considered Hollywood to be *"la ville la plus grossière et vulgaire de la planète."* Nevertheless, we have remained dear friends, and sometimes we even go on Caribbean cruises and Mediterranean vacations together.

    I have never told Danielle about her rival, and she has never asked, but she knows there was someone. I mean, there has always been that suspicious, old, bronze, Buddha head I wear around my neck. Not to mention the recurring dream that wakes me up every few months, with a woman's name on my lips, a name that is not hers.

Part IV

CHAPTER TWENTY-EIGHT

The Last Word

. . . Cybèle was just like us, Zack, one of a kind from the day she was born, and you would have loved her with all your heart. I wanted a part of you to keep, and I got it. Every time I looked at her, every gesture, every facial expression, I saw a little Asian you. She excelled in school. She went to university in Hanoi and studied medicine in Beijing, where she met her husband, an intelligent and outspoken computer engineer from North Korea named Chin-Ho Kim. Shortly after she gave birth to our granddaughter, they flew to Pyongyang to visit Chin-Ho's parents. Tragically, they disappeared one day while out walking in Mangyondae Forest Park, leaving Katay behind in her pram, and no one ever saw them again.

Distraught though I was, I flew to North

Korea, where the Kim family happily obliged me with full custody of Katay. It seemed they were suspicious about the nature of the disappearance and had fears for her future. It took some time, and there was strong resistance, but with my good standing in the Communist Party, and the aid of a Laotian Embassy official who was once an old, Pathet Lao comrade of mine (you remember Poo-Ying, don't you?), I was eventually able to spirit our granddaughter out of North Korea. I am so proud of Katay, Zack, despite her talent for mischief, and I know you will be too. She is every bit as strong as we ever were, though I pray she will never have to prove it the way we did. With her mixed Lao, Thai, Chinese, Korean, Swedish, Scottish, and Irish blood, she is a veritable United Nations, and I believe she offers living proof of a brighter tomorrow. Of course, here in Laos the "brighter tomorrow" is already upon us, for we are so flooded with American tourists and fast-food franchises that I wonder what in the world we were ever fighting about. Anyway, Katay is dying to meet you, and I believe she will soon impose upon you to help her attend graduate school in the United States. As to your proposal that we meet sometime soon, I must say this, my dear one. Let us remember what we remember, leave the past in the past, and look to the future. I know that you and I will spend our next lifetime together, and that our love will last forever. How do I know this? I had a dream the night I received your letter. I was a young and pretty girl again, coming out of an elevator, with a big, handsome young man who looked just like you. Other young people surrounded us, and there was a huge placard on the wall before us. "Congratulations Class of 2040!" We stepped out of the building into a deluge of rain and started crossing a grassy, college common. "Here, let me help you," you said. You took off your jacket, held it over our heads, and we walked off together into the storm . . .

Prochaine Vie!
Nittaya

CPSIA information can be obtained
at www.ICGtesting.com
Printed in the USA
FSHW010027290721
83591FS